Desert F

Lee Perry was born in 1984 in Pemb
Sussex and he served with the Territorial Army before embarking upon a career in education. A graduate of the Open University where he studied Classics which has always been a life long passion, he now lives and works as a teacher of History and Classics in Kent. He enjoys travelling to France, in particularly Normandy and is a regular visitor to the Lot region of South West France where his family and beloved dog Lily reside.

Desert Rose

'I have always had a passion for History, especially the Second World War. The resilience, bravery and endurance of humanity in a world fraught with terror and tragedy are at times inspirational and our future generations have a great deal to learn about humanity's actions of the past, both positive and negative.

This story is about just such endurance and how family and love can play an important role in getting people through the toughest of times, therefore this novel has been inspired by three wonderful friends that are no longer with me, Joe Clarke, Frank Feeley and Andrew Brown, men who served Britain in the Royal Artillery during the North African and Italian campaigns in the greatest conflict the world has ever seen. Since I was a young boy I had stood in the shadow of these wonderful, heroic and humble veterans and it was they who inspired me to join the army and later embark upon a career in education. I have always tried to inspire my students of History the way that those wonderful veterans inspired me and can only hope that this novel also serves as the inspiration of just how important following your dreams and working hard towards them can be. I dedicate this book to the memory of the thousands of servicemen and women who fought and endured in the sands of North Africa between 1940 – 1943. I dedicate it to the countless students I have taught over the many years of teaching who have made me so utterly proud and instilled hope in me that we can learn from our historical mistakes of the past.

Lastly, Desert Rose is also dedicated to my family, in particular, my mother, who for so long has been the strongest root that has supported me through troublesome times of grief and uncertainty, she is an inspiration of self-sacrifice and the greatest Oracle that has guided me.'

The author

Desert Rose

Lee Perry

This paperback edition is published by Lee Perry, 2019
An imprint of Lee Perry

1st edition 2019

ISBN: 978-1-9161090-1-8

Printed by Amazon

This novel is entirely a work of fiction. The names, characters and incidents portrayed in it are the work of the author's imagination. Any resemblance to actual persons, living or dead, events or locations are entirely coincidental.

For Frank, Joe and Andrew, my friends

A New Arrival
March 5th 1920

'John, can you get the door?' Mrs Jenkins called out.

The little boy ran across the wooden landing, imagining he was a fighter plane in a dive and almost toppling Mrs Jenkins, the housekeeper, over on his way. He reached up and unlocked the chain before opening the door. There, in the dark porch, stood Uncle Tom, his dark green uniform proudly displaying a small line of colourful medal ribbons. He wasn't really his uncle of course: it was a nickname that John's mother had given him because no matter what, Tom was always around at the right time. Whenever there was a knock on the door, he was the visitor that little John hoped for the most and today it was particularly special for it seemed a lifetime ago since he had last seen Tom.

'Hello John,' he called and in response to the young boy plunging into his arms. 'You're getting bigger each time I see you. What is Mrs Jenkins feeding you?'

'Whatever I can get my hands on!' was the sarcastic response from the kitchen.

'Uncle Tom, it's been nearly a year, where have you been? Have you been fighting?' cried John with excitement. 'Have you brought your rifle?'

The soldier laughed. 'No, I haven't brought it and if I had that would be really silly of me; it's far too dangerous to have those things around the house! I have, however, brought you a present.' He lowered his pack from his shoulder and rummaged through until he pulled from it a small wooden box. John took it, running his hands over the rosewood surface before opening it to see the treasure inside. 'Toy soldiers – I hope you like them. I picked them up whilst in India.'

'Thanks, Uncle Tom!'

'Now where is your mum?' The little boy pointed to the stairs. 'Is she alright? Was it a boy or a girl?'

John fiddled with the little figures before shutting the box and placing it upon the table. He bowed his head a little, muttering, 'It was a girl.'

'I see and have you been to see your new little sister yet?'

John shook his head and frowned. 'I don't want to and besides she isn't my real sister because she belongs to him: she is only half my sister. Why did she have to marry him? What was wrong with my real dad!'

Tom guided him to a chair and sat down next to him, placing his arm around the boy's shoulders as Mrs Jenkins crept up to the doorway to listen curiously.

'We have spoken about this before, haven't we? I have already told you that your father was a great man, my best friend. But listen John, Ted loves your mum and your mum loves Ted. He won't ever replace your father and I don't think he is trying to, but he has been good to your mum and looked after you. Try not to give him such a hard time.'

'Well, where is he then?' the boy mumbled. 'I will tell you where, in America. His money is more important and his American family. I wish he would stay there.'

Mrs Jenkins sighed from the doorway whilst gently wiping a pan with a tea towel. She couldn't stay silent any longer. 'Oh John, it takes time for the boat to get from New York to England: I showed you on that map the other night.'

'He always abandons us,' sulked the little boy.

Tom placed his head in his hands and then looked across at John's confused eyes. 'That's not true; he has done a great deal for all of you. Now just because you might not like your stepfather doesn't mean you have to dislike your sister, does it? It is just a little baby up there who doesn't understand any of the problems you, your mum – or anyone else for that matter – has gone through. She needs a big brother to look after her: she needs you. I promise you, it will all be fine. Let's go up and see her together shall we?'

Tom always put things into perspective and the little boy suddenly felt a sense of duty as Tom's words winged their way to his heart. His mother always said that he was better behaved when the old soldier was about: perhaps that's because Tom helped him understand things, because Tom's voice was the closest he would get to his real father.

They left Mrs Jenkins to her chores in the kitchen and met the doctor coming down the stairs who emphasised to Tom that Helen was simply the worst patient.

'It's good to see you again, Tom,' said the doctor. 'Been a while since I last saw you – India was it?'

'Far side of the world again, last year was Iraq! But tell me, doctor, how is Helen?'

'Strong willed. She should be laying down, but is already up and about. Poor old Mrs Jenkins will be running out of jobs to do soon if Helen has her way. However, it was the easiest baby I have ever delivered. It was quick with no complications.' He turned to hear the newborn crying. 'But she should rest and I would like you to encourage it whilst Mr Watson is away. I don't know anything about his business in the States, or when to expect him back.'

Tom rolled his eyes. 'I will see what I can do.'

They met John's mother on the upstairs landing. She looked as frail as the day before when she had given birth. She wore a pale complexion with eyes that had forgotten sleep, but as the doctor had said there was also a great sense of defiance and strength. The new baby had cried a great deal over the last few hours and she had clearly been trying her best with Mrs Jenkins to help. She was obviously pleased to see Tom. Her arms opened and they embraced as old friends do when apart for so long.

'My dear Helen,' Tom began, presenting her with some exotic perfume he had brought back with the toy soldiers. 'I hear Ted is…'

'…On his way home,' she replied with a weak smile. 'I'm coping; don't worry and Mrs Jenkins has been a saint over the last few days. I know what the doctor has asked you to say and please, I am genuinely fine. It would be nice if she would stop crying and sleep though. She hasn't stopped for most of the evening now and as for John, he just point blank refuses to see her.'

'Not anymore. Isn't that right, lad?' Tom checked and John nodded somewhat reluctantly in agreement. 'Right. Let's go inside and see her, shall we?'

The room was lit by a small bedside lamp and the air was filled with a warm powdery smell. As they approached the cot, the crying subsided a little until, with Tom and his mum by his side, John caught the first glimpse of his sister from amidst the tangle of pink wool. Her eyes remained closed and her little hands clawed at the air in frustration.

'She is beautiful,' Tom whispered. 'Why don't you hold her, John? Sit down on the bed and hold her.'

He kept his arms folded for as long as he could, but eventually with Tom smiling at him, John relented. His mother lifted the tiny bundle that gurgled and squirmed and then with a face full of happiness, placed the baby into John's lap whilst showing him where to place his hands.

'This is your sister and her name is Sophie.'

Only moments ago the young boy had no intention of accepting this intruder into his life. It had been easier to imagine she didn't exist, just like her father, but suddenly the anger and frustration subsided. She felt warm and fragile. An overwhelming fear of dropping her made him tense up and be alert.

Tom smiled. 'I think she likes you; she has gone all quiet. From now on she will look up to her big brother, follow you around everywhere and think that you are the be all and end all. Imagine that!'

John smiled at the thought and felt a sense of responsibility shiver through his bones. 'I'm going to look after you,' he whispered, looking down upon the wrinkled face, and in response to his oath, the little baby opened her eyes. His mother gasped and held her hand over her mouth to prevent the sobs of pride from being too loud, as a tiny hand reached out and grasped John's little finger.

'What does that mean?' John asked, looking to Tom for the answer.

'It means that you are the first person she has reached out to. You're the first person she has touched. It means she loves you.'

'Will she let go?'

Tom walked over to look closer at the intense stare that the baby was giving the boy and with a chuckle replied, 'She will eventually.'

'I don't want her to.'

The Desert

13th June 1941 – North Africa

It was mid-morning and the burning sun beat down with invisible rays on John's head. The air was still cold; it took time for the desert to warm up after an incredibly cold night. Over his Khaki trousers and jacket, he wore his thick, heavy, itchy greatcoat, standard issue from His Majesty's Army. As soon as the temperature rose the great coat would be unbearable to wear, but out here it was difficult to make a clear choice; it was either too hot or it was freezing cold.

Battalion headquarters had called John back from the front line to pick up the latest orders and pick up and brief his new platoon officer. Lieutenant Bailey had been invalided out of the company temporarily only two days ago and there was no certainty he would return any time soon. From his seat in an old captured Italian staff car, John watched the empty expanse of the desert pass by, interrupted only by the occasional bump. His driver Corporal Orchard had acquired the car by some mysterious means a week before and the suspicious grin had left John not wishing to ask how. The car had been stripped of most of its original colour by the blasting of sand which frequently filled the desert winds giving it an aged appearance. The corporal had painted a crude union jack upon the bonnet, in order to keep hungry but friendly RAF aircraft at bay.

'Are you okay sir?' Orchard asked, wrestling with the wheel over potholes and sharp rocks.

John smiled and nodded in response whilst he pointed to the direction of Battalion HQ out of habit rather than necessity, for both had made the trip many times already during the week. Ahead the emptiness was soon broken by what looked like a cluster of pyramids which with time became tents and parked vehicles. Orchard followed John's outstretched arms as he pointed to a suitable place to park and then brought the car to a dusty halt.

Even before the car had stopped John had noticed his replacement officer. He was a smart, clean-shaven young man, not much younger than himself, but out here a week aged you a whole year and the experience of carnage and suffering added extra lines to your forehead.

John felt like an old man as he looked upon the young curious figure sitting upon the remains of a mudbrick wall.

'That can't be him can it?' The corporal whispered.

'I bet you a week's pay he is,' John replied as he stepped out of the car.

The young officer, his brass so clean it glinted in the sun, saluted. 'Captain Baker?' he asked.

John half-heartedly saluted in return. 'That would be me, Lieutenant.'

'Lieutenant Moore, sir, Brian Moore. I have been assigned to D-Company.'

John pitied Moore immediately; it was going to take time to adjust to life in the desert, especially from that comfortable bunk he had probably been sleeping on for the past few weeks in Alexandria. Now he would have to sleep in the open desert amongst scorpions, spiders and all other manner of creatures, including his men. John expected that he had probably not seen any creepy crawlies yet, let alone the snakes and out here they seemed unusually larger than normal.

He noticed Moore's eyes fall upon Orchard. 'I do apologise, Lieutenant, this is corporal Orchard.'

The corporal's oily hand saluted rather untidily with an enthusiastic smile that would have normally belonged to that of a troublesome and somewhat naughty child.

Without any further verbal exchanges, Moore began to place his personal belongings into the car, whilst the corporal threw his equipment onto the back seat. Once he had settled down the new officer kept his gas mask firmly clutched in his hands upon his lap. He then noticed the absence of one on the corporal. 'Where is your gas mask corporal? You know as well as I that it's an offence not to carry it at all times!'

Orchard did not reply; instead, he smiled. To the experienced soldier, Lieutenant Moore was just another new officer, fresh out of basic training that had been reading too many rule books and was testing his new found authority.

'Well?' The Lieutenant demanded.

'Um, sorry sir, I left it behind, but I assure you it's with the rest of my kit. We don't worry too much 'bout gas out here, sir; both us and Jerry seem to have a mutual understanding about it.'

'I see,' was the weak response and Moore looked to John for some kind of reassurance.

'There are some things that you will learn are not essential out here,' John began, as feeling down to his waist realised he had left his back at the front too. 'We don't always carry our gas masks, but they are never far from hand.' He then turned to Orchard and beckoned him over out of Moore's earshot. 'I'm going to pop over to headquarters and collect the orders ok?' Orchard nodded. 'In future, we better make sure we have our bloody gas mask to hand, he does have a point. Now I shall only be a minute, look after the Lieutenant…' Orchard began to head back to the car. '… And Corporal…'

'Yes, sir?'

'Be gentle,' John pleaded, but as he turned away and headed into the oasis of tents, he could already sense the Cheshire cat grin that had found its way across Orchard's face.

John wandered through the camp, giving the odd salute and trying not to trip over the ropes of the many tents before finding the one that belonged to Major Love. Inside he found the Major's aid, a young lance corporal that he always forgot the name of, who was busy sorting papers and maps. John's entrance went unnoticed for a while.

'I am here to see the Major.'

'Captain! Oh, I am sorry sir, I didn't hear you come in. You have missed the Major by a few minutes, he has been summoned to division headquarters at the last minute.'

'Division?' John queried. The fact he had been summoned to division could only mean one thing, something big was on the horizon. The corporal confirmed as if knowing that he had revealed too much already. John always knew the signs when something was about to happen. One sign was normally brand new equipment which meant an attack was imminent, like the time they got new rifles and Bren gun spares they didn't need before their baptism of fire at Halfaya in Libya. Replacements were normally a dead giveaway and lastly, the absence of the Major to division headquarters was a sure sign something was being planned. 'Well I was here to pick up my orders from him, how long will he be?'

'Oh there is no need to wait, sir,' the corporal left his maps, some of which slid to the floor in a noisy heap and took from the Majors untidy table a handful of documents. The Major always said that his mess was controlled chaos and that despite how it looked he knew precisely where everything was. The corporal clearly didn't though, but after sifting through some of the clutter found what he was looking for. 'Are your telephones still working sir?'

'They were this morning, that's when the Major spoke to me and told me to come here.'

'In that case, he will contact you as soon as he is back, that's assuming they don't get cut again, especially if Jerry starts that blasted shelling! Mind you, saying that it's been remarkably quiet the last few days.'

'I'm sure it has, back here.' John added.

'These are your orders.'

'I have told the Major that replacement radios would make life easier.'

'He knows sir and you should get some new batteries for yours tomorrow.'

And that was another sign of imminent danger, John thought. He looked at the type on the head of the first sheet which read 'Battleaxe' in big red letters before sighing. 'A little bit medieval wouldn't you say?'

'I'm sorry sir?'

'It doesn't matter corporal. Was there anything else?'

'There was just one more thing Captain Baker. I have a Lieutenant Moore outside to replace Lieutenant Bailey from your company. It's a shame; the battalion just isn't the same since Lieutenant Bailey departed, we all miss his humour. I better take you to meet him as you may not know where to...'

'That won't be necessary Corporal,' John interrupted. 'I found him on the way in, Corporal Orchard is seeing to him now.'

'Orchard is looking after him?' he dropped the rest of the papers onto the floor.

'Yes he is which is why I can't really delay, but if that is all I will head back to my dugout.'

The Corporal, whose name still escaped John saluted smartly and returned to his mess of maps as John headed outside to his ride.

The old car that had clearly been battered and bruised in some past battles, whined and jerked forward, kicking and billowing up the dust of the desert as it went. John sat quietly in the front and looked through his orders between occasional glances into the rearview mirror to observe his new officer. Moore's head twitched and turned like a curious owl, at times towards the towering dunes and at others towards the sky. He had clearly never seen the true extent of the desert before, perhaps travelling here via the coastal road where there could still be found little patches of green. Clearly, some things were going to be different from what he had been expecting. He gabbled incoherently and answered his own question 'How far is the front then Corporal, about three miles?'

'About that sir,' shrugged Orchard.

The wheels on the staff car dug continually into the dust, kicking it up into dangerously obvious clouds behind. The vehicle cumbersomely clanked along groaning with frequent asphyxiated gasps as if each one was it's last. Ahead the sun was rising further into the clear blue sky, bursting brilliant shards of light in every direction and as it rose so did the temperature.

'I presume you have acquired this vehicle recently?' Moore tentatively asked, as they bumped and ground across the sand trying to find something tactile to grab onto in order to keep his posture and composure.

'Acquired? Hmmm, you could say that' Orchard chuckled. 'This is my baby!' he boasted, baring a perfect set of pearly white teeth and grinning once again like a Cheshire cat.

'Where are you from then, Lieutenant?' John asked, still sifting through his orders and coming upon a small file on his new lieutenant which he skimmed over.

'Surrey,' Moore replied.

'That's a bit far out isn't it?'

'I understand that most of the battalion are from Sussex?'

'Indeed they are or certainly were, except the corporal here off course, isn't that right corporal?' Orchard nodded in agreement, still smiling. 'The corporal is from another part of the world, completely alien to most of us, where is it again corporal?'

'Peckham,' Orchard announced proudly. 'Rye Lane round the corner from Jones and Higgins. Know it, sir?'

Moore shook his head. 'Perhaps I have, I am not sure, not Rye Lane anyway. Is it nice there?'

'Paradise sir, although not as nice as where you're from I imagine, all those green fields, open spaces, gated houses and country pubs.'

'Oh, you've been to Surrey then?'

Moore's response was perhaps honest and innocent, nevertheless, it was the first time John had seen Orchard get caught out as he replied, 'No I haven't. Never really left London, to be honest.'

'Oh, I see Peckham is in London.' Moore continued.

Orchard went from seething at the ignorance of the man to glowing again as if the very mention of London filled his heart with warmth. 'Yep, good old London, I'm a London boy me, London through and through. Born in London and will die in London, with a pint of pride down my throat and a busty woman on my arm.'

'Thank you, corporal,' John jumped in amused. 'I see here in some papers I have on you Lieutenant that you have done some extra training whilst waiting to be assigned to a company. Mine clearance training with the Royal Engineers, am I correct?'

'You are sir, I spent a few weeks with them. I had a few weeks spare in Cairo, I didn't know what to do with the time and after hearing that Jerry is quite resourceful with mines I thought it would be a good idea to know what to do if I found one.'

John was secretly impressed, 'I couldn't agree more, did you see the pyramids whilst there?'

'No sir.'

'Aye?' Orchard squawked with surprise. 'You didn't see the pyramids! Their one of the tenth wonders of the world! First thing I did when I saw them was to scribble my name on one of them bricks.' He went sheepishly quiet when he saw John scowling at him for his sacrilegious behaviour.

'I am afraid I didn't see them, Corporal, well not close up as you did. And it's seven by the way.' Orchard looked confused at his comment so Moore filled in the gaps. 'Seven Wonders, there are not ten. Anyway, I have seen the pyramids before so I felt I could afford to miss them.'

'You have been to Egypt before?' John asked surprised.

'Yes, in my youth.'

'Teens you mean,' Orchard interrupted.

'Teens? Oh yes, I see what you mean,' he corrected himself over Orchards huffing. 'My father was based out here, only for a couple of years. It was to do with the Arab Bureau, I didn't understand it at the time.'

John began to sense a ranking officer, something that any ordinary officer began to fear. The last thing he needed was a family connection to the higher echelons in his company's midst. 'Your father was in the army?' he asked cautiously.

'Lieutenant colonel,' Moore replied and both John and Orchard repeated the rank out loud with some surprise.

'Is he still a Lieutenant colonel?' John asked, his eyebrows raised.

'Retired sir.'

John settled back into his seat, unaware just how twisted and contorted his posture had become. 'You know who was involved in the Arab bureau don't you?'

'Lawrence of Arabia,' Moore cut in proudly. 'I met him when I was five as my father had to work with him briefly, I don't remember it though and didn't really understand who he was at the time.'

'I doubt you would at that age.'

'And you, sir?' Moore now turned his attention to John. 'Are you Sussex born and bred too?'

John thought for a minute, his little sleepy village was a place you only knew if you were local and after naming his village and seeing Moore's puzzled face in the mirror simplified for him, 'near to Eastbourne.'

'Oh, how lovely near the seaside,' he smiled. 'The corporal was explaining what had happened to the Lieutenant I am replacing,' Moore continued his face a little paler now. 'I am very sorry about Lieutenant Bailey.' John frowned and looked towards Orchard who smirked and then deliberately turned his head away. 'Welcome to the desert,' Moore said to himself with a sigh, pinching his forehead between his thumb and middle finger.

'What was that sir?' Orchard queried tauntingly.

'Oh nothing Corporal, I was just talking to myself,' said Moore wafting his hand dismissively.

'That's not good sir,' Orchard said with a smirk. 'Not good at all, you've only just got 'ere and already you're going do-lally.' Moore shrugged his shoulders at him. 'Do-lally sir. It's what we Tommie's in the Desert call those who are a bit funny in the 'ed.'

'Well I'm not do-lally,' Moore retorted. 'I was just making a comment that's all. I always thought the desert was supposed to be…' John glanced in the mirror again as the Lieutenant thought for a moment, clearly in order to avoid any further clever comments from the inquisitive Corporal. 'Well, I guess what I mean is, that the desert has always had a sense of romance to it.'

'Wouldn't bring my Mrs 'ere,' was Corporal Orchards crackling reply and with it, John couldn't help but chuckle. Moore also loosened up; John could see the smile in the mirror. The ice had melted.

A grinding distance later a small cluster of emerald green palm trees appeared on the desert horizon and coming in the opposite direction was a field ambulance; a comforting sight to the wounded, but a solemn one to those yet to be at the front. John continued to observe Moore in the mirror.

Eventually, under the palms, some old ruins came into view made out of mud brick, long abandoned by families of a distant past. After the tinkling bells of the ambulance had passed, they overtook another vehicle, this time an armoured car parked randomly in the shade of one of the palms. When Orchards' crippled staff car doddered up alongside it, John watched Moore's face pale even more as he could see it had been knocked out, its hull black and charred from the flames. As for the crew, three small mounds of earth lay in a neat row beside the car, decorated with coarsely engraved stones rummaged from the landscape marking their final resting place. John did not have the heart to inform him that he and Tom had buried them three days ago.

It was not long before Orchard brought the vehicle to a gentle stop. 'Here we are sir, home sweet home.'

John could see the hope of comfort drain away on the young officers face as the uncomfortable realisation began to set in. He helped him with his large pack and patted him on the shoulder with a smile. 'You get used to it,' he said and beckoned him to follow.

They walked on into the emptiness until they came to the maze of trenches, whilst in the far distance were a few scattered shell craters that scarred the desert like craters on the moon.

'This way Lieutenant,' John said beckoning him down into the cool, shady trenches. Inside the labyrinth, men rested and sheltered from the sun. Some of them were drinking their tea rations, some were cleaning equipment whilst others lay still reserving their energy. The trenches had once been occupied by Italians; a clue had been a small empty bottle of olive oil by the entrance of the trenches and a lone Carcano rifle propped up next to a sleeping Lance Corporal. Further into the maze Italian propaganda leaflets carpeted the floor. A few twists and turns later, around the narrow corridors with their corrugated iron walls revealed a dugout. Inside were the occupying company officers and some tatty Italian propaganda posters, zealously quoting; Gioventi Fascista. Il fascismo non vi promette ne onori ne cariche ne guadagni ma il dovere e il combattimento. 'Fascism does not promise you honour, or load you with gain, only duty and combat,' John translated for him, noticing Moore's curious eyes.

'I can speak a little French,' Moore replied weakly.

'Another holiday with your father?' John smiled, but Moore remained silent turning his gaze towards the centre of the room.

As their eyes adjusted to the gloom, the company officers were leaning over an old wooden table that was propped up on one corner with what looked like a grey Italian tunic. A map was spread-eagled across the table and bathed in shafts of sunlight from a gap in the undulating, rusty corrugated iron roof above.

'Gentlemen may I introduce our latest member of the family, this is Lieutenant Moore,' John called out.

There was a moment of silence as the small group of men looked him over. Moore's uniform had been exposed to dust on the journey, but still retained its smart and stiff appearance, whereas the men that stood before him had uniforms with a far more weathered visage, as if taken from a forgotten trunk in the attic. Even the pips that perched upon their shoulders or the stripes upon their arms were dusty and faded.

John beckoned him closer. 'Well, Moore, come in and I will introduce you. Firstly, in briefing it's all very informal here. We are all on first name terms so you can call me John.' He then pointed to an older man whose face initially was shadowed in the shade of the dugout. He was well built, upright, clean and well shaven and impeccably dressed compared to the others. As the figure ventured forward the telling lines and battle scars of combat were written all over his ruddy complexion. There was nothing about war and battle that this man had left to learn. He had seen his fair share of conflict and not just here in the desert. This, of course, was nothing new to John, but clearly, Moore was taken aback a little by the imposing figure.

'This is Sergeant Major Tom Hill,' John said introducing Moore to the experienced old soldier. 'Tom is the backbone of D company don't ever forget that.'

Moore shook the Sergeant Major's hand, the grip firm and strong. His hand was rough, carved with small canyons of age.

John then introduced the remaining two other officers, both would have seemed young to Moore, but their faces were also weatherworn in their appearance. Keyes jerked forward over the table volunteering his hand. He wore his goggle typed rimmed glasses that had since been chipped in one corner, but which still fitted and complimented his circular face. His thin pursed lips made it appear that he struggled to smile, a feature that John had still not worked out for himself as if it was a natural flaw to his appearance or perhaps something was troubling him deep down.

Then there was Anthony. His strawberry blonde fringe dangled loosely and closely to the side of his face and constantly flicked forward as they shook hands. His penetrating deep blue eyes pierced you with overbearing sincerity and his public school image bubbled through with everything being 'smashing' or' jolly good' at the end of his sentences. John couldn't help but feel that these two would get on like a house on fire, reminiscing of their holidays abroad that daddy's had taken them on.

'Remember to call me Anthony,' he encouraged.

'Well, I'm Brian, Brian Moore.'

With introductions over after Sergeant Scott was forced to see to a problem, John placed the contents of the envelope upon the table and together they looked upon the plans for 'Battleaxe.' He watched with interest to hear the new Lieutenant's take on the plan but as partially expected he remained quiet.

'So there it is,' John said with neither confidence nor pessimism as they neared the end of the briefing. 'We have been on the run for some time now and it's about time we hit back. The plan is called Operation Battleaxe. This plan involves hitting Rommel and hitting him bloody hard. Crete has fallen and we desperately need to relieve Tobruk. We attack on the fifteenth of June, that's three days away. We will leave our current position here at 06:00 hours and head for this ridge.' His finger pointed to a blank area on the map in front with only a number to indicate that there was anything there at all. 'In the meantime, we have been ordered to hold here. For the time being, I want you to make the best use of these old trenches, reinforce them as best you can, any questions?' John finished fervently.

'This Battleaxe, is it going to be like that last show we embarked on sir?' Keyes asked his face seemingly weighed down with a thousand worries.

John knew what Lieutenant Keyes was referring to, all too well. The last major battle they had been involved in was in the Halfaya Pass, which the men had renamed rather appropriately 'Hellfire pass'. The casualties had been enormous for both sides. John's Company had managed to get away with only light casualties, but the experience of this badly planned engagement by those above was still imprinted in the minds of many of his men.

'I don't know,' he responded honestly. 'I hope not.'

'Shall we settle in, or shall we keep equipment packed away ready to move?' Anthony asked.

'Better keep them packed,' boomed Tom, interrupting for the first time in his deep Sussex accent. 'We might have to pull back at a moment's notice, especially if the battalion is in a holding action.'

'I agree,' John said. 'We all know how unpredictable Rommel can be, so let's not assist him in being unprepared. Be ready to move at a moment's notice. Don't get too comfortable here. Keyes, I want one section of Second Platoon to position themselves out front on the OP.

‘It’s quite exposed out there,’ he replied and Tom agreed with a grunt.

‘I know,’ John sighed. ‘They can use the shell craters for cover and send a runner if they hear or see anything and don’t forget that about a mile in front of this position there is an Indian unit out there.’ Keyes nodded in agreement. ‘Otherwise, we’ve all got things to get on with so let’s jump to it. I can see Lieutenant Moore is itching to get acquainted with his new Platoon.’ Moore smiled, but as the other two Officers left he loitered hesitatingly. ‘Problem Lieutenant?’ John asked.

‘Not really sir. I just wanted to say again how sorry I am about my predecessor.’

‘You mean Lieutenant Bailey?’ John checked.

‘Does it matter?’ Tom transgressed.

‘Well I know it must be difficult, I don’t want the men to think I am trying to replace him in spirit as well as duty,’ Moore stuttered. ‘The Corporal mentioned just how popular he was, his humour and all that sort of thing.’

Tom sniggered a little and John found it hard to refrain from smiling. ‘What did Corporal Orchard tell you, Lieutenant?’

‘Very little sir, but mentioned that it was a bit, well a bit of a mess though.’

‘Indeed it was,’ John chuckled, sensing one of Orchard’s practical jokes. ‘Lieutenant, I should have warned you a little earlier, but Corporal Orchard is not only one of the finest soldiers I know, but one of the most mischievous I know. Our previous officer Lieutenant Bailey who started with us back in England simply had a very serious case of dysentery. In fact, we are hopeful he will return to the unit as soon as possible and replace you, not that we are unhappy to have you of course!’

‘Dysentery?’ Moore echoed in disbelief. All the way here he had clearly been imagining a far different scenario from Orchards wicked and yet imaginative mind. He looked around the dugout befuddled before his eyes found Tom’s.

‘It was very serious dysentery,’ Tom added in such an infringing tone that John couldn’t help but laugh out loud.

‘I see, well if you will excuse me, sir, I better meet my men.’

'Would you like Orchard to show you to your platoon?' John offered.

'It's quite alright, I will ask for directions.'

'Turn left when you go out and then straight on for a hundred yards. Their all yours,' John said and returned the salute that Moore gave him as he left.

With a big grin across his face and shaking his head in disbelief at Tom's interjection, John folded up the map on the table and then as if by magic two tin mugs appeared in its place filled with tea. 'Good idea,' he said still smiling at Tom. He ran his hand through his hair to watch the dust sprinkle to the floor and then collapsed upon an old stretcher that had become his bed for the last two nights.

'Don't let that tea go cold,' Tom remarked, lighting a cigarette and then puffing away at the entrance to the dugout as if to be polite.

'Trust me I won't; I bloody need it.'

'That's what you said yesterday when you fell asleep just after I made it,' Tom muttered through clouds of cigarette smoke spiralling ambivalently into the pale blue sky. 'What do you make of this new fella then?'

'I'm sure he'll be fine, he seems focused and positive if not a little nervous.'

'He's young,' Tom said in a rueful veteran tone.

'We've all started young. I'm sure you were that keen once,' John heckled. He rolled over onto his front and looked up at his old friend. 'What about my father when he was young?'

The Sergeant Major paused for a moment; drawing in his cigarette and making the moment last for as long as he could. He then warmly looked at his young Captain. John thought how strange it was that Tom had been a family friend since before he was born, seen John through his first days at school, his training as a young officer and now he was his subordinate, not like back home where it felt as though he was pretending like it was a game. They had now been in some of the most gruesome battles in North Africa to date and Tom had always said that it was in the fire of war that his young protégé would find his feet and his voice. Yet despite the role reversal, where back in England John felt in command only from behind a desk and through paperwork, it comforted him to look upon such a familiar face.

'Your father was as impatient and as eager as I was. In fact, everybody was enlisting and conscripting themselves in, keen to get it over and done with. We thought the last war would be over as quickly as it had begun. Many thought they would knock themselves out as heroes and come back from that war with shiny medals on their chests. Jesus if only we had known,' he said looking at his hands. 'Even now, twenty-five years later, I can smell the stench in my nostrils; hear the screaming in my heart, feel the cold damp mud around my feet and the blood on my hands. It will never wash off, it will never go away,' he reminisced ruefully.

'That was cheerful!' John joked.

Suddenly the bright shaft of warm light that had been beaming into the dugout was broken and in the doorway was Corporal Orchard.

'Come on in Corporal,' Tom said grabbing another mug from a small wooden shelf that was the remains of an old ammunition box lid wedged between some sandbags, 'Tea?'

'Right you are, sir,' Orchard replied settling himself into the corner of the dugout.

John sat up and jabbed at the Corporal, 'no more messing about with our new Lieutenant, Corporal, understood?'

Orchard smiled broadly. 'Sorry sir, it won't happen again' and then under his breath muttered, 'well not for the rest of the day at the very least, I'll wait until tomorrow!'

John swirled his tea around in his mug clockwise and then anticlockwise making the most of the refreshing nectar. 'I told you back at Battalion to be gentle.'

'I don't fink he will last,' Orchard perked up. 'When I drove him here he was finking too much, could see it in his eyes. You know the flicker when you fink. Honestly, all the way 'ere, fink, fink and more finking.'

John looked at him puzzled. 'What has thinking got to do with how long he lasts corporal?'

'Well sir it's dangerous you see?' said Orchard emphatically, edging his posterior forward and out of the corner he was squatting in, as if on a secret mission with a message that no one else should hear.

'No I don't see. Why is it dangerous?' said John warily.

‘Got to be in the moment, sir, or they’ll get yeh! They’re bashing ‘em out in their nappies from training these days. He’s not potty trained yet. Probably get caught napping!’ he quipped closing his left eye and pulled his right index finger to his thumb in a shooting gesture.

‘Talking of babies, Orchard what have you done about that bloody awful set of wheels you commandeered yesterday?’ said John awakening from the realisation that he had been caught again by the cheeky corporal’s banter.

‘Well, I was rather hoping we could keep her sir,’ remonstrated the corporal raising his eyebrows and fluttering his eyelids imitating the gestures of a female to gain favourable odds.

‘Draws too much attention,’ Tom coughed soberly amidst the rattling of the spoon in the tin mug. ‘If it doesn’t break down soon the ruddy Luftwaffe will have us all just from following your dust trails!’

‘That’s very true,’ John said. ‘Don’t use it anymore.’

‘But it’s bloody great for getting to and from Battalion HQ, sir.’

‘Well as of today we have a new one of these now,’ John twisted his torso around so he could point to a field telephone sitting idly on a clump of sandbags. ‘So you can stop running that old piece of junk.’

‘Very well sir,’ said Orchard in dismay.

John finished his tea and with a thumbs up he thanked Tom. There was a brief silence. In the background, all that could be heard was the sounds of men calling out and the occasional clicking and rattling of equipment, but soon a new sound grew. At first, it could barely be heard in the distance, but a minute later it rumbled through the narrow passageway of the trenches and into the dugout. Running outside they all looked skyward to see and hear an angry swarm of German bombers.

‘Stukas,’ a solitary voice called from the crowd of spectators that now all craned their heads to the sky.

From above the dugout a three-man Bren gun section, their gun on an anti-aircraft stand tracked the mass of planes ready and waiting to see if they would turn towards them. But after a while, it became clear as the planes droned onward that their target was elsewhere.

Not long to go, John thought. Those Stukas were being used to soften something up ready for an attack, so it wouldn’t be long before something headed their way. He returned to the shade of the dugout, with Tom following.

'They might make a move before we do.'

'You ought to get some rest sir; you were up all ruddy night,' Tom said.

John knew he was right of course. His eyes felt like lead balls and it had been difficult to concentrate in his exhausted state. He knew there was a possibility that the enemy might try and make a push. Just knowing that there was a chance, kept his eyes firmly open, but that wasn't the only reason.

'I know Tom, but you know I can't sleep, not now, something's brewing. Rommel has been far too quiet lately.'

'That's because he is focusing on Tobruk. You know full well that you won't be able to make good decisions in an unfit state and besides, that's not the only reason you don't sleep. You're thinking about it all again,' his tone was one that suggested there be no more silly questions. 'You're thinking about your journey.'

'My journey, is that what you are calling it now?'

'It's what I call it,' Tom sighed. 'And you are worried about her, which I know is natural, but you can't do anything about her out here, besides she will cope better than you give her credit for, her letters are filled with confidence and none of it is false. So do me a ruddy favour and get some ruddy rest; I will wake you if anything happens.'

John knew he could trust Tom and besides he was right, he was an officer and the company depended on him. How many times had he walked amongst his men encouraging them to take any rest they could? A fresh soldier functions better than an exhausted one. It was time to follow his own advice.

'I will try, I am tired, but I am also at that stage sleep won't come easily.'

'It's anxiety. Think of a happier time, a memory perhaps, one without sand. Have you got one?' John nodded. 'Good, whatever it is and whenever it was, start from there and try and remember every day that came after, try and remember exactly who you saw, what was said and what you did.'

'Was I good a brother to her?'

'The best,' Tom replied.

'What about now that I am stuck out here?'

'An even better brother, because she is free to breathe a little,' Tom chuckled.

'I wasn't that bad!' John cried throwing a lump of earth at him playfully. 'Very well Sergeant Major, the Company is yours, wake me if anything develops.'

Tom nodded and walked outside to give him some peace.

At first, John thought he would just lie there and that sleep again would be an elusive hope. The air was humid and his body sticky and uncomfortable from the heat. His attempts to relax often caused him to think of home, but that then led him to become restless, because from here the cares and worries that he had left behind were out of reach and beyond his control. As he stirred, from outside he could make out the voice of Tom talking to whom he thought to be Sergeant Scott. He was already drifting through a peaceful ocean of darkness and then without even realising it, as he visualised the green fields of Sussex and the white picket fence that embraced the garden at home, he was asleep.

Sophie

May 4th 1938, Sussex, England

It was one of those stereotypical English springs. The countryside was yawning and stretching from the hibernation of a bitter winter. In the rousing meadows and fields there were newborn lambs bleating and bouncing, birds were dipping and darting, chirping and chattering in and out of the hedgerows, making ready for their coming broods. The mornings were glistening with delicate dew and the air breathed its gentle breezes.

It was also the perfect type of day for a wedding. The sun had kissed the hours enough to cast off any greyness that had been loitering in the sky. John stood on the edge of his Uncle Richard's lawn, which was bathed in the evening's sunset, reflecting on the day. It had been a grand wedding, horses and carriages and all the usual pomp that was to be expected to celebrate the union of his highly respected Uncle Richard and Richard's new bride Joy. John didn't quite know the ins and outs of how they met and he couldn't quite remember how long they had been together, but he never did like to pry into other people's business much. The reception was in full swing: A sweet and romantic melody accompanied by lush, stimulating string arrangements and a strong tenor voice undulated in the background. John held a glass of Champagne in one hand and the tie, which had been clutching at his neck all day, in the other. The heels of his shoes rested on the stone terrace whilst his highly polished toes tapped to the rhythm on the lawn's edge, which like the rest of the lawn was covered in cherry blossoms chipped from the branches of the tree in the centre of the garden and sprinkled like confetti by the clement evening breeze.

John was quite a novice when it came to weddings, having attended very few. His first introduction being his mother's second marriage to his stepfather Ted, a successful New York banker who had been part of the second wave of American forces that arrived in Europe in 1917 and loitered after hostilities ended. They had met quite by accident during the interval of the London production of *As You Were* at the Pavilion Theatre located on the corner of Shaftesbury Avenue and Coventry Street. 'Our eyes met and that was that, your mom and I. It was fate!'

Ted, in his broad Yankee accent, had informed a very disconcerted young John, who had resented the distraction of his mother's new-found attention. Ted had a smile that crept up one cheek like a cartoon character and when he laughed he bobbed his head – both of which made John want to thump him in the face. The only masculine influence he respected was his father's lifetime friend Sergeant Major Hill, or Uncle Tom as he was known to both Sophie and John when he was at home. Tom fuelled him with stories of their camaraderie and escapades and had actively served with John's father in the Great War, promising to look after them in the event of his death.

John had immortalised his father and needless to say he would protest most vehemently at the prospect of moving to the States or having a 'Yankee stepfather' when it was mentioned more than once. Fortunately for John, Ted's love affair with England became as passionate as his love for John's mother. He managed to arrange his business in the City on a permanent basis when he was completely recovered and commuted home to the States once a year. For John, this was an added bonus as his travels kept Ted away for months at a time. It also delighted his mother because he returned bearing exquisite gifts still unobtainable in post-war Britain. He lavished upon her provocative silk lingerie and the latest American fashions, making her the most enviable lady in the area! Nothing was too good for his girl and the post-war blues made for a general feeling in those days that life was short and should be enjoyed.

John's only real recollection of the disastrous event was the attempted presentation of a New York Yankee baseball cap, ball and bat which his mother had gently encouraged him to open at their wedding reception. He had thrown the half-unravelled package to the ground, relishing the anguish and disappointment in his stepfather's face.

'More like she married him on the rebound after father's death, based on expediency rather than on love,' John would retort if his name was brought up in conversation in later years. The only good, in his opinion, that came out of the marriage was his little stepsister Sophie, whom he adored.

His next personal introduction and education on the subject of marriage had been brought about by Anne, his first – and to-date only – love to whom he had given his entire heart. Anne or Annie, as John's mother called her, had fitted cosily into the family. She got on particularly well with John's mother as they both shared a passionate interest in their local Women's Institute, but Anne wasn't the typical next-door-type girl and needed constant attention. Sophie had remarked that she was too 'high maintenance' for John, a very astute and, as it turned out, accurate observation for one so young and as inexperienced as she. The army kept John away a lot of the time, so looking back, the result was inevitable. His own 'close shave' to the institution of marriage had been very clinically severed from Anne last year, not long after his mother's death, a double whammy at the time. She had eventually left him after a very 'on and off' two-year relationship for his supposed best friend since primary school, George Cutter (the ultimate betrayal). Today of all days seemed to bring his 'lucky escape' very close to home again, despite having to constantly repeat the circumstances to all who questioned Anne's notorious absence from his side. Furthermore, this apparent misfortune had brought on many looks of sympathy that were beginning to become – on what was supposed to be a happy occasion – quite frankly, an embarrassment.

'Oh, John, poor dear, I can imagine how you feel and what with your mother's passing not so long ago as well,' patronized Great Aunt Prue on his mother's side, in between ramming her third vol au vent into her ravenous mouth, losing the remnants of the puff pastry casing all down a very expensive fox fur that was wrapped around her already heavily bejewelled neck. The fur had obviously not seen the light of day for many a year, because it smelt as though it had just died. She put out her hand and squeezed his arm, smiling and continued condescendingly, 'But then I heard that fidelity wasn't exactly her forte, was it?'

'Another?' John asked, removing her grip from his arm and transferring the silver platter that she had been foraging from furiously into her hand. He took his leave but unfortunately walked straight into the next bombardment from cousins Agatha and Amy. John couldn't believe it; it seemed bottomless, this false pit of concern.

'It's so unfair, poor love. It must all be so raw. If only we lived closer,' they said in unison and with an 'isn't he brave expression' stretched across their duplex faces.

'Well, life goes on doesn't it?' he had said with a smile to match their false concern.

Now, whilst the band played and the vultures looked for other gossip to pick apart, he stood in the solace of the garden away from it all, his foot still tapping upon the damp grass.

Meanwhile Sophie had been watching from over their Uncle Richard's shoulder her brother's relentless torment with helpless amusement. She looked on him lovingly and pitifully. Every so often she shrugged her shoulders teasingly when his eyes would catch hers, pleading to be rescued from any more interrogations. He held everything together; he was her whole world and the only real family that she cared for. John was only on leave for the weekend and being away for such vast quantities of time as he often was, she was becoming continually frustrated throughout the evening at being separated from him. In the house where friends and family were gathered, there was the constant droning on about who was doing what and where so-and-so had been. For Sophie, the continuous empathy for their family plight was becoming tedious. She really wasn't interested and didn't care to remember the names and faces that made her acquaintance throughout the day, but continually smiled politely and responded courteously as her brother had taught her to do, despite the burning desire to tell them all where to go.

Deep in her thoughts, she reminded herself what family should have meant and to Sophie it should have been a part of who she was, where she was from and what she would become, a part of her identity. It was supposed to give her a sense of belonging. Sophie and John had been through so much in their short lives, but not once had this family been there to intervene or help them feel that they belonged anywhere, other than in the microcosm of their own backyard. The majority of the family members on their mother's side had distanced themselves to the extreme, afraid of the reprisals from John's dictatorial grandfather and trapped in the Victorian mind-set of keeping the family name from any possible public scandals, an attitude that should have died with him all those years ago. Since the Great War, long-standing class barriers had started to break down. The break was subtle, the erosion had begun even in their family, but for Sophie – still in her tender years – it was all still a bit of a sham and as far as she was concerned, their half-hearted interest was too much, too late.

Now she found herself longing to escape outside and find her brother, away from the falseness that surrounded her. Aunt Marjorie wouldn't stop talking about how happy she was that her daughter Brenda had married a wealthy businessman from Streatham of all places; already within a month this rich stranger had apparently become the son she had never had.

'He virtually paid for the whole wedding. He insisted!' she emphasised. '"Only the best for my Brenda." Mother-in-law he calls me now. He wouldn't have it any other way you know.' Then with a sharp intake of breath she continued, catching Sophie out of the corner of her eye, 'Oh my dear, how is Delsie these days? I didn't get time to chat with her on the day; well you know what it's like? It's your turn next I hear?' Aunt Marjorie jibed, clapping her hands tightly.

'No,' Sophie sighed drearily.

'Well, I distinctly remember Delsie telling me the wedding was set for September,' Aunt Marjorie insisted.

'Well I'm sure that you're right, Aunt Marjorie,' tweaked Sophie, 'but I am Helen's daughter not Delsie's! And I wouldn't have it any other way,' she said very loudly and indignantly as she flicked up her nose and set off in the opposite direction.

Aunt Marjorie was left standing with her mouth ajar. 'Well really!' she said with embarrassment, looking around to see if anyone was watching.

Cousin Clara however, was the one who had got up Sophie's nose the most. She had met a Lieutenant in the Guards and brought him along to the wedding to show him off in his immaculate red uniform, and show him off she did. Everyone was impressed and compliments were flying in all directions. The perfect gentleman that he was, he played up to every moment of it.

Nobody had said how proud they were of her or John. Sophie's brother had done just as well and had recently been promoted to Captain in the Infantry. There had been no admiration of or congratulations on his worthy achievement, but then John was not the sort to crave attention. He normally wore his uniform with pride for King and Country but today he had favoured something more casual, a simple suit. She noted that Cousin Clara was heading in her direction, waving frantically for her attention. It was obviously her turn next. Sophie reflected on the consequences for just one moment and immediately took an avoiding turn and bumped straight into her Uncle Richard.

Today he looked very dapper in his navy, combination, five-guinea, elegantly-tailored Montague Burton suit with the overwhelming pungent fragrance of an ochre orchid in his button hole. He caught her in mid-flight and he wrapped his welcoming arms around her waist. Like her brother, Sophie was fond of her Uncle Richard. He had always been her mother's favourite and she his, the youngest of eight and her only brother to survive the Great War. Richard had been the apple of his father's eye and his mother's silent benefactor in times of crisis and because of this was seen as the figurehead of the family. His face, like many young veterans', had character in that he had been made older than his years. He had found solace and comfort in his sister's house and family when, upon his return from the Navy, he found that Spanish flu had claimed the life of his young wife and their only son. These days he was sometimes a little slower to react and give support, as he was now in the very feminine and possessive clutches of his new bride Joy, but he tried and Sophie and John always appreciated that.

She suddenly realised that her uncle was speaking to her and deep in thought she had not been listening to a word he was saying. Luckily she had noticed that Joy was admiring the picnic set that both she and John had picked out as a wedding gift. It didn't seem much when compared to the gifts of other family members, but it was all they could afford and a great deal of thought had gone into it.

'We hope that you like it?' Sophie replied assuming that it was the picnic set that Richard was talking about. 'Mum used to tell us all about your explorations and exciting picnic trips up the river when you were both younger. So it seemed to be made for you. Perhaps you will take a trip together and use it sometime?'

The bride prodded precariously around the basket's contents, thanking Sophie and John for their thoughtfulness. Tucking her hand through Richard's arm, under the glare of the chandeliers above, a ray of light became trapped in the prisms of the huge diamond ring displayed on her fourth finger and it glinted provocatively flicking mirrored shards in all directions. She beamed with delight at the effect.

'It has been a glorious day. You look beautiful Joy, and the dress is absolutely stunning,' Sophie said sincerely to Richard's bride. Joy wore a cream strapless gown, with a sweetheart neckline accentuated by a lace ruche that ran down the entire bodice, the skirt of the dress pinched in at the waist with a real detachable yellow orchid. It complemented her bouquet which was made from orchids provided by her father's gardener who had grown them specially in his greenhouse. All the way down the back, the dress was finished with beautiful lace buttons; Richard had bought Joy some pearls as a wedding gift amongst a trillion other things. Slightly blushing, she toyed with and twisted them around vainly with her fingertips as she absorbed Sophie's compliments. Sophie thought how she resembled Betty Grable, but an older version of course. Richard smiled and nodded approvingly at her kind words and then, sensing her eagerness to get away, he loosened his hold.

'You do look beautiful, Mrs Beaumont,' said Richard, taking his new wife by the hand and kissing it gently. 'Shall we?' he invited and he guided his new wife to the dancefloor.

A round of applause erupted as the bride and groom appeared on the dancefloor and Sophie paused briefly to watch. She smiled with relief that her uncle appeared to be so happy before tiptoeing outside and down the terrace to the edge of the garden where John stood deep in thought.

Sophie slipped her arm through her brother's and said, 'Found you,' then with a light shiver, added, 'Penny for your thoughts?'

John stroked her arm and gazing upwards, he sighed, 'I worry about you Soph, being at the house on your own. Mrs Jenkins is coping alright, isn't she? I mean, she is getting on a bit now and…'

'Don't even suggest it, she loves our house and is part of the family. She is absolutely fine. Trust me my darling big brother, everything is fine.' She squeezed his waist and gave him a big smile.

John sighed. 'The army is keeping me away for longer and longer periods. There is a lot going on in Europe at the moment, such as…' He paused, a frown crawling across his face.

'I read the newspapers sometimes; you don't have to explain.'

'You know, Uncle Richard wants you to come and stay here with him and Joy for a while. They have both spoken to me about it today and it might be for the best.'

'I don't think so,' retorted Sophie, devastated at the suggestion. 'Mrs Jenkins is a great housekeeper and I help out all the time. I'm fine.'

'I fear for you, Sophie, I really do. I might be away a long time. You're too young to be left home alone. Mrs Jenkins isn't getting any younger and I'm not sure that I can afford to keep her for much longer on my wages. I might even have to sell the house.'

'Absolutely not! Mum would never forgive you.'

'Well, mum isn't here anymore,' he said cautiously.

'John, it's our home. You couldn't you wouldn't. I'm not coming here and that's that! I won't, I won't,' she implored. 'Oh what a horrible, horrible day, I can't take any more of this.' She slumped to the ground, bursting into tears. 'Now I'm a burden to my brother!'

'Hey, hey,' comforted John, pulling her shoulders into his chest. 'You can never be a burden, Sophie. You're my little sister and I love you. It's just that times are a little difficult and uncertain right now and I can't see a light at the end of the tunnel!'

'I wish Mum was here, she would know what to do,' said Sophie with exasperation.

'If Mum was here we wouldn't be in this mess,' John said in one big deep breath.

The garden was beginning to form wandering shadows as the warm orange glow of the sun sank lower in the sky. John thought to himself that it was a shame his mother couldn't be here to see Richard get married and was sure she would have approved of Joy and put Sophie to rights. He thought that his mother and Joy would have got on well. They were remarkably alike in character: strong, independent, resourceful, warm, both sharing similar family struggles. Joy had lost her husband to the trenches as so many had, worked her way to the top in the clothing industry and brought up a daughter all by herself. She doted on Uncle Richard and him on her.

'I think he sees some of our Mum in Joy,' John said, not realising that he had spoken his thoughts aloud and correcting himself quickly as he saw Sophie's eyes blacken.

‘Well I don’t like her,’ Sophie said, half of her delicate beautiful face bathed warmly in the depleting sunset. ‘She’s false and if I lived with them, it wouldn’t be long before I was demoted to a maid taking care of the chores. I’ll be like that, that Wilt Dizzy film that we went to see last month, running away with all those gnomes and she’s really a wicked witch.’ She gasped, frightening herself.

‘You mean Walt Disney and Snow White silly,’ chortled John. ‘I don’t think she would turn you into a maid and I don’t think that Uncle Richard will appreciate you calling his new wife a wicked witch, especially when she looks like Betty Grable with a few years added,’ he remarked checking over his shoulder.

‘Oh gosh, I had exactly the same thought earlier on,’ she gasped again. ‘She does though, doesn’t she?’

‘What?’ said John, miles away again as other thoughts distracted him.

‘Look like an older Betty Grable? I wonder if Uncle Richard thinks so?’ She giggled excitedly.

‘Lucky old Richard.’ John winked. ‘You know you might grow to like her and become the best of friends. After all she has impeccable taste and you have Uncle Richard in common.’

‘I’d rather get a job,’ she replied. ‘Can we go home now, *pleeeasse?*’

‘What? Halfway through? That would never do. How is the party going anyway?’ queried John.

‘The party’s great. It’s just the guests, all pretending to be something they’re not. Aunt Marjorie thought I was Aunt Delsie’s daughter and Cousin Clara…’

‘I know, I know, I’ve had enough too. Thanks for rescuing me from Aunt Prue by the way.’ John smirked.

Sophie apologised profusely, saying that she had tried her best to get to him.

John turned to his sister and realised in her earnest stare of sincerity how much she resembled their mother. It hit him sometimes just how much he missed her and there were days when he genuinely couldn’t look at his sister because of it. She looked radiant and quite grown up in her dress, which she had slightly altered from one of their mother’s that had been made especially for such an occasion but rarely used in the latter days. She hadn't thrown anything away. She couldn't. She had inherited her mother's stature and figure as well as her brown hair that fell about her bare shoulders in small curls and her deep brown chestnut eyes which brought her pale complexion to life. For a minute, John shuddered. It was just as if she had come back to life. Feeling a ghostly chill around their shoulders, they put their arms around each other and together ventured bravely into the awaiting jaws of the party once again.

As they stepped into the ballroom, John reminded her calmly, 'Remember, black sheep that we are, we are here for Uncle Richard, nobody else!'

'I know,' she replied. 'The rest of them can go to hell for all I care,' Sophie said and John knew she meant it.

'Have I told you how beautiful you look today?' John asked. He took her hand and led her onto the dance floor where for a brief moment they danced so as not to regret not having done so when they returned home.

'Just before we left,' she replied.

'I like what you have done to Mum's old dress. You have a natural talent with fashion.'

'I know where this is going and yes, I am well aware that Joy works in the clothing industry, but the answer is still no.'

'Alright, alright, I admit defeat.'

'I was thinking though…' she began.

'Oh dear Lord, is that wise?'

She gently hit him on the arm. 'I was thinking that it might be nice to invite Tom round for dinner one evening. Perhaps some of your officers would like to?'

'You remind me of Mum today.' The thought had been there all day and it just had to be said. 'In fact I can see so much of her in you.'

'Stop changing the subject! We can all sit out on the terrace at the back of the house when the weather is a little warmer. I can pop out into the orchard for fresh fruit – I was thinking strawberries.'

They continued to dance, swirling in large circles so that her dress would billow a little, which she clearly liked to see as John noticed her head tilt down to watch every so often. There was soon a gentle tap on John's shoulder.

'May I?' interrupted Uncle Richard. He twirled Sophie around a few times, much to her delight as the crowd watched and she became centre stage before returning her to John.

'I think that we are about to be off now.' Richard winked. Joy slid gracefully alongside him in her going away suit, clutching her bouquet. It was of course (as Sophie would later surmise to her brother) the perfect suit to complement Uncle Richard's attire. Sophie had seen a similar one in one of the latest magazines. It was worn by one of the other famous film stars that Joy didn't resemble – probably Olivia de Havilland or someone like that. It was a Mainbocher copy in navy Forstmann wool. Its collarless peplum style was offset by pockets at the bust and hips. She wore it with a paisley printed ascot and a thin, patent belt. She had a tilted straw Homburg hat on her head and black gabardine shoes with patent trim on her small dainty feet. She had added white doeskin gloves that really set off the ensemble nicely. Sophie knew all about fashion. After all, it had been their mother's passion too.

'Is milady ready?' asked Uncle Richard.

'Oh Richard, really.' Joy shied with a sheepish grin, yet clearly loving every minute of the attention she was getting. She really did look the part. To all the expectant ladies' amazement anxiously waiting for the throwing of the bouquet, Joy promptly handed Sophie the flowers. The once excited bustle now faded to silence as Joy spoke dramatically and for all to hear.

'On behalf of me and my husband, I wish to thank you all for coming today, it has certainly been an experience. I want to thank you all for welcoming me so warmly into the Beaumont family.' She then turned to Richard. 'Well, what a family you have here my dear. What can I say? Sophie. Thank you for being the nearest thing to a daughter today, for my Katherine couldn't be here. I hope we become friends; you will always be welcome in this house' – and looking at John continued – 'both of you,' before pecking them on their cheeks.

Her eyes a little watery, she steered Richard to the door and they left in a flurry of rice seeds and flower petals, quickly handed out in little napkins by the staff during her succinct speech.

'Well that was one in the eye for all and sundry,' said John, staring at Sophie gobsmacked. 'Good old Joy, where did all that come from? I didn't see that one coming. Wicked old witches, gnomes, maids and chores eh?'

'It doesn't change anything and I don't care,' snapped a resisting Sophie, although it was clear she had difficulty hiding a smile when looking around at the reactions of the remaining crowd. 'I'm not coming to stay here and that's that.' She then patted her brother on the shoulder and left him alone to get something to nibble from the remainder of the spread.

The guests had begun to spill from the house down to the path towards the awaiting taxi that was to take the bride and groom to their honeymoon destination. Europe was in the grip of moving borders, uprisings and changing governments. Political speculation and rumours were rife. Joy loved to travel and Paris would have been heaven in May but Richard and Joy had decided to stay closer to home on this occasion but as to where… No one was privy to that information except themselves. Richard had done well for himself along with the natural progression of inheriting the family estate in Sussex. He had bought Joy a small country house outside Exeter, much to her delight. It was anybody's guess where they were going, but Exeter was probably where they had gone to. You never really knew with Uncle Richard. He could be a wily old so-and-so and take you by surprise now and then.

John followed his sister into the drawing room

'I don't want to go back in there,' she whispered.

'I know. As soon as the car has gone, we will make our excuses, say our goodbyes and then we can go home.'

'Thank you,' she said in relief.

The celebrations were naturally coming to an end at midnight anyway with the last few guests departing. A few, unlike John and Sophie, had a long journey ahead and had been invited to stay. Others had arranged to stay at a bed and breakfast in the village. Staff and doors were clanging and banging – trolleys loaded with crockery by now – and attempting to clear up some of the debris. People were clambering over and between each other to and fro and in and out of rooms, and it seemed a bit chaotic to say the least, so nobody noticed them slipping away.

It only took them half an hour to walk home from the wedding and the exhaustion of the day soon settled in. They quietly unlocked the door so as not to wake the neighbours. Next door was unlikely to have heard them anyway, but respectfully, they still crept inside, pecked each other goodnight and took themselves upstairs. John threw off his jacket and collapsed backwards on his bed, closed his heavy eyes and began drifting off to sleep immediately. He began recalling the day's events, confusing in his almost unconscious state his mother, Joy, Anne and his sister among the throngs of people, but he was dreaming and the dream – never meaning to last – eventually dissipated into darkness.

He suddenly found himself awake with a start to the slamming of a door. He didn't know for how long he had drifted away and for a minute he wasn't sure where he was, but he was still fully dressed. The comfort and familiarity of his own room kicked in and his eyelids started to flicker once more. Then the door to the back garden slammed shut down stairs. There was no mistaking the sound; this time he roused himself and clicked on the bedside light to look at the time. It was 2:30 in the morning.

Somebody was awake and it sounded like they had just gone out into the back garden. Reluctantly he raised himself from the bed, pulled himself to the window, rested his elbows on the ledge and peered into the darkness. Slowly, as his eyes focused, he made out a figure perched on the end of the terrace. It was Sophie.

He grabbed his jacket from the top of the bed and headed downstairs. Anyone else would have been in a rush, but to John this was nothing new. Once outside and in the garden, he walked across the terrace.

The moon was full, shimmering over the garden in gentle blue shards and the air was fresh and crisp.

'I'm sorry,' she sobbed, realising that her brother was approaching her. She could barely breathe through the sobs.

'What's wrong?' John asked.

He noticed that she was only wearing a flimsy nightgown and so put his suit jacket over her shoulders. She shivered as the heavy jacket fell about her shoulders. Her arms were wrapped up around her knees, which she had pulled in tight to her chest.

He sat down next to her. His legs stretched out, putting his heels onto the damp grass, next to her pale bare feet.

'It's been three years,' she sobbed, her chin resting on her knees.

'Jesus, I didn't realise,' John replied. He put his arm around his sister and stared up at the moon. Of course he knew it had been three years. It had not been an easy thing to forget and never would be. It was the same charade that he had played every year at this time. Every year she would remember, and every year he would pretend to forget in the futile hope that one day, she would be able to let it go.

'You'll catch your death out here,' he said to her. 'Come on, let's get you back to bed before we wake up the neighbours.'

She didn't move and instead continued to stare down to the bottom of the darkness in the garden. She had managed to control herself a little, but small crystal tears still clung to the bottoms of her eyes. Those that had previously escaped left delicate tracks across her soft skin, for other tears to follow.

'Sophie, we must get you inside. You have barely any clothes on and it's cold and damp now.'

'Are you ashamed of me for what I did?' she sniffed,

'Why on earth would you say such a thing?' John demanded, unnerved by the question. She had never made a comment like it before. 'Of course I'm not. Why would I be ashamed of my little sister?'

The tears that had been holding on followed the tracks left by the others. Despite its regularity it still hurt him to see her old wounds reopen.

'It was all my fault, all my fault. Oh, God forgive me,' she pleaded.

'Sophie.' John gently shook her. 'It was never your fault, never. It was all just a tragic accident.'

'John, promise me,' she begged, looking imploringly at him with her round chestnut eyes glistening with more tears ready.

'Promise you what?' he asked, standing, pulling her up and trying to lead her inside.

'Promise you won't make me go to Uncle Richard's. Please don't punish me. I'll get a job. That's what I'll do. I'll get a job, and then I can stay here.'

'No one is going to punish you,' said John in frustration. Then, wearily, he said, 'You don't need to get a job, Sophie. We'll manage. I'll manage. Haven't I always looked after you since Mum? I don't blame you for anything, Sophie. I love you, and you're my little sister. Come on, let's get you upstairs.'

He struggled, tired with the weight of the day.

'The weekend is nearly over all ready,' Sophie sighed sadly. 'You'll be gone again soon?'

'Yep,' he said, hugging her tightly. He loved his sister more than anything in the world and he still remained uneasy and uncertain about leaving her again when clearly nothing had changed. He had so hoped that she would have seen what he saw in Joy: someone whom she could look upon as a role model.

'When will you be back again?' she asked cautiously, already knowing the answer.

'When I can,' he replied.

'I hope they don't send you too far this time, although it makes me feel better knowing Tom is your Sergeant Major and that he is always with you,' she reasoned, her emotions ebbing.

'Sophie, I don't have a choice. You do know that, don't you?' he implored. 'I might be called away at any time and when you need me, I might not be able to get back for you. Not because I don't want to be, but because I just can't be. That's why Uncle Richard…'

'Oh, yes, yes, yes, I understand!' she surrendered. 'I understand. I hope you never get sent too far away, but if you did… promise me you'll try to get back. I don't want to lose you too. I'm not too lonely because of Mrs Jenkins, but I do miss you when you are not here. I'll be waiting here for you until you come back, as always,' she said in-between short, sharp breaths.

'That's my girl,' he said, squeezing her before leading her up the narrow staircase and finally into her room. He tucked her tightly into her bed, switched off the lamp light and crept towards the door. 'Goodnight,' he gently whispered.

Dinner on the Terrace
June 1938

'What dessert shall I make?' Sophie called out, her bare feet gently pressing upon the soft grass between the avenues of apple trees. She was heading towards the strawberry field now bursting with a display of voluptuous bright red fruits nestling on beds of straw in evenly spaced identical rows that ran horizontally at the end of the orchard.

Behind their cottage was a working 'pick your own' farm, with large orchards of a variety of seasonal fruits and vegetables. It belonged to Mr Maynard who had inherited the farm from his father's father and people would come from miles away during the varying seasons to fill their baskets with his delicious fresh produce.

His wife had a little wooden hut at the entrance to the farm, which displayed what was available and announced you could buy the farm produce there if you hadn't the time or notion to 'do it yourself' and pop your laden baskets on the huge clanking scales that towered over the doorway.

Their mother used to weigh Sophie on them before and after they had been to the fields and every time Mr Maynard's wife would always comment on how she had grown in just half an hour because of all the goodness in the fresh fruit and vegetables that she was eating. Carrots would enable her to see in the dark, strawberries gave her colour in her cheeks and apples would keep the doctor away! It was just a wonderful place where all your senses would explode into life: the aromas and scents, the textures and tastes, the palettes of vivid hues all blending into one glorious experience.

Now was the time that Sophie liked best when all the soft fruits were abundant in the fields: strawberries, gooseberries, black and red currants, raspberries and of course her most favourite of all, cherries that were all just ripening and the perfect ingredients for a summer pudding.

She had not wasted her time whilst John had been away. She had become a very skilled little cook under the watchful eye and experienced guidance of Mrs Jenkins since her mother had gone. Her own recipe book was growing by the days.

The farm was a valuable asset at the bottom of the garden. It had virtually everything they needed. Old Maynard and his wife had always said they could help themselves as long as they didn't catch them wasting anything. Sophie and John would help themselves on occasions, but Sophie would always keep a record of what they had taken and pay Mrs Maynard every penny she owed when she went to collect the eggs on Fridays.

The only time they went scrumping was usually in the autumn when the apples had fallen naturally from the tree or still dangled precariously on the branch, waiting for a strong breeze to finally sever their stalks. By then the 'pick your own' hut was closed for the winter. John was normally home around the autumn for a while and Tom would often stay for a few weeks. It was her favourite time of the year when they were both around. Although Tom had yet to use the apples to make the homemade cider he so often threatened to create.

John loved the orchards; they reminded him of his Grandma Baker who used to work on George Ralling's farm, pruning in the spring and picking in the autumn. Cox, Worcester, Bramley and Laxton, superb apples to name but a few and then there were the sweet pears on the far side. He remembered helping to bottle the pears with her – apart from those that melted with mouth-watering juices in his mouth – and then there were her scrumptious apples pies. There was always fruit on the table and always something irresistible cooking in her oven. She had been the last tie to his father and these memories were a precious limited selection he would share with Sophie.

At the end of their garden, next to a rather rickety potting shed was a small black gate, almost hidden by brambles and the shade from the looming fir trees that towered above. Gardening was not one of John's fortes and since his mother's death had played little part in their lives. Mrs Jenkins kept the worst under control for them and Tom would tinker when he stayed occasionally, but the bottom of the garden nowadays still looked rather dark, dingy and unloved. It had always appeared a bit spooky to John, encouraged unhelpfully by Ted's graphically described ghost stories as a child, so he had always been nervous about descending into the depths of its shrubbery. It seemed silly now, especially when, as he approached the gate, you could see the dramatic shards of light awakening the orchard floor and scattering pools of sunlight stepping stones. 'Magical,' he thought to himself.

'Sooooo,' called Sophie again. 'What dessert shall I make?'

'I will leave that up to you,' John replied. 'You're the cook.'

He opened the gate and ducked under the wild honeysuckle full of bees whirling and buzzing lazily collecting the pollen from the flowered vine that wildly wound itself along the hedgerow.

'What about something with strawberries in it? I think I said that once before?' she called from somewhere far ahead.

'Tom likes strawberries,' he called back.

'I know,' she chuckled, suddenly appearing from nowhere, brushing his ear with her voice. 'When he stayed with us through last summer a whole bowl disappeared over night.'

'That seems to answer your question then, strawberries it is with sugar and fresh cream,' he murmured. Then licking his lips and rolling his eyes, he caught her up in his arms. 'What was that strange dessert that our mum used to make with strawberries?'

Sophie laughed out loud. 'You mean the strawberry surprise?'

'It had other things in it, bits of sponge, cream and there was something else.'

'Don't ask me, but I know exactly what you're referring to, it was horrific. I know for a fact that you ate it all out of politeness, because there is no way anyone could have liked it!'

'Of course I didn't like it, but why did she keep making it and where on God's green earth did she get the recipe?'

'She made it up silly! The only reason she kept making it was she thought we liked it.'

'Tom liked it, didn't he?'

'No!' she laughed. 'Tom hated it! He said to me once when mum wasn't listening that once you had eaten trench cuisine you could eat anything.' She began tickling him, which he hated. 'All that suffering we endured from Mum's strawberry surprise was your fault for pretending it was so good!'

He suddenly and playfully pushed her into some thick grass he had seen that looked thick enough to break her fall. After a shriek and a tumble, she regained her posture and launched herself at him in an attempted to retaliate although her brother was prepared and she found her attempts to wrestle him to the floor were in vain and they continued to walk for a brief perfect moment in time without a care in the world, but it couldn't last.

John's company had been given their orders to move to the docks in a few weeks, ready to sail to foreign soil. Nobody knew where they would be heading and nobody had thought to even guess where they might end up. The inexperienced greeted the news with excitement and fervour, an opportunity to see foreign climates, people and places. John's reaction was quite different however. Adolf Hitler's influences and his bullying tactics had gone from strength to strength and Germany was throwing her weight around in the political arena. There was a chilling uncertainty running down many nations' spines and now the resonant sound of war was looming on the horizon and John knew it.

As they rummaged through the straw gathering the luscious fruits in abundance, as many being eaten as were collected under the watchful smile of the benevolent summer sun, the reality of it all seemed so far away. It couldn't last and John played out a hundred different scenarios in his head as he tried his best to figure out how best to tell her.

John had invited some of the Officers from his Company to their home for an evening meal; a suggestion Sophie had been encouraging for many months if not years now. What John probably had in mind was a friendly quiet evening with his men. After all, they had been given some leave from the barracks and no doubt intended to make the most of it, but Sophie wanted it to be special. It was a glorious summer evening so she had suggested that they all eat outside on the terrace. She was very excited. Apart from Uncle Tom, she had never met any of the Company about which John would often talk. It had been a strange change for her since her brother had been promoted. He was hardly ever around anymore, and his visits were ever briefer, especially with all the training and the responsibilities bestowed upon him. But on days and afternoons like this one, she loved having him home.

For the remainder of the day, Sophie spent her time busy in the kitchen getting the supper ready. Mrs Jenkins on one of her few days off had thoughtfully left all the vegetables prepared and now they were gently bubbling in their pans on the range, the enticing aroma of a chicken casserole wafted in and out of John's nostrils.

'Mmmm, that smells great,' John gurgled in her ear.

She finished coring the strawberries they had picked and strategically placed them circularly within a sweet pastry base, topping them with whipped cream.

'Almost ready. Put this on the table would you?' said Sophie, thrusting a basket full of warm crusty bread into John's hands. 'Everyone should be arriving soon.'

No sooner had she uttered these words than the first knock at the door came. It was Tom, of course. 'Thought I would arrive a little earlier otherwise you wouldn't have time to do anything with these,' and from various pockets inside and outside of his jacket he produced an array of spirits.

'Oooh cocktails.' Sophie clapped excitedly.

'Only for the grown-ups though, eh?' John winked at Tom over her shoulder.

'Well, really, you'd best get on with chores yourselves then,' exclaimed Sophie and then realising that they were pulling her leg, she sniffed, 'You two!'

'It's good to see you again my dear,' said the old Sergeant Major, giving her a heart-warming cuddle. 'Something smells good.'

'It's only chicken Uncle Tom,' she beamed, her arm releasing her mother's oldest and most trusted friend. 'I'll put your jacket upstairs in your room for you. I presume you're staying tonight?' she remarked. He was as much a part of the furniture as the furniture itself these days and had always been considered part of the family. 'I think you should.'

He looked beyond her towards her brother before responding. 'Don't mind if I do.'

For John, Tom was the only link left to his father. He loved to hear about their youthful exploits and his heroism in France during the Great War. He had gotten to know his father through Tom's eyes. It was a comfort to him. For Sophie it was slightly different. She adored him; Tom was the one family friend that her mother had always said could be relied on. She trusted him completely. A steadfast surrogate father figure to his best ability under the circumstances, dependable through all the turbulent times they had been through.

Before long the terrace was teeming with laughter, the chitter and chatter of voices rolled in and out of varying topics of conversation between appreciative mouthfuls of mains and dessert. Afterwards, compliments, cocktails, cigarettes and cigars flowed generously and as dusk finally slid behind the curtain of darkness, the crickets ceased their calling and silence fell temporarily in the surrounding meadows until the chain reaction of nocturnal vibrations filled the air. Sophie lit the candles and the luminous body of burning gas fluctuated against the depths of the evening. The quivering wings of insects attracted by the brandished light made the flames flicker and dance; moths tapped the windows and fell disorientated on the table and terrace floor.

All three of John's Company's Lieutenants had managed to arrive, although Lieutenant Thomas was considerably late due to getting lost. Captain Simon James, the Battalion's Medical Officer had put in an appearance. Sergeant Scott brought his rather dry sense of humour to the table: mixed with Lieutenant Bailey's comedic banter and Lieutenant Keyes who seemed quite sensitive, it made the evening a memorable one.

Sophie had loved every minute of the evening. She was the perfect hostess to his new military family and it was nice to put faces to the names she has heard so much about of late.

'That tart was bloody marvellous,' said Bailey. 'I think even Lieutenant Keyes enjoyed it.'

'Yeah, but he is a bit of a tart!' Scott joked in his one-toned voice, as he continually blew perfectly formed rings of smoke from his cigarette, each inside the other forming a chain.

'That's clever,' Sophie said admiringly, 'but it's bad for your health.'

'He's bad for everyone's health,' Keyes chipped in, getting his own back and scoring an invisible point in the air with his finger.

'It was a lovely meal and company,' complimented Lieutenant Thomas, trying to bring some sobriety to the conversation. 'You must have been slaving away in the kitchen all day. Would you like some help with the dishes?'

'Would you like some help with the dishes?' mimicked Bailey in a high-pitched voice. 'If you want to do dishes, Lieutenant Thomas, get back to the barracks on the double and while you're volunteering, my underwear needs washing as well… Sorry Miss,' said Bailey acknowledging Sophie's look of dismay, 'but he's a tart as well.' In unison they all collapsed into boisterous and crude laughter.

'You want to be careful, Lieutenant Thomas, chatting up the Captain's sister,' said Scott waving the knife he was paring an apple with. 'You'll be in the firing line before you know it, you mark my words,' but as he threw himself back in his chair looking pleased with himself, he leaned too far and fell off the chair. Even Sophie had to join in the hysterical laughter that followed as he scrambled back onto the seat, embarrassed. This time Lieutenant Thomas scored an invisible point in the air with his finger.

'Seriously,' asked the Lieutenant again. 'Would you like some help with the dishes? I'm a jolly dab hand at it you know.'

'Thank you, Lieutenant Thomas. You wash and I'll wipe,' she instructed as they headed indoors.

'Call me, Anthony,' he said rocking up and down on his toes quite nervously.

'Anthony,' she repeated, trying it out for what she hoped would not be the last time.

John leaned back in his chair watching them go and Tom watched him watching them.

Deployment was a word that weighed heavily on their minds and so it was inevitable that it had been brought up as a matter of course and conversation earlier in the evening. Nobody could disagree with Bailey's comment of 'Not whilst I'm eating,' but it had reared its ugly head again. For Sophie it was the first it had been mentioned, a streak of resentment for her brother's silence filled half her heart whilst the other drowned in despair, but the good hostess that she was kept her calm on the exterior. There must have been a reason why her brother had not told her and the sheepish look he gave her when Keyes brought it up – along with Tom's rolling eyes when he caught them both – told her perhaps enough.

'I would just like to know where they are sending us so I can gather medical supplies,' Captain James commented.

'Surely the army will sort out your medical supplies?' Sophie quizzed as she returned to gather more dishes and the like.

''Course they will,' he said callously, 'but if we are getting sent to the jungle, then there is no harm scrounging a few extra supplies to counter the local diseases, like malaria for example. You know there is so little known about tropical diseases, snake bites, spider bites, among other things. There are all kinds of other critters waiting to pick us off one by one out there. There is so much shit out there in the jungle, you just don't know what you're heading for. Just a little nick or nip in jungle conditions, wham!'

He slammed his hand down onto the table, causing Keyes to jump.

'Next thing you know infection on infection, sickness, fever, dead! I saw it all the time. The army gives you plenty of supplies for what they think you'll need, but they never really know how much you're going to use and nine times out of ten, it's never enough.

'The medical and surgical advances have come a long way in the past twenty years, it's ironic that out of the last war the field of cosmetic and plastic surgery has come along leaps and bounds, but we still can't stop a bloody mosquito or some unseen bacteria or virus in the air or water from wiping out an entire company, just like that.' He clicked his fingers in the air.

Sophie was captivated. She had thought about a medical career herself.

Captain Simon James was an interesting and informative character and had only been assigned to John's Battalion fairly recently. He was well educated and an experienced and eloquent medical man who always wore a cheeky smile below his small greying moustache. He was dedicated to his profession and as death had been a constant companion on the battlefields of the Somme to the point of emotional immunity, he tended not to get too involved with people on a personal level, but was very personable and intriguing. John's commanding officer was Major Harold Love. He had apparently sworn that there was no better Medical Corps man in the army than Simon James. She couldn't help but feel comforted that he would be close by her brother in the future.

'Environmental-related illnesses can be as common a killer as the battlefield itself,' Simon continued.

‘Such as?’ Sophie asked, twisting the stem of an empty wine glass between her thumb and forefinger.

‘I’m going to have another slice of this strawberry tart if I may, before you take it away?’ Simon digressed, already leaning over the table for the knife. ‘Such as, young lady, that I would really like to get my hands on a supply of sulphanilamide to coat wounds as a first line of defence against infection. Extra quinine wouldn’t go amiss either, especially should we end up in the jungle. Remember what I said about the creepy crawlies?’

Sophie nodded, her mouth wide open as she concentrated. ‘You slammed your hand on the table when you told us.’

‘Did you know there is a type of louse that burrows under your skin, lays its eggs there and the larvae eats you alive?’

‘Uh Doc!’ Bailey almost choked with a cry. ‘Straight up?’

‘Straight up,’ confirmed Simon, wiping away some of the cream from the corner of his mouth. ‘There is so much shit in the tropics you just don’t know what you are heading into.’

‘Oh, of course,’ said Sophie waking from her trance and trundling back to the kitchen to find Anthony in full swing at the kitchen sink. ‘More I’m afraid,’ she said with a twinkle in her eye, grabbing a cloth to dry the rinsed crockery waiting on the draining board.

‘You really are a fab cook,’ praised Anthony.

‘That’s Mrs Jenkins’s influence I’m afraid,’ Sophie sighed. ‘I didn’t want to go live with my Uncle Richard when my mum died and John arranged for Mrs Jenkins to stay on as housekeeper as he was going away more and more. So she encourages me with all the housekeeping things that will help to make me a good wife one day. She’s getting on a bit but she is amazing. You know, she can make something out of nothing!’

‘Sounds like a good teacher and I think you’ll make someone a lovely wife one day,’ remarked Anthony.

‘That’s very kind of you,’ Sophie said, as she stacked the last plate with a clink. Her cheeks felt ever so warm. ‘Best get back,’ she hinted. She had felt sorry for him being the brunt of the taunts for offering her assistance and she wanted to avoid any further embarrassment for him. The torment had started before the evening had even begun by him getting lost and turning up late on his motorbike in a bit of a fluster and the night was still young. Sure enough as they returned to the terrace, Bailey piped up, now having become a little the worse for wear from his sixth Tom Collins of the evening.

'Aw, did he wishy washy his handy pandys then?'

'We did wash our handy pandys thank you,' Sophie responded, much to his surprise. She then rounded on him, 'I bet if your wife were here you'd have been jumping up saying, "Yes dear, no dear, three bags full dear." Fortunately for you she's not, but I'm sure when she sees the state of you when you get home, the repercussions will be a drop in the ocean compared to this *gentleman's* experience!'

'Woooohooooh!' called out Tom and drew his first finger into his thumb as if pulling an imaginary trigger at Bailey. Bailey's jaw dropped for the second time. He then cupped his hands together and clasped them to his breast as if he had been shot through the heart.

'You know,' he eventually replied with a little grin. 'You are right, I can't go back home like this: she will kill me. Sergeant Major, brace yourself because I am sharing with you tonight.'

Sophie laughed at him as he winked at Tom and poured another glass whispering to her as he did, 'If I'm sharing with him I'm going to need this!'

Bailey truly was on comical form this evening. Unable to contain themselves any longer, everyone joined in with heartfelt laughter and sarcasm. Sophie never wanted it to end; the house rarely contained so much happiness. It helped wipe away bad memories and warmed her heart in the fresh spring air. There was another reason for her to smile: for the second time in only a few minutes she was sure that Anthony had been looking at her across the large table.

John, settling back in his chair, was surprised at her defensive reaction over Anthony and he noted the pair of them clearly enjoying each other's company as the evening progressed further. Tom caught his eye with a very large smile upon his face and a subtle wink, but John was not pleased with what he deduced was taking place at all. All jokes put aside, what was going on here? Was Anthony chatting up the Captain's sister?

'Over my dead body,' he quietly said to himself.

'Did you say something?' Tom asked, leaning over. 'That was a bit of a surprise, eh?'

'She felt sorry for him that was all. You know what she's like. It's her maternal instinct to defend the underdog,' he excused.

Tom raised his eyebrows and drew on his cigarette, saying nothing which provoked John further.

'She is still a child and very naïve. She's only eighteen. She doesn't realise,' he now said defensively.

'I took younger children to France twenty years ago,' he grunted. 'Looks and acts pretty grown up to me. I've known many a woman who was mature before their years.' He smirked, but quickly put his glass to his mouth to hide it as John shot him a glance.

'They've only just met,' John protested.

'Who's being naïve, now?' asked Tom sympathetically, heading towards the drinks cabinet to pour himself a whisky. He always poured himself a whisky before retiring for the night.

John wondered what he had meant by his last comment and followed him into the living room. 'They aren't in a relationship,' a fact he said to himself. 'They've only just met!'

'You say something again?' Tom said as he poured his whisky into a small glass.

She had no admirers, no beaus. She had never had a relationship. There was no one in her life except him and more than anything, she would never blindly attach herself to the first one that came along without his guidance and least of all, a fellow officer. Would she? Had she? He rubbed his chin with thought.

A doomed expression torpedoed John as he walked back outside and watched as Anthony whispered something in Sophie's ear and she giggled. He felt his body sinking as he watched her pressing her lips together, smiling at her glass and mentally retrieving her thoughts. She was drifting away as high as a balloon, further and further away and John realised he was in danger of losing the ribbon that held her.

A nervous uncertainty set into his brain that he had never considered before. The possibility she might blindly attach herself to the first person that came along without his guidance and mistake it for love. She caught his stare and smiled back meekly.

'Right lads,' Tom bellowed as the clock announced the arrival of one in the morning. 'The lady will be needing her beauty sleep and I'm not just talking about Gladys over there.' He pointed to Sergeant Scott.

Keyes prodded Scott gently and then signalled Bailey to give him a hand. 'Come on me ol' mucker, it's time to make a move. We don't want Gladys finding she's got a sister in the morning.' Keyes laughed.

'Who is Gladys?' Sophie asked Anthony quietly.

'Ah well, it's a bit difficult to explain without actually showing you,' he winced. 'I don't know if Captain Baker would be pleased if I did.'

'Uncle Tom?' she questioned with intrigue.

Tom looked to John who simply shrugged his approval and then grinned. Tom then beckoned Scott over and propped up by Keyes and Bailey simply said, 'May we see her?'

Scott released the top two buttons of his shirt. 'Let it be a lesson to you,' he slurred and as he undid more buttons an erotic tattoo of a nude woman was revealed in all her naked splendour.

Sophie was not as naïve as John perhaps liked to admit, but Gladys did take her by surprise. She stepped back, catching her breath and covering her mouth with her hands.

'A few years back,' Tom began as if telling a fairy tale. 'Many years, I might add, just before the First War, Sergeant Scott here first trod the drill grounds of the Navy. Believe it or not, he didn't smoke or drink then, coming from a very temperate background.

'On leave one day he fell in love with a girl called Betty. Nice lass, by all accounts. The date was set and he looked forward to coming home and marrying her at the end of his final voyage. Then, when the ship docked on his last night, his mates decided to throw him a farewell party and this was the result.'

'I couldn't go home and marry her after this, could I?' Scott stated.

'Oh I don't know…' Sophie replied and then looking at it again added, 'but probably not.'

'I did a runner and reenlisted with the army a week later. Gladys has been my only wife ever since.'

Tom could see Sophie wavering to the side of sympathy. 'Don't feel too sorry for him,' he said. 'As demented psychopaths go, he positively enjoys taking it out on the parade ground, shouting and insulting new recruits. If he seems like he has got nothing else, remember he has got the sexiest chest in the army.' He chuckled and tweaked Scott's cheek with his thumb and forefinger.

Whilst Keyes and Bailey began dragging Scott from the patio, Tom assumed the role of chauffeuring the guests to the door to a waiting taxi that had been pre-booked from dropping them off earlier. They were all profusely expressing their gratitude over and over again and all profusely drunk. Anthony, riding his motorbike home and still very sober, collected his goggles and waterproof jacket from amongst the array of coats hanging on the coat stand. He tarried for a moment, tapping his pockets for his keys, finding them and raising them in the air as if they had been pulled from a magician's hat. Sophie smiled.

'Thank you, Sir, thank you, Miss Baker. Spiffing evening,' he bowed and kissed her hand.

'It's Miss Watson, actually,' she commented tentatively. 'John is my half-brother, we shared the same mother but not the same father.'

'I'm so sorry. I didn't mean to offend,' he flapped. 'A pleasure to meet you Miss Watson, I don't suppose…'

'No she doesn't,' interrupted John, virtually shoving him out of the door. 'Goodnight Lieutenant Thomas, thank you for your company and ride home carefully,' said John edging him further.

'Goodnight!' Sophie called after him, but the door had already slammed shut.

'Nice lad, didn't you think Sophie?' asked Tom, his glass now shy of whisky.

'What on earth are you playing at telling a complete stranger our family business?' demanded John. '"He's only my half-brother!"'

'I didn't say it like that,' Sophie protested, shocked at his wrath.

'No she didn't,' agreed Tom.

'You stay out of this!' He pointed aggressively at Tom. 'This is a family matter!'

Sophie gasped in horror at John's remark. When he realised what he had said, he screwed his eyes up tightly and winced remorsefully every time the words repeated themselves in his head, praying that the ground might open up and swallow him whole.

Tom pouted his lips together and swallowed the last drop of whisky before placing the empty glass on the side table. 'Over-reacted there, son,' he said and then very emphatically pronounced, 'I mean, Sir.'

Sophie threw her arms around the old soldier. 'I'm so, so sorry Uncle Tom,' she said, and then turned on her brother wailing, 'What's got into you? How could you say such a thing? You've spoilt a really loving evening.' She kissed Tom on the cheek, shook her head disapprovingly at her brother and ran upstairs.

The silence was deplorable; somebody had to say something. It was Tom who broke silence first to pour oil over troubled waters.

'As I said earlier,' he said quietly and deliberately. 'Looks and acts pretty grown up to me and has a fire in her belly that one, just like your mother had. You see John, I don't see a weak, insecure, incapable, nervous little girl in need of being looked after anymore. I don't think you do either: maybe that's the problem. You are the one that's afraid of being left behind and alone John, not Sophie,' and with that he patted John on the shoulder and took himself up the stairs to bed.

'I'm sorry,' John said after him, aching to put his mistake right and Tom paused on the stairs.

There was so much more Tom probably wanted to say. This second silence was more painful than the first. Slowly he turned, his gaze looking beyond John, as if into a world that only he could see. Now they were there face to face again.

'Tom,' John murmured reaching towards him as he ascended the stairs now. 'Tom, I didn't mean what I said about family. It was unforgivable of me.'

Tom held the banister to steady himself and gave John a warm smile. He reached to where John was and placed his hands upon his shoulders. His eyes meeting John's and drawing a breath, he said, 'Forgotten already.'

Story Time

'You liked him, didn't you?' Tom asked Sophie in the kitchen next morning. He settled down at the small oak table whilst John, suffering with a slight headache from the night was clearing up outside.

She looked to see where her brother was before settling down opposite him placing a cup of tea in front of him, 'Well, he seemed nice.'

'I can sense a smile even though I am not looking at you,' he chortled. 'Common interests?'

'Don't know really. We didn't talk much, that's why I can't understand what all the fuss is about! And anyway, you are all going away soon. You can't get to know anyone in the space of a few weeks, can you?'

'Well, I don't know about that!' he said warily.

'Really? I sense a story and one I haven't heard before. If there is another story you haven't told me, you need to tell me now,' she pleaded. 'Is it a true story? I love your stories, Uncle Tom.'

'No, no,' he tormented. 'I think I've upset your brother enough for this weekend and it wouldn't do to be heard within earshot of a young lady.'

Making a point of looking all around her as if checking to see if there was anyone or anything around, she sat herself comfortably on the kitchen table, swinging her shapely legs in and out from under the table leaf. 'See, there are no ladies here, so don't hold back on my account. Did it all happen within three weeks?' she asked cheekily.

'You could say that,' he said reflectively. He pulled himself up on the kitchen table beside her and began. 'When I was first in France with John's father, we were stationed just outside a little village near Amiens. A very pretty little place called Contay. There was a bar and tabac at the furthest end of the village, which was out of bounds to the platoon, but we all used to take it in turns to sneak out to get our snout and an occasional drink. The barmaid was a pretty dark-haired little thing called Madeleine and she took quite a shine to me and, well, amongst other things, how shall I say it? She was very welcoming, very welcoming indeed and she spoilt me more than any of the others!'

'More than John's father Jack even?' Sophie asked, quite innocently.

'Jack?' questioned Tom and then on a quick about-turn, he said, 'Oh, Jack. God no, he wasn't one of the others. He had Helen at home to think about. Devoted to her, he was. He was a respectable officer and wouldn't be caught in a place like that. No, John's father would cover for me many a time and enable me to swap on the late guard shifts, so I saw her as often as was able or if I got a spot of leave, for instance. Her goose-feathered bed and a hot bath tub beat the trenches hands down. What she could do with her hands, well, I can't tell you. But it all got a bit risky,' he stated solemnly.

'What with all the Germans and everything?' asked Sophie sincerely.

'The Germans?' Tom sounded confused. 'The Germans? Oh no, they weren't a problem – well, not at that point. It was her bloody husband that was the problem. He kept coming home on leave from Verdun at the same time I did, purely coincidental I assure you, and it was technically becoming more and more difficult to find a private spot, pretending you're fixing something in the cellar and risking him catching me with my pants down all at the same time!'

'Sergeant Major Hill!' Sophie exclaimed, flicking him with the tea towel. 'She was married?'

'Oh yes, she was a needy little thing,' he chuckled.

'Then what happened?' Sophie asked, bewitched by this time.

'Oh well, I ran out of reasons for being there so often. All the locals knew what was going on and I wasn't her only admirer of course! It was only a matter of time before I caught something and it was going to be more than just trench foot! But when we got moved further up the line, it was too far to keep popping back and the whole affair sort of lost its momentum.' His tone deepened and darkened. 'Then Jack got killed and my nerves couldn't take it anymore. Life is more important than a quick fumble under the sheets when you're in the firing line, but I thought about her sometimes, poor little Madeleine. I went back after the war had finished,' he said quite lightly. 'Just to, well I don't know, just to see how things were, I suppose. You know skeletons in the closet, laying ghosts to rest and all that. The place was derelict. I asked after her at the bar and at the post office and an old local woman told me that after her husband had been killed at Verdun, Madeleine had got caught providing services to the German soldiers in more ways than one. They hung her from the old chestnut tree on the verge outside her own bar. The Germans that is, not the French! "*Putain*" the old lady said to me and spat at my feet, "*Bâtardes,*" I spat in reply. I borrowed a trowel from her potting shed, dug up some poppies that I'd noticed growing in the wheat field at the end of the lane as I came into the village and replanted them under the tree. Then I left. There was no point in being there anymore.'

'Oh, that's sad,' said Sophie, tears welling up in her eyes. It was rare that he would open up like this; normally the stories opened and ended on a jovial note.

'That's War,' was his simple reply.

'Shall I put the kettle on?' suggested a meek voice. Her brother had been listening for some time and whilst being lost in the story, Sophie hadn't even noticed him enter the kitchen and lean up against the cupboard next to her.

'Have you heard the story of Madeleine?' she asked him. 'It's so sad.' She jumped off the table, snapping them all out of the melancholy of the moment to get the cups and saucers out from the front room dresser.

John had heard it once before when Tom was half cut in Aldershot. It had taken him by surprise then and hearing it again reminded him of a private life that so few had been initiated into.

'I know what you are going to say,' Tom cut in before John could begin. 'Not all my tales have a happy ending, but I am running out of the happy and fluffy ones.'

John responded by shaking his head dismissively. He was just pleased that the previous night had been forgotten. Tom, however, clearly felt differently.

'Look at her John. She's a grown woman now and totally capable of looking after herself.'

John sighed and, keeping his voice low, said, 'She is still vulnerable.'

'We are all vulnerable.'

'Don't you remember?' John said, almost shouting in a whisper.

'Of course I remember, but perhaps it's *you* that's holding her back so she can't move on. You can't keep her caged up in childhood forever.' He appeared to check himself. 'What I am trying to say is, she won't need a guardian angel forever, John, and she won't need you forever. Sooner or later you will have to come to terms with that. I think the biggest problem right now is admitting to yourself that you actually want to let her go.'

'Of course I do,' John replied, snapping but still whispering. 'I just don't think he is a particularly good choice.'

'Choice?' Tom laughed. 'There hasn't been a choice yet. For God's sake man, nothing might develop out of this at all.'

Tom was right of course.

'What if it is different this time?' John asked.

'What if it is? Could have already been the spotty butcher's boy from down the road last summer for all you know. Were you here? No. It's all about trust John, trusting each other to make the right decisions in life at the right time. Give the girl some credit.'

'Couldn't be worse than that, could it?' said John feebly.

'What?' Tom asked, appearing to be confused at which part of the lecture he was referring to.

'The spotty butcher's boy from down the road. You don't think that she would, do you?' He seemed to shudder at the thought.

'Him? Of course not, I was merely giving an example. Take an old soldier's advice, John. If you love something, let it go: that is the true test of love and is always the one thing most appreciated, even if they don't remember to tell you. Have you ever considered that with you being a parent, your sister lost her brother?'

'My mother said that to me when I lost Annie. The first bit of your speech anyway,' he recalled aloud.

'Well, there you go. It must be good advice then,' he said warmly.

'I miss my mother. I wish she were here. This is tougher than the army,' he said wearily. 'I'm not too good at this hormone, birds and bees lark, am I?'

John truly loved his little sister and would protect her no matter what. She was all he had left, but he'd gotten himself all tangled up on this one and Tom's words – especially about losing a brother – had really hit home. His heart ached.

'At least you know Anthony,' Tom added. 'And anyway if he's home, you're home. What's the harm in that? You can keep an eye on things. Serving together, there is plenty of time to get to know him better.'

John let out a sigh and gave Tom one of his 'I hate it when you are right' looks, which were becoming more frequent as the years went on.

'Okay,' John began, his head nodding although his brain wasn't in total agreement just yet and still processing the details, as if it were signing an agreement with a great deal of small print. Sophie walked past with the saucers and began making the tea. John continued addressing Tom, but out of Sophie's earshot. 'Maybe it is time to let her go. We will see how it goes, but if he breaks her heart, I swear to God I will break his neck.'

Tom winked. 'You have made your mother proud. Time to let her stand up on her own and when she needs you' – he began walking out into the garden and called out behind him, 'you won't be far away.'

A Night Out

It was by pure chance that Sophie caught sight of Antony walking down the path to the front door. She perched herself on the arm of the couch and watched through the tangle of ivy that had begun to take over the window. He flicked and picked at the lapels of his uniform and then at the crown of his cap, which was tucked under the right armpit of his uniform. He raised his slightly pointed chin and pushed the knot of his tie as high as it would go comfortably between his crisp starched collars and glanced down at his highly polished boots. Fidgeting and rearranging his posture yet again, he twitched his shoulders back and rested his long lean trouser legs equidistance apart as if on parade under the order of 'at ease'. Finally, he reached forward, un-tangling the weathered bell cord from the clutches of the climbing rose that encased a porch-way type trellis around the door well and pulled. Stepping back briskly, he resumed his position, puffed out his chest and waited.

From his behaviour Sophie wondered how long it had taken him to muster up the bravado, but he was here now at April Cottage. He glanced nervously around, taking in the scenery of the front garden, licking his lips as his mouth had become a little dry. In his left hand he held his gloves and what appeared to be some tickets.

It had seemed an eternity until the nose of Mrs Jenkins the housekeeper peered around the door. When she saw the lieutenant's uniform, she came out more brusquely to the doorstep, wringing her hands dry into her apron.

'Captain Baker isn't here,' she remarked quite curtly. 'He's gone up to the big house to see his uncle with the Sergeant Major.' She jerked her head back indicating an easterly direction. 'He won't be back till late mind, so do you want to leave a message? Who shall I say called?'

'Um, well no actually,' he babbled profusely. 'I've come to ask, I mean, call upon Miss...' and before he could splutter another attempted word. Mrs Jenkins interrupted him, grinning impatiently.

'You'll be wanting Miss Sophie then I suppose,' she quacked, raising her eyebrows above her horned-rim tortoiseshell glasses, folding her arms and pumping up her bosom, a formidable foe that would have deflected any advancing army. 'Is she expecting you?'

'Well, no, not exactly,' he croaked.

'Wait there,' she said and slammed the door shut, leaving him staring at the tired, cracked woodwork of the front door.

Sophie hurried to look busy as Mrs Jenkins entered the front room, but there was no fooling Mrs Jenkins who took one look at her, huffed and returned to the front door.

'You'd better come in then,' she said, ushering him forward into the hallway. 'She's in the front room. You know where it is, I believe,' she sniffed, pointing ahead and then shuffling off in the direction of the kitchen.

Anthony tapped and entered through the door at the same time to see Sophie hurriedly arranging the cushions neatly on the sofa. She looked up.

'Hello Lieutenant Thomas. What a surprise! John isn't here I'm afraid. He's gone up to the Great Hall to see Uncle Richard.'

'Yes, Mrs Jenkins told me,' he began. 'But I actually…' He thrust forward the tickets, which turned out to be cinema tickets as his speech lost its momentum. 'I wondered if you might like to join me. There's…'

'Some tickets in your hands?' Sophie smiled encouragingly and warmly, trying to help.

All of a sudden he seemed to let his guard down and it just came out all in one go. 'I am a real cinema buff, Miss Watson and I know it's a bit short notice, but my friend Billy plays the cinema organ at the Astoria Cinema in Gloucester Place in Brighton. Jolly clever chap actually, should be on the stage, known each other since well, anyway… When I'm home on leave I let him know and he gets me concessionary tickets when something special is on. To cut a long story short, I have two tickets to see *Goodbye Mr Chips*. It stars Robert Donat and Greer Garson and is for this evening. I wondered if you would like to accompany me? With your brother's permission of course.' He breathed a sigh of relief for he had finally said it.

‘Oh,’ said Sophie quite taken aback at his invitation. ‘As I said, my brother is visiting our Uncle at the Great Hall and I’m not sure when he’ll be back.’

‘Quite,’ said the Lieutenant disappointedly. ‘Should have thought really, silly me and I guess he will be away for some time.’ Posturing himself up and stepping back apologetically and embarrassed, he continued, ‘Just a thought, perhaps another time?’ He quickly turned on his heels and made for the hallway. He chastised himself all the way to the door and met Mrs Jenkins coming from the kitchen. ‘I’ll see myself out,’ he said, tipping his cap politely then placing it on his head.

Sophie caught up with him on the doorstep. ‘I didn’t say that I didn’t want to come,’ she said jaggedly. ‘I just said that I didn’t know what time John would be home. How would we get there? It’s quite a journey from here,’ She asked tentatively not relishing the thought of a trip on the back of a motorbike even though it was the middle of the summer.

‘Oh, well in my car of course, unless…’ he stumbled in surprise.

‘No, no your car is fine,’ she said dismissively and relieved.

‘What time shall I be ready for?’ she enquired casually.

‘Um, five o’clock?’

‘Five o’clock it is then Lieutenant Thomas,’ she confirmed.

Antony smiled and tipped his cap to Sophie, then tipped it towards Mrs Jenkins, who was again resting her well-endowed bosom upon her folded arms, sourly observing the shenanigans taking place. He almost skipped down to the gate at the bottom of the path and then dramatically he leap-frogged over it.

‘Well I never,’ Mrs Jenkins remarked. ‘He nearly broke the gate then!’

‘Lieutenant!’ Sophie called out.

‘Yes?’

‘Is *Goodbye Mr Chips* the one with John Mills in?’ she called.

‘I believe it is,’ he called back.

‘How wonderful. I love John Mills,’ she cooed. She waved enthusiastically and closed the door.

She let out a gentle sigh and fell against the wall. It was then that she caught Mrs Jenkins giving her a strange look.

‘I best not ask,’ she said walking back again upon her earlier footsteps.

‘There is nothing really to ask about,’ Sophie replied with a half-truth.

‘My dear, I am happy to see you meeting people and having fun, but’ – she paused at the cupboard under the stairs where she collected a duster and some polish – ‘a soldier in your brother’s company was perhaps not the best choice.’

‘Well luckily there hasn’t been a choice. I have only met him once and I want to see it as a friendship,’ she replied.

‘He is very well-spoken, when he could get a word out.’

‘He was nervous.’

‘Sounded like he was from the same stock as your mother.’

‘I don’t understand what you are getting at.’ Sophie’s mother was from the Beaumont family, very well-to-do in these parts.

‘Nothing my dear, please ignore an old woman’s scepticism. Your mother fell in love with two soldiers, John’s father and yours, and it didn’t end well for her. I’m just worried that you might go the same way.’

Sophie wasn’t sure she liked her tone and although a little cryptic, she wasn’t sure she liked what she might be implying. ‘Well it might not go anywhere as I said before.’

Mrs Jenkins looked genuinely apologetic and with a cheeky smile dusted the conversation away by dusting Sophie on her way past, causing Sophie to fight her off.

Sophie spent the next hour charging through her wardrobe to find something fitting to wear. After three costume changes, she decided on a fine wool crepe suit in lilac. The jacket moulded around her upper body, widening her shoulders and emphasising her breasts. The skirt fell into beautiful godets and pleats with a subtle flare where the hem sat several inches below her knees. She faintly and artfully applied her makeup, drawing her pencil thin eyebrows together and dabbing a hint of her mother’s lipstick on her lips. She swept up her chestnut locks to finish. She twisted and turned, checking front and back. She looked long and lean and quite pleased with herself.

‘Going somewhere?’ asked John inquisitively peeping round the door.

Sophie jumped, giggling nervously and said candidly, 'You're back.'

'I hear from Mrs Jenkins that we had a visitor while I was out. He didn't waste much time then did he?'

'Lieutenant Thomas has two tickets for *Goodbye Mr Chips* at the Astoria and has very kindly invited me to accompany him.' She watched her brother in the mirror. 'He acquired them quite by chance, hence the rush and I have said yes.' Then she took another glance at herself in the long mirror. 'It might be fun. John Mills is in it and I want to go. He seems very sweet, John. What's the harm? He's one of your lieutenants so I'll be perfectly safe!'

'Not looking like that you won't,' he scoffed resentfully. 'I would have loved to have seen that film. I like John Mills myself. I love the flicks. We don't go often enough. Hey, I've a great idea, what time is he picking you up? I could be ready in a jiff and we'll all go together?'

'Oh! John,' she squealed in alarm. 'Please don't.'

John let out a very emphatic sigh, but suddenly seemed to be recalling something as his eyes searched the heavens and he began nodding as if in agreement with something personal. 'Sophie, do we get our meat delivered by the butcher's boy?'

'What an odd question. Since when have you worried about whether we get our meat delivered?' she purred inquisitively, picking up her delicate, violet lace gloves that complemented her ensemble.

'Well, do we?' he persisted.

'We no longer have our meat delivered, John. In fact I doubt there will be any deliveries for the foreseeable future from Freddy Southon's, because poor Charlie the delivery boy fell off his bike into the open cellar of The Three Feathers last week while the draymen were delivering. Poor Charlie, he'll be in traction for weeks.' Then continuing idly in thought she said, 'I wish he'd do something about that terrible acne and those awful goggle-type glasses. Oh and now what with that bushy thing that looks like a caterpillar on his lips, it makes him look ridiculous. The spitting image of Professor Calculus in the Tin Tin books.'

John chuckled to himself and followed her down the stairs into the parlour.

'You are acting very strange at the moment. What's got into you?'

The pendulum of the grandmother clock in the parlour swung evenly to the soft rhythmic sound of the tock and as five o'clock drew near, the winding and grinding of the gear mechanism amplified into the Westminster chimes and the hammer struck the bell five times.

'Five o'clock, I'll remind myself that punctuality isn't one of his better qualities,' John said belligerently, but no sooner than he had said it than the knock came at the door.

Sophie grabbed her bag and kissed him on the cheek. 'Don't wait up.'

'Christ, Sophie, it's only a film at the flicks. How late will you be then?'

'Flora Thompson's book *Lark Rise* arrived by post yesterday. You remember Mum's friend from Dorset? It's in the bookcase and might be good reading,' she said now opening the door.

'Nope,' said John contentiously and grabbing his coat he leapt to her side. 'I think I might just go and investigate the cellar down at The Three Feathers!' He squeezed past an open-mouthed Antony, acknowledging him with a nod.

'Sir,' saluted the Lieutenant. 'Evening Sir.'

'Good evening, Lieutenant.' John waved dismissively as he strutted down the path. 'Not too late mind,' he called as he jumped over the gate and headed for The Three Feathers, passing a baffled Tom coming the other way with a small portion of fish and chips in hand.

'Well, Miss Watson,' admired Lieutenant Thomas. 'Shall we?' He put out his elbow for her to take his arm. She pulled the door shut and positioned the key under a strategically placed flowerpot half hidden by a small conifer and took his arm, smiling.

Tom by now was walking down the path and had obviously pieced together the puzzle by now. 'That's why he was in a grump.' He smirked. 'Where are you two off to then?'

'The key is under the pot. We're off to see a film!' Sophie squeaked as the pair of them dashed past.

Anthony had barely any time to say hello as they left Tom by the gate dumbfounded, but she had enough time to see what she thought looked like a smile beginning to find its way across his puzzled expression.

The Lieutenant opened the door of his baby blue 1936 Austin 7 saloon and Sophie elegantly stepped in. She sat resting her hands and handbag on her lap. She looked all around her, taking in and feeling the luxury of the tactile leather interior. He jumped in and bounced up and down in his seat to find a comfortable driving position and proudly remarked, 'My twenty-first birthday present from my parents. It has a worm and wheel steering mechanism, four speed and reverse gear box, with synchromesh in second and third and I love her!' He grinned like a Cheshire cat.

'Really,' said Sophie, trying to sound fascinated. John had spent a little time with her trying to teach her to drive, but she hadn't really got the hang of it yet.

'Do you drive, Miss Watson?'

'No I don't. John's the driver in our house, but I am doing my best to learn. I have a bike though.'

'I'd be only too happy to assist,' he offered, pointing to the steering wheel.

'No you're okay, I think,' she smiled. 'Perhaps, however, we could be a little less formal. You don't have to keep calling me Miss Watson.'

'Okay Miss Watson, I'm Anthony,' he introduced himself again with a childlike grin and put out his hand.

Sophie played along, 'I am pleased to meet you Anthony. I'm Sophie.' Her outstretched hand met his and with a laugh of spontaneity they shook hands. Anthony turned the key in the ignition and pulling the starter lever, the car jumped to life and away they sped.

They reached Gloucester Place in no time at all or so it seemed to Sophie. There was a light shower as they crossed the road to the Astoria but they reached the foyer of the grand building relatively unscathed. The queue had virtually disappeared as they ran up the steps. At the top, the upright and immaculate concierge dressed in his splendid wine and gold braided uniform, opened the portals for them as if they were royalty, bowing as they stepped through the highly polished glass door into a richly ornate art deco interior. There was a café restaurant to the right of them as they entered and it oozed the tempting smell of roasting coffee beans.

There were still a few people queuing to get their tickets from the lady in the kiosk. She had obviously lost her sense of humour after dishing out her thousandth plus ticket of the day and appeared to be melting in her temporary glass prison.

The atmosphere was electric and people were criss-crossing the foyer in all directions, looking at their tickets and then scanning for the correct arrows on the pillars and walls that marked and pointed to their seating destinations.

Anthony and Sophie had tickets for the upstairs centre stalls and the Times New Roman markings took them up a highly polished marble staircase that led them to a brightly lit galleried landing. Two usherettes each guarded a swing door.

'Tickets please,' one of them asked and Anthony handed them over. She tore them in half, giving Anthony one half and the other half to the second usherette who promptly threaded it on a piece of string before she pushed open the swing doors into complete oblivion. With nothing to guide them except the roaming beam of her flashlight, they followed the usherette to their seats.

They were good seats, Sophie thought as they settled themselves into a comfortable position. As the organ covered in coloured glass panels was illuminated from behind with lamps that changed colour automatically, she could see the full stage.

'Wonderful view,' she whispered delightedly as the organ gave its own rendition of the current popular tune "Begin the Beguine" followed by "Jeepers Creepers," which had them both singing and acting out the hand gestures to each other.

The safety curtain rose and the credits rolled: 'Metro Goldwyn Meyer presents, *Goodbye Mr Chips* starring Robert Donat and Greer Garson, directed by Sam Wood and produced by Victor Saville' flickered on the stage screen. The whole auditorium erupted with the intensity of clapping hands, and then silence fell as the film's magical hold began.

She thought about holding his hand in the dark at least once. Even the curiosity of what he might do if she leaned her head against his shoulder had crept into her mind, but for now it was nice to have company, a friend, someone fresh.

One hundred and fourteen minutes and a small delicious vanilla tub of ice cream later, Sophie was beside herself as they left the Astoria. It was the best film she had ever seen and she barely took a breath between her oohs and aahs! Anthony found it all quite amusing as he gazed fondly at her enthusiasm.

'Oh that music!' she cried attempting her best to imitate it with da, da, da's and de, de, de's. 'I love "The Blue Danube". I can play it quite well on the piano,' she chirped.

'But you don't have a piano?' Anthony quizzed.

'Up at the Great Hall, my Uncle Richard's home, there is one. My mother taught me. Uncle Richard's wife Joy uses it and is very good. Oh Anthony and then when he saves her in Austria, the scenery! Oh, have you ever seen anything so stunning?' She bounced backwards, swinging her bag as they crossed the road to Anthony's car. 'Have you been to Austria, Anthony? I bet you have. Did you go to Vienna? Have you seen the Danube? Is it really that blue or only to those in love?' she gabbled furiously, firing questions at all angles in her excitement.

'Well actually, I have,' he replied. She had barely enabled him to get a word in edgewise. 'I've been twice, both times with my parents and it is a stunning place, I have to say. I've been very fortunate as my father speaks German, Spanish and Italian and obviously working for the British Consulate in London, he does a fair bit of translation and administration work. So Mother and I were always popping off somewhere to meet him. He used to get shipped all over the place which was very fortunate indeed,' he reflected.

When he spoke of his family, she wondered what they would think of her. They sounded a million miles away from the lifestyle that she led. There were times that she wondered how she could ever be good enough for a man like Antony.

As he opened the door of the car for her to get in, she stopped in front of him and searching into his face, their lips almost touching, she enquired again teasingly, 'Soooo, is it only blue to those who are in love or is it a dark murky grey, green colour.'

‘Well, dash it all Sophie, I don’t really know to be honest. As a twelve-year-old boy I can’t say I really took any notice. It was just a river at the time.’

His lack of intuition at the opportunity that she had just given him left her embarrassed. With that, she disappointedly got in the car, sighing. The conversation was a little awkward on the way home and she knew it was herself that had enabled it to be so. A small drizzle of rain pitter-pattered upon the screen and the wiper blades did their best to clear the drops.

‘I really have had a wonderful evening,’ he began. ‘You are lovely company.’

His words helped. They rekindled the flickering flame of hope from within her. she had enjoyed her evening also and found the temptation of romance running wild through her veins. Was it real? Was it infatuation? Or was it simply a desire for adventure and a chance to prove to her brother that she was able to lead her own life and make her own decisions? She pondered for a moment and realised it was probably a little bit of them all.

‘I have enjoyed your company too. Will I see you again? I mean there are lots of places for nice walks or we could go out for something to eat one afternoon.’

‘You mean you would like to go out again?’

‘I don’t think I can make it much more obvious,’ she said.

John was up and waiting on the front door step when they pulled up at April Cottage, so if either of them had developed or had any romantic designs in mind at the point of their parting, the window of opportunity had well and truly passed. Sophie was not sure what to think or say, seeing John with his folded arms on the doorstep, she decided that a fleeting but polite exit may be best under the circumstances. She alighted from the car and then leant back in saying earnestly, ‘Thank you so much for a lovely evening, Anthony. It was very kind of you and I really enjoyed it.’

‘Me too,’ he replied and then sincerely and confidently for the first time he said, ‘You look beautiful this evening.’

‘Oh… thank you,’ she said, quite taken a back. Clearly as the evening had progressed his confidence had grown.

'And, I was damn proud to wear you on my arm Miss Watson. See you tomorrow at eleven. Shut the door, there's a good girl, better dash.'

'Wait, what's happening at eleven?' she thought as she slammed the door, but he was already gone. 'How strange!' she bounced and smiled all the way up the path to her waiting brother and pecked him on the cheek saying, 'I had a great time; isn't going to the cinema the absolute? It's the best film I have ever seen and sooooo romantic, but sad. He dies you know at the end, Mr Chips.'

'We all do, Sophie,' John said patronisingly and then following her into the parlour, he asked, 'Better than *Snow White*?'

She smirked at him, 'That's completely different. Anthony...'

'Oh, it's Anthony now, is it?'

'Anthony,' Sophie continued, ignoring her brother, 'was telling me on the way home that before they built the Astoria at Gloucester Place, there was a row of houses demolished to make way for it. One of them was number sixteen and that had been the home of no other than Christine Edmunds, the chocolate cream poisoner, found guilty in 1872 of the murder of a four-year-old boy!'

'Riveting I'm sure. Well, if that's the extent of the conversational material throughout the evening, I'm already bored, tired and going to bed.' He yawned. 'Goodnight.'

'Oh, goodnight,' she said surprised. 'Anthony is picking me up at eleven in the morning. I don't know where we're going; it's a surprise,' she said, calling out after him.

'Probably the local wax museum, that's full of dummies you should both feel at home there! Have fun,' he called back sarcastically.

Sophie had no idea how to dress the next morning as she didn't know where she was going. She flitted and fluttered through the wardrobe until she saw one of her mother's old summer dresses at the very back. She lifted it out and laid it against her, pulling the waist of the dress into her own waist. It was a delicate yellow cotton dress, very simple, very summery and it felt right. It complemented her olive complexion and chestnut hair beautifully.

Her nose was pressed against the bedroom window when Anthony arrived and she shouted to what seemed an empty house, 'He's here!'

She darted down the pathway so quickly that Anthony hadn't even stopped the engine when she hopped in beside him.

'Miss Watson!' he exclaimed, taken totally unawares.

'Good morning,' she chirped. 'Where are we going then? I wasn't sure of the attire for this outing. Will this do?'

'Perfect, dressed exactly for the occasion and it's a surprise.' He winked. 'Glorious day though, I was worried the weather would not be on our side.'

'It's outside then,' she thought.

He pulled up and stopped the car where the South Downs crossed the River Cuckmere at Alfriston. He went to the boot of his car and pulled out a tartan blanket and picnic basket. He then opened the passenger door of the car and like the historical legend of Sir Walter Raleigh and Elizabeth the First, he swept his arm across the front of his torso directing and rotating his hand, portraying the chivalrous knights of old, throwing down his cloak inviting her to step out of the car into the bright sunshine upon it.

'We are just East of Alfriston between Eastbourne and Newhaven. The river crosses here, then continues through the village and up through the Downs.' He pointed across a spectacular view of undulating scenery rolling through the valley. 'It's not the Danube, of course and there are no Austrian Tyrols. You don't need to be rescued either: well, only from me of course!' he jested nervously. 'But it is the most beautiful of days and the perfect spot for a picnic and the best I could do under the circumstances.'

Anthony sprawled the tartan blanket across the grassy meadow floor and beckoned her to be seated. Opening the door to the backseat of the passenger's side, he pulled out some cushions for comfort. Then, seating themselves on the blanket, he threw open the basket to reveal an array of delicious summer fruits and a bottle of homemade lemonade, neatly presented between two crystal glasses, porcelain plates, silver cutlery and a sugar shaker. There was a little drawer at the bottom of the basket that exposed a neatly folded lace table cloth which he spread between them evenly, with a napkin each.

Sophie was speechless at his thoughtfulness and the romance of it all. They wiled away the afternoon, declaring each other's hopes and fears, proclaiming dreams and ideals. They laughed at each other's misspent youths, confessing their loves and hates, gaining knowledge and understanding of things and feelings previously unknown and bringing to light similarities of something that was already there. They were discovering each other.

Sophie looked into Anthony's face and stared for a minute, she was so close here in this perfect moment of time, but as she allowed herself to get closer, he appeared to retreat. His eyes darted around in all directions, every so often catching hers before looking elsewhere. His strawberry blonde fringe had fallen to dangle loosely on his cheeks. He nervously tried to wipe it back into its Brylcreemed place with the palm of his hand. She stretched out her hand, smiling warmly, to help him, thinking how debonair and handsome he looked, but he caught her hand in mid-air from reaching his face. His eyes, now braver, looked deeply into hers. She didn't smile. She wasn't sure what was about to happen. She was so close now she wouldn't dare let him go. She unashamedly inched closer making her intentions as obvious as she could. Then he made the decision. Wrapping his hands around her wrists firmly, he pulled her towards him gently, saying, 'May I kiss you, Miss Watson?'

With all of this day's and her life's emotions welling up from the very substance of her being, her soul was screaming, 'Yes, yes!' Inside, her heart fluttered as she gave herself heart and soul to him, saying, 'I thought you were never going to ask.'

In that moment in time she imagined her later years, when she would recall the stories of her past to her eagerly awaiting grandchildren at bedtimes and she would say of this perfect day. 'Whatever our souls were made of, his and mine were the same. We loved each other dearly with a love that was more than love itself.'

How had this happened? She remembered Tom's story and it helped a little to deal with any niggling doubt about the speed with which this kiss had arrived, the speed at which she had simply let herself go, given in, opened up, surrendered. It didn't matter if it wasn't real and it didn't matter what it might become: all she wanted now was a never-ending kiss. His inexperienced lips and hers had now met and it was a relief to feel so connected. It was love she would tell herself every day after. It was meant to be and it felt so right. There was nothing else to compare it to, for her experience of love in this case was limited, but that didn't matter. What could you compare it to and why would you try?

John would later tell her to be cautious, Tom would probably stay neutral and possibly encourage when John wasn't in ear shot, whilst Mrs Jenkins… Sophie wasn't sure what she would make of it all and quite frankly it didn't matter, not at this moment in time.

It would take many days for her to reveal the new relationship that began to blossom and flower as the summer began. She changed the subject when John was around and arranged to meet Anthony in different locations in an attempt to throw John off the scent. She even lied to him on occasion – something she had never done since childhood. She told herself it was necessary to avoid interrogation, but the reality was that she also didn't like seeing him get upset and wanted to spare him the worry. On every occasion when they were due to meet, John would huff and puff. He would wander around the house with no real aim and take hours to settle.

It was Tom whom she told first whilst he was in the garden attempting to tidy around the gate that went into the orchard.

'How long has this been going on?' he quizzed, standing on a step ladder whilst cutting back long fingers of honeysuckle.

'Since June, not long after the dinner we had on the terrace.'

'That's nearly a whole month. Does your brother know?' She knew that her silence was enough to answer for her. 'You need to tell your brother.'

John knew she thought, he always knew. Tom of all people should have understood that John had an ability to just know things.

Tom looked down to her. 'He deserves some honesty from you. Secrets are all very well for surprises and birthdays, but this is different.'

'You know how he will react.'

'Well, if he already knows as you have clearly surmised, then there is little to worry about. It's respect Sophie that's all.' He came down to her level and placed his gardening gloves onto one of the ladder rungs. 'Do you love him?'

She hesitated. She knew that she did, but would Tom accept such a strong reply so soon? 'I don't know, possibly with more time.' She felt it was a good response, fair and what both Tom and John would probably prefer to hear.

'Well congratulations. I am very pleased for you, but let your brother know, officially like. If he is involved, it will be easier to digest. I know he can be overbearing, but he is probably coming to terms with the fact that you are growing up and that, for someone who is as protective as him, is difficult to deal with.'

She wrapped her arms around Tom and as he returned to the bushes, she headed back towards the cottage. It was time to tell John.

John was surprised at how well he took the news. Not that it was really news to him – he had been waiting for weeks for Sophie to spill the beans. He attempted to do the parental talk and was embarrassed at his own clumsiness to handle the more delicate of subjects. If the announcement of Anthony as Sophie's partner had taught him anything, it was as Tom had warned him: she was no longer his little sister.

His acceptance of the situation and the blessing he gave them both was not easy and had a 'if it lasts' tone to it. John didn't perform well as an actor and so when he tried to be genteel it tended to come across patronizing. When he was in a foul mood, he couldn't help but pull rank, even when out of uniform. A part of him found it amusing that Antony referred to him as 'Sir' at all times. It was not difficult to process the news, but it was clearly difficult for him to know how to behave in a manner that was either welcoming or accepting.

There was, of course, another issue John had with it all, the timing. He used this as his biggest reason, much to Tom's protests that there was more to it than that, but it was a legitimate reason. The Company was due to be shipped abroad in a matter of weeks and in briefings with the Major it was clear that there was no turning back when it came to the hostilities with Germany. Maginot lines and the sudden drive for recruitment were not done without a reason, he told himself. There was a chance that they may not come home from this adventure, that Anthony might not.

He fought his thoughts day and night, consumed by them. He thought of ways of breaking them up so that when the inevitable came it would be easier, but that was not him thinking and not his usual mentality. If anything, he had to get on with things, accept Anthony more readily. After all, they had now fallen in love, whether it be war or natural causes that broke them apart, it would still be painful. There was nothing he could or should do. It was the first time he had been powerless since he was a child and it was not a natural feeling.

Newhaven Dock
August 10th 1938

D company marched in a perfect formation through the rain-soaked night and into the docks. Two long columns of well-dressed soldiers were led at the front by Sergeant Major Hill. Each soldier carried his webbing, equipment and weapons, whilst behind them came several trucks carrying their kit bags and heavy equipment. Their tin helmets wobbled on their heads and made strange music as the muzzles of their rifles joined by the heavy rain took turns to tap upon the broad rim of the helmets.

John and the rest of the officers arrived at the docks in a staff car, looking with torchlight at the unfamiliar maps of their destination and guessing where their camps were to be. The destination had been revealed the night before as Egypt, somewhere outside the city of Alexandria.

Family and loved ones who knew they were departing, lined the docks to see them off onto the awaiting vessel one last time. Tom halted the men at the entrance to the docks and after speaking to the harbour master, who had greeted him with a message, fell the men out giving them the opportunity to take a rest or run over and bid their last farewells to any of their loved ones present in the crowd. Those that had already said their goodbyes at home caught up with a quick cigarette and a bit of idle chit-chat.

The officer's staff car had pulled up behind some monstrously large Bedford Lorries and the three Lieutenants and John stepped out onto the wet and slippery surface beneath their feet. It had been raining for most of the night and although it had begun to ease off, the clouds looked like they would open up any minute for a final downpour.

'Look at them,' Bailey said, pointing to the mass of the company who were by now swelling the ranks of onlookers, wives, children, friends and lovers under canopies of umbrellas.

'They're making the most of it and so they should,' Anthony said, putting his great coat on. 'Amazing to think we won't see family for what; another two years?'

'Doubt it,' Bailey added. 'As soon as we arrive in Pharaoh land they'll take one look at you and send you straight back. I give them a year before they get fed up with us and send us home.'

Through the drizzle walking towards the officers, they could see Tom approaching. Out of uniform, he was simply Tom, but in uniform, he was quite an imposing Sergeant Major, the father of the men, one who deserved respect, even from the young and inexperienced officers. This was the man who would really get them through the troubles ahead and John knew it.

'We've got a bit of time spare before the remainder of the Battalion gets here sir,' Tom said. 'Apparently, they are delayed back at the barracks. I took the liberty of allowing the men a breather and a final moment with their families.'

'That's fine Sergeant Major,' John replied saluting, he then took Tom to one side. 'You old softy, I wouldn't have it any other way. What's the delay anyway?'

'I don't know, the harbour master just told me that he had been telephoned by the barracks. They want the Major to telephone back when he arrives.'

'Well I'd best inform the Major then,' John said.

The Battalion commander, Major Love, had travelled with them in his beloved Humber staff car to watch John's company embark on the ship. Now upon seeing the company parading their emotions amongst the crowds or standing idle on the dockside and generally appearing in disarray, he was trumpeting through the rain which had recommenced falling from the dark clouds above.

'Captain Baker!' he stormed.

'Yes, Sir.'

'What the hell is going on? What are your men lingering about on the dock for? They should be lined up ready to board.'

'Apparently, there's a delay, sir, was just coming to find you.'

'Delay, what bloody delay's that then?' he bumbled under his bushy but waxed ended moustache.

'At the barracks, sir.'

'At the bloody barracks?' he squawked in parrot fashion. 'Who said?'

'The Sergeant Major, sir, was told by the Harbour Master that as soon as we arrived you are required to call the barracks as soon as possible, sir.'

'Well, why the blazes didn't you bloody well say so?' he said, his moustache twitching to and fro and his body twisting nervously in one direction then the other as though he couldn't work out what to do next.

'Because we've only just found you, sir, this way I think sir,' said John sensing his predicament.

'So what are we doing about this ramshackle lot running a mock on the dock?'

John steered him in a direction away from the Company, but as he did Bailey decided to equip them all with his sense of humour by adding, 'didn't realise you were a poet, sir.'

'What! Humph, haven't you got something better to do Lieutenant, like round up this lot?' he snorted unimpressed with Bailey's comment and waving his baton in all directions.

'Well sir, two years is a long time,' John began. 'I thought it a nice gesture for the men to see their loved ones, so many turned up to see them off. It's their last chance and all that, but if you disagree, I'll get the Sergeant Major to get the men to fall in immediately.'

They were away from the crowds now and took what shelter they could under a loading crane. 'I don't disagree. I suppose you are right and I would feel the same,' the Major said. He scuffed the floor deliberately with his polished brown shoes as if massaging the earth. The Major had a tendency to run through what appeared to be personal conversations with himself, John found it difficult to tell if he was speaking directly to an individual or this reflective inner self. 'Yes, quite, yes, I see. Might never be back I suppose.' He mimicked back clearing his throat. By now the rain had intensified and everyone had started to dive for cover under any form of shelter that they could find. The rain had started to run from the peak of John's cap down the front of his tunic. Tom had now approached but kept a distance. 'Right, right, decision time,' spluttered the Major under his breath then coughing. 'Right, Captain Baker, I best pop to the Harbour Masters office I suppose and see what those scallywags at the barracks are doing about this damn hold up, I suppose if it was my last night in

Blighty I would invite my officers to pop down to the pub while I was waiting for the ship to load, wouldn't you?' he winked. 'Keep up the good work then,' he saluted and with an assured quick pace marched off towards the Harbour Masters office. He then slowed down and looked back for a moment, John pointed to the direction of the office and the Major continued.

Tom shook his head incredulously and muttered to himself, 'it's beyond me sometimes the army,' then turning to John, he said, 'best make sure the men are ready for when the rest of the regiment get here, silly old duffer might be back sooner than we think if he doesn't get lost!'

John grinned, 'do you think he will ever find the Harbour Masters office?'

'Well put it this way, I think we've probably got time for a quick one as he suggested' and he pointed in the direction of the pub which they had marched past on their way to the docks and was situated on the end of where the wharf wall commenced. 'I will give the old man some credit, the pubs a good idea. Might be your last proper drink.'

'Before I have to get used to dirty desert water.' John replied.

They both rallied those interested and Chinese whispered a rendezvous to those who wanted to remain and set off for what could be their last pint in England. It took a while for Bailey to even believe the Major had really suggested it. 'You don't mean to tell me there is a brain behind that twitchy moustache of his after all?'

Major Love had been a young medical officer during the First World War. He had served alongside General Townsend in Mesopotamia. The disaster at Kut in Iraq and Turkish imprisonment in which he had seen thousands of his soldiers suffer, had left him a man who cared very much for the hearts and wellbeing of his soldiers. John was one of the few who knew these details, whereas the majority only saw the bumbling façade that John had begun to believe he put on deliberately.

Some felt the Major was too old and wouldn't cope through the reality of battle. Tom was different; an old soldier of the Great War himself, he had heard about the stories from the Majors time in Iraq and at Kut. Despite his occasional mocking, he firmly believed that the Major was an incredibly able officer and the right man to lead the battalion abroad, if not a bit dithery about directions at Harbours.

'What's the name of the pub?' asked Keyes.

'Who cares what it's called, if there is beer there, let's go, I'm catching my death here,' Bailey began and then after forgetting the chain of command he looked apologetically at John. 'If that's alright with you sir?'

John looked back at his men who were still savouring every moment with their families and loved ones. The few who had no family or loved ones present were now mingling with those who had, being introduced to wives, friends, sweethearts and children.

'Go on then,' John replied to Bailey who was clearly itching for a drink. 'I will pop along after I have dealt with things here.'

The three lieutenants disappeared whilst John headed through the rain towards the harbour master's office in order to find out what the delay was and cover their backs.

Sophie began to worry that she had missed John, she didn't recognise any of the uniformed men on the dockside when she arrived. After searching through the rain, which every now and then found its way in small rogue drops down the back of her coat she spotted Tom. He was looking around the crowd of unfamiliar faces, with a typical stern face that had become synonymous with that of any Sergeant Major. She had never seen him in this mode before and she couldn't help but pause as if checking it was the same man she had always known. He winced as the rain spat into his aged face and then when he saw her the stern face broke into the familiar smile she recognised. She broke through the last of the populace of glistening umbrellas and raincoats and threw her arms around.

'Hello Miss Watson' he said pecking her gently on the cheek.

Drenched to the skin she said with relief, 'I thought that I might have missed you. I got held up at the Great Hall. Uncle Richard was going to bring me down, but Joy's daughter was coming up from Exeter to see her this weekend by train and he wasn't back by four from picking her up at the station, we presumed it was late, so rather than missing you I caught the bus.'

'I didn't realise that Joy had a daughter?'

'She doesn't see her very often as she is a sister in one of the hospitals in Exeter. Very career minded. She has just passed all her exams to become a Matron apparently. She wasn't at the wedding this year because she did a stint in Africa studying tropical diseases. Seems a bit odd to me not coming to your Mother's wedding, but there you go we can't all be the same can we?'

'Sounds just the ticket for Captain James, if you ask me?' Tom commented.

'Ooh yes, perhaps we could get them together sometime,' giggled Sophie, her eyes averting and scanning for her brother or Anthony. 'Have I missed John?'

He shook his head reassuringly and she tried to glance over his shoulder as he replied, 'John was here a moment ago, so he should still be about somewhere.'

'Why are you still here?' Sophie enquired. 'I am really pleased you are of course, but I was so sure that the boat would have at least been pulling out of the harbour by the time that I got here. And Anthony?' she asked dismissively as if it was a second thought.

'We are delayed apparently so the boat has to wait as do we for orders, which I think John has gone to find out about with the Major. In answer to the most important question, however, well your young man has actually gone with the others to the nearest pub.'

'My young man?' she queried.

'I don't know how you want me to refer to him, partner, lover?' he smiled.

'Well, it's early days yet as my brother would prefer to say,' she said firmly. 'But we are going to write to each other while he's away,' then continuing she struggled to contain her happiness as it revealed itself with a smile. 'You know Uncle Tom it's been a lovely summer!'

'I'm glad,' he smiled in return. 'Can I give you a little bit of advice from a wounded old heart, just so you don't make the same mistakes I did?' he spoke with an air of ill ease, frowning and showing the lines of age that reappeared across his forehead. 'Be honest with each other, say everything you want to say don't keep it inside,' he said tapping his breast. 'Say what you feel, when you feel it, never leave things unsaid, be true to yourself, otherwise there becomes too much water under the bridge.'

'Why do I think there's another 'Tom tale' to be told here?'

He chuckled, 'maybe there is, but I'm going to have to save it for when I get back, or perhaps a letter?'

'Yes a letter, send it to me in a letter, although I don't think I can wait that long for one of your stories!'

He kissed her once again, but this time on her head as she hugged him tighter. 'You are indeed a comfort to my poor old soul,' he teased lightly.

'I love you, Uncle Tom,' she said with a tear in her eye and it was then that she noticed the men around them watching their exchange. Some had expressions of confusion, some were smiling, whilst others looked surprised. It was then as Tom noticed them watching that he returned back to Sergeant Major mode.

'Let's get you out of the rain shall we?' he pointed to one of the soft-skinned lorries. 'But just bear with me,' he winked and then turning to the men he barked. 'And what the bloody hell are you lot staring at? Haven't you got family and loved ones to spend time with?' There was a sudden sense of panic and the men were almost falling over each other, boxes and weapons. Some returned back to the conversations with loved ones that had been on hold. It amused her that they reacted as they did, for she knew it was all an act, she knew the man behind the bark.

Meanwhile, John had found the Major as he was emerging from the Harbour Masters office. 'Captain,' he called. 'Captain it turns out that Captain Frasier fouled up on his logistics. They are two Lorries short back at the barracks. What I want you to do is group your men and get them back in order, unload two of the Lorries and send them back to Captain Frasier.'

'Very well sir,' John replied.

'Where are your officers by the way, down the pub I expect?'

John panicked, for a moment he wasn't sure whether it was a question or a statement, had he misunderstood the Majors comment earlier about the pub?

'Well, actually sir they may well be. Forgive me I must have misread your statement earlier.'

The Major gave him a sharp look, 'John, are your officers in the pub or not?'

John swallowed. 'They are sir.'

'Good man, let's get this sorted and then we'll join them for a quick bevvy. I'm dying of thirst!' he croaked clasping his throat in jest.

The rain was coming down in the bucket loads now. The families and loved ones with their brave Tommy's were sheltering as best as they could under the colonnade that lined the railway station running alongside the quayside.

On his way back John found Tom chatting to someone hidden by shadow in the back of one of the lorries, he guessed who it might have been from the way Tom was conducting himself.

'Sergeant Major,' called John.

'Yes sir,' he replied with a smart salute.

'I have found out what the holdup is,' he said returning the salute. 'I need you to get the men back in order and have these first two Lorries unloaded by hand as quickly as possible on the dockside then transfer their cargo on board.'

'I thought we were loading the lorries onto the boat as well?'

'We are, but it turns out Captain Frasier is two lorries short and they are needed back at the barracks, so these two have to go back.'

'Very well, it won't take me long to unload, but it will be hours before Frasier's lot get here!'

'I know, but there is nothing we can do about it. Food will be provided in the galley when the men are on-board and that means whilst there is a delay we can sneak off for that cheeky pint after all! You may as well start with this one here.'

'Well before you do sir, you ought to know that there is a very precious cargo on board this one,' Tom said with a delightful smile.

John walked to the back and looked up inside to see his sister, just as he had suspected. 'Well Sergeant Major,' he began with a cheeky grin on his face. 'After inspection of this one, I would say we might as well throw this lot over the side into the channel then. I can't see what use it will be to us where we're going.'

Sophie let out a playful cry of surprise and then jumped down next to him.

'Over the side indeed!' she scorned and gave her big brother a warm cuddle.

'I thought that I had missed your departure. Uncle Richard got delayed collecting Joy's daughter, so I had to catch the bus and well you know,' she waved her hand dismissively. 'Tom knows the whole story, but I'm here now, better late than never.'

'I thought you would get here somehow, call it intuition. Come on let's get you out of the rain, everyone else is at the pub around the corner,' John said. 'I'll just finish here with Tom, won't take a minute with all hands on deck and then we'll go and find them.'

'You go on ahead, sir, I'll sort this lot out,' Tom offered.

'Are you sure?' John asked. 'Many hands make light work.'

'No problem sir, I've got enough men to unload five times as many trucks, I'll gather them now and then get everything including the men on board.'

They saluted and he walked off barking orders at the men, who with a few groans and moans soon returned to line up in their ranks. With that done, Tom began embarking the men on board leaving a small section to unload the two lorries.

John wrapped his overcoat around his sister and after grabbing an umbrella from the boot of the staff car, walked her round to the street where the pub was at the very end.

Sophie strolled slowly. 'Is Anthony at the pub?' she asked keeping her eyes looking towards the pavement.

John had grown used to 'the situation' as he liked to refer to it by now, but he found it difficult to hide his true feelings still. She knew he disapproved, but he had however through the assistance of Tom been helped to see a little more light on the matter. He still had days of conflict in his mind, days he hoped that despite his unchanging opinion of the relationship, that with the likelihood of them all being away for a fair amount of time, the whole situation might just fizzle out. Then there were days he saw how excited and happy she was and he even had to admit to himself that it was a nice relief. Despite his disapproval, he was still a gentleman he told himself and never made a scene when the two of them were together, but couldn't help airing his frustrations when they weren't. He didn't really know why he didn't like Anthony and when he was alone and the subject on his mind, he came up with a new reason each time. So despite his effort, he was still a little hostile to the bemusement of them both. He just couldn't help it.

'He will be in the pub with the others.'

'I know we have discussed this before, but can you not try and warm to him?' she pleaded.

'I don't dislike him,' John said.

'So what is it then? You barely speak to him and when you do you belittle him. He is kind and attentive and I like him John, please try?'

'Look,' he said. 'I'm not stopping you both being together, I just don't think it's wise. You could get hurt. You're both acting like a happily married couple and yet you have only known each other for… well it's a matter of weeks.'

'Like you say its early days, John, we are still getting to know each other and I would like you to get to know him too.'

'I do know him though,' he snapped somewhat amused by the comment.

'No,' Sophie said in an impatient tone. 'You know him as a soldier and an officer in your company. He's a good soldier, you have said so yourself. I want you to get to know him as my …' she paused a moment, looking at him out the corner of her eye as they walked along the cobbled road and past the terraced cottages.

'Well, what?' he asked.

'…as my friend, my partner even.' The umbrella shook as John shivered at the very sound of the word. It made the situation sound more serious than he hoped it really was. 'Please John, stop this. He really cares for me and I really care about him. I'm being serious this time.'

'I know, I know, I just worry.'

She stopped him and made him look at her where he could see a growing confidence in her eyes.

'I know you worry,' she said placing her cold hand on his cheek. 'But there is nothing to worry about anymore. Anthony is a good person, I like him and John, I am not a child anymore.'

They were very grown-up words and as the rain bounced gently off her face, for the first time he heard the changing tone in her voice, a strong mature determined tone that he began to feel responsible for bottling up.

'I just don't want you getting hurt,' he said. 'You are all I have got.'

'I know, maybe I will and maybe I won't,' she whispered. 'But for the first time, I feel free of the past and alive.'

She put her arms around him and lay her head on his shoulder. John put his arm around her and kissed the top of her head. His protective instincts started to be overwhelmed with pride, but letting go would still take time.

As John held her in his arms, Sophie thought how lucky she felt to have a brother who loved her as much as he did. It was overbearing at times, but it was a love that was true and difficult now to imagine a life without.

She gently pulled away and said, 'Promise me you will try and stay out of danger and come back home safely, all three of you?' Her brother nodded and smiled, but it was a weak smile, almost uncertain. 'And look out for each other.'

She caught a glimpse of the young brother she once remembered, the boy who would play with her, read her scary stories at night and chase her around the garden. His eyes were heavy, weighed down by worry. 'I'm scared Soph,' he whispered, his anxiety catching her by surprise. 'I'm scared I won't do my duty. I'm scared I'm going to mess things up.'

She took him by the hand which she thought she felt tremble and reminded him of a comforting fact, one that helped her when she imagined the danger they might be going to. 'You will have Tom as your trusted Sergeant Major, just as your father did.'

The pub was almost full to exploding and there was a buzz of anticipation in the air. The normal animosity found between soldier and sailor where ego and drink was concerned seemed distant and there was a sense of camaraderie in the air, they were all in the same boat in respect of their destinies and their destinations. Sailors from the massive merchantman that sat in the dock were bound for Africa and were drinking their last pints before transporting John's men to one of the furthest corners of the world. Locals and regular dock men leant against the far end of the heaving bar spellbound by the invasion. Like Fred Astaire in one of his dance routines, the landlord was tripping and skipping from one end of the bar to the other trying to keep up with the constant demands coming at him from all directions. His face wore an expression that suggested all his Christmas' had come at once, smiling with the thought of the revenue to hand.

The three Lieutenants sat in a corner out of the way, hugging a blazing open fire stacked high with logs. Drying and warming themselves to the accompaniment and miraculous appearance of non-other than Captain Simon James, who like a genie from a bottle had appeared from nowhere and John was quick to comment that it had something to do with the involvement of alcohol.

Sophie stuck to a fruit juice for various reasons, she had never really enjoyed the taste of alcohol, she would suffer a lemonade shandy out of politeness at times, but as a general rule she didn't touch alcohol. John as usual ordered a whiskey and she left him propping up the bar to go over to her new beau. Anthony jumped out of his seat with surprise when he saw her coming towards him, as he thought they had said their goodbyes the previous day. Her face beamed with happiness as his arms found their way around her waist. She was still soaking wet, but Anthony didn't care and he kissed her gently on the cheek.

The remaining seated officers put two fingers to their mouths pretending they were going to be sick, which was no doubt a light relief for John's embarrassment.

'What are you doing here?' Anthony asked excitedly. 'I thought that….'

'It was meant to be a surprise and I would have been here earlier but Uncle Richard still wasn't back, so I had to catch the bus and ….oh it's a long story, another time, it's not important, I'm here now,' she said and pushed her fingers through his and he squeezed their hands together gently.

'That's wonderful, but you're soaked. Come and sit down with us, you'll dry off in no time.'

He took her drink from her and gently guided her to the table in the corner, he pulled out a chair and she sat with them around a large round table with the glowing fire behind her. Her toes felt wonderfully warm in no time.

'Do you remember everyone?' Anthony asked.

'Oh yes,' she replied.

'How are you, Miss Sophie?' Simon asked.

'I am fine,' she said combing her wet hair with her fingers. 'How are you, Captain James?'

'I am much the better for seeing you again my dear. I still think fondly of the fantastic meal you made us out on the terrace, those strawberries...' he shook his head to gesture that they still had a magical effect on him. 'I am looking forward to a future invite. How are the career decisions going these days? Still toying with the idea of medicine?'

'Actually,' she replied. 'I have, but Anthony took me out…'

'Did he now?' Bailey interrupted joyfully. 'You sly old dog you!'

A bundle of laughs filled the corner and even Sophie joined in with her tell-tale giggle that Anthony found so adorable.

She felt so at home with John's officers and found their company easy and comfortable. Any normal average girl would have found Bailey's comment either a little degrading or embarrassing, but Sophie was quite used to the banter these days, something Tom had introduced her to in order to deal with his own dry sense of humour. As Bailey had already experienced, she always gave as good as she got.

'Go on sweetheart, you were saying,' Simon said.

'Oh yes, what was I saying? A few weeks back Anthony took me to the cinema, to see goodnight Mr Chips which is about a school teacher…'

'…And you're thinking about the teaching profession?' Simon interrupted.

'I don't know. What do you think?' she asked him. 'I find medicine quite interesting and your comments about tropical diseases were fascinating. I'm still very much interested in being a nurse.'

'Well thank you, little lady,' he smiled courteously. 'I'm glad to have been of service.'

'That's one of the reasons I was late, I was hoping to meet my Uncle Richard's stepdaughter today, she's becoming a Matron in a hospital in Exeter and has just come back from Africa where she was doing a sabbatical studying tropical diseases, but I guess the train was late because Uncle Richard wasn't back in time to drop me off at the docks, but I'm looking forward to meeting her and hopefully she'll give me some good advice!' waffled Sophie for the third time.

'Sounds my kind o' gal,' Captain James chuckled.

'Well it's funny you should say that,' said Sophie putting her hand to her mouth sheepishly. 'That's exactly what Tom and I said earlier, the Sergeant Major I mean.'

'You'd better get her address for me Sophie and then, perhaps we can compare notes,' he said with a twinkle in his eye and nudging her.

'Really Captain James you are as bad as all the others!' Sophie gasped.

'On a serious note, let me know how you get on and what you decide, if it's in the medical profession, I might be able to pull a few strings for you, John will have my number!' he said in a jovial fashion but genuinely and as he smiled his little moustache twitched.

'Thank you, I will,' she said.

'Right let's see what that brother of yours is up to,' he said rising from his seat and moving towards John.

Sophie leaned on Anthony's shoulder their hands still clasped together.

'Do you all know where you're going yet?' she asked openly.

'Yep, we're off to the land of the Pharaohs for a bit of sand, sand and more sand.' Bailey quipped, taking to the floor and shuffling across it mimicking the Wilson, Keppel and Betty act. 'Egyptian sand dance, do you think I should take it up professionally?'

All that were seated around the table shouted in unison, 'get off!' in comical pantomime fashion.

'I take that as a no then and stick to the day job?' he rounded disappointedly.

'I wouldn't count on that either.' Keyes winked.

'A little dance Lieutenant?' he pouted his lips in jest and held his hand out to Keyes as if a dancing damsel in distress.

'Get off!' Keyes pushed him away and pointed Bailey to his seat.

'Egypt,' Bailey then finished. 'We all found out yesterday.'

‘Wow that’s fantastic, you will get to see the Pyramids and the Sphinx,’ Sophie cooed. ‘I saw a photograph that Tom bought back once.’

‘Didn’t know the Sergeant Major had been to Egypt, mind you, I suppose he’s been everywhere. Egypt doesn’t do anything for me personally, no grass or fields,’ said Keyes. ‘It’s not exactly a holiday, is it? Going to have hardly any time for sightseeing I should imagine.’

‘Oh, I’m sorry, I didn’t think,’ said Sophie apologetically.

‘And I’m sorry, that was rude and unbecoming of me, I know you meant well,’ said Keyes in return. ‘Besides if Adolf kicks off it will kick off in Europe, I suppose we should be grateful that we will be well out of the way of it all.’

There was a little comfort in what he said, the desert and enchantment of Egypt would be far from where the action would be if war did break out.

Anthony squeezed her a little. ‘To be honest Sophie, I don’t think we will be seeing anything exciting. Were to be stationed outside Alexandria, not Cairo.’

‘But there is a train that goes from Alex to Cairo,’ Bailey winked nudging Keyes as if to tell him to lighten up. ‘If we do pop into Cairo we will take some snaps for you.’

‘If you don’t spend all day in those harems,’ Keyes retorted.

‘All part of the culture,’ smiled Bailey.

There was a moment of reflective quiet. Sophie sipped her drink and then sipped it again as nobody spoke. Simon stood over them, looked into his glass and rolled the liquid around the bottom watching it. It was a heavy atmosphere that suddenly descended upon the fun they were just having, the realisation that the world was on a knife-edge, no matter how hard they tried could not be hidden. It was clearly on their minds, clearly draining them of every ounce of calm and normality. Sophie worried about them, all of them. So recently acquainted, yet so familiar a family these men had become, something both her and John had lacked for some time. They reminded her of the goodness in life.

She looked over to John and whilst Simon sidled up next to him she could still make out the worry in his expression. There were lines on his forehead when he frowned, just like the lines that appeared on

Tom's forehead when he did the same. It hadn't sunk in yet that this was their last night together.

By the time Simon approached John the major had arrived on the scene and was jiggling in the doorway creating a puddle of water at his feet courtesy of his saturated attire.

'Still wet out there, sir?' said the Landlord gliding from the far end of the bar. 'What will we be having?'

'Whiskey and a dash,' the Major ordered and then turning to John who stood next to him raised his glass. John acknowledged the gesture by raising his. The Major swirled the whiskey around in the small glass for a moment and then promptly downed his drink in one, crashing his glass and a shiny new sixpenny piece down with it saying, 'another.'

Simon patted John on the shoulder, 'how about you, another?'

'Why not,' John replied.

'Another sir?' Simon called to the Major.

'Ah Simon!' the Major said startled to see him. 'I didn't realise your people were here already? And don't mind if I do, it's good to see you, my dear fellow.'

John watched as his commanding officer swallowed the second glass in as many minutes before holding the glass out for the third time.

'And another for him,' Simon motioned the landlord. 'Yes we are all present and correct, sir, arrived at the docks about an hour ago. I hear there is a hold up with the rest of your lads?'

The Major informed Simon of events before turning to John. 'Everything alright Captain Baker you seem a little quiet?'

'I'm fine sir just enjoying a tipple. Sergeant Major Hill is dealing with the holdup.'

'Yes that reminds me,' the Major said gesturing to the landlord. 'I don't suppose you can spare the bottle?' The landlord obliged and the Majors grin grew ever wider. 'That's the spirit, sir!' Simon cheered.

The Major and Simon had always got on well, especially when the drink was concerned. They had known each other before John had joined the company and Tom had hinted that they both had an uncanny way of producing a bottle as if by magic. John never commented on it, for he was aware that drink may be the comfort that both he and Tom might need from time to time in the future.

'Are we all ready to go Captain Baker?'

'Pretty much sir, the lorries will be unloaded by now and the company on board.' He took the last sip and turning to the remaining officers he raised his glass and continued this time for them to hear. 'Cheers gentlemen, time to be off, another ten minutes and the boat awaits!'

'Cheers,' they all replied their chairs grating across the floor as they stood up.

Despite the pub still spilling over with uniforms of all ranks and regiments, Sophie, John and Anthony unexpectedly found themselves alone in a crowded place, each not knowing what or when to say something to one another. Anthony decided it was appropriate to take his leave, first and kissing Sophie on the cheek and whispering, 'write soon.' He tenderly squeezed her hand, let go and left quickly without looking back.

'Bye,' she said timidly, beginning to raise her hand in response but he had gone.

She turned to her brother who saw the look in her eyes and sighed. 'You'd better go now if you want to catch him, he'll be on a route march to the dockside.'

It was the first time he had acknowledged her needs and not only that but he was encouraging her to go to him and Sophie felt overwhelmed by the gesture, for this was the one thing that had been missing, her brother's encouragement.

'You know how much I love you don't you? And that you'll always be right here,' she held her hand to her heart. 'The most special, the most loved and the most wonderful brother anyone could ever have? All the things we have been through…' John gestured her to stop and she hugged him with all the strength she could muster from her inner being. 'Keep yourself safe. Goodbye,' she whispered and ran from his empty arms to the door. She paused a moment and looked at him before going out into the pouring rain. He put his cap firmly on his head, shrugged his shoulders to help his heavy greatcoat sit on them right and then weakly smiled at her, pointing towards the door and mouthing the word 'hurry.'

Sophie stepped out into the rain. She looked from left to right and right to left peering through the rainy haze that made her blink as every drop fell on her eyelashes, not knowing in her haste which direction she should go and then she saw him. She didn't know what had made him look behind at that moment, but they saw each other and she ran into his open arms. The swollen clouds continued to bless them with its load and Anthony pulled them into a doorway for shelter. John passed them a few moments later a bottle in hand, covering his head with his rainwear and calling out, 'not too long Lieutenant, we've got a boat to catch.'

The rain chinked and clattered on the cobbles of the street. In the films that Sophie enjoyed so much the rain always added a sense of romance to any encounter with lovers, but now she was soaked to the skin and so uncomfortable that it was difficult to think of much else but the dry warmth of home.

'I think,' Anthony began. 'No,' he corrected himself. 'I know……that I'm in love with you Miss Watson.'

'Really? Do you really mean that? Because I feel it too.'

He smiled and let out a relieved howl of laughter. 'I was so worried then that you might say something different or say it was too soon!'

'No, no not at all. It feels right, doesn't it? I've never felt this way before, it's strange.'

It was strange, the feelings that had bubbled up inside her made her feel as though she was floating. Sometimes the feelings she had hurt, a painful stab that reminded her of how vulnerable she felt at times. Whenever a car had pulled up outside the cottage she went to investigate and there were days when she avoided going out after convincing herself that he would surprise her with another spontaneous day out. She imagined scenarios between them when she was bored, scenarios where he rescued her from a silly situation, nothing serious like a fire or anything, but times when she was alone or needed some excitement and he would be there to whisk her off in his little blue Austin. She had a photograph of him on the chest of drawers by her bed and she would talk to it as if it were a magical portal to his thoughts. It was quite childish she thought and this was the only thing that worried her, but love changes people, that's what it does. The loss of control is a regular feature of love, or so all of her books and Tom's stories had told her. The unnatural feelings were actually natural and that is what she told herself.

As she looked back to him their lips met, his strong and positive kiss sending shivers of excitement that tingled down her spine and she wanted to stay there forever in this lingering moment. They had kissed so many times before, but this time it meant more, it was the last kiss, a symbolic one, it had to be the best so that it remained in her memory. She ached for more time, but he had to go.

'Go,' she ordered reluctantly. 'I know you have to.'

'You will write won't you?' he asked nervously walking backwards away from the doorway.

'Every day,' she promised, blowing him a kiss.

And then he was coming back and she fell into him again and longingly they embraced and kissed again. Their lips parted and Anthony said to her softly, 'close your eyes, Sophie...... can you see us down by the river on that day?'

'The Blue Danube,' she replied with her eyes still firmly shut.

'That's where we'll always be in my heart,' he said. 'Count to ten, Sophie.'

And still, with her eyes closed she counted to ten, trepidations looming in her body, she tried to reach for him unsuccessfully with her hands outstretched to feel where he was, to find when she opened her eyes that he was gone.

Sophie wanted to scream, the feeling was there, but she held back, partly conscious that he might hear her and run back. She didn't want that because she would have to say goodbye again. She considered walking down to watch the ship leave, but in the end, her heavy heart pulled her back against the wall and doing her best to control the sobs the rain fell in unison with her tears.

Within the next half an hour the officers were embarking onto the ship. Tom had already seen to it that the ordinary ranks of the company were on board. The rest of the battalion along with Captain Frasier had arrived and were also boarding the ship. By the time the boat was well out into the channel, the rain had stopped and a full moon that had once lurked behind the clouds burst its brilliant light upon the water. Lights from the shore twinkled like stars and the white cliffs of the Seven Sisters could be seen reflecting in the now still water.

The boat was an old liner and was therefore very comfortable. A bar and restaurant upstairs catered for the officers whilst downstairs the ordinary ranks shared cabins and bunks. A galley would supply the men with the finest food they would eat for a long time. The bottom outside deck was also available so that many of the men could stretch their legs or cling to the railings as their stomachs tensed with seasickness. The voyage would take several weeks and would be for John the fondest memory he would have of his time with the men. At this stage, it was still peace-time and their voyage to Egypt was an adventure, the war had yet to rear its ugly head and spoil the atmosphere, although its presence was never far away and loomed its ugliness regularly within the conversation.

Tom had gone to place his kit in his cabin which he was to share with Sergeant Scott and although most of the officers were hovering in the bar, he returned to find John in the same place he had been since setting sail outside at the stern of the ship. It was cool outside and the monstrous engines rumbled underneath him making the boat shudder with a grumble.

'Everyone has settled in downstairs sir,' Tom said, leaning over the railing next to him to look down at the bubbling wake.

'Thank you, Sergeant Major.'

'Most of them are asleep already.'

'I should think so too, there was a lot of kits to load.'

He watched the lights of Seaford pass by and then Brighton came into view. It looked lovely from the sea, a thousand sparkles bouncing and reflecting, created the illusion of an upside-down city in the water.

'Beautiful night,' Tom admired.

'Do you think we will ever see them again?' John asked.

Tom looked surprised at the question. 'The lights? What on earth makes you think we won't?'

'Because there is going to be a war Sergeant Major, I feel it in my bones and so do you. You know it and so do I. This silent denial between us all can't go on forever.'

There was a look in the trusty Sergeant Major that told John he was right and the eruption was fast approaching. John took a deep breath in and then let out a large and long sigh as if he could feel the tension in Europe on the sea air. Everything he had been doing since joining the army was building up to this point and he hoped now that he could live up to his father's name and that Tom's wisdom and experience would help him get through the worst of what was perhaps to come. As for Tom, John couldn't help but wonder if it felt just like the last time, the calm before the storm.

'Then I don't know sir,' Tom replied. 'I can't honestly see what Hitler would want in Egypt, so I think we will see the lights of Brighton and Eastbourne again. But you never know, perhaps Heir Hitler has a bit of a fancy to Egyptian things,' he smiled.

'Or a fancy for the Suez canal,' John added. 'Let's hope it's a short time, do our duty and damn well get ourselves home.'

'Did you get to say goodbye to your sister?' Tom asked.

'Pretty much, I let her go to Anthony.'

'Silly bugger, stop worrying about them,' Tom chuckled.

'He thinks he is in love with her,' John remarked.

'Maybe he is, time will tell. Just have to ruddy hope that Adolf keeps his toys in his pram now won't we?'

From below decks, Corporal Orchard arrived. Orchard was one of John's most able soldiers, his aid in the company command section who regularly ran errands for him. He was, however, a real diamond in the rough, a cockney character whose cheeky antics and quick mind John knew would be its own reward in the trials to come. He had unpacked his belongings and was bored already, finding his way to rear of the ship a cigarette perched on the end of his lips.

'Bloody chaos down there,' he muttered.

'Really?' John asked.

'Yeah, too crowded for me and I get sick! How are things for you, sir?'

'Fine Corporal, just fine.'

'I bet they are! I expect you've all got fancy cosy cabins eh?' he said with a sarcastic grin across his face. 'I'm only joking sir, sorry if I was getting out of line.'

But John didn't mind his humour, combined with Tom and Sergeant Scott it was no more unbearable and he liked Orchard's sharp mind and ability to turn the most serious of occasions into a comedy show. Instead, he decided to play the game and return the compliment. 'That's alright Corporal and your right they are very cosy, in actual fact, we have nice quilted mattresses, two extra pillows and the whiskey cabinet of course!'

'No!' said the Corporal his lower jaw nearly hitting the floor. 'You've got a whiskey cabinet an' all?'

'Now you have done it!' Tom huffed joining in. 'You know what he wants now, don't you? He wants a spare pillow!'

'Spare pillow? I want a bloody drink, not a spare pillow or a quilted mattress! All the galley has is bloody Navy rum.'

'Nowt wrong with a bit of rum Corporal.' Tom chipped in.

'Have you really got a drinks cabinet?' but John's grin gave the game away. 'You nearly had me then sir. I tell you what a couple more minutes pulling my chain and I would have been close to mutiny.'

John returned to the now fading lights again. The cool air and sound of the sea against the hull were soothing. Orchard came alongside and watched too.

'Do you think we'll be back?' he asked, just as John had earlier.

'Here we go again,' Tom mumbled.

'I asked Gypsy Rose Lee the same thing earlier,' John chuckled. 'His crystal ball isn't working.'

'Oh sorry,' Orchard replied. 'Perhaps it was a bit morbid wasn't it, but it does make you wonder.'

'Well we're not at war yet,' Tom snapped.

'Yet,' huffed the Corporal.

John turned his back on the lights, looking around the deck at some of the other men wandering to and fro, giving the odd nod to officers in the other three companies. 'But if and when we are, then I promise I'll do my damned best to get us all home in one piece.'

Tom put his arm on his shoulder squeezing it a little and nodding.

Orchard threw the stub of his cigarette over the railings. 'It might be a bit of a tall order that sir, but know this, D company is my family, that makes you our father, if you watch out for us, I will watch out for you.'

With those words he left, entering the inside of the ship, conveniently through the bar where drinks had just begun to be served to the officers only without anyone noticing him.

'God help us.' Tom sighed with a gentle wink.

A New Life
13th June 1941 - Sussex

It had been over two years since D company's departure and Sophie missed their cheery sound. The dinner on the terrace seemed another lifetime ago and sometimes even felt like it may have been someone else's memory, for so much had now changed. The sleepy villages were bustling with olive drab traffic, the pretty coastal walks across the Downs crisscrossed with grey barbed wire, even the skies no longer held just the sound of morning sparrows, but also the roar of Merlin engines, although of all the sounds of war the planes were her favourite.

The distant yet still vibrant sound of sirens was the least favourite. The first year of the war they howled out the coming of death across the hills, followed by the faint twinkling lights of Eastbourne fading one by one in the distance. By the second year of the war, they had become intrusive and nauseating as her mind became ever more used to the sights and sounds of war. The plight of so many hiding in their shelters became the norm and with time Sophie was becoming bored with the war, her concerns about Britain soon took second place under her concerns about a good night sleep.

Sophie's twenty-first birthday had come and gone without too much occasion. Uncle Richard and Joy had sent a beautiful bouquet of flowers and a silver key to represent her coming of age. Mrs Jenkins baked a cake with what ingredients she could muster of her own and other local well-wishers additional ration coupons. John had sent a very special message in one of his letters with Tom and Simon amongst others signing their regards and their apologies for their absence at the bottom. In John's last letter a small felt patch of a brown rat upon a black background fell out, it's significance she assumed would be understood later.

Anthony had sent a vinyl record of Johann Strauss' 'Blue Danube' on a 78rpm Decca recording label that she would be able to play over and over again to remember their day by the river Cuckmere. How he had managed that feat was the biggest surprise of all, but it was now her most treasured possession, although she hid it away at times concerned that the label might cause some to talk.

As she had expected stress and worry was a constant companion, but what took Sophie by surprise was the anxiety that came with waiting for the mail, of not knowing what was going on over in the desert and how quickly the absence of letters turned from fear to frustration. The newspapers had only so much use in that they gave a broad spectrum of the war, whilst gossip and rumour had to fill in some of the gaps. There was nothing that would tell her how Anthony or John was except direct letters, of which as time went on became fewer and fewer. Mrs Jenkins blamed U-boats, but the reality was far more likely to be that there was little time for the men to write. Uncle Richard helped to explain this to her as the fog of war.

'Soldiers like nothing more than to communicate with home,' he had told her. 'But the reality of war gives them little time to actually write. Tom and John will be too busy working, cleaning kit, doing drill and training the men.' He had conveniently left out the other big factor they might be engaged in. 'But I tell you this Sophie, although they may not be able to write, you have no idea the value a letter from home has out there.'

She bared her Uncle's advice in mind when writing shortly after, this time to Anthony. She liked to write individual messages and what she wanted to say to him was private. She imagined the letter to be folded up and placed in his breast pocket and her mind convinced herself that it would be looked upon over and over again when the times got rough. She hadn't confined her news to just Anthony and John; she kept constant correspondence with Tom and Simon James as well. She wanted everyone to feel well informed of what was happening at home, in case their news was as fragmented as hers at home.

It felt like her whole family had gone away and only she was left, but there was Mrs Jenkins of course who now popped in only every other day, partly due to retirement and partly because she had spent so long over the years being involved with the family she classed Sophie and John as one of her own. Sophie wondered if she couldn't completely let go, but the new arrangement suited both parties well.

Sophie had kept her promise to her brother and remained in touch with Uncle Richard and Joy up at the Great Hall on a fairly regular basis. As John had hoped, Sophie's attitude had mellowed a little and a few bridges had been crossed. She had found some of Joy's strengths compliable with her own. Since the wedding and the grand speech that slapped all the ugly relatives in the face, she had really warmed to her and the outbreak of war saw all of them sharing so much in common, for Joy's daughter Katherine was also sent overseas, her experience in tropical diseases something the army could not afford to overlook. Sophie's brief acquaintance with Katherine had given her someone else to write to, as well as the push she had needed towards doing her bit for king and country.

It was Katherine, not Simon James, although his advice had been second to none, who had found her a place volunteering three mornings a week at the Newhaven Down's hospital. Sophie really enjoyed it now and it changed to become her full-time vocation by the end of her first year, but it hadn't started that way. At first, the job was a quiet one, local accidents, most of them children learning to deal with the new alien surroundings that war had bought them were the regular visitors. She remembered now with a little grin that fateful first day, the cuts, the grazes and the little old man who was her first victim with a needle. The matron had huffed and puffed in the background, her foot tapping consistently on the floor whilst she observed.

Then came the real baptism of fire between the 26th May and the 4th of June in 1940, when Sophie and nine other nurses were placed on a train and sent to Folkestone. That spring had so far been glorious with nothing but talk, newspapers and the odd green truck passing through the sleepy villages that hinted at any reality of the war. The train journey was full of excitement, a journey into the unknown. They left inexperienced, not exactly sure what they were heading into as the train pulled into Folkestone train station. Their uniforms were white and blue, none of them exposed to the reality of war. Dunkirk changed all of that.

The wounded, most of them evacuated soldiers and oil soaked sailors, were brought into the hospital from the harbour, scarred and blistered in various forms. She remembered now how her feet had slipped upon the blood and how sand had been poured almost as freely upon it to help the grip. Most of all she remembered how impossible the blood was to wash from her hands, especially under the fingernails. She had begun as a nervous wreck, walking dazed from one crisis to another. She remembered looking at herself in the mirror of the toilets and how pale she had become, a ghost of her former self.

Her hands had shaken uncontrollably, so much so that at one point she dropped a bowl and its bloody contents spilt and spread across the floor. Getting down onto her knees she gingerly began picking up the sodden dressings with the tips of her fingers, guiding them as best she could back into the bowl. She then wiped away a wisp of hair that had fallen into her contorted face and it was then that she caught the gaze of a wounded man a few feet away. She didn't know what it was about his gaze that did it, for he simply stared, not a single blink or movement. His mind was elsewhere no doubt, perhaps still on the other side of the channel and all that was staring at her was an empty shell. She even wondered if he was dead, but his chest heaved ever so gently under the blanket. He simply looked straight through her as if she was not even there, with no sign of any emotion. Perhaps all sense of feeling had been drained from him over on the other side, she wondered if only his soulless body had returned. It was his gaze, his emptiness that caused her to realise that her plight, her suffering and torture was nowhere near his. She returned to the bloody bandages on the floor and this time picked them up with a firmer grip. She ran her hand through her hair to keep it from her eyes and this time wanted to feel the blood stick and dry to it.

'That trip was what did it,' her matron had told her. 'That is what woke you up and that was when you became a nurse.'

She was right of course, but Sophie couldn't pinpoint a precise moment that caused her to change, there were so many moments in that evacuation that shaped her and hardened her, from the soulless soldier, learning how to apply a tourniquet, to the different types of exit wounds and how to treat burns. Perhaps if she forced herself to pinpoint a moment and one where it did feel a switch had been flicked it would have been Ryan Townsend.

Ryan was bought into Folkestone on the 29th May 1940, she remembered because she wrote everything down in a big diary she had started since John and Anthony had left. He had a wound caused by shrapnel she thought could be patched up, but the doctors and surgeons did not. For a whole week, she visited him, reading letters from his pack and even helping him write his own letters home. They became friends and she became a rock. Every time she saw him he smiled and she could tell that she had made a difference just by her presence. It was the 5th of June that she turned up to check up on his progress, her little pencil tucked behind her ear at the ready and it was that day that the bed was empty. It was the first time that her emotions took control, up until then she had done so well to numb the effects the horrors had inflicted upon her, but Ryan was too much. It was there in a cupboard under the stairs that she swore never again to get attached to a patient. Never again would she allow herself to be controlled by the circumstances. She was reborn.

Sophie returned to Newhaven with a reputation as the Florence of Folkestone as the evacuation came to its conclusion. It was inevitable that some of the last ships evacuating the French and remaining BEF, this time from Normandy, would head for whatever ports they could. The few liners, trawlers and warships that limped into the harbour at Newhaven were nearly bursting full of exhausted, oil-soaked men. They coped well considering it was only a small hospital, intended for the population of the town and men who served in the nearby fort and harbour itself. After that spring the hospital settled down and had been a lot quieter, the occasional soldier, sailor or airman would arrive, but it was local civilians who had been hurt from German bombing raids or simple daily accidents and general health procedures that took up most of the hospitals time now.

It was not long after Dunkirk that reports came back from the fighting in North Africa against the Italians and it was then that her new found inner being would really be put to the test. She read the newspapers more heavily now, but as Uncle Richard had pointed out, it was unlikely she would catch a glimpse of John's company. Her heart was heavy, but it coped, especially when an agreement was made with Mrs Jenkins to keep the radio turned off when at home.

On this particular day she attempted to take her mind off the war by taking a detour home through the woods. She dismounted her bicycle and pushed it through dry dirt paths and between the pillars of oak and chestnut. There was a stream that trickled and gurgled across smooth stones that broke up the path. One of her earliest memories, perhaps even her first, was her brother walking her across the stream, holding her hand and helping her across the stepping stones coated with slippery moss. Back then it had seemed like a raging river and each step perilous, but now a single well-placed step took her and the bicycle across. She paused upon a fallen tree and watched the water, remembering the sounds that children make when playing and concentrating her mind to visualise their childhood here, before making her way up towards the fields that bordered their home.

Passing through the door she went upstairs to change and afterwards found Mrs Jenkins in the kitchen hard at work.

'You will wear the carpet out,' Mrs Jenkins said.

Sophie felt as though she had barely been home five minutes, but the reality was probably more like twenty and she had indeed been shuffling around the rooms looking for something to do.

'You can help me with these spuds if you like or continue to wear the carpet out which is what you are going to do if you carry on the way you are.'

'I doubt that,' Sophie smirked her foot tapping upon the wooden floor.

'Well thank goodness for that then. It was your mother who wanted carpet down here and it was your father that wanted the rustic feel,' was the reply. 'What were you doing in your brother's room yesterday?'

Sophie thought for a moment and then remembered that she had been looking through some of John's photographs.

'Memories,' she replied. 'I was looking through the photo album.'

'Plenty of memories here if you look hard enough. Oh, by the way, there was some post for your brother, I think it might be some payments due, but I didn't open them.'

Sophie found them on the side table and opened them, sighing when looking at the digits. 'John's pay is so inconsistent.'

'Yeah but you are earning now. How was work today?' Mrs Jenkins pushed her spectacles to a more comfortable position upon her nose as Sophie shrugged to her question. 'But I have said before my dear that it may be time for me to go. You could save a fortune and you don't need me anymore.'

'A fortune? Mrs Jenkins, you cost barely anything and don't come round nearly as much as you used to. No, it's not that. I can just about manage, but I do need a little more income. John needs his pay and can only spare what he can. God knows what he might need to buy out there.'

'What about renting out the spare room?'

It wasn't the first time it had been suggested and Sophie hated it when it was referred to as the spare room, it was mum's room, it always had been and always would be. She couldn't deny that it had become a spare room, it was where they billeted Tom on his many visits, but its décor and atmosphere had never changed.

'I couldn't,' she whispered.

'John's room then, just for the time being until this bloody war blows over. There are plenty of servicemen working locally, especially the Navy down at the docks. Your uncle might know someone who is looking for somewhere to lodge.'

'What if John returns before the war is over?'

'Oh goodness me Sophie, it doesn't matter what room it is, so long as you tell yourself that it's temporary, which it is.'

She thought for a moment, jostling with the idea in her head. The fact was that when John returned there would still be a room free. She always made sure she thought of his return as a certainty, even when others would use the term 'might' from time to time. The memory of her mother's passing and witnessing the many helpless deaths of young men in her care the year before had but one benefit, it had helped her come to terms with the loss in her life. It was that uncomfortable reality that made her decide to reluctantly agree.

'Mum's room then,' she said. 'But where will I store all her things?'

Mrs Jenkins put down the potato that she had only half peeled and embraced her. 'We can put them in the loft love, I will help you.'

The ladder into the roof was old and creaky. Sophie climbed up into the darkness that bit by bit gave away its secrets stored for many years by the gentle light from a paraffin lamp. She had never been up here before, when things had needed storing it was her brother or Tom who ventured up here. There was an old mirror leaning up against the chimney stack and various boxes covered with a very thin layer of dust. Her old pram and cot were also visible in the gloom, broken down so that they could be passed up through the narrow hatch in the floor all those many years ago and it was here that they had resided ever since. Mrs Jenkins gingerly climbed a few rungs and passed the items they had boxed up to Sophie. John and Tom had already once cleared her mother's clothes, not long after her death and most of her mother's jewellery was now in a box in Sophie's room. It surprised both of them how little there was to move.

'That's the last,' Mrs Jenkins called up to her.

'What is in all these boxes?' Sophie called down. 'There are quite a few. Are they John's?'

Mrs Jenkins paused a moment. 'I couldn't tell you my dear without seeing them and even then it would be a guess. Perhaps they were your mother's?'

'My mother's?'

'Quite a bit of hers was put up there.'

'I know, but I don't remember John moving any of these, the boxes are all blue, does that ring a bell?' Sophie asked trying to piece the pictures together. She looked down to Mrs Jenkins when there was yet another pause.

The old lady simply looked back at her with a strange smile upon her face, one that almost insinuated she knew more than she was giving away.

'Blue boxes? Oh no, they belonged to your mother. I remember her asking your father to put them away up there, just before he died funnily enough. All I can remember was the largest blue cardboard box wrapped in a piece of string. About this big,' she gestured like a fisherman does after nobody saw the great catch of the day. 'Struggled to get it up there he did. Take a peek it's about time the dust was cleared.'

Sophie looked back into the gloom and after scanning around the corners saw a box amongst the rest that fitted the description. She crawled over to it and removed some small shoe boxes of photographs and postcards that sat on top. She pulled the string to one side and opened the largest box. Inside was a treasure trove of memories, large books, envelopes and loose letters. She gently lifted one of the books, some photographs fell from the limp pages and after picking them up she opened the book at a random page to reveal her mother's handwriting with a date perched at the top, July 14th 1925. She sifted through some more pages, again the same layout, her mother's wonderful handwriting that she had tried so hard to copy in her youth and another date, this time August 24th 1925. She opened the next book, October 17th 1931. They were diaries, filled with her mother's thoughts, feelings, photographs, postcards and pressed flowers. A tear pricked her eye but she fought it back.

'Mum's diaries. I have found mum's diaries,' she crawled over to the hatch. 'I never knew she had diaries. Mrs Jenkins?'

But Mrs Jenkins was no longer at the bottom of the ladder.

'It's started,' Tom said over a distant rumble of enemy gunfire.

'That's one hell of a barrage,' Sergeant Scott added.

Both men stood on top of the parapet and watched as the German guns pounded away at the British lines. Fortunately, in their sector, the German shells were dropping short, they exploded in distant thuds about a mile away, lighting up the lilac and blue sky. It was a sure sign that things were soon going to heat up.

'Looks like they'll make a move before we do,' Tom said.

'Think we ought to take cover Sergeant Major,' Scott advised, in his calm one toned voice, a cigarette dangling from his lips as always. Every soldier smoked, but Sergeant Scott was not every soldier.

Tom jumped down into the trench; Scott followed. By now the light was fading and the wind had picked up from nowhere, getting stronger and stronger by the minute. It began to blow the sand and dust across the floor of the desert, whistling strangely as it went. The ground looked as if it was alive, twisting mini but growing whirlwinds of dust; it was an awesome sight billowing and buffeting into dunes that scratched the burnt earth in undulating movements.

John was asleep, just as Tom had left him at mid-morning. He had barely moved a muscle at all, so exhausted that not even the distant thud of shells had stirred him. But now as Tom returned to check on him he began to twist and turn as the thoughts of home became a bad dream of frustration and worry.

'Wakey, wakey now sir,' said Tom nudging him.

'He alright? He's sweating a bit?' Scott remarked making himself a brew.

'Having one of his bad dreams again, he's concerned about home,' Tom replied.

'About his sister?'

'Probably. Does he worry about anything else?'

John roused and was soon awake, his eyes were sore and itchy and his head was thumping as if it had been struck by a mallet.

'What time is it?' he asked dazed.

'Late evening sir,' Tom answered. 'You've had a good long kip, sir. Sorry, I had to wake you up, but Jerry has opened up with his artillery.'

'Good God, I feel awful,' John said, taking a mug of tea that was being offered by Sergeant Scott. 'Why didn't you wake me earlier Sergeant Major? I can't believe you let me sleep for so long.'

'You needed a rest, sir. Everything is under control. You haven't missed anything up until now.'

'Dodgy one, sir?' Scott chipped in. 'You were tossing and turning like a mad man.'

'Was I?' John replied. 'Maybe I was, had a bit of a bad dream. How close is the bombardment Tom, I mean Sergeant Major?'

'About a mile, it's landing near the Indian brigade to the north. There is another thing,' he perched himself in a corner. 'You don't have to keep calling me Sergeant Major all the time; we have spoken about this before.'

John smiled. 'I know Tom and I am sorry, I keep doing it don't I? I think it's just habit in front of the men.'

'Well at the moment the Sergeant hardly fits the category of men.'

'Speak for yourself,' Scott replied quickly.

'Besides,' Tom continued. 'They don't think anything of it, so long as they don't call me Tom. Bloody hell they all think I'm your bloody father anyway!' He laughed.

'Or grandfather,' chipped in Scott dryly.

Tom shot him a look. 'Haven't you got some cigarettes to liberate from somewhere?'

'Sergeant Scott, could you give us a minute?' John asked.

Scott nodded and left through the blackout curtain that gently flapped like a flag at the dugout entrance, his cigarette still perched between his lips and a brew in his right hand. It was the typical Scott pose that the men had come to be familiar with.

Tom moved to the entrance of the dugout. The wind had picked up even more and in it John watched as grains of sand pricked into his leathery burnt face causing him to grimace and turn away.

'I can't seem to settle,' John said frustrated. He rose from his bed and paced up and down beside his old friend. 'It's been a while since I've heard anything. What if she needs money?'

'We are all in the same boat there!' Tom guffawed trying to lighten the atmosphere. 'You're sending your pay home when you can and anyway no news is good news, you know the lines have been pretty tight the past few months. Mail will get through eventually. She'll be fine, you can lead a horse to water but you can't make it drink. She's stronger than you think; independent, just like her mother,' he coughed gruffly. 'I assure you, you've got weaker men here that need you now,' he said slapping him paternally on the back. 'Remember you've got them this far, you're doing a grand job. Don't bring your worries to work son. If it interferes with your duties here none of us will be going home and what then?'

No matter what difficulty abroad or at home, Tom's pep talks always hit the spot, just like when he was a boy. What would he do without Tom?

'Your right and they won't, Sergeant Major,' he sighed and looked his old friend in the eye. 'I'm sorry Tom, I keep doing it, I think it is just because of where we are and because of the men and…'

'I know,' Tom smiled reassuringly. 'And it doesn't matter if anything it's professional.'

'Right,' said John, clapping his hands together. 'What's next on the agenda?'

The wind howled now and the late evening sky was an inky dark blue as night took over. There was still the distant thud and whistle from the German guns, but it had dissipated and was not as concentrated as earlier.

'I just worry sometimes, I have these dreams and it sets me all back. You've seen what she gets like,' John said harrowingly. He slumped back against the sandbag wall of the dugout. 'She shouldn't have gone through what she went through.'

'You're referring to her father again I take it?' Tom sighed.

'You know how I felt about him, but I never wanted her to go through anything like that. She didn't deserve it.'

'No one does and it was a long time ago,' said Tom bluntly. 'Listen, John, we have had this conversation many times and the truth is…' he paused and checked himself, rubbing his forehead. 'I don't know what I am getting at. Why don't you try writing to her again, get your thoughts onto paper and out of your head,' he suggested dismissively, lighting a cigarette and strolling out into the wind.

'Tom?' John called out, but he was gone.

There was paper by the field telephone and a pencil for jotting down messages. He didn't want to write to Sophie, it was difficult to know what to say. He couldn't tell her where he was or what he was doing. Anything considered detrimental was blacked out by the censor for fear of any information getting into enemy hands and being used. The thing with Sophie was she didn't want to hear pleasantries and there were few of those to speak of out here. She wanted to know the ins and outs of everything and to John, it made for bad reading, Anthony probably had the same problem he mused.

He paused for a moment, as sand began to trickle like the inside of an egg timer between the gaps in the dugout which had appeared from the vibrations of the recent shelling. The wild, prolonged wailing of the wind wafted in from outside. As it got caught in the sheeting of the entrance of the dugout, its pitch changed to a shrill that pierced the ears.

'Sand storm sir,' Sergeant Scott said, entering the dugout without a single shred of surprise in his voice. 'Getting pretty nasty out there too.'

'Sounds like it. Sergeant, how is the company doing for supplies?'

'We got plenty of ammunition, although not for the Tommy guns. Water ain't a problem and neither is food,' he raised his eyebrows, checking his thoughts to ensure he had covered everything. 'We raided a load of medical supplies off that ambulance that came to pick up Private Hamilton and that's about it.'

'Morale?' questioned John.

'Very good sir,' he said, with his usual hint of sarcasm. 'The men love it here and said that tomorrow with your permission they're going to dig a swimming pool under one of those palm trees.'

'And seriously?' he questioned again.

'Ain't too bad sir, it could be better though. Don't take it personally they're good lads. They went through hell in that last attack and it's knocked their confidence a bit. Now they know there's gonna be another one they are a bit stressed and yesterday that air attack really put the wind up em.'

John knew that his men had been under a lot of pressure. They were exhausted, they all were. The heat, the sand, the winds, and the humidity all took its toll. The pounding of guns thundering all around them forever in the background played on the nerves and as the Sergeant had pointed out already, there was the stress of knowing what was coming.

The Halfaya pass would not be forgotten easily. It had been paid for in too much blood and sanity. Now they occupied scorpion infested Italian trenches under constant air and artillery attack. This had been the first day that they had been able to rest. Fourteen men had been wounded and one killed and not a single rifle had been fired at the enemy for the past week. They had not seen an Afrika Korps soldier or an Italian for nearly a week either. Only the artillery and Stukas sometimes reminded them there was a war on.

'Writing to your sister?' Scott asked.

John shook his head, giving up on the idea as the telephone rang. It was strange hearing a familiar sound in such an unfamiliar desolate place.

'Hello, D Company,' John said picking up the cold receiver.

'Hello, Captain Baker. John? It's Major Love.'

'Hello, Sir.'

'Sorry I missed you earlier, Lieutenant Morris settled in?'

'It was Lieutenant Moore sir and yes I think he is fine.'

'Ah yes, Moore that is what I said was it not? How are things on your part of the line?'

'Not too bad sir,' John responded. 'The men are holding, but it's pretty miserable here.'

'Don't expect it helps with this damn monstrous sand storm that's kicking up. Now listen, Captain Baker, John this is very important. The enemy is probing forward on all fronts; there is nothing friendly in front of your position anymore. That Indian company has pulled back. In fact, I am with Captain Clarke's B Company now and they have just started to filter through his lines.'

'Are we to expect an attack?' John inquired. 'It's an unusual move to probe on all fronts at once, the Italians don't normally do that,' there was silence on the other end of the telephone for a moment. 'Sir?'

'Sorry John, got a bit distracted then. We can hear tracked vehicles or at least we think we can. No doubt some of these assaults will turn out to be feints, but keep your guard up. I want this position to be held, do you understand?'

There wasn't much to hold John thought. 'Yes sir,' he replied.

'Anything alters I'll contact you later. In the meantime hold, that's an order. Must fly, got to get back to Battalion. Good luck Captain Baker' and with a 'click' the Major was gone.

John took a deep breath and held it for a moment and then looked at Scott; his cigarette drooping precariously, stuck on his dry cracked lips.

'Orders sir?'

'We're to hold, Sergeant Scott, same as before. The Major seems to think there is some activity ahead of us and they might try and push through. I want you to stay by the telephone in case our orders change. I'd better go and have a wander, see how the men are doing and pass on the news,' John said. Thoughts of letters and Sophie were now firmly locked away in the recesses of his mind. He grabbed his tin helmet, his webbing belt and from his respirator bag a pair of gas eye shields that he used as goggles.

Outside the wind blew fiercely its mournful laments imitating the cries of a dangerous wild animal. John squinted to prevent the wall of sand that now sliced his face with its razor-sharp claws from penetrating his eyes. He edged slowly forwards, towards First platoons position. In between the ululating shrieks of the wind the distant crackling of gunfire could still be heard.

John surged forward, fumbling to put his belt on with one hand whilst the other tried to shield his vulnerable face; the eye shields were virtually useless in these relentless gusts.

A shadow appeared ahead of him, the visibility was so poor it was impossible to make out who it was and they couldn't have been more than a few yards ahead.

'You alright Captain, sir?' called out a voice that was barely recognisable over the grains of sand that beat like hailstones on Johns steel helmet. 'Captain, sir?' the voice repeated.

It was Private Dean, the platoons Anti-Tank rifle gunner. Beside him was Private Woodgate and the Boys rifle, which was covered with some old Hessian rags to keep the sand out of the guns working parts. John put a thumb up in response and then slowly fought his way on through the precipitating storm.

Sand, sand and more sand, it perforated through his skin, splintered his face like a thousand needles. It attacked and infected every orifice, up his nose, in his throat and it even jammed itself in his ears causing agonising and searing pains through his head. Keeping his head low didn't do any good, as the powerful gales advanced through the trench, propelling themselves around and reverberating back up into his face.

Laboriously he trekked finally seeing an outline of more figures up ahead. It was First Platoon. Many were sheltering down in the bottom of the trenches, under any available resource that would hold back the mercurial tide of shifting sand, but some still peered over the parapet into the swirling, progressive wall of dust. Amongst them was Anthony, who with sheer persistence against the billowing blasts, sat upon the parapet, watching for any sign of trouble. Incredulously he was peering through a pair of binoculars.

'You won't see anything through those!' John screamed above the gnawing blizzard.

'Well its better than jolly well hiding down there,' he screeched back, pointing to the floor of the trench.

John beckoned him down from the parapet and together they squatted against the trench walls.

'Thought I saw something earlier,' Anthony said. 'Like a shadow, but I could be wrong.'

He leaned against the wall of the trench dusting himself off as best he could. Around him huddled his men, all seeking some kind of protection from the storm. Some wrapped themselves up in greatcoats; some could only crouch against the sides of the trench for some form of refuge.

'How are the men?' John asked, not that he needed a reply; all the faces around him had had enough of the conditions they found themselves in, their discomfort and contempt of their plight very plain to see.

'Need you ask? They are bloody awful. Thank god we have these trenches, or we would be stuck out in the open like C Company, poor sods.' He reached into his coat pocket and from it withdrew a flask. He offered John a tot of rum.

'You know full well I don't drink on duty,' he said with disapproval.

Anthony, covering the lip of the rum flask as best as he could, swigged a mouthful. He let out a gasp of thirsty relief and wiped the residue from the corner of his mouth with the back of his hand.

John scowled at him. 'When you have finished setting a good example, our orders are to hold this position. There is nothing else in front of this position now but the enemy and they might try a push on us during the night. I hardly think a tot of rum is going to help.'

'Better than dysentery,' he winked back cheekily.

John was about to walk on, but Anthony grabbed him by the arm to stop him. The move was bold, especially in front of the men. John wheeled around to look at him, but before he could say anything Anthony got the first word in.

'Listen,' he pleaded. He must have known that the grabbing of the Captain's arm was a step too far, which was reflected in Johns enraged face. 'We've been out here nearly two years. Can we not at least try and get on, even if it's for the sake of the men? After all, we have the same interests at heart, do we not, sir?' His desperate eyes awaited the response.

If John's face looked enraged, then it was outdone by the anger that welled up from within, stimulated by Anthony's comment. The same interest indeed, John thought, but by now he was coming to the boil under his collar. Was this man taking the piss out of him or was he overreacting? What was happening to him? He couldn't think straight. He deliberated for a moment. He shouldn't let bitter differences get in the way of duty though, that much was true. The men were demoralised enough as it was without him bringing his personal life onto the battlefield. Saving face he took on a different air and snorted lightly;

'Take your hands off me, Lieutenant.'

Anthony did so, his hands now free, awkwardly fiddled with his jacket.

'I'm sorry that was very unprofessional of me sir.'

‘It was bold,’ John squinted. ‘But your right of course,’ he said gracefully tapping Anthony on his shoulder. He could feel the gaze of the nearby men and tactically retreated.

He then leaned into Anthony’s earshot. ‘Don’t ever bring her into it again.’

‘I try not to, but to my mind that is the true nature of this problem,’ Anthony replied. ‘I think I know what you want, what you have always wanted, but I will not leave her.’

He reminded John of his stepfather Ted and how much he always tried to please his mother, showering her with gifts in the early days, perhaps it was that too that infuriated him. John gave him one last glare and continued further along down the trench. He didn’t want Anthony to leave her either, but in his pride couldn’t admit it either and left the Lieutenant to stew over his lack of response.

At one point, John had to break cover from the trenches to try and find Second Platoon and as he did he presented himself yet again to the full force of the sand storm. Vulnerable, he struggled to stay upright, falling to his knees a few times in the prevailing winds. Every time he got back to his feet he lost all sense of direction. The trenches were only a few feet apart in places, but once you had wandered a few more feet into the storm it was so easy to get disorientated.

Out of nowhere two figures rallied to his needs and pulled him from the ground into a shelter where he was reunited with Second Platoon huddled together.

John called to Keyes, ‘anything Lieutenant?’

Suddenly the restless fervour regressed almost as if someone had just flicked a switch and John could hear quite clearly.

‘Not sure sir. Some of the men keep thinking they can hear something, but they don’t know what it is they are hearing. The bloody sand storm has made it impossible to tell if there is anyone in front of our position.’

‘If there is they are not going to be friendly. I had the Major on the telephone earlier and he suggested vehicle movement. But in the meantime, our orders are to hold, understood?’

Keyes nodded and then returned head first into the receding but still restless blizzard of sand and dust, peering over the top of the trench.

By the time he reached Third Platoon the storm was clearly dying down. Visibility had increased, but only just and John no longer had to scream orders over the agitated nomadic gusts as the storm tried to motivate itself again periodically.

When he arrived at Third platoons position he found Tom with Lieutenant Moore.

'We have to hold,' he repeated. 'It is possible they might probe our positions all along the line and they may try it here first, it could even be a full assault.'

'It was pretty obvious something was brewing with those Stukas earlier, what about the Indian company?' Tom asked.

'They have pulled back; whatever approaches from in front is to be regarded as the enemy.'

'Sir, sir!' an urgent voice called from further down the trench, it belonged to Private Carlson a young and eager lad from Canterbury.

'What is it Private?' Moore called out taking the lead for the first time.

'The guns sir, the guns have stopped!'

He was right, John had failed to notice it over the whirling of the dust and debris kicked up by the sand storm. Now with the storm almost exhausted and a lull in its ferocity it was impossible to doubt it, the German artillery had stopped firing.

'Visibility?' John asked another young soldier who leaned over the top of the trench.

'About twenty yards or so, sir, but it's getting dark now as well so that doesn't help.'

'Lieutenant Moore, keep a strong lookout and listen carefully for anything that may give away an enemy presence,' John said.

Moore, keen to see his first taste of action nodded eagerly.

Tom followed John back to the dug-out. The sand storm was dying off very quickly now, it had gone almost as quickly as it had appeared and it was easier to pass by the soldiers who crammed nearly every corner of the trench system.

Without warning the screaming sound of artillery began crashing down again, this time all around them. The shells came whining down from the heavens, screeching like the brakes of a train pulling into a station. The shelling was much more precise than the previous barrage had been, the thudding so close that sections of trench began falling in and half burying its occupants. The darkness was riddled with vivid orange, white and yellow flashes, but as quickly as it had started; just like the sand storm the guns fell silent. It was a brief barrage, a sure sign that the enemy was on its way and getting into position.

From outside the dugout, John could just make out First Platoons trenches through the blackness, just to his left. To the right somewhere in the dark was Second Platoons position. Peering over the trenches cautiously John waited.

'Ready?' Tom asked, leaning on the parapet next to him with his revolver in his right hand. He then barked the orders to stand to.

Looking to his left John watched Sergeant Scott position himself next to Tom. He gripped a 303 rifle, ready to take on the juggernaut that could be heading their way. As usual, precariously dangling from his lips was another cigarette.

'Put that cigarette out now,' ordered John. 'Or you'll make us all sitting targets!'

'Old wives tale,' he retorted, but he did as he was ordered taking a good strong last draw. John shook his head in disbelief. 'What?' Scott moaned, opening his hands in exasperation. 'Might be my last!'

Beyond Scott, Private Dean appeared, hastily loading the large Boys rifle, whilst Private Woodgate placed spare magazines next to him ready to load.

John looked back at Anthony. Even though there was a growing darkness, he could just make out his silhouette raised above the inky skyline. The bloody fool was sitting on top of the trench again where he could get a better view.

'Orchard,' John called out and soon the Corporal appeared. 'Tell Lieutenant Thomas to bloody well stay in his trench, if I can see him so can the enemy.'

'Yes sir, anything else?'

'Yeah, make sure you say please to him,' he muttered, to which he caught Tom rolling his eyes.

'Very good sir,' and Orchard hastily ran off.

John listened intently for any sounds. He could hear a rumble, what he couldn't make out was whether it was the warm calming wind filling his ears with fictitious sounds, or whether he could hear the tell-tale sound of tracked vehicles.

Orchard soon returned. 'Well?' John asked him, referring to Anthony.

'I informed Lieutenant Thomas that it would be wise for him not to present himself to the enemy sir,' Orchard replied with a triumphant grin.

'Good,' John said.

'May I also add, for the record, that Lieutenant Thomas's reply was somewhat colourful.'

John grinned; Orchard always had an amusing way of reporting things.

He looked across once more towards First Platoon. Anthony could not be seen anymore and neither could anybody else, obviously he had seen the error of his ways and taken cover.

Even the gentlest breath of a breeze had now dispersed and the ever darkening sky above was now glittering clearly with the painted heavens. Not a grain of sand polluted the now clear starlit sky above them.

They all continued to listen. Tom even closed his eyes, straining his ears to pick out any odd sounds. It was the waiting game, or so some soldiers called it. This game could go on for hours, even days. It required patience instead of skill and often had men turn mad with boredom. Men would claim to hear the strangest things in the silence, but it was merely their subconsciousness, seeking out any sound that would bring the game to an end.

Suddenly in the darkness a repetitive squeaking could be heard. As the seconds passed it got louder until it was unmistakable. It was an armoured vehicle. It couldn't be seen, but the squeaky, grinding sound of metal on metal from the tracks of the vehicle cut through the blackness. The sound of rifle bolts sliding the first round into the chamber soon reached his ears. They were followed by the clicking of cocking Bren guns. The vehicle was closing in now, the closer it got the more the ground vibrated in front of them. John's breathing became heavy and slow as he tried desperately to tame his excitement, tinged with fear.

The vehicle soon came into view. It lumbered out of the dark like a hungry bear. As quickly as it had appeared it halted.

Italian voices could be heard on the softening wind. They made no attempt what so ever to be quiet, a sign they were unaware of the rifles pointed at them. They called out to each other, sometimes confidently; sometimes with what must have been a joke, as men hidden in the darkness laughed.

It was strange to hear laughter from the enemy, it caused the opposition to become familiar and it was that very sound that caused John to lower his rifle.

The men of the company watched the vehicle, its identity shrouded a little by the dark. Private Dean peered at it down the long barrel of the anti-tank rifle, waiting for the signal to pull the trigger. A few more minutes passed and the vehicle jerked backwards in reverse, back into the darkness.

John's company waited silently and patiently to strike, just like the scorpions that they shared their trenches with. After a couple of hours silence resumed and the threat died away.

'Keep alert,' John said to Scott and then turning to Tom whispered in his ear, 'I think that was it, just a false alarm, but we will keep the men vigilant.'

Tom nodded.

Once again John did the rounds as he had come to call it. He checked that each of his soldiers was okay and helped to lift their spirits. The biggest challenge was Second Platoon and lifting the spirits of Lieutenant Keyes.

Keyes was a strange soldier who didn't believe that the lessons of war were ever learnt. Because of this he had little faith in the inheriting abilities of future generations. He feared that for all the good they were doing, the sacrifice of life and limb, the thankless tasks that they were performing for the freedom of mankind; that ultimately his men and the men of all freedom fighting countries in the world were being wasted. He couldn't understand the sacrificial murder of cultures, religions, creeds and colours. As for the politicians; this was an area to avoid in discussions and John had only fallen into this trap once before learning his lesson very quickly. To Keyes, the politicians were prolific fat cats, only interested in lining their own pockets and boosting their own egos. 'You mark my words,' he would say. 'This will all come to no good. This, which we are all fighting for, well what is it for?' He was a kind and gentle man and a good friend to John who voiced his opinions only on special occasions. Why he had chosen to join the Infantry with such ideas was the biggest mystery of all. John was surprised he wasn't at home conscientiously objecting.

Despite his lack of faith and it was generally thought it had something to do with his upbringing, he was an outstanding officer and comfortable in the desert and in the presence of his soldiers. He smiled as John appeared from down the trenches and offered him a cup of tea.

'No thanks I had a mug earlier,' John said.

'We saw the tank,' Keyes said. 'It was an L3 Tankette, Italian.'

'Seemed bigger than that to me,' John said unable to believe that all the worry had been over such a small and lightly armed vehicle. 'Could have had a go at it with the anti-tank rifle then.'

'I think your decision to stay low and quiet was the better one,' Keyes responded, fiddling with his top left breast pocket. He was trying to put a small piece of note paper away along with a pencil.

'What's that?' John asked curiously.

'Oh nothing,' Keyes responded, but he was hardly convincing.

'Are you sure it was nothing? What is it notes?'

'Just something I was mucking around with,' Keyes replied and when he looked at his captain's eyes filled with deep curiosity he felt obliged to explain. 'It's a poem I'm working on.'

'I didn't know you wrote poetry,' John said with surprise, but it began to make sense, soldiers with morals tended to make good poets. 'Can I read it?'

'I don't write poetry, this is my first attempt. And no you can't read it. One, because it isn't finished, and two, because I'm a bit embarrassed about it.'

'OK, your bag,' John said. 'We'll call you Keats from now on,' he teased.

'And that attitude is exactly why I keep it to myself,' he waggled a pointed finger at John.

'Seriously though,' said John with sincerity. 'I would like to hear it, see if it's any good.'

'I might never finish it,' Keyes replied.

'I'm sure you will,' John replied comfortingly. 'What's it about?'

'Sacrifice,' was the short and blunt answer.

John could see where the poem was going already; it was going along the same lines as Keyes' personal opinions.

'You know Lieutenant, as bad as war is,' John put forward. 'Sometimes we have to stand up to the bullies. If we don't fight back and stand our ground, the choices are made for us, we are forced into suppression and our ability to think for ourselves is gone. If that happens our spirits would be broken and we lose the true value of ourselves. Sometimes we have to fight, for ourselves, for our rights, for what we believe in. It's not about getting the first punch in or anything like that. It's about leaving it too late to fight back.'

'It's about survival you mean?'

'Well, yes. That is exactly what I mean,' John said triumphantly beginning to walk away.

'But what if we could see the bully coming? What if we could find a way around each confrontation without having to throw a punch?'

John thought for a moment and then called back. 'Then I would say, what a wonderful world you would have created, but sadly worlds like that don't last and never will. Ying and yang, good karma, bad karma, angels and demons, God, The Devil. Opposites attract Keyes. As long as there is good, there will always be evil. Gosh, that was quite deep!'

'I agree, I've never heard you talk like that before!' Keyes laughed.

'Better write it down!' John chuckled back to him.

'Mrs Jenkins?' Sophie called, putting on her coat by the door and checking she had all her belongings. She tapped her pockets to hear the jingle of the keys, some spare schillings for the bus and her lipstick. 'Mrs Jenkins?'

'Yes love?'

'I won't be needing any dinner tonight, I'm going to work late and get some dinner up the road after my shift.'

'Very well, I will just focus on the cleaning then, when you say up the road you mean your uncles I take it?'

'Yes,' she replied releasing the chain from the door.

'And you are getting the bus today? I hope so those grey clouds out there look menacing. Might as well be night time,' Sophie nodded in response and opened the door. 'Identity card?'

'Got it.'

'Money and keys?'

'Bye,' Sophie called out walking down the path to the lane.

She only just caught the bus and as she sat down and it passed the post office she realised that she had forgotten to get some more envelopes and stamps. She wanted to tell Anthony about so many things again and also update Captain James about her nursing.

The clouds were indeed gloomy and the day was dark. It was misleading that it was a June afternoon especially since it had been a sunny start to the year. She wondered if it was a precursor to some bad news. Since the war had started she had become quite superstitious, everybody had. Little trinkets now became lucky charms, the number of magpies suddenly had real meaning and cracks in the pavements had become more than just a tripping hazard. She knew it was silly and dismissed it openly to herself, but as she stepped off the bus she made a conscious decision to avoid the three drains in her path.

She soon arrived in Newhaven just as the distant rumble of a spring storm announced its arrival. As she walked past the docks a large grey ghost of a ship sat at the quayside unloading what she knew would be wounded soldiers, she didn't know how she could tell the cargo of a ship by just looking, but after Dunkirk, she could just tell. It shouldn't have been something that surprised her, but the only active frontline at this time that she knew off was in Africa. Where had these wounded men come from was a question that begun to cause her to slow her pace and look through the tall fence.

The wounded, most amputees from what she could see were being helped inside the hospital, but five soldiers who hadn't quite made it home on the boat were laid in a neat row outside. They lay under green and brown sheets, the very sheets that they would use in the field when it rained. Three of them had labels attached to their boots and the remainder had only their bare feet visible at one end. An empty ambulance had just begun to load the stiff cold bodies to transport them to the mortuary.

It wasn't that they were dead that had made her slow down as she approached the side entrance of the hospital; after all, she had seen many corpses during the spring of last year. What caused her to pause was the conversation she overheard between the two ambulance men saying, 'It's a bloody shame, poor bastards catching a tropical disease whilst on board the ship to finish 'em off like that, ruddy bad luck getting wounded in the first place but to be robbed of coming home, well, it just ain't fair.'

It was the word tropical disease that had caught her attention. She moved closer to look at the corpses and although they were covered over discreetly and respectfully, one of the cadavers revealed its shoulder and left arm which protruded from its khaki sleeve. Khaki, it was a colour associated with only one theatre of war. Every photo she had received from her brother or Anthony had them wearing it and although the photos were in black and white shades, there was no mistaking the tan tones. Not only that, but the outstretched arm showed signs of sunburn.

The distant dunes of the desert were not so far away anymore and all because of that most powerful of words, 'tropical'. It made the war so much more personal and her body shivered with fear which it had not done since those early days during the evacuation last year. All those letters she had received had already told her where they were, out in the sandy ocean of peril, but now it was official as if a ghost had come home and tapped its cold fingers on her shoulder.

Her mind was full of questions, but the hospital telephone bell was ringing and bringing her back to her own front line, she dashed through the entrance doors to her station brushing it from her mind. The matron was waiting for her surrounded by more khaki-clad figures. The colour was everywhere.

'Miss Watson you are cutting it fine!'

'I'm sorry,' she replied, dropping the receiver which was recovered by another nurse. 'I just paused for a cigarette.'

'Yet you don't smoke. Come with me.' The matron beckoned her into a small side room and then looking over her shoulder at the wounded shuffling their way past smiled. 'They have just come back from the Middle East, Iraq I think,' she said. 'They have been shipped home to create space in the hospitals over there as they can no longer fight. Not the part of the world where your fellow is, well not quite, but I guessed it suddenly hit home. You have gone very pale.'

Sophie breathed in deeply. 'I'm sorry, I just had a moment.'

'Well I guess you are entitled to that,' the matron said. 'You thought they had come back from Tobruk hadn't you?' Sophie shrugged unsure what she had been thinking. 'Oh dear. Well, you can rest a little easier knowing they are not from there,' she sighed. 'Not that it makes it any easier. They have been bought back home for good, but will be here a few days until we can relocate them home.' She flipped through the paper on her clipboard. 'I have a new nurse in today, was wondering instead of your usual duties if you would show her the ropes. Timid little thing, but eager.'

Sophie protested, finding her voice again. 'But I was due to…'

'I know what your duties are today, but a change of scenery might do you good and I think it's time you began stepping up. It's been a year Miss Watson. You can help me run Seaford wing for the next few weeks and train up the new girl,' she ticked something on her paperwork with satisfaction. 'She is waiting upstairs and her name is...' she checked her notes again. 'Oh yes, Isabella Howard. She likes to be called Bella, something to do with her Italian ancestry,' she then whispered. 'We have had her checked out and her Italian family are a few generations back, moved here in the last century. Good luck. Oh and one more thing, I have moved Lieutenant Buckland upstairs so that he gets a little peace and quiet, see to him will you?'

Sophie nodded after rolling her eyes at her colleagues and went upstairs to the Seaford wing. Today the hospital appeared a little busier than usual and that didn't include the influx of men from Iraq. There was much to do on Seaford wing and now Sophie had a shadow.

'Bella?' Sophie asked. The girl was young, her eyes locked onto everything that moved and she jumped at every noise like a skittish deer. 'Are you ready?'

The girl gave an over-exaggerated nod and then struggled to keep up with Sophie's pace as she marched down the corridors. Sophie could sense her head twitching and turning to look in every cabinet, every doorway and at every passing white cloaked figure.

'There is no need to be nervous. Where are you from?'

'Brighton.'

Sophie enquired about her training and family, all of which seemed perfectly normal. In-fact Isabella was in exactly the same position Sophie had been only a year earlier.

'We have a busy day,' Sophie said looking at the growing list of jobs. 'Today just watch and help me when I ask, I want you to get used to the place first.'

'At least we don't have to deal with those men downstairs,' the girl said. Sophie halted and frowned at her. 'I don't think I am quite ready for wounds just yet, did you see some of them?'

'Well, you better get ready!' Sophie snapped. 'And for your information, those men are only here until they can be sent home. For them the war is over and whilst that at first appears to be positive, they have to rebuild. Their wounds were dealt with back at their last hospital, but when the freshly wounded do come in I can assure you it's far worse!'

'Gosh I am so sorry,' the girl gasped. 'I didn't mean to sound uncaring. I can see I have offended you.'

'You haven't offended me,' Sophie sighed. 'It's not been a good start to my shift that's all. Shall we?'

Bella helped Sophie look at a young boy, who with his three friends had been hurt messing about down near the beach. He had been tangled up in one of the barbed wire fences that had grown as ivy does upon a tree all along the sea wall. Thankfully two Home Guard soldiers had helped to cut him out and bring him to the hospital.

Her final duty of the afternoon was to check on Lieutenant Buckland, a Motor Torpedo boat commander who had been struck down with pneumonia whilst out at sea. He lay comfortably in his bed when she approached him.

'Hello my favourite nurse,' he smiled. 'I thought you were downstairs today?'

'Hello, Lieutenant you look much better I see.'

'I feel better as well,' he said sitting up politely. 'I was hoping to get back to duty after the weekend, but when I saw you again I seemed to change my mind, I've never wanted to be ill so much! Who is this?'

'This is Bella,' she introduced and watched as her shadow went weak at the knees.

'What a lovely name, Italian roots I am guessing.'

She chuckled and played with her uniform. Sophie one eyebrow raised checked the Lieutenant's chart. 'You will have to refer to her as Nurse Howard.'

'Of course,' the Lieutenant smiled. He attempted to puff up his pillow and Bella intervened, she almost curtsied when he thanked her.

'Miss Howard, it's been a long afternoon, perhaps you would care to take a break?' Sophie asked in an attempt to shake her shadow off for a moment. The young girl looked confused and slightly disappointed. 'A cigarette break perhaps? I will come and fetch you when I am ready.'

'Necessary?' Buckland enquired, watching the girl make her way to the end of the ward and looking over her shoulder every so often until out of sight.

'You were enjoying yourself too much,' Sophie smirked.

'You know there is only one nurse for me.'

She chuckled at his boyish advances. Something she had been unable to do whilst there was an audience. Lieutenant Buckland made no effort to hide his flirtations and Sophie found it charming, it was harmless fun and nothing more. If anything it made her feel appreciated and helped to put a smile on a constantly worried face. She knew he wouldn't be at the hospital for much longer; he had made a speedy recovering considering the seriousness of his condition.

'What would my Anthony say if he heard you flirting with me Lieutenant?' she joked.

‘I don’t know, what should we tell him?’

‘We?’ she laughed.

‘Oh I see, I have to do all the work do I?’ he laughed. ‘Well, in that case, I will say that you simply couldn’t keep yourself away, I mean three times a day you come to my bed!’

‘Only because duty demands it,’ she laughed as she put back his notes and began to move further down the ward.

His young and vibrant laugh echoed after her, ‘Duty? I’ve never heard it called that before, but if you insist, you’ll miss me when I’m gone.’

She looked back at his mischievous face shaking her head and smiled. Of all her patients he was one of her favourites, his cavalier and audacious manner never failing to make her giggle and laugh, but then she remembered Ryan Townsend. No attachments, she reminded herself.

‘Will you be with me tomorrow?’ Bella asked as she returned to Sophie’s side, she walked so close for the rest of her shift that Sophie couldn’t help but think of her as a small yapping terrier. ‘And the day after? Gosh, I would hate to be with someone else, you have been so good to me today I can’t thank you enough.’

‘Tomorrow you can help me take blood.’

‘Yes, yes of course.’

When her shift had finished she plucked her coat from the hangers and checked her watch to see how long she had before the bus. Twenty minutes roughly and as she left the front door into the fading light, Bella followed.

‘Bus? I have to get the bus too, same stop, just different direction.’

Sophie gave her a weak smile, she justified her rudeness by reminding herself she was tired.

‘I’m going dancing tonight with my Gerald,’ Bella continued, lighting a cigarette. ‘Boy he can dance!’

‘Gerald being your partner?’ Sophie enquired.

‘One and only.’

‘Really, I wouldn’t have guessed the way you were behaving around Lieutenant Buckland earlier,’ the moment Sophie said it she regretted it. Petty was not in her nature.

'The Naval officer? He was very handsome, but no I have my Gerald, the first and only man I will ever love. He is a reserved occupation so can't go abroad, thank goodness, I would be lost without him. How about you nurse Watson? I sense that there is, in fact, a little spark between you and the Lieutenant.'

'Me?' Sophie was struck by how familiar her trainee had become. 'No! I'm not interested in Buckland. He has been stuck in my ward for over two weeks that is why we are familiar with one another. I have a partner, his name is Anthony.' Bella waited anxiously for more. 'And he is in Africa in the army. He is in the same company as my brother.'

The young girl's jaw dropped. 'The other nurses mentioned you this morning!'

'They did?'

'I didn't realise it was you they were referring to, I'm not familiar with anyone yet you see. They didn't say anything horrible, just that you had lots of loved ones in the same place. I thought that was unusual, all of your family in one place, at least they have each other.'

Across the docks and through the town of Newhaven a distant air raid had begun and towering columns of white light cut open the darkening blue sky. The blackouts which had been enforced since the beginning of the war had made every night since ever more dark. When Sophie cycled home at night, even with the benefit of a small bicycle lamp and a glorious bright full moon to help her, it was still a hazardous journey and so was thankful that today she took the bus.

'Yes,' Sophie murmured. 'They have each other.'

'And so do we,' Bella said, tugging her arm.

Harry

14th June 1941 - The Libyan Desert

'Lovely clear evening sir,' Tom said, peering into the dugout with a pink and peach coloured sky pasted behind him as the sun began to fall.

John sat upon a pile of sandbags, his back leaning up against the wall of the dugout whilst he cleaned his revolver. Six rounds of .38 calibre bullets sat to attention upon the little wooden table and one by one he carefully slid them back into the chambers of the gun.

'Any activity outside?' John asked.

'There were a few aircraft about five minutes ago sir, but otherwise nothing.'

'There's or ours?'

'I do believe they were ours for a change.'

Tom disappeared back out into the trench system. John could still hear him barking orders as he advanced further down the line.

The whole day so far had been very peaceful, no artillery, no air attacks and no fumbling with equipment either. The men of D Company had been taking things easy and resting. They needed it, for tomorrow morning they would advance on the ridge that already after yesterday's briefing had earned the nickname 'Hangman's Hill'.

A quick glance out from the dugout entrance revealed three sleeping privates, curled up on the sandy floor, hugging their rifles as if they were teddy bears. John had been up all the previous night expecting an attack which never materialised. He had heard tanks or so he thought, but nothing except the small Tankette had appeared out of the darkness.

His eyes were heavy and leaning his chin in the palm of his hand he tried to nod off, even if it was to pretend, just to make himself feel as though he had attempted to rest his eyes.

As his eyelids drooped further and further, almost to the point of no return to that momentary state of unconsciousness between sleep and where dreams play, making you think that you have been away a long time, a sound reached his ears. A strange sound, not from inside or outside and not a sound of war either. His tired brain acknowledged it as a kind of scratching sound and he slowly opened his eyes, looked around, but there was definitely nothing there. Perhaps his silent mind now freed from the onslaught of thought was picking up the gentle breeze blowing, or the sound of his own breathing.

The sun made him feel tired and lazy. Heat exhaustion was a constant companion settling itself into your psyche due to the sun's rays. The constant waiting and vigilance could play tricks on your mind and of course, the other trigger for seeing and hearing things could be boredom which was a huge problem, it affected every soldier. Being in the desert didn't help either; its barren landscape had nothing in it to focus on. Everywhere you looked it was the same. John always referred to it as an empty beauty.

He picked up his revolver again and started to fiddle with it, but pretty soon he realised that there really wasn't much more he could to to it. It was ready, set and immaculate. He even wondered whether to clean it again, but there was even futility in that thought and he decided against it. So he closed his eyes again.

Tom in the meantime made sure that boredom had less of a chance to sink in. He thought of boredom as 'the other enemy'. In actual fact he was allergic to the word, especially where his men were concerned. 'Forewarned is forearmed,' he would say. 'We all know something is coming and we are better for being prepared to face it, so guns to the ready and keep those eyes out there.'

He had gone on one of his many wanders, first, he visited First Platoon and with Anthony's permission went about checking the platoon's weapons. The rifles were pulled through and the Brens stripped down and once he was happy wandered over to Second Platoon to do the same again.

His very presence put the men on alert, as the presence of any Sergeant Major would. Sergeant Majors had a reputation to uphold after all and Tom was working hard to do his bit to keep the reputation alive. When the men saw him coming, they immediately set about to look busy, John never forgot the time he watched when one Private even re-tied his boot laces.

When Tom reached Lieutenant Moore's Platoon there was even less to do. The young Lieutenant, fresh and keen to set about his new job, had already had the weapons inspected and put his men to work bolstering up the defences. There were plenty of sandbags upon the parapet, but Moore had seen fit to add more, just to keep his men busy. Tom was impressed to see Moore inspecting each sections arcs of fire, after motioning with his hand to carry on, he watched for a brief moment and then returned back to the dugout.

John was still in the same place as when Tom had left him, his chin resting in his hands. 'Why don't you get some rest?' Tom asked.

'I can't,' John replied.

'Big day tomorrow, it will do you good,' he said. His strong Sussex accent always became stronger when his more caring nature was revealed.

'Maybe later,' John agreed, to keep him quiet.

Tom sat down next to him with a grunt, facing the opposite wall and picked up Johns revolver. He examined it for a moment and then began checking the working action.

'Missed a bit there,' he joked, pointing to the side of the barrel which was of course immaculate.

John returned a sarcastic smile and then leaned back against the sandbag wall with one eye shut. He had been thinking about home and his warm comfy bed as the sand slipped and slithered uncomfortably under his fidgeting weight.

'What's on your mind?' Tom asked.

'Oh, I was just thinking about home,' John said wistfully closing his eyes trying to recollect the picture and the moment in his mind that was now fading.

'Ah, home,' Tom smiled to himself. 'Home is where the heart is.'

'Do you go somewhere special in your mind when troubled?' John asked him.

'Are you troubled?' Tom asked concernedly.

'No,' John laughed. 'It was just a question. I didn't say that quite right did I? I meant, well, is there somewhere you like to think of, or a favourite image that your thoughts carry you to, or a favourite place you like to go when you have time to think?'

The Sergeant Major thought for a moment, the revolver sitting on his lap. 'Well there is the parade ground at Aldershot when it's frosty; looks very pretty and who can resist the image of Jean Harlow pinned up on your barrack wall, or mouth-watering thoughts of a good old Sussex pint,' and he smacked his lips in jest.

He was joking, John thought, well apart from the Sussex pint and thinking about it probably Jean Harlow the little blonde bombshell that had risen to stardom through John's late teens and early twenties. To the men of the Company, the Sergeant Major had never had a life outside the Army. To them, he had been born on the parade ground. It was not true of course, he was as normal as any other man, but he quite liked playing up to their imaginations.

'And is there anywhere else on the other side of the barbed wire fence of the parade ground that is special to you?'

'Not that's repeatable,' he said with a wink.

'Oh,' said John, hoping that he was going to go into one of his renditions.

'Glorious sunset out there though, looks as though the sky's on fire,' he leaned towards the entrance of the dugout and briefly pulled back the blackout curtain. 'Could do with a pint now though,' he sighed remorsefully.

'God, so could I,' agreed John, the thought arousing his senses whole-heartedly, the glands in his mouth awakening and releasing the saliva now rising in his cheeks, watering the channels of his throat to then be swallowed into oblivion, unsatisfied that the smooth but bitter taste was just a mirage. 'Out the front door,' John began again, gesturing with his hands as if he were really there, 'Up the lane and left, then down to the Three Feathers, grab a quick pint, take the style on the left and a small track that goes up onto The Downs. When you get to the top on a clear and really sunny day, you can see Eastbourne on your left and sometimes Seaford out to the right. On a summer's day, the sea is an azure blue and the cliffs are a diamond white, the perfect place to finish your pint and admire the view.'

They sat for a moment in silence, each adrift in their own recollections to be interrupted by a quiet grating, abrasive, scraping sound.

'There, listen,' John beckoned.

'I can hear it too,' confirmed Tom 'What is it do you think?'

They were now both engrossed with the strange rasping sound.

'I don't know. I heard it earlier, but I couldn't make out what it was, I was beginning to think that I was imagining things,' John whispered.

'Probably loose sand or a bloody snake.'

As suddenly as it started it stopped again, just as it had done before. Tom looked around the dugout, moving and discarding false alarms like papers and box crates of ammunition, curious as to what it could be. As he was doing so, Captain James entered through the blackout curtain.

'Hello Simon,' John called out cheerfully, it was good to see another friendly face and normally Simon came bearing gifts and today he did not disappoint.

'Bought you a gift,' he said, a bottle of Rum in his hand.

'Where the bloody hell did you get that from?' Tom asked, astonished and wasting no time in taking possession of the bottle.

'I was in Mersah Matru last night, only got back an hour ago as I was picking up some supplies. While I was there a gorgeous Australian destroyer pulled into the harbour, well off-shore actually and a boatload of Aussies came ashore. I thought to myself, "I bet that's laden with some goodies" and I was right.'

The tin mugs were out and soon the Rum was going down well. Both John and Tom were careful not to overdo it, but Simon, famed for being able to source alcohol from the most unlikely places was having his fill. He sat on the step of the dugout, blocking the entrance in front of Corporal Orchard, whom on hearing the rattling of mugs and sighting the doctor earlier guessed what might be going on.

'Pardon me sir; is this a private party or can anyone join in?' Orchard said peeking over the shoulders of the doctor.

'Piss off,' Tom laughed in jest.

'Now, now, that wouldn't do, Sergeant Major,' Orchard replied. 'You know what the neighbours are like around here. You might be at a disadvantage to have the seduction of alcohol knocking at your door tonight. The more it goes around the less the danger of being caught out. I would, of course, like to volunteer myself in assisting you all to remain more sober and alert than you would be if left alone to your own devices!'

'You can still piss off,' Tom repeated laughing an even heartier laugh.

'Grab your mug Corporal,' John said generously. 'But Mum's the word.'

'Oh yes sir,' he replied excitedly and soon he was passing his mug through the dugout entrance. John put a dribble in and passed it back. Then it was just the three of them again and a golden silence.

'What's that noise,' Simon said inquisitively.

Both John and Tom listened again and from behind the makeshift table they could hear the sound that John had first noticed earlier.

On the table was an old metal box in which Sergeant Scott kept his cigarettes. He didn't have an ordinary cigarette case like most; for he smoked so many that a box the size of a biscuit tin was needed. Next to the tin was some biscuit crumbs and the noise was coming from behind the tin.

They watched, three pairs of curious eyes waiting to see what would appear. Tom tapped the box with his baton and scurrying out from behind, munching a scrap of biscuit appeared, as surprised as they were to see him, a Jerboa, a small desert rodent. Its great big curious eyes looked up and warily watched the three soldiers, as it picked up as many of the scraps as possible and then having sized up the situation it just continued to graze the contents of the table. Its soft ginger fur rippling nervously as it twitched with every inhalation.

'It's a bloody rat,' Tom exclaimed.

Simon was laughing at the boldness of the creature, whilst John was fascinated by its lack of fear. He moved his hands carefully to see if the little fellow would run, but the Jerboa continued looking for more food as if aware that Johns movements were no threat.

John slowly sifted through his pack and found another biscuit. Breaking it up into small crumbs he slowly laid it on the table. The animal hopped straight over to the food, ravenously collecting his bounty.

'That's alright little chap, there you go,' John said, placing the remainder of the biscuit down.

'Bold little fella isn't he?' Simon remarked. 'I must admit it's the first one I have seen.'

'It's a bloody dirty rat,' Tom interrupted. 'You're a doctor Captain James, you should know better than to be encouraging that rat, we have enough scavengers like Corporal Orchard to cope with, without the help of disease-ridden rodents. Out of the way' and he brought the Webley up as if to shoot at it.

'Sergeant Major!' John scorned and Tom backed down. 'Touched a nerve have we, not one of your weak spots is it, a phobia perhaps?' and in response Tom showed him that he had removed the bullets which he laid on the table along with the revolver.

'It's only a rat and no I don't have any issues with the adorable little Mickey. They were a great deal bigger in the last war,' the old soldier muttered. 'But they do spread disease sir and I'd rather not share my rations with a rat if you don't mind, it's bad enough having to share my rum with Corporal Orchard!'

'Oi, I heard that!' shouted Orchard from outside and coming in to see what all the fuss was about.

'Oh Sergeant Major have a heart, he's quite an adorable little rat isn't he?' Simon said cheerfully. 'And besides he is Gerboa, I think they are a little cleaner than your friends from the last crusade.'

John found the whole situation amusing and was strangely fond of the little creature; it was endearing and different, a branch away from the everyday humdrum soldier stuff. It was hard to believe that in this harsh unforgiving environment something so small and delicate could survive; perhaps there was hope for the company after all.

The Australians trapped and besieged in Tobruk had been nicknamed 'Rats' by the German general of the Afrika Korps, General Erwin Rommel. Similarly, the 7th Armoured division just to the south of their location had the Jerboa as there divisional insignia. It seemed appropriate then that this little ball of fluff and boldness should come along at this moment. Something in the way it looked at John after handing it a treat of more biscuit crumbs, told John this wouldn't be the last he would see of the animal. After taking every crumb that lay on the table, the Jerboa soon disappeared back behind the cigarette tin, hopping off without making a sound.

'Well that was something different, either that or I've had too much to drink,' Simon said.

‘Wish I had a camera. Sophie would have loved that wouldn’t she?’ John asked, looking to Tom who nodded in agreement ruefully.

‘You will have to tell her in your next letter,’ Simon said. ‘Has she sent you one lately?’

‘She has and she sends you her best regards as always.’

‘I’m glad she has settled into her nursing. What’s happening back in old blighty?’

‘Not a great deal by the sounds of things, just air raids and more bad news from the rest of the world. Mind you her letters are normally a week or so in getting here. Her last letter said the Bismarck had been sunk.’

‘Ah well I read that in the papers,’ he replied.

‘But the most worrying news is that the Army has decided to put a bloody ack-ack gun at the end of my garden. Apparently, she can barely sleep at night when she’s home,’ John giggled.

‘She’s never up till midday anyway, probably do her good,’ Tom added in jest.

More rum went around and soon the party was joined by Sergeant Scott.

‘Well, well, well,’ he said like a policeman who has caught three naughty teenagers, a big grin beaming across his face. ‘What have we hear, a secret party?’

‘And I suppose you want some as well?’ Tom said out loud.

‘Well, one of us needs to be able to hit the target, but as you’ve offered…’

‘We didn’t,’ Simon butted in with a childish giggle.

‘And let’s not forget,’ Scott continued. ‘I’m a better shot than any of you pissed or sober, Cheers!’

There was a lot of laughing by the time Scott had made himself comfortable, it was a sound which had been sorely missed in the silence of the empty desert. Scott told some of his dirty stories about his more youthful day's training, to which Tom, no doubt involved or a witness, kept quiet and just nodded from time to time, both of them had served together previously.

Then a little more relaxed and to John’s delight, Tom even managed to remember some amusing stories from the Great War and it still amazed John how even in the most demanding and terrifying situations some of the funniest things could happen. Even John could remember some funny moments as a young training Lieutenant, but the mood went more solemn when Scott turned and directed a question at Simon.

'What about you Sir?' he asked. 'I hear a rumour you were in India, I bet you got up to some mischief over there, I know my old man did.'

Simon poured some more rum into his mug and looked to the ground. Behind him the sun had settled on the horizon and the peach coloured sky from earlier was darkening into bright reds and fiery oranges.

'Afraid not,' he replied. 'I was on the frontier of Afghanistan, near the Khyber pass for most of my time there.'

He nodded his head from side to side as if trying to shake a bad memory from his mind. Simon was normally so full of heart and had become the life and soul of the group since Bailey's temporary departure. Bailey was sorely missed, normally teaming up with Simon for a real comical act.

'What happened there?' John asked.

'In India?' Simon sounded hollow, the drink beginning to sink in. 'This and that, let's not ruin the party. I never talk about it. Not because I don't remember much. I remember every bloody minute of every bloody hour of every bloody day,' he said darkly the rum doing some of the talking.

'You don't have to tell us,' Tom added. 'I understand.'

Despite the get out clause Simon had started now, the liquor unravelling his tongue. 'I served with an Indian company in 1919. I was attached to them for three months in the Khyber Pass. Apparently, we won a great victory there over some little tribe, but I don't remember any cheering, not like here with you good people.

You wonder why I am a genius with wounds, or so they say! Well, I'll tell you. The Afghans had guns as we did, but when they got in close they would resort to all manner of weapons, clubs, swords and daggers, tools more associated with medieval times. I had to adjust to what I was taught, sew up wounds that I never expected to see. One Indian boy would have his skull smashed in, whilst another would have their stomach ripped apart, their insides…' he gestured with his hands.

The audience of three sipped their rum, listening carefully at the traumatic wounds the doctor described to them.

'I know what you're thinking,' he continued. 'That there can't be much of a difference between a shrapnel wound one of our boys might have out there to that that I saw in the Pass, but I assure you there is. Dirty wounds, inhumane, but then war is inhumane.'

There was a long silence as the men thought about what the doctor had just told them. His head hung down as if wishing that he had said nothing and his face was almost contorted with painful memories. Suddenly his head raised and a grin beamed across his face as he looked in the direction of the table, something had cheered him up and it was the Jerboa, it was back.

'What the bloody hell is that!' Scott exclaimed.

'He appeared this afternoon, that's our desert rat,' John said as if it were now fully adopted into the Company as a mascot.

'So we are now encouraging a rat,' Scott said matter of fact, but Simon disagreed.

'You'll hurt his feelings you know Sergeant. There's a big difference between a rat and a desert rat you know.'

'Which is?'

Simon thought for a moment. 'Well, one lives in the desert, you stupid bugger!'

John fell about laughing whilst Scott looked bewildered.

'Tell you what though,' Simon joked, knowing what would wind the Sergeant up. 'He likes your cigarettes; I think he's been using the tobacco for his nest.'

'That does it!' and Scott was up and out of his seat in a flash.

He leaned over Tom and took the tin form the table. In a sudden panic the Jerboa made a dash away from the looming hands, but the only place available in that split moment was John's arm that leaned upon the table. Running up his arm, he paused to take stock of the situation, perched from John's shoulder. He was safe there, remembering the generous gift of biscuit he had received earlier.

'Love at first bloody sight,' Scott joked.

'What shall we call him?' Simon said.

‘Don’t be bloody daft,’ Tom jumped in. ‘You’re not seriously going to name him; it’s a ruddy rat for God’s sake, you’ve all had too much sun. It’s turned your heads.’

‘Couldn’t agree more,’ Scott added, cradling his tobacco tin as if it were a precious child.

John laughed at the seriousness in Tom’s voice and then gently ran his finger across the tiny creatures fur coat. ‘Soft,’ he whispered.

‘You’ve gone soft,’ Scott said. Mind you, I had a bunny rabbit called Harry once,’ Scott added and after a brief pause of silence to take the comment in they all fell about laughing. It was not the comment they would expect from the stern sergeant, a comment to which Tom found so funny that he was almost crying at the man whose humour was only ever as dry as the desert around them. ‘What?’ Scott said innocently. ‘I was only a little lad, we found him in the garden stuck in some chicken wire, couldn’t let dad cook it I was sensitive then.’

‘Well that settles it then,’ John chuckled. ‘We shall call him Harry’ and scooping Harry gently in his hand, he put him back on the table.

As Harry scuttled off for more scraps, the darkened sky from behind Simon began to light up. Flares and the tell-tale flickering of artillery dazzled the darkness. The British guns had begun to pound the enemy positions ready for tomorrow’s engagement.

‘The peace and quiet is over gentlemen,’ John said. ‘And so is our drinking session. Let’s get back to the war shall we?’

With a groan one by one, they headed outside. John took one last glance back at the table where Harry continued scrounging for food. Then killing the soft light from the hurricane lamp, he left the room in darkness.

Opening the past

Newhaven, June 15th 1941

It was quite late in the day when Sophie arrived at Lieutenant Buckland's bedside with the prescription trolley ready for the night shift. She had made certain already that Bella would see to other vital tasks, by now willing to admit even to herself it was because she enjoyed his attention and wanted it to herself. He was getting dressed, his smart naval uniform with embroidered cuff rank insignia was dazzling. If she had thought he was handsome already, the uniform and Brylcreem hair now only made him more so, although she still felt he looked a little 'grey around the gills,' a favourite expression her mother used to use.

'Hello,' he said looking deep into her eyes, she found it hard to look at him directly. 'Is there any more news from Egypt?'

'Nothing for a while now,' she replied. 'Why do you ask?'

'Only out of curiosity. My cousin, he is also in the Navy, although on destroyers, much more glamorous than my old tub, he just wrote home and turns out he has ended up in Malta. I thought to myself that wasn't far from your brother's neck of the woods.'

'I don't think there are many trees where my brother is,' her dry comment roused a small grin from him.

'You know what I meant. You have a lovely smile, am I going to see it before I leave?' She shied away and fiddled with the pills dispenser. 'No news of Anthony either?' he flicked tiny dust particles from the top of his cap. Sophie shook her head in response. 'You know if I was a lucky guy like Anthony, with a girl like you on my arm and I knew you were waiting back home for me, I would find any excuse I could to get back home to you and I'm sure he will too. I promise you are in his thoughts every minute of every day.'

Her time with Anthony seemed so long ago that she wondered at times if it was real. She knew that she should have felt guilty enjoying Buckland's attention, perhaps it was its innocence that enabled her to not feel that way or the fact that it was a temporary arrangement she could walk away from. For now, any guilt that was there was hidden away, disguised in some way that she couldn't see. Either way, it was his last day and she knew there would be no harm to her soul to enjoy his attention one last time.

'You've been discharged I see,' she changed the subject airily.

'I'm saddened to say Nurse Watson; I have to be going,' he sighed placing his cap neatly on his head. He coughed a little, holding his chest to fight the slight pain of his cracked ribs, a remnant scar courtesy of his condition. 'It has been a pleasure which naturally has been all mine!'

'You still need to be taking it easy though.'

'Indeed, which is why I won't be returning to the sea any time soon. I had an offer of a new posting, temporary until I am better, although I can keep the post if I want to.'

'I would ask what it was, but…'

'Yes I know, everything is confidential these days. Although you couldn't help me with this address could you?' he rummaged in his pocket and pulled out a slip of paper.

'Is that not confidential?' Sophie asked.

He chuckled, nodding at his own stupidity and put the paper back into his pocket. 'I'm sure I will find it. Well, Nurse Watson, it's like this, I have to be going.'

Sophie felt the blood rush to her cheeks at their moment of parting and there had been too many of late. This time the military patient she had come to like was leaving alive and well and she should have been pleased, but now that the moment had arrived it felt wrong. Sophie felt there needed to be more to this moment than a simple handshake.

In a panic, she fumbled for words and looked around the room for anything that might help her make more of this, but as she turned back to him she simply held out her hand and said flustered. 'Thank you, it was nice to have met you.'

The moment the words were uttered she regretted them, ashamed, embarrassed and her inner thoughts were screaming disappointment at her.

Buckland frowned and slowly took her hand. 'It was nice to have met you too.'

He grabbed his kit bag, threw it over his shoulder and gave her a casual yet still smart salute before marching gallantly off. As he reached the swinging doors to the corridor he turned and called, 'Hey,

Miss Watson, if you change your mind about Anthony and if you ever fancy the company of a disgraceful, foolhardy but humble sailor, look me up!' and he waved as the ward doors swung to and fro.

'He can steer my boat any day!' said a passing staff nurse. 'What's his name and where's he from then?' Sophie's arm was nudged crudely.

'Archie,' whispered Sophie. 'Lieutenant Archie Buckland' and the doors crashed closed behind him. The dashing naval officer had gone and even though she had only known him for a couple of weeks, it was a friendship she suddenly felt she would miss, she longed for affection and it felt her only source had just left through the double doors. It was now that guilt began to make itself felt. Was it wrong, she wondered, to hope that this was not the final parting? Would they meet by coincidence somewhere in some other place at some other time? She hoped for it, longed for it and then remembered Anthony, scorning herself for having any such feelings.

The rest of Sophie's night shift was uneventful, the first two hours were spent with Bella, who was determined to invite herself round for afternoon tea. Sophie's description of April Cottage had clearly made an impression in the mind of the girl who felt her little rented townhouse could simply not compare. The third hour was spent in the shelter whilst a flight of bombers headed for London and the final few were spent doing menial chores. As the sun began to rise the following morning and the long night shift ended, she rushed home, one thing firmly in her mind.

It was one of the few nights that Mrs Jenkins would not be waiting for her and with that in mind, Sophie paused at the bakery, her ration book at the ready. She craved a sandwich, one with crusty bread, but also another peek at her mother's diaries. When Anthony and her brother were not at the forefront of her mind, which was rare, her mother's diaries were. Every night she had dived deep into the thoughts and feelings of her mother's past life, enchanted and soon addicted to them. It bought her back to life somehow.

She had kept the lamp at the top of the old ladder that took her up into the roof. Its gentle flame flickered its magical glow upon the boxes as she sifted through the many books, eventually settling on one of the oldest. Sophie had always loved reading, John had read to her as a child and as she grew into her teens she would read out loud, frequently visited by her brother, who would often lean on the doorframe until he had figured out what she was reading.

Tonight the chapter was simply 'January 24th 1916' and as Sophie began to read through her mother's swirly handwriting, full of immense detail, she was taken back in time. She could see her mother, Helen, standing upon the platform, she could smell the strong aroma of coal from the billowing steam and smoke of the train and hear the hustle and bustle of the crowd.

Helen looked around at the canopy of different hats that stretched as far as the platform allowed her to see, she couldn't help but feel they resembled a large flower bed with their range of colours and adornments. Her arm was strongly looped to Jack's, who walked her carefully through the crowd towards one of the carriages, his other hand every so often brushing upon hers. She looked occasionally at the faces of the women she passed with a sense of satisfaction as she caught them gaze at Jack's uniform and the two pips that stood proud upon his sleeve.

'Are you alright?' he asked gently, his voice was always gentle. 'It won't be long and when I return...'

He didn't need to finish his sentence; the wedding had been firmly in her head since he had asked two months ago. She glanced at the ring upon her finger, an air loom of Jack's family. It had belonged to his mother and before her, his great grandmother and the very thought of them made it suddenly feel heavier. There was no need to rush the wedding, by now it had become plainly obvious the war might drag on another year and although her father had offered to put together a wedding that would never be forgotten, it was Helen who wanted more time to plan and prepare it. She told Jack it was that her creative instincts wanted to take some control away from her father. The truth was she didn't want to be a war widow. She knew so many people now who had got married in a rush and every single one of them had lost their new husband in France before the year was out. She wasn't prepared to take the risk and tempt fate.

'What about when I am on leave?' Jack asked. He opened one of the carriage doors and disappeared inside, laying his kit bag on the seat before returning to the platform. 'We could set a date as soon as I know when I am due back.'

She shook her head and suggested that she wanted to wait until the war was over. She never once mentioned her fears.

'Well there is nothing more I can do to change your mind,' he shrugged. 'Will you be alright?'

She nodded again. 'Will you?' she asked.

'Off course, I've got Tom to protect me, isn't that right Sergeant?'

Through the crowd of hats came Tom, he wrestled his kit bag back through the mob and stepped up into the carriage with Jack, tilting his hat to Helen as he passed.

'I will do my best to keep an eye on him, Miss,' Tom said

Jack gave him a pat on the shoulder as he passed. 'If anything happens to me, this man you can always trust,' Helen looked upon the sergeant one more time, making sure she could remember his face. 'And Helen, I mean anything. There is no other man I trust more in this world than Tom here.'

He had mentioned Tom so many times, but this time was the first time she had met him. He had been quiet in the car on the way to the station, leaving her guessing as to his character. She had been curious about him, watching his mannerisms and trying to ask him questions that he had answered vaguely or not at all. He was a mystery, she knew nothing of his family or his history, but Jack couldn't praise him high enough. 'Tom didn't let you in unless he was sure about you,' Jack explained. There was however an air of confidence about the man. Everything he did was quite methodical. The little that she had managed to get out of the sergeant was that he had fought at Mons in the early days of the war. Jack filled her in on the rest. 'Held off fifty Huns alone with a single Vickers gun, although Tom never talks about it,' Helen had been told. Jack told her that there was a type of soldier that you knew would make it through and although she didn't know how she could tell, she sensed that Tom was just such a soldier. It was a thought that comforted her. When looking at Jack, who saw the whole thing as one great big adventure, she was not so sure.

'I love you,' he said.

She had been fighting the tears all day and had been successful up to this point. She had no control over them now and they flowed freely from her eyes, she did however manage not to sob out loud, afraid of embarrassing herself. Jack wiped the tears away.

'I love you more,' she put on the best smile she could now, forcing it across her face so that he could see it. 'Sergeant Hill? You will look after him, won't you? I need him back.'

Tom returned a smile that appeared just as difficult to put on. 'I will do my best Miss.'

The following morning, Sophie decided to call in unannounced to Uncle Richards' for a surprise visit. The diary of 1916 had been a long and emotional journey for her the night before. It had left her surprised, for she had never realised how much her mother had loved Jack, but as he was John's father and not her own it had perhaps never been a natural curiosity. Their love had been very strong and their parting at the station very familiar, she remembered how difficult letting Anthony go at the docks had been. She felt now that she had a unique link to her mother, a shared experience, of love and loss. A sudden coincidental breeze blew some dry leaves towards her into a small whirlwind, it helped encourage her imagination to think that perhaps her mother's spirit agreed.

Her shoes crunched upon the gravel driveway up to The Great Hall of her uncle's. She had been popping round quite a lot recently, in the afternoons it had become a convenient destination for a bite to eat and in the odd mornings, Joy would be there playing the piano in the lounge. Joy played most mornings, it was one of her passions and Sophie envied her talent. She walked up to the side door and as had become custom did not even ring the bell, but walked straight inside to the reception room. Her feet tapped upon the black and white tiles in front of the staircase that had always made her think of a giant chess board and threw her coat over a chair.

The Great Hall had stood as the seat of the Beaumont family for over one hundred years. Its past echoed an honourable family, but from what Sophie had heard about her grandfather, who was the last of the old breed, it was an esteemed family she cared little for. They were the past and her Uncle, now the keeper of the family name, was an entirely different generation. Despite Richard's warmth, something that was new to the generation and her mother's banishment when she did not fit the mould, the house still retained its past pretentious demeanour. It was just a house she reminded herself.

She admired the burst of sunlight that beamed in through the high windows and bleached some of the black tiles so that they blended with the white. All it needed she thought, were some suits of armour. As she raised her hand to shield her eyes the rest of the room came into focus, including a man who was standing in front of her, a man she recognised instantly.

Her lower jaw would have dropped to the floor if it could have and her heart seemed to have stopped as if stunned at what appeared to be a destined encounter.

'Nurse Watson?'

She didn't know why he questioned whether it was her or not, even she had by now realised this was no illusion.

'Lieutenant Buckland!' she attempted to smile, but the expression of surprise was difficult to alter, by the time she had begun to shake off the shock, Buckland's expression of surprise turned to one of suspicion.

'What are you doing here?'

His eyes rolled and darted as his brain attempted to compute the odds of this chance meeting and she suddenly realised that he was increasingly nervous. It made sense, she thought, it was an incredible coincidence and from his point of view was probably not a coincidence at all.

'Have you followed me here?'

She remained speechless and knew that being so would only make things worse. She had hoped to meet him again, but in this scenario, she was unable to pull herself away from the surreal circumstances and was also lost for words at the concept of what his mind was thinking. There was no doubt that the word 'spy' had entered his head at this point and the crazy fact was this was her family home and yet those words just would not dislodge from her mind.

'Nurse Watson?'

Joy appeared from the top of the staircase and it was at this point that Sophie no longer needed to find her words. Joy as always smiled and opened her arms to her niece as she approached, putting her into an embrace that said all the things Buckland needed to see in order to put him at ease.

Joy turned to see his startled expression, uncertain as to what had just transpired. 'Lieutenant Buckland, thank you for waiting, my husband will receive you now. Are you alright?'

'Fine.'

'Are you sure? You look frightfully pale.'

'Top of the stairs am I correct?' he asked.

Sophie imagined his awkwardness and his sudden need to escape was suggested by the sharpness of his manner. He was already moving before Joy confirmed. 'First on the right.'

Joy smiled at him as he passed and then turned back to Sophie, guiding her into the kitchen. She placed the kettle onto the heat, sliced some bread and gestured Sophie to help herself. The bread was still warm, its fresh smell comforting her nostrils. Joy began to prepare the teapot as the kettle announced its readiness with a high pitched cry.

'I take it you are going to explain the situation out in the hall? I watched from the top of the stairs.'

'He was a patient we discharged only last night. I never thought I would see him again and there he was.'

'Well, he didn't seem too pleased to see you.'

'I think,' she checked herself. 'I think he thought I was a spy who had followed him.'

'Why on earth would he think that?'

Sophie explained about the address he had mentioned and how her sudden arrival perhaps had taken him by surprise. Joy agreed it could have been misconstrued.

'Why is he here?' Sophie asked between mouthfuls of the delicious fresh loaf. 'I was as surprised to see him as he was me.'

'I can't really say. Your Uncle has been recruited by the Navy again. I know, I was as surprised as you, only I was more verbal in my disappointment.

Anyhow he has a new role, something to do with the harbour and the fort down in Newhaven, what it is I couldn't say, even if I did know. The young Lieutenant is going to be working alongside your uncle. I can't say much more than that.'

The tea was poured into the cups and Sophie watched the milk swirl in little clouds until it became one with the tea. She had hoped for a chance to see him again and although the circumstances could have been better, she couldn't help but feel excited about it. The only thing that filled her head was the chance to see him before she left. She hoped she could smooth over the way in which the reunion had taken place, a fear of not getting that chance was making her grow nervous.

She had been silent for some time now as she sipped her drink, aware now that Joy was studying her thoughtful expression.

'How's work?'

Sophie explained that she had a trainee nurse and gave a general overview of things, but she didn't go into much detail. She turned the conversation onto Anthony, something she enjoyed talking about when she could and no doubt Joy was used to the routine. The only problem was there was little to say of late. The letters had dried up, so had any news from Africa and she was left with only speculation.

'I haven't heard from Anthony for a while or John.'

'Oh you know it takes time for mail to get home and no doubt they are busy winning the war. No news can be good news.'

'Have you heard from your daughter, Katherine?'

Joy nodded, sipping her tea and pointing to an open envelope upon the kitchen table. 'It arrived this morning, makes a change, our estranged relationship means I get very little from her. I hadn't quite started reading before your naval officer arrived at the door.' Sophie picked up the envelope and pulled out the tatty contents. 'You would think she would write on something with a little more quality, I wonder if its toilet paper sometimes.'

'John and Anthony's letters are the same, the YMCA paper is thin and easily rips. It makes it difficult to keep, which I do,' her eyes glanced across the loops and curls of Katherine's handwriting. 'Well, she seems to be in the thick of it, although she doesn't say where she is.'

'She wouldn't because she knows I would worry. When she does I can barely pronounce half of the places she has been to, your uncle tries to show them to me on a map,' she shook her head. 'Sounds awful, but I would rather not know.'

Before long the small talk was interrupted by Uncle Richard. Like Buckland he was in his naval uniform, it was the first time Sophie had seen him this way that was not a dull photograph from the last war. It scared her, so many wore uniforms now that you were lucky to catch someone in civilian clothes.

‘All finished?’ Joy asked and after catching the young lieutenant’s eye, pointed to the kettle. ‘Tea, Lieutenant?’

‘Actually my dear,’ Richard began. ‘The Lieutenant must be going. We have sorted everything out here that needs sorting, but I must whizz him down to the docks. Problem with accommodation.’

‘Well, there is plenty of room here for the Lieutenant.’

Richard disagreed and explained how it would not be proper. ‘Of course, I have no objection to him being here, but Admiralty would rather he had his own space. It’s important that when he rests he is not resting in his working environment.’

‘Oh Richard, really? There is a war on, needs must,’ Joy protested, but Richard would have none of it. ‘There is of course another alternative,’ she looked to Sophie. ‘But it requires Sophie’s consent.’

‘Of course!’ Richard laughed. ‘Sophie has a spare room with her brother away, two rooms in fact.’

Buckland began to protest. ‘I’m really not sure sir, poor Miss Watson could probably do with all the peace and quiet she can get. I would feel like an intruder.’

‘What do you think Sophie?’ Richard asked.

Sophie was in two minds. She could certainly do with the rent and had only recently been debating the problem with Mrs Jenkins. Her uncle already knew that they had emptied her mother’s room so it would be impossible to object. There was however the other issue and that was having Buckland in the house with her. She had enjoyed his attention in the hospital and secretly wished to see him again, but that was in the hospital environment, where enjoying his attention was a guilty pleasure and it was easy to seek out and walk away from. If Buckland was living with her, it might not be so jovial and then there was another possibility. Sophie couldn’t help but wonder if his advances in the ward, for all their innocence they may have had, might hide a real passion for her. That was attention she could certainly do without.

‘I don’t know,’ she stuttered.

‘Honestly Miss Watson, there is no obligation and I totally understand,’ Buckland turned back to Richard. ‘I will find something, Sir. It may be that I head towards Eastbourne and besides I am sure the Admiralty will sort something out.’

Richard rubbed his chin, a family trait that John also had. 'Shame, it would solve so many problems. You will be near work, near me if I need you here and solve Sophie's financial problems.'

'Fine,' Sophie had spoken before knowing she intended to. 'It's fine, he can stay at the cottage. I cleared out my mother's room only yesterday, it might as well be used.'

'That must have been a difficult thing to do,' Buckland stated.

'It was, but Uncle Richard is right, you need a room and I have one.'

Richard was delighted with the arrangement and Joy also pleased. Buckland, however, remained quiet about the arrangement and continued to press Sophie, checking that she was sure it was what she really wanted.

It was, she told herself. It did solve her problems and perhaps the company would do her good. There was also something else, something she believed unseen. Perhaps she was meant to help him? It couldn't just be a coincidence that their paths had crossed under such strange circumstances so soon. She wanted to see where this was going, even if she didn't admit it to herself.

The Olive Branch.

It was approaching four in the morning and already the sun was rising in the sky and lighting up the horizon. There were nearly two hours before the men were to advance on Hangman's hill. They sat cramped up in the trenches checking and then re-checking their equipment. The re-checking was partly to do with being totally prepared for what might be coming, but it was also to keep the nerves at bay and take their minds off what lay ahead.

The enemy which were highly likely to be Italian had been shelling the nearby positions for most of the night and although the shelling was not particularly accurate it was not a good sign, as it more often than not was an indication that they were expecting an attack.

Sergeant Scott walked up and down the entrenchments of First Platoon. The men's faces were in darkness, hiding the fear that was surely in their eyes. He checked on each soldier as he went past, to some he asked if they were okay and to others it was a simple but necessary pat on the shoulder or back.

John was in his dugout which was cloaked in darkness. Outside all that could be heard was the distant crackle of gunfire and every now and then a dull flash gently bathed the dugout in a warm yellow glow, but it was only for an instant.

'John?' a whispered voice said from the entrance.

He looked to see who it was and recognised the dark silhouette as that of Anthony.

'John, may I come in?'

A part of John wanted to be alone, he liked to spend time thinking before a battle, but another part of him decided that perhaps it was time to put away childish things and heal old wounds.

Tom had given the opinion of late that Anthony had proved himself again and again on the battlefield and even more so on moral grounds. He clearly felt for Sophie's sake and John's that Anthony deserved a chance. They were all living on the edge these days and life was too short to bear grudges.

John knew he had to resolve the issue sooner or later. The company had all been through and faced many battles together and the way in which his sister wrote about Anthony in her letters told John one thing, she was really happy and if they were home tomorrow she would want to be with him and she wouldn't want to have to choose between them. Even though it was only a written relationship these past two years, her feelings were real and they weren't going to go away.

If the roles were reversed John knew that Sophie would have only encouraged him in his quest, she had never liked Annie his last and only partner, despite his mother's fondness of her and at the end of the day despite expressing her opinion frequently and her own protectiveness of him; she had never acted as negatively towards Annie as he had Anthony. The choice and how he made it had always been his, wrongly or rightly. She had only ever been supportive.

Time and the shared experiences of warfare together were beginning to mellow his attitude and he knew what had to be done.

John beckoned the Lieutenant in and invited him to sit at the small wooden table. Anthony thanked him and fumbled around in the dark for the seat.

'Put the blackout curtain down and light the lamp,' John advised and soon both of them sat facing each other in the dim light.

Anthony looked at John and in return, John looked back. There was an uneasy atmosphere between them, but this time it was different. Before Anthony could never put a foot right in John's eyes, but this time the air was one of awkwardness and most of it was coming from John's side of the table.

'Drink?' John invited, reaching for the bottle of rum left on the table from earlier. The bottle was nearly empty from the small party they had enjoyed earlier, but there was still enough for a last quiet drink.

Anthony was taken aback for a moment and John knew that he was thinking about the fact that only earlier he had been reprimanded for a small sip of rum from his hip flask.

'I thought you didn't drink on duty?' he asked.

John half expecting the remark grinned and looked at him. 'You don't know me very well do you?' he said leaning his mug on his knee.

'Appearances can be deceiving, but I do genuinely believe there's a time and place for everything, including a drink.'

'Well I thought I did, but maybe I was wrong, that last night before embarkation at Newhaven, you had a drink then what was it?'

'Whiskey.'

'I thought that perhaps you didn't drink generally and particularly in front of Sophie because of her father?'

The young man was being a little too clever now for John's liking. Bringing up Sophie's father was always a step in the wrong direction. 'What do you want Lieutenant?' John snapped.

Anthony looked down at the mug and his fingers nervously tapped upon the table. 'I have said the wrong thing again perhaps this was not a good idea,' he rose from his seat and headed to the doorway.

John was already finding the discussion difficult, but he knew that he had to break through the tension that he was so used to. 'Sit down,' he sighed, placing his mug upon the table and with a cringe he apologised.

'I just wanted to talk,' Anthony said 'and a chance to break this stupid act we have, I'm sorry I know that was blunt, but I've had enough.' He looked to John as if to gauge his reaction, but John kept silent. 'I know you are very protective of her. I also know that we have spent very little time together in your eyes, but I can only tell you that I love her and that my feelings won't change and I feel pretty confident that hers won't either.' He paused again as if waiting for John to interrupt, but he remained silent. 'I love her John, so many words can't describe it. All I wanted was to talk to you.'

John remained thoughtful, admiring his courage and after a little sip of his rum replied, 'I appreciate your honesty and believe it or not I understand. You are right, we do actually want the same thing and that is for a young lady back at home to be happy.

It's a hard habit to break when I've got so used to being like this for so long, you know why I'm like this don't you? Off course you do, she would have told you about our mother and her father.

But after two years of being stuck in this place, in another man's words, life is too short and seeing how happy you make her, even if it is only in writing, Anthony, it's time to step down from my high horse and let her go.'

Standing up John raised his tot and their mugs chinked and clinked together. John couldn't believe how easy it had been to say and his soul felt all the better for it. Anthony however, was not so convinced.

'I don't know what to make of that.'

'It was sincere if that is what you were getting at?'

'Good,' he then took a sip of the rum and coughed from its potency. 'Where the hell did you get this stuff?'

'Captain James.'

'Silly question wasn't it?'

'It tasted better earlier, I swear. I'm sorry if I have been so hard on you lately,' John began his body tensing, he was not used to apologising. 'I have been pretty unfair.'

'Forgotten,' Anthony stated. 'And as you said, I understand.'

'No, I'm not sure you do, not fully, but hear me out first. We might not make it through tomorrow and god knows how we did the last time. I should have made this effort back then, before the Hellfire pass, but we had never seen war then, we were all still naïve.

Tom always talked about it and it wasn't until then that I understood. You're a damn fine soldier Lieutenant there's no mistaking that, I have let my own personal pride get in the way of our relationship for too long. It's time to stop. Sophie could end up with far worse a man, so for what it's worth, I'm sorry. Here's to better times, to friendship and Sophie.'

'Sophie,' agreed Anthony, his mug meeting John's again. 'You know John, I would be just the same if I had a little sister like her.'

'You would?' John chuckled, the tense air blew away.

'In fact, I would probably be worse,' Anthony continued.

'Don't think that is possible,' John replied.

'Have you heard from her?'

'Not recently.'

Anthony sighed, 'I ask because I received another letter the other day and, well I don't know if this sounds crazy, but it's as if she has changed.'

John knew exactly what he meant. Her letters were getting shorter and shorter, whilst her tone was sometimes a little curt with him.

'I think I know what you mean,' he chuckled. 'Tom tells me that she is the same in his letters. He seems to think that it is just the war, after all once you have written about it a few times what more is there to say? Besides, nursing must be a stressful role under the circumstances. But then Tom might be wrong, perhaps she has changed, haven't we all a little?'

'I guess we have, especially after tonight.'

'I will drink to that, even though its actually morning,' John reminded him.

They sat in silence for a moment in the peace. The distant crackle of guns the only sound and for a moment the war seemed a long way away.

'Why do you always allocate my platoon a supporting role and never let them lead an attack?' Anthony said in the gloom.

John looked upon his face, trying to make out with the limited light his facial expression, for John thought he knew in an instant what he was trying to get at, but even so as he tried to read him, his expression was blank. As company commander, he always had a reason for his decisions, but this one, a decision he made so frequently, revealed a chink in his armour.

To make matters worse Tom had now arrived and perched himself on the step of the dugout.

'You have given the same order again for today's engagement where my platoon have been put in reserve,' Anthony continued. 'I very rarely question your judgement, but time after time my platoon is placed out of context. Surely the whole point of First Platoon is that we have trained damned hard to head the assaults and neither the men nor I for that matter, can fathom why second or third platoon always get the job.

'Just think of it this way John, it doesn't do a lot for my image in front of the men and their confidence in my leadership. I'm in the army to be a soldier; I'm in it for the battle, Sir, not for sitting on the fence or hanging out the washing.'

John didn't need to look at Tom, he could feel his curious gaze and sense the grin that was spreading across his face, even though there was only his silhouette to see.

'He has a point,' Tom couldn't help but add his tuppence worth and John wondered if he was enjoying the moment a little too much.

'Wait, is it because of Sophie? You mean this whole time you were trying to keep me out of harm's way? You were trying to…'

John cut in tactfully, 'I don't think there'll be anyone sitting on fences from now on, Lieutenant. I take your point and I thank you for your honesty, you'll get your day soon, but tomorrow I need Keyes up front and I need to see what our new chap is going to do.'

'Surely it would make sense to keep Lieutenant Moore in reserve, he is still going to see some action.'

'My decision has already been made. Besides we are just getting to know each other and you're no good to me dead or wounded if we are to catch up on lost time some more,' John caught Tom from the corner of his eye. Tom give him a nod of approval. 'You best get back to the lads, get them prepared. Thank you, Anthony.'

'Thank you,' he said with a very positive salute and took his leave as he pulled back the dugout curtain.

Tom imitated a cough and called to him, 'Lieutenant, I am sure there was one more thing?'

Anthony stood rigid to the spot and licked his dry lips nervously.

'Now?' he quizzed Tom, who responded with a gentle nod and whispered something that John couldn't make out. 'John there is one more thing. I am worried we have made so much progress in one night that I might now undo it all in a single sentence, but Tom's right, it's best to ask now.'

John's heart was thudding against his chest. He ran through in a split second a whole list of things that Anthony could be about to announce. Naturally, they were all negative, but the worst, the very worst was that Sophie was pregnant. He dismissed this almost as fast as the idea had come to him, for they had been out here for two years now and that would be impossible. No, he thought, it must be the other kind of announcement he dreaded.

'I seem to have lost momentum because of my nerves,' he said stalling nervously then blurted out, 'I would like to ask your permission to marry Sophie if she'll have me.'

There was an awkward silence and John and Anthony both looked to Tom as if for some divine intervention. John sensed that Anthony might have already sent a letter home, or had certainly drafted the letter, he wasn't stupid. He might have only got to know Anthony the way he should have done in the last hour or so, but he knew him all the same. He was also acutely aware of how awkward or even impossible he would have been, had Anthony approached him earlier. The reality was that he didn't blame him for avoiding the confrontation that would have been inevitable.

'Wish you had asked earlier' and before Anthony tried to explain, John continued. 'But I understand why you didn't. I am not sure these are the best circumstances Anthony, but I will try hard in future to not only be the commanding officer you need, but the brother in law you need.'

Anthony's face beamed with a pure joy John had not seen since back in England, at one point he looked close to throwing himself on his newfound brother in law, but instead refrained and held out his hand for John to take.

'Welcome to the family,' John said.

'Sophie was right about you when she said that people seldom understand you, but I do and I think I always have. I am looking forward to you being my brother as much as I am Sophie being my wife.'

'She hasn't said yes yet,' Tom added. 'But I am sure she will,' he jumped up with glee and with them either side of him, he patted Anthony on the shoulder, saying, 'proud of you lads, damn proud, brothers in arms, that's what we've got, brothers in arms. Well done.'

'Do you think I have time to write?' Anthony said, checking his watch.

'If you get going now you might,' Tom replied and ushered him out of the door whilst Anthony attempted to give John a salute.

'There is more to all this than meets the eye, isn't there?' sensed John looking straight at Tom, 'but I don't expect I'll get to the bottom of it any time soon.'

'Don't underestimate your own ability, it's been a very productive day so far,' Tom remarked, his face twitched a little as he held back a grin.

'Everything seems to turn out just about right when you're around,' John said warily, 'always such good and sound advice and not just to me either, by the look of things.' Tom looked through his large pack, avoiding John's gaze. 'You know you are the closest thing I have to a father and I thank you for that.'

'Well that is a lovely compliment Sir, thank you.'

'All this matchmaking you get up to, when not playing the ferocious Sergeant Major, is it because...' he paused. 'Do you regret the army? You have never had a wife or children.'

'The army is my wife John and I've had more than enough children with tantrums and tempers to bring up as soldiers in this world, but I'll let you into a little secret. You've always been my favourite!' He rose from his seat and glanced at his watch noting the time. It was getting on for four thirty. 'As I said, Captain Baker, just a few minutes ago, I'm proud of you, sir.'

'Actually Sergeant Major Hill,' said John. 'I'm proud of me too. After all, we only have a certain person's welfare and our common interests at heart, don't we? Do you think that she will say yes?'

'Does a Jerboa like biscuit crumbs?'

Tom flicked his head sideways twice to imply to John that he should look to his right and there perched on the edge of the table was Harry again. His scurrying little paws cleaning his whiskers after yet another hearty meal.

John looked down at his watch as he walked across the rough hard ground. It was ten minutes into the attack. Artillery shells, exploding in all directions, this time thankfully belonging to the Royal Artillery had been whirling through the air and pounding the ridge up ahead. Columns of pirouetting dust devils marked the area where they had been striking, but now the gunners had paused, waiting for a moment to reload before commencing another full-on outburst.

The enemy had taken a beating, but just how severely they had been hit only time would tell. There was an eerie quiet about the place, except for the gentle rumbling of the tanks, barely a sound of battle could be heard during this momentary lull, both sides taking the opportunity to regroup and rearm.

His equipment weighed him down and made his shoulders ache, no matter how many times he tried to reposition the straps on his shoulders his posture didn't improve; instead, it made his equipment seem heavier and evermore uncomfortable, the heat adding yet another physical encumbrance to his already drained torso. But he wasn't alone in that respect.

Ahead of him were six Crusader tanks, slowly creeping forward with the platoon warily following in staggered formation behind. The engines of these mammoth beasts crackled and moaned, chugged and puffed as if they had been wound with a clockwork key, every now and then bursting into life and rising to a quickening pace. Then as if they had become bridled stallions their energy tempered and restrained to a snail's pace in order to allow the battalion's soldiers to keep up.

These formidable, bulging, bulky chunks of metal were never designed to tardily cross the desert floor and this necessary but languid pace inevitably played on the nerves of all those concerned in this wide open space of vulnerability.

To John, the whole scene had reminiscences of a herd of elephants and cautious zebra approaching a watering hole. The tanks advanced slowly, churning up the dust gently in their tracks like a tractor ploughing the earth. The men positioned warily behind them.

Somewhere out there in this inhospitable place there were lions stalking them. When and how long would it would be before they were pounced upon, scattering and panicking like stricken prey in all directions, time would tell.

D Company advanced in the very centre of the battalion with the remaining company's either side of them. John took up the most central position he could find amidst Keyes' Second Platoon and a few yards behind one of the tanks. To his left was Moore's Third Platoon and to the right Anthony's First Platoon.

He wiped the sweat from his brow and then slung his rifle over his shoulder to take a quick look at his map. He always carried a rifle and encouraged the other officers to do so as he believed it made them look less obvious as officers to the enemy and they were more of a weapon than the revolvers they carried at their hip.

John knew only too well how useless a revolver could be in the open spaces of the desert. In the last attack he had spotted an Italian soldier running for cover, John could see him even now as clear as day, his face red with exhaustion and the plume of purple feathers on his helmet making him stand out like a sore thumb. John had brought up his Webley and fired three times and each time he had missed, there hadn't even been a kick of dust to represent the fall of the shot. He cursed and then watched miserably as the figure fell instantly at the same time as the shot which rang out from the rifle of a passing private. It was clear that a rifle was what you needed out here in the desert if you stood any better chance of making it through.

'Is everything alright sir?' Tom called out over the whirl and whine of the tank engines.

He was just behind John, walking calmly as if out for a stroll. He was smiling and John couldn't help but wonder how he could stay so calm in such a tense and fearful situation.

John nodded at him and then looked at his map, he didn't know why he was looking at it again, he could see the ridge up ahead and looking at the map wasn't going to tell him where the enemy was going to be. It was the enemy that would make the first move; they would tell him where they were, but by then it would probably be too late. The Lions were ready to pounce and he just hoped that the six

Crusader tanks would be mighty and strong enough elephants to enable him to get his zebras to safety.

Unlike John, Tom probably did not allow worry to consume him. He had survived the First War and no doubt had every intention of surviving this one. John wondered if their advance brought back the memories of Cambrai, the Somme and Passchendaele. At Cambrai the British had first used tanks in a mass attack; Tom had witnessed the birth of the new weapon and seen it mature. The men including, Tom and Jack's troops, walked steadily behind the lumbering, cumbrous machines, using them as cover, just as D Company were now. It had been a tactic that worked well, but now years later, warmongers had perfected new tactics and were using new weapons, these lumbering giants could be just as easily the prey. Walking cautiously behind a neat row of tanks, John couldn't help but wonder if Tom was worried this battle would be no different than that fateful engagement where he had seen his father perish. If his soul carried any form of disquiet, his cheerful smile showed no signs of it and he held it forthrightly encouraging the men and putting them at ease, with his proud chest protruding forward, he maintained his constant pace.

John, putting his map case down by his side continued to walk on. The ridge began to loom ahead, but still all was relatively quiet. Enemy shelling could be heard in the distance north, but it was difficult to hear over the grumbling and churning engines of the Crusaders. His own apprehension began to wonder just how much longer they would get away with this exposed positioning they were all in. It couldn't be long now.

He looked to his right and caught a glimpse of Sergeant Scott; sure enough, a cigarette drooped from his lips. He turned again, walking backwards for a moment to check on the rear. Lance Corporal Lewis was directly behind him, sweat pouring from his forehead as he carried the massive radio on his back. Behind him was Tom, still smiling broadly and behind him Simon, who John was surprised to see so close to the action considering he shouldn't have been there.

Before he could question Simon's presence, John noticed four black spots appearing on the horizon above Simon's head, but it was difficult to tell if they were on the ground or in the air through the heat haze. His pace slowed for a moment fumbling for his binoculars his heart racing with anxiety. The specks were in the air and getting closer by the second due to their incredible speed, aircraft, but were they friendly or enemy?

He peered through the binoculars as the aircraft became more recognizable and breathed a sigh of relief. By the time he had lowered them, he could clearly see four Hawker Hurricanes only just a few feet off the ground streaming towards them. They roared overhead, their instantly recognisable Merlin engines humming, bubbling and crackling to the cheer of the audience below that watched with awe as they sped overhead, fiercely boosting the troop's momentum.

'Fantastic,' said Lewis. 'Wonder what they're after?'

'Enemy vehicles and position I should imagine,' John said, watching them fade into the distant blue and as they did small puffs of black smoke appeared in the air around them. The anti-aircraft guns were only just beyond the ridge and John brought his binoculars back up to his eyes.

He looked ahead at the small black puffs of cloud and could see the Hurricanes trying to dodge them before they went out of focus. He then lowered his binoculars to focus back on the ridge. Still there was nothing. Surely the enemy could see them coming by now and surely if they left it any longer it would be too late, why did they do nothing?

Thoughts began racing through his mind. Perhaps there was no enemy on the ridge and they had pulled out. Perhaps they hadn't been spotted yet, but John quickly put that theory out of his mind, the Crusaders, although going slow were still stirring up small dust clouds that would have been visible for miles and he knew the enemy was there. This terrible waiting game brought trepidations and fear and they were all sensing it.

No sooner had the dreadful thought of ambush entered his mind, the first shell whistled down from the heavens, its wail a scream like a downed and dying aircraft. It crashed to the rear of First Platoon spewing dust and rock fragments throughout the air at a terrifying speed.

'Cover,' someone yelled further down the line and to John's horror his men began to drop to the ground.

Tuning his mind in as if it was a wireless that had been out of frequency he knew there was no cover here and therefore there was no safety. The tanks could not go on without infantry support and with the ridge only a mile or so ahead there was only one thing left to do and that was to advance as quickly as possible. If the company got closer to the enemy, their artillery would be useless and they would be safer.

'No, no, no! Get up, get up,' he screamed to the men around him. Another shell garishly pierced the sky and fell around them. 'Come on advance, push on! Sergeant Major, get those men moving forwards!'

Tom was already getting to grips with the situation, running amongst the stragglers, grabbing the ones that lay on their bellies and pulling them up before kicking them forward with his own boot.

'Come on lads,' he yelled. 'Keep moving forward. Move, go, go, go, we're sitting ducks here!'

The tank drivers had clocked on by now what was going on. It was difficult to hear anything inside those huge iron coffins, but the thud of the explosions that had now begun to reign down was enough for them to speed up. The men were also beginning to organise themselves, jogging just behind the Crusaders to keep up and stay behind cover to get out of the killing zone and field of fire.

John continued to yell out encouragement to his men and check that the line was still holding, the last thing he needed was a platoon to fall behind or even rush ahead. He wanted everyone exactly where he could see them.

Another shell landed not far away and blew him to the ground. Dust was in his eyes and his muscles, particularly his calves which ached from the strain. So painful was the pain in his legs that it felt as if one more move, even slightly, would force his bone to punch through his shin. In a moment of blindness, his hands fumbled around on the desert floor searching for his rifle. Eventually the tell tale signs of a wooden stock told his hands they had found it and by now he could see again. Dusting his sand covered clothes off, coughing and spluttering, he continued on, helping another private to his feet ahead of him.

To the left Moore was doing well, the young inexperienced Lieutenant's men were holding formation and keeping up with the tanks. From where he could see John counted no casualties and was impressed with the fresh Lieutenant who appeared to be keeping his cool.

The line ahead was good too and to the right also, so far nobody had been hit or wounded, but more shells were coming in. They whirled and sprayed and punched through the air announcing themselves and although impossible to see, John found himself looking up from time to time to try and catch a glimpse of one. The ground shook when they hit, splitting the ground into cavernous craters and tossing him aside like a rag doll. The fountains of grit and sand particles flew and stung like a swarm of bees distorting his view.

Regaining his focus, he roared, 'fix bayonets!' and he heard the order echo from soldier to soldier.

They mustered up from the depths of their souls every emotion they could possibly draw, fear, panic, anger, exasperation, hatred, passion, conveying bravery and fearlessness, never faltering in their heroism despite their trembling and sweating, they looked ferocious as they ran onwards like a ravenous, bloodthirsty stampede; their blades glinting in the sun, John just hoped they could get close enough to use them.

It was just after the order that the first casualty was taken. It was Private Wellesley of Second Platoon. The shell landed just in front of him and blew him into the air and almost back on top of Sergeant Scott who went to his aid. John could see a leg was missing and his rifle had been split in two like kindling. His shirt and trousers were in tatters, but he was still alive, screaming for his mother.

John felt sick, this was it, the lion had pounced.

Another screaming shell, the detonation sent more stones hurling through the air, mimicking shrapnel. It lambasted a soldier running ahead, striking the side of his helmet and knocking him to the ground, after a moment of dizziness the young lad shook himself, nervously looking all about him he was then back on his feet and running ahead.

John looked over to his left. Moore was still advancing, but his platoon was taking hits and many of the men full of zeal and life were suddenly dropping to the floor like flies that had been swatted. One soldier sat on the ground clutching his knee whilst his mates ran on. Another just ahead was walking back with the help of a friend holding a dressing to the side of his head. Ahead of them a small crater, charred and smouldering marked the last place of another young soldier.

John surged onwards the ridge now only yards ahead and he could see a long entanglement of barbed wire that clearly marked the enemies' whereabouts.

A quick glance over his shoulder reassured him that Tom was still with him. The Sergeant Major had in his right hand his rifle, whilst his left held a handful of Lance Corporal Lewis' shirt, he was dragging the poor man who still had the full weight of a radio set strapped to his sweat-soaked and bloodied back, rubbed raw through the searing heat.

By now they were nearing the ridge and John knew they were close as mortars had started to join in with the Artillery.

Menacingly joining the mayhem was the high pitched shriek of anti-tank shells, they made a horrible loud pinging sound as they ricocheted off the armour of the tanks. John heard it again and looking ahead saw a bright flash as one of the shells glanced off the side of the lead tank's turret.

The gun could have been hidden anywhere up ahead and whilst running, with sweat stinging his eyes, he scoured the landscape ahead as best he could for any sign of where the shots had come from. The Crusaders had now noticed the raining of enemy rounds and in response used their smoke dischargers, spewing white clouds in front of them. The haze they created was thick as fog and as it started to spread the tanks halted and began to reshuffle their positions to try and confuse the enemy.

Bullets began flying now. They ricochet off the tanks and the tank commanders that risked the full view of battle were forced into their turrets to seek cover. The problem was whilst in their turrets their visibility was reduced and the smoke screen they had created would only last so long. They were reliant on the infantry now to find the threat and John knew it was up to his men to find the bellowing enemy gun. The ridge was just yards away and muzzle flashes could be seen all along its length.

'Cover!' a voice yelled and this time John didn't query it, he had already been thrown about by the last near miss. He kept his head down desperately looking through the gaps in the smoke for where the enemy anti-tank gun was located. He knew the key to taking the ridge was to keep the tank support intact. Without it they were naked.

A flash appeared to his right and an even bigger 'whomph'. The muzzle flashes of rifles and machine guns continued and a second later a screeching armour piercing shell ripped through the lead tank. Splinters and shards of steel flew through the air, splicing and blinding one boy who was only feet away. Keyes was thrown to one side, but was soon back up and taking cover behind the now burning hulk. The crew of the tank bailed, jumping from the wreck and diving behind for cover dragging one man free unconscious.

The company had returned fire now and the sound of 303 rifles erupted all around.

'Don't waste your ammo, fire at the muzzle flashes,' Tom was braying.

Bren guns chattered and rifles burst sharp fracturing cracks above the shell explosions and occasional screams of shock and pain. The remaining tanks had moved position now and halted behind their makeshift screen, but the enemy gun was still having a go, firing blindly into the smoke hoping for a chance hit.

John continued to peer through the occasional gaps in the smoke. Suddenly another flash, it was brighter than the enemy rifle fire on the ridge, this time and in the same place he had been looking earlier. That must be it he told himself, but there were barely any significant landmarks to accurately describe to others where the gun was. A small dead bush or shrub was just to the left of where the flash had been and to the right a small pile of rocks that were piled in the shape of what he could only describe as the top half of a person.

'Sergeant Major can you see that small dead shrub and those pile of rocks?' he yelled, pointing frantically at the area.

Tom dived down next to John and peered ahead. 'Got it,' he confirmed.

'About ten meters to the left of those rocks, the ones that look like the top half of a person there is an anti-tank gun,' another flash suddenly revealed its location. 'I want the two-inch Mortars to hammer it with smoke, blind the bastards!'

Tom smiled and raising himself to his feet, gave a thumbs up before running back to the mortar crews who were bringing up the rear.

Now all that was left was to break through the barbed wire and capture the trenches that were hopefully just beyond it. He could then send a small party up towards the area where the gun was located.

'Lewis, get on the radio to First Platoon and inform them I want them to flank far to the right after they have broken through, inform them to look out for an anti-tank gun,' Lewis was on the radio, frantically relaying the message and flinching at the near misses that were coming his way.

Breaking through would not be easy. The enemy had the men pinned down on the open desert floor and casualties were mounting. The tanks were the only cover, but behind their makeshift smoke screen that was now beginning to drift away, the men could barely see the enemy, they had to press on it was the only way.

Keyes and Moore were now heading forward across the open ground to the wire; Bren guns provided cover fire from the rear before heading forward themselves. From where John was he could see in the sky above them a shower of small black objects, some heading towards the enemy, some littering astray and some down on Moore's men. Grenades!

A multitude of explosions ripped through Third Platoon, but beyond the black smoke John could see Moore's men still charging on. The young Lieutenant who only two days earlier seemed so naïve and had Tom and Orchard wondering if he would be up to the task as a platoon leader was proving his worth. He might not have had any experience before this engagement, but his determination, training and courage were all that was needed now. The platoon had begun to breach the wire and Moore was leading from the front, a revolver in his right hand and his men close behind shouting in a blood-curdling bayonet charge. John turned away, he didn't want to see Moore fall which seemed inevitable in the hail of bullets that met him.

Keyes had pushed forward and appeared to be caught just in front of the wire. Mortars rained down all around them as they duelled with the enemy soldiers.

To the right there was very little movement. Anthony's platoon was fighting back, but from behind the safety of the Crusaders. The smoke screen had lifted in a wafting and sultry light breeze and the tanks were beginning to edge forward slowly.

The Mortars that Tom had taken command of had done a good job; John could see that where he calculated the enemy anti-tank gun position to be, a plume of white smoke had blocked its view of their positions. It would buy him time to get closer as he knew there were only a few smoke mortars left, but Tom had thought ahead and instructed the mortar crew to hit the area with explosive rounds as well as smoke to make their rounds last and keep the enemy crews heads down.

The Tanks opened fire on the position where the gun was believed to be now, the smoke acting as a beacon for them, but the new tanks just didn't have the firepower to deal the deathly blow needed.

Finally, up front, Keyes had broken through the wire, but on it lay several bodies riddled with bullet holes, faces pierced with shock, one still alive clawed up at the sky in torment between friend and foe whilst around him on the floor the desert was now soaked with patches of blood.

John turned again to check on the rear. Orchard was just behind him firing his rifle at the enemy, whilst next to him Lewis cowered on the floor looking in the direction of the battle, his face pale. Simon was tending to a wounded private that John couldn't recognise, but soon the wounded soldier was on his feet and edging back towards the rear under his own steam. Simon then approached and knelt down next to John.

'I have just sent Private Banks back to the rear,' he said trying to wipe the blood off his hands with a handkerchief.

'Is he alright?' John asked.

'Patched him up as best as I could, but he'll be okay, just missing half his left cheek.'

John wanted to be sick, but marvelled at how calm and collective Simon was being. He looked again at First Platoon. They still had not advanced and beyond them, A company was held up because Anthony's platoon had yet to cross the wire. John looked again, where was Anthony? They needed to be further forward.

'Orchard, when Sergeant Major Hill has finished at the mortars tell him to assume command here and push on behind Lieutenant Keyes, I am going to see what is holding up First Platoon.'

'Right, Sir.'

John carefully picked himself up off the desert floor and then made his way across the now scarred battlefield, Simon and Lewis followed. They took cover as another shell whirled in above them, but soon after ducking and diving like a pair of boxers in a ring, they made it over to First Platoon. There John found Corporal Woods kneeling and peering from behind one of the Crusaders. He fired a shot and then pulling the bolt back, fed another round into the chamber as the last cartridge flipped and reeled to the floor.

'Corporal, what's going on, why haven't you advanced?' John asked over the rattle of Bren fire.

'Haven't got the order yet sir,'

'What? Where is Lieutenant Thomas?'

'Last time I saw him he was behind that tank over there sir' and Woods pointed to the last tank in the line. The tank had lost a track and so couldn't advance along with the others. Its guns were still firing in defiance of being wounded.

John looked ahead and out in the open he could see most of Anthony's command section, he waved to get their attention and in response a few waved back. The two sections he had should be enough to break through.

'Thank you Corporal, I'll go and see Lieutenant Thomas and see what the problem is, meanwhile you're in command as acting Sergeant of both these sections now. Get your arses together and I want you to move forward, ready?'

The Corporal, now promoted on the spot, nodded in agreement, his head then bobbing down to avoid a ricochet of bullets and flying shrapnel. When John gave the order to go he led both sections, nearly twenty men in total, forwards towards the wire. Grenades were tossed into the air ahead and large plumes of dust and debris towered where they had exploded. John raised his rifle and provided covering fire whilst Simon peeped over the back of the tank to watch. The men continued to charge, some managed to jump the wire, one fell on it in order to allow the others to cross, all the time grenades exploding all around. John reloaded his rifle after firing ten rounds, the first rounds he had fired since the chaos began and then looked again to see how they had done.

'They're through, they've done it!' cried Simon and from his position he could see the men now using the entrenchments to harass the retreating enemy. Suddenly the Crusader they were sheltering behind lurched forwards with a new lease of life in order to join the fight.

'Let's find Anthony,' John said, heading for the immobilized tank at the rear to which he guessed Anthony was behind.

It had already occurred to John that something was wrong, but even with that thought in mind it knocked the wind from his sails as he arrived at a scene of carnage to find Anthony lying in a pool of his own blood, the remnants of number three section crowded around him trying to save his life.

John was numb with pain; he didn't know what to do, he didn't know what to think and so just stood there amidst the enemy fire morosely looking down at the Lieutenant. Amongst pangs of guilt and remorse, he found himself thinking about their discussion only a few hours ago and how even when challenged by Anthony, he thought he had managed one last time at least to keep him out of dangers way, all because he had been trying to protect his sister. He thought of all the times he had been so rude, so difficult and unreasonable. Now was not the time to worry about the past, but he couldn't help it, the feelings welled up inside consuming him with regret of his own behaviour.

He almost let himself go emotionally, he knew that everything was wrong about this situation and he willed Anthony to hold on, deep down inside hold on. Simon was immediately helping others to hold him down. He was in such pain his torso was lurching all over the place from the shock of the hit, as if he was no longer in control of it. There wasn't a great deal of blood around him, the porous and thirsty desert had sucked most of it down into the sand.

Three terrible wounds had punctured his chest, shrapnel from one of the mortars. A bandage had been hastily put onto one of the gaping holes, but Simon had ripped it off and was replacing it with one of his own, all the time trying to hold Anthony down as his body writhed off the ground as if the floor was on fire. Not a sound left Anthony's lips, but his mouth kept opening as if gasping for air, or trying to say something. His eyes were open wide and filled with tension and unease looking from person to person and then finally settling his attention on John.

John paralysed by his imploring gaze screamed at Simon. 'Do something, can't you do something? For Christ's sake this isn't how it is supposed to be, save him' and then bawling at those surrounding him and pushing himself forward to Anthony's side, he thrashed out at the other soldiers, 'give him room, get yourself to the wire, push forwards, get yourself out of harm's way, we'll deal with this.'

John was beside himself with agitation. Simon looked up at him and as quietly as he could without Anthony hearing, said, 'he has lost a lot of blood John, if I'd known earlier, then…' he finished by simply shaking his head and returned to comforting Anthony.

'For god's sake Sir, get down,' a private cried to John and he grabbed his captain and pulled him down next to wounded Lieutenant.

Anthony's eyes followed John to the floor.

'Come on Simon; tell me what to do, what's next?' John said exasperatedly trying to keep calm but his voice was becoming more desperate.

'I heard you the first and second time,' Simon replied busily trying to plug the wounds and stop the bleeding, he gave Anthony a shot of limited morphine.

A shell exploded nearby, it scattered shrapnel and stone across the desert and Simon dived over Anthony to protect him as the dust and debris fell from the sky. John looked on into the Lieutenants dimming eyes and his heart burned with frustration and torment. He could feel the tears welling up inside him and knew they were visible when they began tickling his eyelids.

'Oh god, Sophie. Simon, you need to save him.'

Simon turned to face him. What greeted him was John's pleading visage for a miracle that the doctor knew he could not perform.

'I'm sorry John,' Simon said slowly.

'Simon, you must,' John said, but as a few precious seconds passed, the efforts began to dwindle.

'I can't,' the doctor said, throwing a bloody bandage in frustration, his head drooping down low. 'It's gone too far! I can only make him as comfortable as I can. John, John?' He shook him. 'Captain Baker! We have to get to safety.'

Simon backed away from Anthony, a signal that there was nothing left he could do and beckoned to the soldiers left at the scene to put him on a stretcher to lay him to one side. Too much blood had dispersed from his veins and by the time they would have moved him a few yards he would be dead.

Anthony, still conscious had begun to calm down. The pain was subsiding due to the morphine and his hand started to gently crawl across the dust until it found John's where it gripped it tightly. John looked down at his hand, enveloped by Anthony's and then looked at him despairingly. His heart beat frantically and he found himself praying, praying to God, any God or anyone who could stop this horror that was engulfing this situation right now.

'I'm sorry,' John said meekly drying a tear from his eye. 'I am so sorry.'

Anthony's grip tightened around John's hand and his eyes looked more urgent than ever, he clearly wanted to say something, but couldn't.

'I'm sorry for everything,' John blurted out. 'I don't know what more I can say. Keep holding on, they're doing everything they can. Hold on old chap, you're nearly there. I'm going to get you home to her.'

Anthony winced as they transferred him on to a stretcher. His lips continued moving in an attempt to speak and then the tight grip he had around John's hand surged and gripped even more tightly for a brief moment before it slumped limply over the edge of stretcher and along with it his lips stopped moving. He was gone.

It took a moment as it would with anyone for John to break free from the situation. He stared at the lifeless body and all John could see in his mind was his sister, it was too much for his anguished soul. He couldn't bear it. He had never felt so responsible, he had failed Anthony and he had failed his sister. He took a deep breath and stood up, now he had to get on with the job at hand; there would be time to mourn Anthony and blame himself later. His men needed him now, their eyes were already fixed upon him, waiting for the next order and so taking an even deeper breath and turning away from the body he addressed them.

'Right, time is ticking. We have to catch up to the rest of the Company,' He looked around and they appeared as numbed as he was. 'Simon, can you wait with Anthony and get your people to take him back?'

Simon nodded and patted him on the back. 'Consider it done,' he said congenially showing empathy at the professionalism John was showing.

'Okay, ready lads?'

The men grabbed their equipment. John looked over the trackless tank to where he had earlier sent the other sections off over to the wire. There was now a gap in the wire, created by one of the tanks which had struggled its way up the slippery slopes of the ridge, the rest of the platoon right behind it. John would assume command of First Platoon for the moment in Anthony's place.

'Head for the wire, there is a gap to the left made by the other tank. Form up behind the tank and then advance to the right of section two, there is an anti-tank gun up there somewhere, I want you to locate it before pressing on beyond the ridge.' The men looked at him, waiting for the word as shells and bullets raked the dust around them. 'Go!'

John dashed out from cover, his rifle gripped firmly in his sweaty and blood-soaked hands. The men ran either side of him panting and wheezing in the heat. Ahead was the gap in the wire and beyond it the tank. The ridge, which was only a few feet high, seemed to loom above them and on its slopes were the rest of the company.

To the left in the distance was Moore's platoon fighting their way up to the top. In the centre was Keyes about half way up, one section was still pinned down at the base. Behind Keyes, just crossing the wire John could make out his own command section with Tom bawling out orders to the straggling section of Second Platoon.

Then out of nowhere there was a thud below his feet and the ground swallowed him whole. Above him the clear blue sky seemed to spin and his body throbbed as he fought for air, writhing with every breath that seemed harder to obtain. John was confused; and then casually he seemed to be floating, totally uninhibited, carefree, drifting and complacently unaware of what was happening to him. His eyes looked left and then right deliriously, but all he could see was the blue sky. He could still hear and there was the sound of gunfire and shouting in all directions. There were high pitched cries as darkness enveloped him. He could hear marching and the scuffling of boots upon the rocky ground and then someone was calling his name. It was a soft and gentle voice, vaguely familiar. It was reassuring, calmly calling his name, it was beckoning and willing him onward in an effortless, peaceful and smooth transition. He was sure it was a woman's voice and he could hear her clearly, whispering, 'where is Anthony?'

'Over here,' he heard Anthony reply. 'We are coming, we are ready now' and everything faded from a muffled vagueness into complete silence.

The Dark Room

John's world was surrounded with darkness, he couldn't even conjure up an image of his own from within his mind such was the blackness. He couldn't feel anything either, no pain or any of the senses he would normally feel. He breathed in, but couldn't feel his chest heave nor hear the sound of the air he needed. He blinked, but in the world of darkness he had no idea if his eyelids were moving or whether he was imagining that they were, or whether he no longer had sight.

His ears worked perfectly though. Through them he could tell that he was amongst the living, although he wasn't sure whether he was alive himself; perhaps he was a lost soul wandering between heaven and earth and was stuck in a sense of in-between.

Through his ears, he could still hear the shells whizzing overhead and the loud explosions of the near misses. He could hear screaming too, loud and high pitched. He could hear talking and praying, but it was in another language, a language he couldn't fathom at this moment or understand.

Finally, a dull light began to penetrate through the dark. His brain seemed to be reconnecting with his eyes and the signals were obviously getting there. It was faint to begin with, but as time passed it got brighter and brighter. He hoped it was the sun shining through his eyelids and not some angelic host. As slowly as an opening bud in spring, his eyes began to open and he could see.

In front of him was the glowing sun, surrounded by a wonderful blue sky. As he stared and blinked he could feel the weight of his arms and head again enough to attempt to move. He slowly tried to turn onto his side, whilst around him a collage of sound bombarded his ears. He kept trying and trying to turn, but the energy was just not there. Shells exploded not far away and he could hear people's voices and bustling around him, but he still couldn't understand what was being said. He felt vulnerable and frustrated at his incapacitation. If he was still alive he was a sitting duck.

He could feel a tingling in his lips and he was sure they were moving now, but there were no words flowing. Perhaps he had lost his voice or his hearing and that's why he couldn't hear himself speaking, but that couldn't be right because he could hear things going on around him, or was he imagining the sounds around him too? Why couldn't he get up? Why couldn't he move? What was happening to him or rather what had happened to him? In a last dramatic struggle he squeezed the last bit of adrenalin he could muster and heaved himself onto his left side which left him dizzy, limp and exhausted again. As he drifted in and out of consciousness again, he weakly opened his eyes once more to focus on the face of a man who was laying on a table, his left arm dangled down, his hand clutching a gold chain and locket, perhaps a keepsake from someone special. He stared back at John through glazed eyes, the twinkling light no longer visible. John's eyes rolled down to where he could see the blood-soaked desert floor.

Shadows and figures moved back and forth from behind him, but he felt so sick and confused that he had to remain where he had got himself to as any further movement was still impossible. Frustratingly stuck, he noticed that the lifeless body before him wore a blood-soaked Italian uniform. His curly whiskered beard was showered in clots of dried blood where the bullet had exploded inside his left cheek and left a gaping wound. His lips were slightly ajar and John ascertained from the fresh trickle of blood that dripped to join the growing stain below that he had only taken his last breath a few minutes before. John was still none the wiser as to where he was.

He noticed a large rectangular shadow was cast upon the floor further down towards his feet, which meant that behind him was some kind of tent or shelter. Underneath the dead Italian stood a box of field dressings, some had spilt out from the box and their wrappers lay upon the dust. Taking a guess, John assumed he was at a dressing station and judging from the difficulty in understanding the language he could hear coming from behind him, it was extremely likely that he was behind enemy lines.

He was just taking stock of the situation when into view appeared two more but very much alive Italian soldiers. They gently lifted the dead body from the table and lay him down onto the floor. One of the men then placed a brown blanket covering the soldier, but the other, out of the corner of his eye glanced in John's direction and noticing his consciousness began shouting in English.

'Capitano! Capitano your friend, he is awake,' he yelled jabbing his finger towards John and then as if by magic Simon's face appeared.

He was covered with dust and his cap was in tatters, his lower lip was cut, but a warm and comforting smile was spread across his face when he saw that John's eyes were flickering.

'Jesus Christ, you're awake thank God.'

John's body relaxed on the table with relief. He was alive and amongst friends. He tried hard to speak, but all that came out from his dry, cracked lips was a feeble, 'roll me over.' He tried again to speak, but his lips moved without a sound. Simon understood and carefully he rolled him onto his right side.

'Italian field hospital,' Simon explained and as he walked around the table which John was on, he lay over him just in time to shield him from debris flung into the air by a nearby shell. 'We're just behind enemy lines. Sounds like our boys are counter-attacking.'

The top half of his body virtually came on to automatic pilot again when John grabbed Simon's tunic in panic as another nearby shell smashed into the sand, he felt hopelessly vulnerable lying upon the wooden table.

'Got to get off, get me off of here!' John panted weakly.

Looking beyond Simon he could see more wounded, mostly Italians again lying upon tables and being seen to by Italian medical troops. They lay screaming in agony, some writhing in pain as arteries pumped rich crimson blood onto the baron dirt floor.

'No chance there matey, you'll have to hang on a bit longer I'm afraid, you're safe enough here for the time being, trust me. Back in a jiff, needed over there' and as magically as he came he disappeared again.

Bit by bit, his anatomy was beginning to tick a regular rhythm and his eyes moved around the makeshift hospital. His glance caught more lifeless cadavers laid out on an embankment, obviously the ones that the medical teams couldn't save. He blinked with disappointment and had to ask himself, 'what is the point of all this?' He thought to himself for a moment that perhaps they were the lucky ones, peacefully resting there. Their fate, their war, their suffering, their fears, their sacrifice, their duty, done.

All the corpses were covered with either a blanket or a jacket, but there was one nearest to him at the end of the row which was only partially covered and the head was tilted slightly, staring out from under the darkness.

The partial portion of the visage looked vaguely familiar, he recognised a face of importance when he saw one and he knew this corpse was important to him, John tried to remember, but he couldn't. He couldn't really see and he couldn't really remember. Why couldn't he work it out? He tried to stretch himself closer to focus better but the pain that instantaneously seared through his torso was so great it ripped and gripped in the side of his neck, down to his stomach where he felt as if he was on fire. Reeling back into himself he launched a scream of agony, the very voice that had been unable to get out unfurled itself with a vengeance, his body became an introverted mechanism once again, his eyes now seeing clearer than ever before realised who it was. Orchard, his skin was pale, but it was peaceful too, a gentle smile which had been worn in life was still present now in death. That very smile had served him with true dedication and respect. Tears filled John's eyes, his lips trembled and now his body was listing heavily. 'Corporal?' Off course there was no response, he was dead, but something within him just wouldn't accept it. 'Corporal wake up.' He was tired. Slipping and drifting slowly.

'John? No John, you have to stay awake we're going to get you to a hospital, you must stay awake!' he heard Simon shout, but it was too late. It felt easier for him to close his eyes and let go. He took one more glance at the face he recognised and called his name one last time before he fell back into the darkness.

The Lodger
The Cottage, June 17th 1941

Two days had passed since Sophie had offered to lodge Buckland, although she added the term 'relented' when updating Mrs Jenkins on the news. Today uncle Richard was bringing him around for his first night and it wasn't long before his car pulled up outside, followed by the rumble of a motorbike.

Mrs Jenkins was due to leave an hour before, but her ever attentive curiosity had evidently delayed her departure. She had wanted to know all about the lodger since she arrived in the morning. Not only did she commend Sophie for moving forward and clearing out her mother's room, a decision that she knew had been easier said than done, but then went on to articulate how much she loved a sailor.

'Handsome?' she had asked. Sophie tried at first to shrug off her questions, but this appeared to make her seem as though she was evading the answers rather than trying to show that she didn't have an opinion on the matter. Neither did she divulge that she knew the Naval officer and therefore already knew what he looked like. He was handsome, but not in the same way as the stars on the cinema screen, not like Cary Grant, one of her favourites, despite only seeing one of his films when it was brought over the Atlantic. It was probably his well-kept and tidy appearance, along with his smart uniform that had the nurses swooning. Sophie liked his attention and certainly found his humour a breath of fresh air, but otherwise she would say to herself that she couldn't firmly pinpoint the attraction towards him.

'You alright dear?' Mrs Jenkins asked. 'You have gone a little quiet.'

Sophie left her in silence briefly to open the door, remembering on the way his awkwardness when the room had been suggested in the first place. There was more to Lieutenant Buckland it seemed than humour in the hospital and bravery at sea. His uncomfortable appearance about the arrangement, now mirrored as he walked through the door with a large brown suitcase under one arm, suggested a polite and considerate side. He was fast becoming a mystery.

'Nurse Watson, I want to say thank you again for your offer.'

'It's fine.'

'I had a word with the Admiralty and they are more than happy to sort out accommodation elsewhere…'

'Its fine,' Sophie simply replied again.

Richard followed him inside and guided him upstairs on a brief tour and to what would have once been his own sister's room. Sophie helped Mrs Jenkins to make them a cup of tea.

'How are you getting on with your midnight reading?' she probed, straining the tea leaves.

Sophie wasn't sure what to say, there was a tone in her voice that suggested she should have found something out, but the reality was that there had been little time for her to flick through the pages of her mother's memories, something she hoped to remedy this evening.

'I haven't read much yet, just the notes she kept on Jack.'

'Ah, I see. Your mother loved Jack very much. Don't take offence, she loved your father too, but Jack was taken away from her and she never got over that.'

'My father was also taken away from her, she lost two men in her life and she was married to my father!'

Mrs Jenkins looked austerely into her eyes, so directly that it made Sophie uneasy. 'I told you to not take offence. Your mother married your father because she loved him too and also because she could. She never got the same chance with Jack. Your father…' there was an awkward pause and she appeared to give up with whatever thoughts were at that time running through her head and resigned herself to whatever secondary thoughts had taken their place. She simply reached for the sugar bowl and quietly said. '… Your father could never live up to her Jack and look what it did to him.'

'Why didn't she marry Jack?' Sophie continued. 'Mother seemed to put it off because of the war and some silly idea that if she avoided marriage he would return because everyone else who had got married ended up losing their husband.'

'Silly? It was not silly my dear, it was brave. She could have had a tidy sum of money if she had married Jack, especially when he was killed, but your mother felt it was more important that he had something to come home for, the belief that they could pick up where they had left off. Money was never important to your mother, hope was.'

'But she was left destitute, an unmarried woman with a child and a dead fiancée…' Sophie paused, she could see that Mrs Jenkins appeared agitated and turned the conversation back to the hospital. This seemed to ease the tension whilst from upstairs, Sophie could hear her uncle giving Buckland a history of the house from the top of the stairs. Soon they were down in the kitchen, looking out to the garden and discussing vegetable plots. Mrs Jenkins handed them their tea and they stood sipping their tea and occasionally raiding the biscuit barrel.

Sophie studied Buckland with great interest, this shy and uncomfortable side to him intriguing her, his eyes darted around the room, jumping from item to item, looking up and down the walls and anywhere but Sophie. He was either taking in his new surroundings or avoiding eye contact. She wondered if his discomfort was due to their reunion. Then again this could have been Sophie's imagination, for now she was second guessing everything he did, assessing it somehow as if it had a meaning.

'Do you have a family Lieutenant?' Mrs Jenkins began, a cheeky glint in her eye. 'You remind me of my husband in his prime, many years ago I might add.'

'I'm afraid I don't.'

'Not even a wife or fiancée?' he shook his head in response. 'Pity.'

Uncle Richard, sensing Mrs Jenkins' playfulness quickly jumped in, 'you will be pleased to hear Mrs Jenkins that the Lieutenant will be able to bring back a few special items you might not get in the shops with your ration card.'

She looked delighted at this news and began reeling off a list of groceries she had clearly missed since the start of the war. Buckland barely got a word in and either shook his head or nodded.

After Uncle Richard left, Sophie followed Buckland to his new room.

'Do you need any help unpacking?'

'No thank you, there is a certain way things go, I'm quite particular about it I'm afraid. Was this your mother's room?' she nodded. 'It's lovely, I like the view out over the garden and the orchard beyond. She must have loved it here.'

'I have many memories of that orchard. John and I still use the orchard a great deal. Actually, that was some time ago, it feels like an eternity when I last used it to make a strawberry tart for them all shortly before they left. That's when I first met Anthony.'

'We can always take a trip down there if you like? I love strawberries. Funny all this isn't it? It was only the other day I thought I was never going to see you ever again.'

'I know it's strange,' she replied.

'Perhaps it's fate?' Buckland winked, it was the first glimmer of his old self she had seen. Whilst it should have been a comforting relief for her, she couldn't have his attention under this roof, it didn't feel right.

'No, just strange.' She turned away and headed downstairs, meeting Mrs Jenkins at the front door and following her out.

'Nice lad,' she remarked as Sophie passed her coat and bag.

'He's alright, I knew him from the Hospital.'

'Ah, I thought there was something there!'

'What do mean?' Sophie snapped, she didn't like her choice of words.

'Well, you seemed familiar with each other.'

'In what way?'

Mrs Jenkins sighed. 'Christ Sophie! I only meant that you must have known each other. You have been a bag of tense nerves all day. I will see you in the morning.'

At first, Buckland was an irritation to Sophie, an invasion of her quiet and peaceful life. She was more frustrated about his intrusion than the anti-aircraft gun that had been placed at the bottom of the garden, camouflaged amidst Maynard's orchard which occasionally broke her peace and quiet with a loud crack and thump, shaking the house violently. He constantly asked her if she wanted some tea, or if she fancied a walk. He would take hours to settle, sometimes he would loiter upstairs, pacing backwards and forwards which stressed out the floorboards that whimpered under his weight. He would later come downstairs, again pacing and wandering around, clearly uncertain as to where he should be.

'Why don't you just sit down?' she would quiz him and in response he would ask her if that was alright. This only frustrated her more and when she explained that it was his home too, he nodded and got comfortable with a newspaper. The whole scene would then repeat itself the following day until he soon became more settled.

As the days went by, Sophie noticed that she began to lose her frustration and irritation towards the Lieutenant. She soon came to realise that he had become a part of the furniture and her irritations and frustrations with him were more a reflection of how she felt with herself. She realised quickly that she felt less alone now and his daily flirtations, this time with Mrs Jenkins, amused her and no doubt flattered Mrs Jenkins. At first, she did not wish for his jovial attention, worried what others might think of them both. A small part of her worried that she might betray Anthony in any small way, but slowly it was like being back at the hospital ward with him. His humour was restored and his cheekiness that she so very much enjoyed had also returned. It was a welcome relief from the first few days of uneasiness.

Once settled Buckland had a particular routine every night when he returned from his duties. Tea was the first thing required and normally Mrs Jenkins in her last hour of service for the day obliged. Then there was the flirting. She could tell it was only fun and Sophie would sit in the living room and listen as she pretended to read the newspaper. Mrs Jenkins would spur him on and his responses, gentle, innocent and at times cheeky, caused Sophie to have to sometimes put her hand over her mouth to avoid them hearing her laughter. On one occasion his remarks and her response were so funny that she was bought to tears.

After his cup of tea, which since leaving the hospital had been reduced to no sugar, probably out of politeness as he saw how short they were, Buckland would enter the living room. It was here that Sophie would watch him slump into the armchair and often rub his forehead with thought. She would at this time pass him the newspaper she had been pretending to read and he would catch up with the latest news, or continue from where he had left off before.

'You know it occurred to me today,' he began. 'That you could always fill me in on the news, after all, you have read most of this already.'

She wondered if this was a trap, an attempt to test her on what was in its contents. She looked at him carefully, studying his facial expressions for any tell-tale clue as to whether or not he was toying with her. He continued to read. 'Have you read this?' he asked and preceded to read aloud an article on Spitfire pilots. He was not toying with her after all.

'I must have missed that bit. I don't read everything in there.'

'Ah, I see. You scan through what appears to be important or interesting. A bit like me.'

She studied him a little longer, getting to know his traits. There was the gentle frown that he had when engrossed in something interesting or confusing and a sigh he let out when finishing what he had read before turning the page. She tried to think of some of Anthony's little quirks and she struggled, so much so that she had to leave the room. What was it that he used to do? She suddenly remembered that he would run his fingers through his strawberry blonde hair, he had done it on the picnic down at the river once. Buckland's hair was short and dark, not a lot there to run her hands through, she thought. Then there was Anthony's laugh, it was difficult to remember, but she could remember how infectious it was. With these thoughts rejuvenated in her memory, she felt relief. She wanted to emulate her mother and the love she had discovered she had for Jack. It was a difficult love for Sophie to acknowledge at first, as Mrs Jenkins had pointed out, it was easy to be offended in some way at how her mother had appeared to love Jack more than she had loved Sophie's father, Ted.

With her mother in her mind, she returned to the diaries. The ladder to the roof creaked a little under her weight as she ascended into the dark mysteries of the past. Tonight she had moved onto 1917, knowing that this was the year of Jack and Tom's eventful fight at Cambrai. Up to this point, the letters and diaries had told of nothing but unconditional love, of patience and desire. At times her mother's inner thoughts made for uncomfortable reading, often describing her erotic thoughts and sexual frustrations and it was not uncommon for Sophie to feel her cheeks flush. It was easy to forget now that her mother had been a young woman, learning about herself just as Sophie was. Like herself, the diaries were full of raw feeling and emotion, the kind everybody knows but is too afraid to let the world see.

Before she moved onto 1917 she had to finish the last few pages on 1916 and it was here that there was something new, something she should have half expected, but as she was caught up in her mother's thoughts it came as a surprise as much as it did her mother. Violence, that horrific reality of war had clearly taken its toll on Jack. Sophie imagined the horror and pain of the trenches, the mechanical killing of thousands of young men on a scale that a factory would have difficulty keeping up with.

Tom had hinted about the reality of war, but she could see it clear as day when her mother described Jack's leave and how he had changed. From the pages fell a letter, a draft no doubt, for her mother was meticulous in how she catalogued her life. Sophie had never known until know, just how thorough in the recording of her own past her mother had been. She couldn't remember her mother ever writing anything as detailed as this whilst she was young. There must have been a time, she thought, that her efforts to catalogue information like this must have come to an end. Something must have made her suddenly stop. She forced herself not to route through the remaining books to look for the last year, to look for that moment and try and understand it. She reassured herself that she would get there in the end and skipping events might ruin the voyage she had undertaken.

Instead, she picked up the letter her mother had drafted and her heart jumped into her mouth. It was addressed to Tom. What she held in her hand, as she began to read, was the first moment that Tom became a big part of their lives. It was the very first piece of evidence that her mother had called out to Tom for help. It was nothing that should have surprised her, their story had to start at some point, but holding this letter was to her mind as exciting as Darwin discovering the origin of man.

Dear Sergeant Hill

I appreciate how odd it must be getting a letter from me and may I also add a sincere apology due to the circumstances as you read on. Firstly allow me to express my gratitude for looking out for my fiancée under the circumstances he has sometimes described to me, what you have achieved together is nothing short of a miracle. Your friendship through these testing times and knowing you are by Jack's side every day is of great comfort me.

I apologise for what I am about to write, I only wish that when you were both last on leave I had plucked up the courage to speak to you in private then, but as you can plainly see I am having to write it now, which is perhaps for the best. I am incredibly worried Tom. Your last visit home was far too brief and Jack was no different than the day I first fell in love with him, however when I was alone with Jack and you were not present I noticed a distinct change. A change that gave me cause for concern.

Jack recently wrote to inform me that the two of you have been lucky enough to return home on special assignment to promote recruitment into the Army here in Sussex. Whilst I am full of joy that you are returning home, I would, however very much like to speak to you alone. I am no good at these cloak and dagger letters and so very conscious at how it may appear to you or to Jack as I write it, which is why I must insist that it remain private. I can only hope that when I do see you, all will become clear.

Yours in gratitude
Helen Baker.

Sophie found herself captivated, so much so she had not noticed Buckland's head appear through the hatch. He could have been watching her for hours by the time she had noticed, so gripped by her mother's story.

'Tea?' he asked startling her. He was surprised by how switched off she had been with the real world. 'Whatever you are reading it must be good. I thought you had gone out!'

'My mother's diaries and letters. I found them up here when clearing her room.'

His eyebrows raised in curiosity and from his precarious perch on the ladder he slid a book over to himself. Sophie could see it had 1919 upon the spine. 'My mother was very secretive. She left no diaries or letters to help me piece together who she really was, not like your mother, it looks like everything you could ever want to know about her is here. Parents can be just as mysterious as a Sherlock Holmes classic you know.'

'I didn't think my mother kept any secrets, but now I am beginning to wonder. There is so much in here I never knew.'

'Because they are secrets, or because you never knew to ask?'

It was a valid point, one that she had been going over in her head since the discovery of the journals.

Postman's Knock
19th June 1941

Each postman's knock at the door was always a little nerve racking to hear and each letter that slid its way through the letterbox was always an anxious wait until it was opened and its contents were known. Today's was no exception and the postman's face shone round and rosy from the exertive length of the lane to April Cottage. He waved and then pushed the precious cargo through the door.

Buckland noticed that there was only one letter today and Sophie recognised Anthony's handwriting instantly. She tore away at the envelope with glee, settling herself down at the kitchen table in anticipation. Buckland watched her with interest. Her whole mannerism seemed to change before his eyes. He noticed that Sophie was more complex than he realised whilst being treated by her. She could be mature and at times quite distant. He wondered if she was doing this for a reason, to keep people away or at least at arm's length. He often wondered about these things, but as yet had not come to a satisfactory conclusion. Then there was the other side to her, the one he was seeing tear up an envelope with such unrestricted, almost childish enjoyment. One could be forgiven for thinking this was the first letter she had ever received. It was a very brief note rather than a letter, but its content bowled her over and she hugged it to her chest unable to contain her excitement and danced around the kitchen kissing the paper over and over again. Mrs Jenkins tried her best to step around her with the mop.

Buckland laughed at her behaviour, mostly because it was endearing. Sophie had been wearing a sour face for much of their time together. He worried that his presence was unwelcome sometimes and it had taken time for them to get their old original relationship back on track. He didn't know what was in the letter, he didn't need to know, her reaction told him everything and he was genuinely very happy for her.

'I am guessing then that my chances of running away with you are even slimmer than before?'

She threw her arms around him and kissed him on his cheek. Anthony had asked her to marry him and although she didn't know so, she sensed in his language that John had given his consent willingly. There was of course, no doubt about what her answer was going to be. She could hardly contain herself and immediately took herself off to work.

Buckland sighed as she shut the door behind her. He was truly pleased to see her so happy, but a small part of him perished inside. Ever since meeting her after his accident at sea and even though he knew she was taken for, he had begun to like her. Now those feelings had begun to question their own identity, to argue whether liking someone and loving someone were the same or very different. When did a fondness for someone become love? How did you know when you had transitioned from one to the other? He considered and pondered these thoughts, delaying his departure for some time.

'You alright there love?' Mrs Jenkins asked, her nose twitching into an expression of curiousness.

'Yes I'm fine, wasn't sure I had everything for a minute.'

'Not what I meant,' she walked out to him in the hallway. 'I meant are you alright with the news?'

He pretended he didn't know what she meant, but she was a crafty woman, whose powers of intuition even he had to marvel at.

'You know Mrs Jenkins, in Ancient Greece they would have placed you in a temple on top a mountain and people would have paid you large sums of money for your insights.'

'Or later than that I would have been burned at the stake,' she laughed. 'I don't need to be some divine oracle to know what's running through your mind.'

He smiled and gave her a playful kiss on the cheek before heading to the door and promising her he would be back before six.

Sophie danced upon the air all day at work. At times the matron had to tell her to get off her cloud, despite being happy with her news. There were times that she had to curb her own excitement. She couldn't wait to go and tell Uncle Richard and Joy. Perhaps because of this she found the day to drag on longer than it usually seemed to do.

So it was that her shift came to an end and she now left Bella who was more than capable of fending for herself by now. She was already planning what to write back that evening and repeated the draft of the letter to herself in her head over and over again. She toyed with the idea of simply sending a sheet of paper with 'YES' in big bold capital letters. Now she found herself tearing up to the Great Hall as fast as her feet would carry her, dashing under the 6 great grey archways of the cloister type frontage, flicking the boxwood topiary clipped trees and shrubs that lined it and almost crashing into the aged but solid Elizabethan timber oaked entrance hall door. She pulled the bell chord time and time again impatiently, deciding that this visit deserved a grand entrance rather than her usual entrance unannounced by the side door. The butler reticently opened the door after an obviously long walk from the kitchen and she barged through in the form of a whirlwind, simultaneously acknowledging his presence by saying, 'are they in?' and 'Oh good,' before he had a chance to utter a sound let alone the chance to announce her, the calling of 'Miss Sophie' fell on deaf ears as he spun around confounded.

She found Uncle Richard leaning against the sharp white carved stone mantelpiece of the Tudor fireplace that decorated the main living room. A fire crackled and burned brightly in a compact smouldering inferno. The last few days had been cold for June and very damp although it was a splendid summer day today and the sun beat warm glowing chards of light around the Sussex countryside, the Great Hall's high ceilings and solid stone walls tempered with red rustic bricks kept the warmth and light out, even on such glorious days as today. 'A splendid design,' her brother had always said, 'but it nips at your ankles! Would rather the gatehouse cottage any day, much cosier.' Joy was sitting at a writing desk with her hands clasped over her nose and they were both taken aback at Sophie's sudden arrival and outburst.

Sophie just couldn't get it all out quick enough, her news and enthusiasm for it gushing out all at once. All that she had to say overflowing with ecstasy, dates and ideas that had flurried through her thoughts on the way to the point that everything including the wedding was virtually planned by the time she had reached the Great Hall.

'So do you think then that we could hold it here at the Great Hall, just like you did? Obviously not the same as yours Joy, your wedding was the wedding to end all weddings, but it is the perfect setting, even though a much simpler affair' and she paused to take a breath.

With a fresh intake, Sophie reeled off again, only this time to be stopped in full flight unexpectedly by Joy who shouted, 'Sophie!' ear splittingly and earnestly. Sophie stopped immediately, startled at Joy's intense cry with the sense of dislike for her stopping the flooding of happiness like a burst dam. She glared indignantly at her for the dampening of her elation.

'Sophie,' Joy delicately started again, rising from her writing desk. She looked awkwardly towards her uncle. 'I think you should sit down. Richard and I have just received some very bad news.'

Before she knew it Joy was upon her guiding her to the chaise longue that ran parallel to the fireplace. Joy instructed Styles to order tea from the kitchen straight away and some brandy.

'Oh, I'm so dreadfully sorry; in my excitement, I never gave it a thought that….'

'Quite so, quite so,' Joy interrupted and cuddled her patiently. 'Its marvellous news, fabulous news Sophie and we are absolutely thrilled for you both. Anthony is a lucky man.' She looked back to Richard who remained standing by the fireplace. His posture was as rigid as a statue. 'Darling, perhaps you should…'

'Terrific lad that Anthony,' agreed Uncle Richard, but his tone was far from thrilled and for some time his eyes never left the fire. 'Both made for each other, haven't we always said that sweetheart?'

'We will do everything we can to help you organise your special day as and when your decisions are made my darling,' said Joy encouragingly. 'Richard?' she gestured at her husband.

Richard continued to stand still, it was then that Sophie noticed how red his eyes looked and how tired.

'I don't know what to say to you, Soph.' He sat down next to her and put his hand on hers and squeezed it tightly. That was when she knew. 'It's John.'

Her heart fell to the pit of her stomach. At first it didn't feel real, as if it was a performance being put on at the theatre, the great hall was the set and she had not learnt her lines. She tried to picture her brothers face to help herself cry, but couldn't. In desperation she scanned the room for the nearest photograph and spotted one of herself and John together at her uncle's wedding. It sat upon one of the corner shelves and she lifted herself from the chaise longue and went to the photo, picking the frame up and staring at him. Still no tears came and she got frustrated that her reactions were not what she knew they should be. John, her beloved brother was gone she told herself. It still didn't feel real and so she repeated it to herself, over and over again, forcing her soul to accept the truth. She gasped for breath and reeled in horror disbelieving the very thoughts that overwhelmed her perfect world, shattering, toppling and crashing from her dizzy heights of a few moments ago.

'Oh Sophie, I'm so very sorry, we've only just received the telegram ourselves this morning.'

She wished one of them would cry, in a hope it might bring her hidden tears to the surface, people often cried when others were doing so, she had never been able to understand why, but it was what tended to happen. Looking to her uncle she could sense he had done his crying already.

'I thought today was the happiest day of my life, this isn't right,' she suddenly pulled herself together for a brief moment. 'Why? How did you get the telegram first and not me?'

'Well,' explained Uncle Richard, searching into Joy's face for a little more moral support. 'Just before John left for Egypt two years ago he came up to the house a couple of weeks before. He was concerned that if anything did happen to him, that in the event of his death the news would come here first. He didn't want you to be at home all alone if you received the news.' Then stammering nervously in anticipation of a bad reaction he continued, 'he was only thinking of your welfare Sophie, he did what he thought was best at the time for all eventualities.'

'Because he loved you,' Joy finished for him.

Sophie collapsed into the corner armchair. 'How did he?'

'We don't know much, the information is brief and not very detailed.'

Then her mind jumped to the next worst case scenario. 'And the others?' she demanded.

'The others?' Richard questioned. 'What others?'

'Tom, Captain James and…' then her heart completely collapsed and beside herself with hopelessness she softly whispered 'and my Anthony?'

Joy sat down beside Sophie, rubbing her back. 'Hey, hey I'm sure that everyone else is fine, they'll all have muddled through somehow. Your uncle only has so much information and I am sure they are fine.'

'But not John, why not John? What if they are all gone? What if they were all together at the time?' she wailed on a second wind of emotion, this time with more anger. With so many she cared for it seemed inevitable that she would one day hear some news or open a letter that would bear bad news, so far she had managed to get away with it, but not today and not John, her loving, adoring, passionate, fretful, protective brother. It felt like he had abandoned her, not deliberately of course, but that was how she felt now. They were all her family, she loved and cared for them all.

Styles the butler brought in the tea and brandy. Joy took the tray laid it on her writing desk and started to pour.

'Tea, Sophie with a dash of brandy, it will help,' she replied.

'No thank you, I'm going home, I've got things to do and preparations to make,' she said with a stiff upper lip.

'Don't you think that you should leave the preparations for the wedding for a little while?' asked Richard meekly.

'Oh God and those as well,' she said sniffing. 'But I didn't mean those.'

'What preparations are you talking about then?' queried Joy.

'For when John comes home, the funeral arrangements,' she said surprised that they weren't on the same wavelength and hadn't suggested it as a matter of course.

'Sophie,' Uncle Richard said tenderly. 'I think you better stay here, I think you are in shock.' She gave him a confused glare and he too slumped into a chair. 'John's body won't be coming home. That's not how it works.'

'But he's an officer, I want him home, here with me, with Mum. Tom won't leave him there, he never would, I know it,' she flapped hysterically.

It made perfect sense to her, that was how it should be. She couldn't stomach the thought of it any other way. In her head she could see a little wooden cross in the middle of the vast bareness of the desert. It was crowned with a tin helmet, its chin strap broken or torn flapping in the wind. Slowly the sand began to entomb it, his name slowly devoured by a dune until eventually it was gone forever, forgotten.

'It isn't up to Sergeant Major Hill and they are miles and miles away, the heat, the conditions, Sophie… Sweetheart….be realistic... It just can't be done. I'm so, so, sorry, but its war,' he nurtured.

'It stinks,' she deplored.

'Look, do me a favour and come and stay here. Lieutenant Buckland and Mrs Jenkins will keep the cottage ticking over. I'll telephone the hospital and sort that out for you and telephone Mrs Jenkins to let her know. Come and stay with your old Uncle Richard just for a few days or at least until we get some more information, I could certainly do with the company.'

Joy was nodding fervently in agreement. Trying to hold her own emotions back at Sophie's desperation.

'Can you find out about the others from the ministry with your connections do you think? And Anthony of course, Uncle Richard?'

'I will try, but there are only so many strings I can pull.'

'I don't know what I'm going to do if I've lost him too.'

'I'm sure your Uncle Richard can pull a few strings,' said Joy encouragingly. 'Now then, how about that cup of tea? I think we all need one on this terrible, terrible day.'

Joy was clearly relieved, it became clear later just how much she had been fearing Sophie's reaction, as anyone would. It appeared for now that the worst of the news was broken. Sophie admired how Joy, who was evidently holding back the lump in her throat, was strong enough to bear such sorrows and worries like these with dignity and calm for herself and her uncle. But what if she was wrong? It was war and it was unpredictable pain on a scale none had felt before. A dark fear began to overwhelm Sophie. No matter how prepared she thought Joy's head and heart would be, it might never be armoured enough. There was no doubt that amidst the hurt over John, she wondered about her own daughter. Sophie had forgotten in the midst of her suffering that she was not alone in her torment and it was now that she suddenly remembered that Uncle Richard had lost a nephew also. She held him tight whilst he still remained by the fireplace. He trembled a little and she felt his rigid frame begin to wither until slowly he slumped down to his knees, neither of them cried physically and Sophie knew that he shared the same confused pain she did from within.

An Angel
19th June - Sidi Barrani 1941

'Captain Baker? Captain Baker, can you hear me?'

The voice was sweet and comforting, a woman's voice; John could hear it through the darkness, its warmth penetrating through.

'Captain Baker?'

His voice was crying out into the darkness, trying to answer but it never seemed to get far enough to reach the voice that was calling his name. It echoed around in the darkness he was in, a room perhaps, but there were no doors, no walls and no windows. How then could he get out and how was the angelic voice getting in?

'There are no doors,' he found himself saying to himself and miraculously he received a response.

'There are no doors because there aren't any. Come on now Captain, all you have to do is open your eyes.'

'If I open my eyes what will I see?' he asked, but there was no reply.

Confused in the blackness, he didn't know how to open his eyes, he thought that he already had them open and then as if by magic a bright light pierced into the darkness stinging and burning.

He blinked and blinked again as the light burst through with an amazing amount of brilliance. When everything came into focus all that was left in the picture that he held was the face of an angel. At least he assumed it was an Angel, in the mixed-up state that he now found himself in he was willing to believe anything.

Her face looked down at him and when she saw that his eyes were open and responding to her, she smiled. At that moment there was nothing more heavenly to John than that smile, a very familiar smile. Her eyes were a stirring deep azure blue. Her hair was tied back, emphasising a delicate pair of small ears and a small honey blonde ringlet of hair fell down the side of her right eye accentuating its colour.

'There you are, Captain Baker, welcome back.'

'Are you an Angel?' he said feeling his inanimate body stirring when only moments ago it was dormant.

'Not since the last time I looked! But I'll take it as a compliment,' she laughed gently.

With the substance of his anatomy being energised, courtesy of the saline and dextrose intravenous drip that was delivering the fluids his body desperately needed to rehydrate, he was recalling the Italian field hospital. He remembered the violent shells falling around it and Corporal Orchard.

'I'm alive?'

'Every bit of you,' she confirmed, tugging and tucking at his sheets along the edge of his bed. His smelling sense was aroused by the scent of the fresh linen and antiseptic. 'Do you want to try and sit up? Perhaps not, one step at a time eh?'

'Am I badly wounded?'

'Nothing we can't fix,' she expressed tenderly.

By now John had realised that he must have been wounded in the attack on the ridge and that he was in a hospital. The angelic sister who still stood above him spoke perfect English, but was this an Italian hospital? He remembered Simon telling him whilst in a daze that he would get him to a hospital and this must have been it.

'Is this an Italian hospital?' he asked trying to focus further on from her looking for clues.

'Oh dear, we are a bit muddled still aren't we?' she teased as she glided up towards him with a thermometer which was bulldozed under his tongue to register his body temperature upon waking. She read it, flicked it very efficiently and then scanned it again, she then shrugged her shoulders, went to the bottom of his bed, pulled up the board with his details on and marked the result with a dot on the graph paper, drawing a line from the previous reading to the current one. Then she looked up at him and said, 'I suppose it will have to do, but tomorrow Captain James will want to see some improvement.'

Wagging her finger at him, the sister approached his side and called another nurse over to help her pull John up, each taking an arm, they lifted him punching and prodding and puffing up his pillows behind, before setting him back down. The two nurses pulled the sheets up around his chest so he would be more comfortable and tucked him in. She waved her hand across his eye line.

'How's that Captain Baker? You're looking a bit more with it now, it's the remnants of morphine but it helps to ease the pain. Now in answer to your question, you see you thought I had forgotten, this is a British hospital and you're in the officer's wing; you're in Sidi Barrani.'

Around him, other wounded men sat in beds. Some asleep, some awake and either talking to each other or reading newspapers.

'Simon!' he said alarmed, remembering that he had not been alone whilst at the dirty, blood-soaked aid station. 'Captain James where is he?'

'He's doing the rounds,' she reassured him, 'but he'll be back with a vengeance if there's no improvement. So let's get some fluids into you as soon as possible and a nice cup of tea to get you on the mend.'

There was a real déjà vu about that last statement, it rang a bell he thought and come to think of it so did her face. She reminded him of someone and he couldn't think who, perhaps it would come to him with time.

'Do we know each other?' he asked very genuinely. 'You look familiar, or is it déjà vu?'

'Oh, they all say that,' she chirped quirkily. 'That's an old one, you'll have to do better than that to get my attention. Just sticking to Sister will do just fine.'

'No, I was serious,' said John feeling slightly aggrieved at her remark.

She saw the hurt in his expression and retracting a little she said sitting down on his bed and holding his hand, 'you know the brain plays funny tricks on our thoughts and senses when it is battling to surface from shock and pain. This déjà vu you are experiencing is a syndrome known as or paramnesia, it's the experience of feeling sure that one has witnessed, or experienced a new situation previously, as though an event has already happened, or has happened in the recent past. For instance, seeing me as an angel when you first woke up, although the exact circumstances of the previous encounter are uncertain, this may result from an overlap between the neurological systems responsible for short-term memory…'

John watched as a grin began to spread across her face as she continued to describe more medical terms that she knew were well and truly going over his head. She had made her point to him as she came to the conclusion of her lecture. '…and hey presto déjà vu. If I had a sixpence for every time I had to explain it.'

'Of course,' said John sighing foolishly.

'Now, it wouldn't surprise me if Captain James will be back soon, he went off out about an hour ago, he must be pretty tired himself, he's not left the hospital since you all arrived. He has been checking on you every moment he can, cat napping in between patients and helping out with surgery. You two have been through quite an ordeal I should say, so rest up and try and relax, you're in safe hands for the time being,' she patted his hand reassuringly and eased herself up to go about her duties.

'Thank you, Sister,' he said.

'Don't thank me, Captain Baker, my role is purely pastoral here, Captain James was the cavalry,' she said irrefutably with admiration and strode off in the direction of the nurse's station. 'He really has been an absolute blessing these past few days.'

And that would be about right, thought John; the magician had been weaving his magic again. He closed his eyes willingly this time, confident that her words were her bond and that he was indeed in safe hands for the time being.

He tossed and turned in his sleep, thinking that he was still half awake when in reality he had been slumbering for almost an hour. Somewhere down the corridor a metal instrument bowl crashed to the floor from a trolley waking him with a panic-stricken start.

'Thank you for that nurse, give them all heart attacks why don't you,' Simon muttered under his breath. He stood at the foot of John's bed reading his bedside notes, checking everything was as it should be before taking himself to a spare bed he had got lined up. 'In fact, why not wake the whole bloody ward just as I was going to get some zeds myself! Hey there old chap, wakey, wakey. Have a good doze did you?'

John stirred, grumbling and groaning intermittently for the unusually early and unexpected alarm call. At the very best he had been lucky to get through a night without some kind of drama going on, in the very least it would be someone driving the cows home with their snoring and at the very worst it would be the screams of night sweats and shell shock recollections.

'Hi, Simon,' John said thankfully.

'You're looking better with a bit of colour in your cheeks, I see you've got the baby dragon looking after you then?' he chuckled.

John looked at him inquisitively, 'baby dragon?'

'Sister Hall, well she's a Matron in civvies in actual fact, but her volunteered rank here is Sister hence the title baby dragon. Still, a good looker though eh?' quipped Simon. 'Tough as old boots, she'll have you up and about before you can say Tom, Dick or Harry! No nonsense with that one, that's why she's in the officer's ward.'

'She seemed ......very ......angelic to me,' said John quite innocently and surprised at Simon's rebuff of her.

'Hah,' he cried. 'Don't let the pretty smile and saintly look fool you. Once she's got her teeth into you, she doesn't let go. She's a tiger!' and he clawed his fingers through the air and made a roaring sound.

John looked at him quite amazed, pushing himself back into his pillows as the imaginary claw came closer. 'What happened?'

He couldn't remember waking at any other stage, as far as John was concerned this was the first time his eyes had opened under their own free will since seeing what he thought was an angel and now hankered for the cup of tea that was mentioned earlier. Simon could see he needed the cool touch of water and poured him a glass from the jug on his bedside cabinet.

'What's wrong with me?' he asked probing for more information and just as he did he felt a jolting pain in his right thigh. He stiffened to try and take the pain, but it was unbearable, shooting up the whole length of his body. His hand clutched at the source, but Simon pulled it away.

'Don't touch it if you can, it's freshly dressed and it's quite tight for very good reasons.'

'Jesus that hurts, what's happened to my leg?'

The pain was bringing all his senses back to normal. All sorts of horrific thoughts then suddenly flooded through his mind, the worse one being that he had lost his leg or both legs completely and looking down and seeing both his feet protruding from under the sheets, he breathed a sigh of relief just as the pain ebbed away.

'Morphine wearing off now I expect,' Simon nodded to John's right leg. He passed him a glass of water. 'You were hit in the thigh, the lower part of your left leg and have a nasty bit of concussion. It's going to be okay, you haven't lost your leg and neither are you going to, but your thigh was a nasty sight, it was a bit of a task to stop the bleeding. Should have really had a transfusion, but, well, you know, lack of facilities, scene of the crime and what not! So we need to keep an eye out for a while. Today's a great improvement though.'

John sipped at his water carefully, it felt fresh and cool and he gulped at it thirstily, his hands still shaking and causing him to miss sometimes in his desperation, some even dribbled down his chin. Simon passed him a muslin square.

'So you've been performing miracles again then?' John said in between mouthfuls.

'Not this time,' said Simon sadly, he bowed his head sorrowfully. 'If I was a miracle worker I would have saved more. Doing my bit here is a kind of penance if you like.'

'I'd better do as the baby dragon says then and get myself on the mend. How long will it take to get back to the unit?'

'How long's a piece of string?' quizzed Simon back.

'That bad, eh?' said John disappointedly. 'I can remember certain things, but can't decide if my memories are real or not. I have only just opened my eyes after what feels like good long sleep, but apparently, I have been in and out of consciousness for a couple of days here.

I remember running towards a barbed wire fence, some Italian machine gun fire and that's it at the moment, oh and Corporal Orchard,' he groaned remorsefully.

'Don't worry about that now, just resting is the best thing for the time being; and that's what the doctor orders! It will all come back when you're ready.'

'Simon?' John cried out, his body suddenly took on a mind of its own telling him that he was in serious pain, shaking uncontrollably as if in a fit.

Simon bawled for a nurse and three came running down the ward corridor including Sister Hall. John was coming out of shock, he was reaching profusely and he ached all over as if in a fever. They cooled him down and soothed his brow calling gently and then as quickly as his body had started its raging, it stopped and was calm again.

Simon saw the alarm in his face and tried to assure him saying, 'normal reaction' and instructed Sister Hall to bring a mild sedative.

'Sorry Sister, don't know what came over me,' John apologised, slightly embarrassed as she returned with a bowl and syringe that she handed to Simon, informing him that his camp bed was turned down for him, then scuttled away blushing from his warm thank you, not even noticing John's attempted apology.

John couldn't recollect how, why or what had happened. He hated not knowing. He hated this incapacity. He hated this vulnerability and his impatience and frustration were erupting, 'Simon I need to know now, what if I don't wake up tomorrow. I am accountable for so many things, I need peace.'

'One, you're not accountable for anything, we all do what we think is right at the time, we follow orders, John, that is the code of practice. Two, you are not going anywhere, they'll need a bigger bullet to write your name on and anyway they can't spell in the Kings English this side of the line anyway, so you'll be fine,' he cajoled.

Simon was tired, it had been a very long week for him, he was desperate for a cat nap or two himself and didn't particularly want to relive and account for the recent events right now. In his profession he had attained the knack of being able to brush this type of thing away until really needed to be recalled to the surface again and to get on with the tasks at hand in the field. John, however, wore his heart on his sleeve and took things more personally. He needed to resolve his issues and close each door before opening another. Simon knew this of course and reluctantly started the proceedings of recollection.

'Do you remember the attack on the ridge?' he asked John as gently as possible.

John nodded. I remember most of it, I think. Did we take it?'

'Yes and no,' Simon replied. He cleared his throat before proceeding and leaned his elbow on the side table. 'We lost Anthony, John, do you remember?'

John remembered. It wasn't a sudden memory; it slowly developed like a negative from the darkness into the light, like a developed photograph.

'Does Sophie know?'

'By now? I should think so,' was Simon's reply.

'Poor Sophie,' remarked John. 'It will take a lot of explaining.'

The scene then came flooding back as his blood surged through his veins again, heating his torso. It filled his mind as vividly as if it were being played out in front of him on a cinema screen. He could see himself approaching the tank and as he swept around it there was Anthony lying on the ground.

Only moments ago he had felt far away from reality, but now he was there again. He managed to hold back his emotions at the vision in his mind, the sorrow in Anthony's eyes as he realised his fate was sealed and life's precious thread that had been severed by deaths scissors.

His voice croaked as he replied, 'I remember, I did all I could to keep him out of the danger, for her. She loved him, but he was a soldier, he wanted to fight, that's why we are all here at the end of the day. He thought I was an asshole and punishing him because I didn't like him and that I thought he wasn't good enough. That wasn't really the way it was.'

'I know John; we all knew what you were trying to do,' Simon continued. 'You took First Platoon into the attack after he died, but on the way to the wire you were hit by a mortar. Jesus, John I thought you were directly on your way to St Peter the way you flew into the air.'

'That's how I got this pain in my leg is it?' he asked looking down at his thigh. A part of him longed to see the damage under the bandage, to see just how serious it was, but another part, like avoiding the unwanted mail at the door thought it best not too.

'You had a chunk of shrapnel go into your thigh and a smaller piece into your other leg. I can only assume that the enormous gash on your head was from debris or from where you fell. Inevitable that you'll have memory problems at first and you might encounter some visionary distortion at some point, but it will all be a bit like swings and roundabouts for you, just for a while.'

John adjusted himself to get more comfortable as a syringe pricked and burnt on entry to his vein.

'What happened after the mortar?'

'Well, I thought you were dead at first, I didn't even run over to you because I couldn't believe that anyone could have survived such a direct hit or the blast, but you had. Unconscious and losing a lot of blood, the veins in your leg were pretty severed. Looking back the whole bloody situation was difficult with casualties in every direction and no time to prioritise.'

'What about the men?' John asked. 'What happened to my company?'

'There was a counterattack,' Simon answered and in his mind he could see the whole drama unfolding again, his thoughts jettisoning him back to the battle scene, even to the sensation of the prickling heat of the sun and the cold sweat dripping down his back. He didn't want to go back there, but for John's fractured memory that was where he was now.

John lay on the floor, his life ebbing away as every beat of his heart rhythmically pumped his blood from the gaping wound in his thigh. Simon needed to stem the blood flow. He couldn't carry the Captain far on his own amidst all the chaos and there were no stretcher bearers in sight. There was no cover here either. They were vulnerable and open to the heavy fire coming from the ridge. Simon looked around for help. To his right not far from the trackless Crusader tank he could see a smouldering corpse; the large radio on its back gave its identity away as Lance Corporal Lewis. His heart sank.

Shells were raining down around him leaving more gaping craters everywhere. Past the ever-present thuds and thumps of mortars and shrieking artillery he noticed that he was completely alone. He couldn't see a single man alive, even the mortar crews who had brought up the rear had vanished and there wasn't a wounded man in sight who could lend a hand. Only the dead or dying were present, littered across the cratered landscape with scattered remnants of uniformed material flickering in the breeze. Once smart uniforms worn with pride and polished boots that had marched their way through hell and high water had been ripped from the torso of the wearer and discarded randomly by the fury of battle.

He ignored the isolation and fought frantically to keep the blood at bay. A huge shard of jagged metal, razor-sharp where it had been ripped away from the blast was dug firmly into John's thigh. He could have pulled it out to stop an infection starting, but even in the hazy conditions he knew that the profuse bleeding was probably an artery cut and time and circumstance were against them both now. Removing it would only worsen the situation, he would bleed to death even quicker than he was already, so he packed whole bandages in the wound around the worst parts and then applied a dressing over the top.

Within seconds the blood began seeping through the first dressing and then was covered with sand that seemed to fill the air from the continuing explosions around them. He applied another dressing, tying it as tight as he dared. If the blood seeped through this one he would have to consider making a tourniquet and cutting off the supply completely which meant he would lose his leg, but he was unlikely to make it anyway at this rate. John's breathing was becoming shallower and again a speck of red appeared through the gauze.

'Damn it,' Simon cried. He was sure he had secured it enough, but just as he was about to start a tourniquet it seemed that the seepage seemed to be slowing. He decided to wait for a minute. Time seemed to stand still for that minute but it was clear that the two shell dressings might just have been enough to hold it for the moment.

Now the only problem that remained was how to get John to an aid station. None of the command section apart from the now smouldering radio operator had been with John during First Platoons dash to the wire. Tom had carried on behind second platoon and Orchard and Scott along with him. He had to act and fast, John needed medical attention urgently, Simon had done all that he could. John's breathing and the fact that he was not awake was a very bad sign.

He was now endangering his own life and the chance to save other lives for the sake of one, it was above and beyond his duty and capability to get John to help and safety and he knew it. John would have been the first to have reminded him of that, once everything that could have been done had been done. Take Anthony for instance. There were more casualties that needed his medical expertise who stood more of a chance and his common sense was kicking at his heels telling him to get out and get back, but there wasn't anywhere he could leave him safely and for the very first time in his medical career, he let his heart rule his head.

He grabbed John under his arm and tried to lift him over his shoulder, but the adrenaline that had served him so well during the battle had left him now, draining his body of the heroism and strength that feeds so many soldiers in the heat of the moment. John was literally dead weight.

Simon ripped off his webbing that still clung defiantly to his body in order to lose some extra weight. He tried again to pick him up but only succeeded a few feet before lowering him back to the floor. He became distraught and overwrought, but all he could do was sit down next to John and wait for his body to recover a little.

A bullet pinged across the floor next to him, kicking up a small cloud of dust; soon it was followed by another. Fuelled by frustration and anger with his Red Cross armband clearly visible, he stood up and turned ready to curse at the sniper that was taking the shots and if this was where he was going to die so be it, but he would look him in the eye.

He expected to see the abandoned ridge, the scars of the battle that had swept up along its slopes and the bodies of the men who had been killed in its capture. Instead, he saw what remained of the company running towards him in headlong retreat.

Every so often the men would stop and fire back at the enemy to keep them at bay, leapfrogging their way back to where they had come from. At least thirty men were heading towards him and one of them ran over to where Simon was standing next to John's body.

'Sir, are you alright?'

In his exhaustion Simon could only nod at the young private, but soon his words were active again. 'I need a hand, the Captain is down, quick help me carry him.'

'Captain Baker?' the private asked astonished. 'We thought he was with us over there.'

'Hurry up!' Simon pleaded.

The men began to dash past, their rifles and Bren's blazing back at the ridge. Either side they pulled John's arms up around their shoulders, dragging his flailing feet behind them towards the rear of the British lines. The effort was immense and the whole time Simon was constantly scanning the horizon for the signs of a stretcher that may have been left on the battlefield. His own Medics had been nowhere to be seen since they left their fox holes in the early stages of the assault and so he hoped they may have been delayed and were somewhere just ahead, but as time went on only empty desert presented itself.

Minutes past and they were being left behind, their energy slowly fading. Some of the riflemen gallantly tried to stick by Simon's side. They returned fire back at the enemy trying to give them cover, but caught out in the open casualties were mounting, comrades being dragged away by other comrades, limping and staggering, Simon couldn't keep stopping to tend to them all.

'Go!' he roared pointing back towards the rear 'Just go! Save yourselves!'

Out of nowhere came Corporal Orchard, who seeing Simon and the young private's plight also screamed at the straggling soldiers, encouraging them to keep moving and fall back as he took charge. 'Move lads, move! Find some cover, hurry!' Orchard then looked towards Simon and as soon as he saw who he was carrying with the help of the young and pale private he intervened. He grabbed the other side of his Captain, putting his left arm around his back whilst his right supported the underneath of his wounded right leg. In the process, he pushed the private away telling him to get a move on. 'Go on, get out of here, I'll carry my Captain.'

The sight of Orchard rejuvenated Simon, he wanted to ask where Tom was, but there was no time and no energy.

Sweat poured down their faces, stinging their eyes and driving their eyes to blink spasmodically. All the time the high pitched whistle and wheezes of bullets flew past, flicking the ground, pinging and cracking as they split small rocks into yet smaller stones.

It wasn't long before they were alone again, the straggling riflemen had disappeared into the distant haze up ahead, but neither of them, no matter how exhausted stopped. Simon couldn't let exhaustion get a grip; he couldn't let his friend down now when they had come so far.

To Orchard, the fading Captain meant a great deal. Simon knew that John had been an inspiration to him, encouraging him and always making time for him. He partook in his occasional playfulness willingly, John had not only been a friend but a mentor and role model. As a soldier, Orchard was everything he was because of John. When nobody else would take the cheeky Corporal as a batman, it was John that gave him his first real break and from then the young Corporal had been nothing but loyal.

'I see it as a great honour to have you as part of the Company command section,' John had once said to him. Simon was present that bright sunny day in England. 'I have been watching you in training Lance Corporal Orchard and have handpicked you to join my command section, will you accept?' Orchard couldn't have refused, if anything it was he who was most honoured. 'Good, you'll be promoted to Corporal. Report to me first thing in the morning,' John had said.

Orchard had been so proud to gain one stripe, but to be handpicked and given another, he couldn't have picked another moment from his life where he was more proud. The Captain had always made him feel valued and always knew what to say in a crisis, John's love of his silly humour was also a bonus. Orchard had never forgotten what John had said the night they left Newhaven.

'You promised you would do all you could to get everyone home,' Orchard now panted and at first Simon thought he was talking to him. 'That night on the boat, do you remember Sir? And I promised I would help you.'

Simon knew as the Corporal did that the likelihood was waning with every minute that they remained out here in the open. John was fading fast, but now the Corporal, continuing to huff and puff the vow he had made, pushed up a quicker pace. Simon marvelled at his strength and at his loyalty, like a son carrying a father. It tugged at his heart.

Another bullet cracked past.

'Come on Sir,' he said heartily through harsh deep wheezy breaths. 'You owe me a pint anyway and we need you! You're gonna get us home remember? Besides, you've got the map!' he glanced across to Simon winking, 'nearly there Captain James, hope that Red Cross guarantees us safe passage home if they catch us up and isn't a ruddy target from these ruddy shit snipers!'

Suddenly the weight fell to one side and John's body fell into a heap on top of Orchard. Simon struggled to carefully, like a delicate antique carpet, roll Johns heavy body off the Corporal and it was then that his worse fears came to light. Orchard lay on his front in an untidy bundle on the floor. A red patch growing bigger by the second was in the centre of his back and a pool of dark crimson blood was creeping out from under his chest. The bullet had struck through the centre of his spine and passed through to the front of his body.

It wasn't the way in which Orchard had been killed that fascinated Simon. It was the peaceful smile and reluctant gaze of comeuppance that he had upon his face as if he knew his last remark had ironically caught up with him and his life had ended with supersonic speed. There was nothing he could do; Simon could see he was dead, killed outright by the well placed and considerate shot of a ruddy shit sniper.

The loss of the Corporal made him look behind him and only a few yards away Italian soldiers, some with their tell-tale cockerel feathers swaying upon their helmets were approaching. Their rifles were pointed menacingly at him and the bayonets although small, flashed in the glimmering sun.

The shelling had lifted and was now pounding the retreating company further away. Finally like cautious cats the Italians reached to where Simon was sitting with his hands in the air. Perhaps this was for the best, John was not in good shape and although the bleeding seemed to be holding, Simon could only guess how much longer it would be before his condition became worse.

Behind the Italians, a small group of armoured cars appeared from out of the dust and behind them a pair of small tanks. It dawned on Simon that the ridge had been more heavily defended than had first appeared and that a motorized unit had lain hidden behind it. John's Company and Major Love's battalion had run straight into a trap.

He wasn't afraid of the soldiers that stood rifles at the ready only a few feet away. He hoped that Orchard's infamous words of Red Cross and safe passage would come into play, after all, he was still alive and the Italians were not known for brutality. The first soldier began to say something, but Simon didn't know any Italian. He shrugged to show he didn't understand and in response the soldier ran off towards one of the armoured cars.

He had time now to check on John. He was still unconscious but breathing slowly. In all the stress of trying to reach a safe area, his leg had begun to bleed again. He pointed at his medical pack to the soldiers in front of him and then pretended to dab John's face and looked at them questioningly. One of the soldiers understood the charade and helped to open the pack, nodding towards John. Simon pointed to the spare bottle of water and the Italian passed it to him to allow Simon to carefully sprinkle some of the cool liquid onto John's face and around his lips. He stirred but didn't wake.

From one of the armoured cars an officer, his proud feathers flailing in the gentle breeze that had begun to kick up approached. 'Good morning British officer,' he called stopping a few feet away. 'Your pistols please?'

Simon got to his feet and cautiously removed his webbing belt which held his revolver. 'We have them for self-defence,' he said, handing it to the Italian Officer who in return saluted smartly.

'You have nothing to fear from me Capitano,' he said in a thick Italian accent, he removed the bullets from Simon's revolver and handed it back to him. 'I am Lieutenant Moretti of the 7th Bersaglieri.'

'And I am Captain James of the Royal Army Medical Corps, attached to…'

'I have radioed for a…' he paused uncertain of the word and pointed to John hoping it would help Simon understand better.

'Stretcher?'

The Italian officer suddenly remembered the word with a smile and triumphantly said, 'Ambulance! I have radioed for an ambulance, but your man here does not look good,' he then looked over Orchard and pointed. 'And this one?'

'Too late,' said Simon sadly.

'Ah yes, the shot, it was perfetto, no?' he nodded, knowingly looking down at the tell-tale signs on Corporal Orchards back. 'Perfecto or is it perfect? My English is not a very good.'

'Not the words I would use,' smarted Simon, feeling that it probably was a merciful shot. 'A terrible waste in my opinion of a good soldier.'

He had to hold back his anger, only moments ago Orchard had been shooting at them. He was also selfishly grateful, knowing it could have been him. Armband or no armband, one of them had to be taken down and Corporal Orchard's words as in life had tempted his own fate.

Lieutenant Moretti knelt down next to John, 'A brave man, was he in command?' Simon nodded. 'Very brave, we will look after him if we can, you must come too. I was very surprised why you attack here,' he pronounced, flicking his pistol all around him.

'We follow orders, the same as you,' he checked his leg.

'Si, I understand this Capitano, but you had not enough soldiers, it was very brave, but how do you say…stupid?'

Simon couldn't really argue with that, all wars were stupid. He watched the Italian Lieutenant kneel down again and take a closer look at his enemy as if he had never seen a British Officer before. He appeared fascinated and whispering something to himself or to John, it was difficult for Simon to tell.

'He needs more water me thinks,' Moretti said and taking his own water bottle he gently wetted John's lips. He looked over his body to Simon and in a respectful tone whispered, 'It may be too late for him now.'

'If we are going to an aid station straight away and I can treat his wounds properly, he will be fine. There is not too much damage, but I need proper surgical instruments, do you understand?'

'We will get him to Fort Capuzzo,' and true as his word an ambulance rambled over the dune and before he knew it they were all being loaded on.

The Lieutenant ran back to his armoured car and with a crackle of its engine it lunged forward. He sat as straight as a proud Roman pillar from the top of the turret and as he passed called out to Simon, 'Good luck Capitano, tell him when he wake up, that he is a brave man.'

John sipped a little more of his glass of water, as Simon slumped back into his chair, the ordeal of storytelling over.

The whole bloody thing was so surreal, Simon told him. John was intrigued but also tired, forcing his eyes to stay open as the sedative took hold.

'They took us back to the aid station, not to Fort Capuzzo, we never got that far and they were kind enough to load some of the other bodies onto the Ambulance to be buried. That's when you came to, I think. They were good to us and kept their word.'

'I think I can remember the aid station,' John yawned; he could remember seeing Orchard's peaceful face staring at him. 'Good old Orchard,' he said quietly.

'I buried Orchard at the aid station and three others,' Simon said reaching for John's arm and taking his pulse. 'I kept their tags and pay books.'

Simon told him the names of the fallen, but no matter how much he tried John just couldn't see their faces, even when he closed his eyes tightly.

'My Company, what happened to Tom, Sergeant Scott and the others?', said John suddenly flickering into life again with panic in his voice.

'It's alright, stay calm,' the doctor said reassuring his patient. 'That's why I wasn't here when you woke up. For two days I have been either helping out around here or trying to find where the company is and it turns out they were pulled off the line yesterday, they're here in Barrani and will be here for a few weeks. Apparently, the battalion and several others are being pulled back to Alex.'

'And the Sergeant Major? Is Tom okay?' John asked with concern.

'He's fine and Sergeant Scott too. I spoke to Tom on the telephone and now he knows you're here, he said he will be here as soon as he can.'

The relief was immense as if a ten-tonne weight had been lifted from his shoulders. Losing Tom would have been like losing a father.

'There's one more thing,' Simon said with a concerning tone. 'Promise me you will stay calm when I tell you? Alright then, you've been posted as killed in action, in fact, we both have.'

'What!' suddenly John's thoughts were back to Sophie, what would she do when she found out her brother had been killed and at the same time find out about Anthony? 'Sophie needs to be told that I am okay.'

'It's alright John, Tom will have dealt with everything by now. When I spoke to him on the telephone earlier he said he would let all the appropriate authorities know. When he could, he would be straight over here. For the past two days, everybody had assumed we were either dead or captured.'

'Jesus Simon you don't know what she will do when she finds out!' John began to panic. He remembered his sister's agony at their mother's death and then there was her father, a topic avoided at all costs. He feared she might do something stupid at the loss of both Anthony and her brother.

'Calm down, there's nothing you can do, the right man is dealing with it,' Simon explained almost holding him down in the bed. 'It was just a simple mistake, we were stuck behind enemy lines for nearly two days and nobody thought you would come out alive, including me. There were a lot of soldiers who saw what happened to you and assumed the worst.

Even I have been posted as missing. I promise you Tom will take care of everything. Sophie will be fine. I am sure she won't do anything silly she's a sensible mature woman now. Remember it's been a while since we have been home and things and people change. Besides she has your uncle there, so she is hardly alone.'

He sounded like Tom, John thought. The only calming factor for John was not Simon's words, but the fact that he knew that Tom would indeed take care of everything. Tom always knew what to do, he always did. Even by now he imaged a telegram being sent to Uncle Richard.

'Still awake?' accused Sister Hall towards Simon. 'Determined not to sleep then or are you keeping him up? You both need rest, especially you Captain Baker, I am really surprised the sedative hasn't kicked in yet. You're all so keen to get back to the fighting or compare notes. I don't know what it is with you officers.

Now then Captain James, I really must insist that you get off to bed, as I told you earlier, your camp bed awaits, or if you are staying to assist there is a spare bed at the end of the corridor. Look sharp about it now or you'll be good for nothing tomorrow tired!'

Winking at John he saluted her and responded with, 'yes Sister, goodnight!' and off he strode, most likely secretly relieved that he had been sent to bed.

'Your trouble,' she said, whipping the curtains closed around his bed and brushing down the bed where Simon had been sitting. 'You're all too busy being heroes to take a little time off and appreciate it when it occurs, either naturally or forced upon you. Had you thought about it that way? There's still a lot of mending to be done in that heroic form of yours, you are still in a serious condition, so you're not going anywhere until that thigh has healed. So let's all get some rest from the war tonight Captain Baker before I come back with a stronger sedative!'

Her eyes were captivating and her smile was very arousing, he smiled to himself at Simon's baby dragon remark.

'And you can wipe that silly grin off your face as well, this is no laughing matter,' she said crossly. 'I don't lose patients on my ward and I don't intend to start with you.'

'No sister,' he said now putty in her hands. She looked really beautiful when she was angry. Her eyes shone, the passion of her vocation emulating through. She was quite possibly the most beautiful woman he had ever seen. She made him feel warm, safe and comfortable in her presence and he was entranced. 'You look beautiful when you're angry,' John sighed saying his thoughts out loud without even realising it.

'Well let me tell you, Captain Baker, unless those eyes are shut within two minutes they'll be blacker tomorrow than they are today. Goodnight!' she threatened and yanked closed the last part of the curtain. If it had been a door it would have slammed and fallen off its hinges.

'Wow,' he said hanging on every bit of the worded whirlwind and then presuming she had gone he added to himself, 'I think I'm in love!'

But Sister Hall hadn't gone and hearing the latter she smiled. She wiggled herself down, straightening her uniform to hug her slender figure, repositioned her hat and blushing fully at his accidental flattery, she went about the rest of her duties.

After staying the weekend, with the devastating news of her brother and no further news from Uncle Richard's contacts as yet, Sophie decided that work was the next best thing. It would help her mind from keep going over the news again and again, so re-packing her small weekend case she took herself to work ready for the afternoon shift at the hospital, despite Richard and Joy's protests.

'John would not have wanted me to lock myself away,' she explained. 'Could you ring and let them know I'll be in?'

'Just a few more days,' they had asked, explaining that there might be more news now that the weekend was over. Sophie promised that she would call in again tomorrow just in case and with that she headed to work.

Receiving many condolences during the first part of her nursing roster, it did turn out to be the right thing to do. Bella, in particular, watched over her, a strange sensation when it was only a couple of weeks ago that she was the one in need of looking after herself. Sophie was grateful for the moral support, but still all day there were no tears.

It was late by the time she returned home and it just so coincided with the return home of Lieutenant Buckland. He was hanging up his motorcycle jacket and goggles as she made her way through the front door.

'Hello,' he said looking deep into her eyes that were trying to avoid the sincerity in his. 'I heard from your uncle what had happened. I'm so sorry to hear your news.'

He looked awkward, his hands fiddling with his shirt cuff as he awaited her response.

'Thank you, Lieutenant, I appreciate your sympathy.'

'Couldn't you have had a little more time with family?'

'Trying to get rid of me?'

'No, I meant, well you know to take time out, grieve and what not?'

'That's what my Uncle said,' she sighed. 'He said I am still in shock, I don't think I am, I think…' she paused for a moment wondering why she had been unable to cry, why despite the feeling of loss she had been quite calm and matter of fact about it all. 'I don't think he is dead.'

Buckland looked surprised, perhaps he too thought this was just the behaviour that someone would show if they were in shock, or perhaps he thought she was simply showing the signs of denial. Sophie didn't wish to explain it to him just yet, after all, she was not sure she understood it herself, but she had a strong feeling that John was not dead.

'Are you sure you are ok?' he asked.

'It's hard to believe I know, but yes, I think I am. My head is all over the place, but I really feel, in fact I am sure he isn't dead. The best place for me is here and back to normality, hanging around at the Great Hall won't bring him back, will it? And I've still got Anthony out there somewhere.'

'Well, that was some good news.'

'I know, asking me to marry him, I need to get that feeling of being thrilled back, just as I did when I opened the letter for the first time. Unfortunately, the situation with John..' she heard herself say "situation" and it had a less final ring to it. Now she wondered if she really was deluding herself. '…well, this situation needs sorting first. I should imagine Anthony will know all about it too, I expect he was there, with Tom and the others.'

'Perhaps you should write to Tom?'

'That's a good idea, whilst Uncle Richard is waiting for confirmation and pulling a few strings. I just don't know what to ask Tom.'

'Well there is no need to rush it yet. I am so very sorry,' he said once again.

He hugged her with a genuine concern for her comfort and she accepted it graciously. Pulling her to the front of him, his hands outstretched and then firmly around her arms. She nestled into his chest, breathing in deeply. When Anthony had held her she had felt excited and tense, but with Buckland there was something calm and safe. It was an unusual feeling and as she pulled away and continued to take off her coat, she wondered why she felt calmer in the arms of a man she felt she barely knew and less so in the man she had been with for nearly three long years.

This evening they were alone, Mrs Jenkins did not work every day of the week, but the ritual was still the same. Sophie watched as Buckland went from tea to his usual pacing about, to sitting in the armchair and reading the newspaper she had been pretending to read. She started to treat the whole thing as one big game and chuckled a little when it got to the point that he would ask her if she had read something that she knew clearly she hadn't.

'What is so funny?'

She shook her head dismissively and he went back to his newspaper. She watched him unconsciously and only began to notice it when he noticed her doing it. For a few seconds, although they seemed longer to Sophie, they would look at one another. She then turned away and placed a hand upon her cheek, so he would not see her their red flush. A few moments later she dared herself to look again. It was infuriating and as the evening went on, she found herself doing it again and again, embarrassed each time he caught her.

She wondered if the best thing to do was to retreat upstairs, she could continue her mother's journey in her diaries, find out what Tom's response to her letter had been. It would also break up the temptation of playing this silly game further. No, she thought, it was just a silly game and one that she could stop. She didn't need to look at him again and besides, he was probably too engrossed in the newspaper by now to even notice her looking. With that in mind her eyes wandered over to him again and just as before as if he was toying with her he looked back.

Sophie picked herself up out of the chair and made her way to the stairs, 'Just popping up to read a little more.'

'Mums diaries? Right you are.'

She cursed herself all the way into the dark depths of the roof, muttering how stupid she had been under her breath. He would think she liked him now and that's the last thing she needed, especially now that Anthony had proposed. It was with a sense of aggravation that she slammed down the 1917 diary in front of her, she regretted it immediately when one of the pages began to fall out. She soon found where she had left off and although her mother wrote that Tom would come and see her in secret after her last correspondence, she was too busy thinking about how foolish she had looked in front of her guest.

Eventually she settled down to read, relaxing and telling herself that he would not have thought anything of it. Her mother had written how relieved she was at meeting Tom whilst he and Jack were on leave. Sophie discovered that John's father's bravery had earned him some time back in England and Tom accompanied him. They were to help recruit more volunteers for the war and by what her mother had written, Jack was particularly good at it, Tom not so much.

Helen's feelings for Jack remained loyal and steadfast, but it was clear something had changed. He became short-tempered, aggressive and eager to leave her to return to France. Her mother wrote that he was less sensitive and that she missed his tenderness. Her arrangement to meet Tom in the letter she had recently discovered alluded to a need to understand these changing circumstances. Alone at home, just like Sophie, it must have been impossible for her to comprehend their state of mind, to share their experiences and understand them. And so it was that Helen had decided to meet with Tom on a Sunday afternoon in a busy tea room near Charing Cross station.

It was 1916 and Helen saw Tom long before he saw her. He stood out in his khaki service dress from the ensemble of black, white, grey and mustard coloured outfits of other men. There was also the understandable reality that the majority of the crowd were women, pinstriped dresses and that all too familiar sea of hats again that she remembered the day they had left for France the first time.

As the bell to the door of the tea room announced his entrance, she adjusted her own hat that had made it plain all morning that it was going to be difficult to sit upon her chestnut curls and waved him over. His eyes darted from left to right, reluctant it appeared to look into hers. It was clear that her invitation had made him very uneasy.

'I ordered us some tea, would you like some?'

He nodded with an added smile that he forced upon his troubled face and fiddled with anything that was near to hand. Tom looked behind him a couple of times and continued to gaze in any direction but hers. She reached out and gently took him by the hand, it shocked him as his hand twitched and his eyes finally found themselves level with hers, but he did not pull his hand away.

'Tom I know what you must be thinking, but I assure you that I only asked you here today for help.'

He seemed to relax and gave a gentle nod, 'Ok, what is it I can do for you?'

If things had appeared to be awkward then, they were going to be a whole lot more awkward now. Helen had to explain the changing nature of her future husband, how he was with her when they were alone. Jack had become less intimate as the year had gone on, before the war his hand would often find hers whilst they went for walks, his fingers seeking hers out until they became one. When she played the piano his arm would rest upon her shoulder and she would lean her neck towards it to feel the back of his hand. She had to explain how his eyes were no longer looking at her longingly, but instead looked through her, as though she wasn't there.

Tom listened as she slowly went through her worries, she was careful not to be too loud as it was not always the enemy that was listening. His face went from one of awkwardness to one of pity, imagining how he would feel in such a position. It was a terrible thing to hear how someone he admired and loved, an officer and a friend had changed.

Helen stopped, it was not appropriate to go any further. She had already broken so many unwritten rules in confiding so much with someone she knew so little. She thought of her more intimate time with Jack, how he had asked her to do things to him that were to her mind unnatural, vulgar, humiliating. There was the time he had struck her, she shuddered when she remembered where and remembered how, after doing so he ran out of the room, perhaps taken aback at his own behaviour. No, despite Tom listening so well, so attentively that it surprised her, he was not the person to unload such sensitive things upon, for now she sensed he understood. She would save the intimate things for her diary, a place her tortured mind could rest and confide.

As they went on he did his best to make her laugh, to comfort her and reassure her, all the things that Jack had been unable to do recently.

'It's the war you see, I think that is what is affecting Jack,' Tom said, he looked around the room as if he was still there when he tried to explain. 'Over there, we see things that we couldn't possibly explain or describe. Imagine the worst thing you can think of and I assure you that it still wouldn't even come close to what we go through.'

'I knew you would say that. I think I just needed to hear it from someone who knew him, someone who had shared his hardships. How can I help him, Tom?'

Tom exhaled deeply. 'I don't know. If I needed help…'

He paused and she suddenly saw something in his eyes, something she had failed to see when they were so hard to look into because earlier they had been looking everywhere else. She saw he was suffering too. His contorted face showed lines that she had not remembered before, but they were the same as the ones she had seen appear on Jack's face and the face of a hundred young men and boys she had passed who were on leave that very day. She saw in his eyes an emptiness, a deep well that once before had energy and youth, but now had almost dried up.

'…I wouldn't know what to ask from anyone, if I needed help, I wouldn't know where to start or what to say.'

'Perhaps talking would help? It has certainly helped me today.'

He gave the first genuine smile she had seen. 'Perhaps.'

Helen had ordered a cream tea and now the scones, jam and cream had arrived. She watched as Tom's nostrils flared with excitement. He probably hadn't seen food like this for some time.

'It must be difficult over there, in regards to food.'

'You know,' he began. 'It's not that bad. It's not great, but it could be worse, although I haven't had a cream tea for what seems like years!'

She smiled and gestured him to help himself, happy to see his reaction to the first bite and feeling good that she had enabled him to find some happiness briefly.

'Tom, I wondered if you could do something for me, it will sound quite odd and I understand if you say no,' she reached over for the jam and dared look at his expression as she said, 'When you and Jack are on leave and Jack is with me, I would like it if you were there, with us, as often as you can be. My father will be happy even if you were to stay some nights, it's a large house and there is plenty of room.'

‘Is it really that bad?’ he asked and she still didn’t have the courage to look him in the eye, partially ashamed. ‘Forgive me. That was insensitive.’

‘It’s alright,’ she said. ‘I thought that perhaps we could help Jack together, as well as each other. You probably have a family or a wife to get back to, so I understand if you can’t,’ he shook his head. ‘A girlfriend? Children?’

‘I have nobody, just Jack and the men in our platoon.’

Once again her hand reached out to his and once again he did not pull away. She noticed that his eyes glistened with tears that he fought back gallantly. In that empty well she had looked into earlier she could see a glimmer of hope and she had just put it there. She wondered now if in helping Tom it would help her. ‘I am going to write to you Tom and I want you to come and stay with us. Today I realised that we are both very lonely and both need a friend.’

‘Sorry to disturb, but wondered if you wanted a cup of tea?’ Buckland called out.

Sophie was transported back from 1916 to the present. She was no longer in Charing Cross, but back in the dimly lit attic. It was the second time Buckland had startled her and she had been so engrossed at her mother’s generosity that she had not noticed his head appear through the hatch. At first she wanted to shout at him, tell him to go away, that this was her private place and he had intruded.

‘Kettle has just boiled you see.’

‘No thank you,’ she snapped, barely looking at him.

‘I’ve caught you at a bad time, I apologise’ and he disappeared back down the ladder.

Sophie felt guilty now, her abruptness felt necessary at the time, but now she realised it had been rude and uncalled for, he was only offering a cup of tea after all. She thought about how her mother had befriended Tom, something that she had never thought to ask her in her youth. She thought about how beautiful it was that she had instigated a friendship they both needed and that neither of them at that point in time knew would last a lifetime. She wondered if she should instigate the same with Buckland, if their chance meeting was really fated all along as he had once suggested, that there was a reason for him being here. She had lost her brother and not really opened up about it, perhaps she should try with him, after all, like Tom in the tea room, he was here and maybe he had secret pains too.

She sifted through the rest of the diary over the odd photograph and letters. Her mother really did keep everything, from receipts, bus tickets, to small drawings and little poems that she had created, bookmarked with pressed flowers.

By the time Sophie had reached the end of 1916, after the Somme and into 1917, Jack was a shadow of his former self, he wrote rarely and the letters back and forth to Jack now began to go via Tom. It was Jack's trusted sergeant who passed on her mother's correspondence, as when she wrote directly to her beloved Jack there was seldom a reply. Tom had never mentioned the Somme she recalled, it was as if his war had started at Cambrai a year later. As she sifted through the last few pages, the first letter for some time to be written by Jack was to ask for confirmation on her pregnancy.

It was incredible, her mother was now pregnant with John, for the first time he had come to exist in her mother's memories and for Sophie she had regained her brother in some way after just losing him.

'But he isn't lost,' she said to herself.

She understood it now. As clear as day she understood why she knew wholeheartedly that John was not dead and why there must have been a mistake.

'It's because I didn't feel anything,' she explained to Buckland upon returning downstairs. He was in the kitchen pouring the kettle and when he nodded to it she smiled and agreed to accept what he had offered earlier. 'They say that some twins can feel when the other one is in pain, sad or angry. They say that they can also tell when they are apart if the other has died.'

Buckland tried not to frown at her explanation. 'Urban myth most would say, but continue.'

'I didn't feel anything. I know it's hard to explain, but my brother and I are so close that I would have expected to feel something. Something real and yet it didn't feel like that.'

'I want to reassure you and give you hope Sophie, but you were not twins.'

'Are! Are not twins, enough of that past tense.'

He tapped the teaspoon on the side of the cup, something her brother would do to get any last drops off. 'Ok, it is possible there has been a mistake and maybe, just maybe he is alive. You need to wait and see what your uncle finds out.'

'I just know.'

She began to tell him about what she had been reading in the diaries, running through the events now that she was an expert on them and relaying her mother's thoughts as if they were her own. It was a natural thing to do, once she had started she simply couldn't hold anything back and it was probably a huge relief for Buckland, who now understood her ups and downs.

'There is one more thing I have to do. I need to write to Tom, not about John, but about what I am reading in my mother's diaries.'

'Do you think that wise? I mean will he will want to go over it all?' Buckland asked.

'I don't think it is going over it all, I just thought it might interest him, he can write back and fill in the gaps, tell me more stories like he used to. It will be like he is still here. There is so much I never knew and I need to ask Tom to find out his side of the story. What do you think?'

Buckland rubbed his chin with thought. 'I don't know,' he murmured. 'The past is the past for a reason. You can't change any of it.'

'I'm not trying to change any of it!'

'Hear me out,' he looked at her as a professor might do when about to say something important, all he needed was a pair of spectacles for his eyes to peer over. 'All the things in our past we cannot change and that means there are bound to be things that people like Tom for instance, don't want disturbing. Things he might feel are buried that should stay buried, things that you might dig up.'

Sophie pondered on his wisdom for a moment seeing his point, but telling herself that there was probably nothing her mother wrote that Tom would be unaware of, after all, she was writing about his own history and surely that was no secret to him.

John had been resting in the comfort of a hospital bed for nearly five whole days. He had got a great deal of attention, but all in all, he was on the mend although be it a little bored and desperate to be reunited with his company. Tom had been to see him every day and Simon, although back with the company, was constantly in and out of the hospital using his specialist knowledge to help Sister Hall, the resident doctors and the pretty little nurses, as he had come to call them. He had become a charming and popular asset to the hospital.

Perhaps what surprised John the most was seeing Tom so emotional when he entered the hospital. Tom had believed that John and Simon had been killed; in fact the whole company had been fuelled by stories from those who had seen them on the battlefield last. Only a handful of privates had seen Simon and Orchard dragging their captain back towards friendly lines and those who had witnessed it had even then truly believed the Captain was dead.

The final surprise visit had been the ever-amusing Lieutenant Bailey. Recovering from his horrific bout of dysentery. On his second day in the hospital Bailey had crashed through the double doors crying out, 'where is he, I know he's in here and I know he's faking it!'

Bailey had arrived during the week and taken command of Anthony's first platoon, as well as temporary command of the company and every now and then popped in for advice and suggestions, as well as to see how John was. His comical sense of humour put a big smile on John's face that could only be beaten by his boyish grin when Sister Hall was nearby.

Although John was bored and desperate to get back to take command of his company again, there was one huge reason that kept him quite content in his bed, Sister Hall.

'And how is Captain Baker this evening?' she sounded most bewildered. 'Popular as ever and flooded with visitors again. How does he do it I ask myself? Well, the quicker my nurses can get to work on you the better the chance you have of getting out of here sooner, but at this rate, it will be Christmas!'

'You like him really,' Bailey teased the Sister. 'My mum says there is a fine line between love and hate and this would be a classic example I reckon.'

'Are you going to be here all day wasting my time and patience?' she demanded.

'I tell you what,' he said crudely raising his eyebrows. 'Seeing as you and my Captain are a happy couple now, I wondered if you could introduce me to any of your single staff. There was a lovely brunette who greeted me as I came in this morning, Sister Hope was it? Well, I was hoping…'

'Stay here much longer Lieutenant Bailey and you won't be able to leave unaided!'

'Ouuuuch,' he said as she wrapped her strong fingers around his left ear and literally dragged him out of John's curtained cubicle.

John was beside himself with laughter as Bailey came back rubbing his ear. 'Thanks for rescuing me from the jaws of the dragon! Tight grip she has there, mind you I know I hit the nail on the head there because she overreacted! Sir, my mum always said…'

'Are you still here?' she roared, descending on Bailey again. 'Haven't you got a home to go to? This soldier needs his rest!'

'Well you'll have to find him something to keep him occupied because he's getting bored, his brain needs stimulation,' he nodded indignantly.

'And that's what you are doing are you?' she smiled dangerously casually 'Doctor Bailey is it?'

'It has a certain ring to it, but I didn't mean it like that,' he panicked holding up his index finger then grabbing his ear protectively as she got closer, not sure what she was going to do next. 'You can't keep him all trussed up in here, your breaking his spirit, he's dying, choked up in all these blankets and talking of blankets, Sister, isn't it about time you gave him one of those blanket baths? If you don't mind me saying so Sir, you do chuck up a bit!'

'Right that's it,' she protested. 'My patients do not 'chuck up' Lieutenant Bailey and I am of a right mind to call in the MP's.'

Sister Hall swung the bedpan she had in her hand in jest at him and John didn't know who was surprised the most out of the two of them, Bailey as he got hit with the bedpan or Sister Hall for not missing him as she was supposed to and hearing it clunk around his head like a tolling bell. There was a brief silence due to the shock and then John howled with laughter, simultaneously joined by Bailey and finally unable to resist seeing the funny side of it all, Sister Hall herself.

John would never have thought it from the first day that he had been brought into the hospital, but he was growing on Sister Hall and even with his limited experience of women, he could tell. She was ambitious and career orientated, business was never mixed with pleasure and she was steadfast in that approach. Just talking to other nurses revealed that she was renowned for her dedication and professionalism, but they also disclosed, although much of it was their professional opinion, that she was beginning to like this strong but delicate character and found herself by his bedside at every available opportunity. John had already noticed, at first it was just fleeting temperature checks, water changes or checking his progress chart. All simple tasks her nurses would normally carry out, but she earmarked for herself when his cubicle would become a hive of activity. He wondered if his popularity intrigued her and if there was a part of her that enjoyed the fuss and attention in the form of compliments that flew in her direction from the various members of his company that popped in throughout the day.

So it was that John simply digested it all and would find himself watching her glide in and out, giving as good as she got with his cheeky visitors, protesting his own innocence of course to their schemes and dreams, for fear of reprisals, rejection and miscomprehension. He always retained his charm and politeness when the boys were in town for fear of letting his guard down to be too much like one of the lads, but she was confident of his authenticity and he of hers, he needn't have worried. As the days progressed so did John. His wounds were healing slowly, but they were healing and his manoeuvrability was encouraging.

He continued to lead his company, even from his bed where he would empathise with his fellow officers and NCO's. Even in his incapacitated state they still sought his guidance and he continued to give it.

‘I’m looking forward to seeing my company again,’ John said cringing with the pain from his thigh as he lifted himself upright in his bed on her latest round.

‘But you see them virtually every day, I don’t know why we don’t put the hospital where your barracks are and be done with it,’ she chirped. ‘It would make life so much easier.’

‘Do you think it will be too much longer before I can be discharged for duty again?’ he asked earnestly.

She paused a moment. ‘So soon? Captain, it’s been barely two weeks and wounds like this leave heavy scars, so we must make certain that a full recovery is made otherwise all manner of things can go wrong.’

‘As in?’ he questioned.

‘Well the wound is particularly deep and although your main artery was not severed, the stitches and delicacy of your wounds alone would be prone to splitting and bursting, if the new tissue and muscle hadn’t started to repair itself. Then there is the danger of infection…’

John stared into her big blue eyes, he could get lost in them, he thought. He imagined himself as a sailor drifting upon a vast blue ocean of turquoise and azure blue, with no sight of land in any direction, yet totally relaxed. Her skin was very pale for someone who worked under the intensity of the desert sun, but the power of the light had brought more prominently to the surface of her skin small freckles upon her arm, like little stepping stones. Her blonde hair, bleached a little, was hidden most of the time by her uniform, but today small curls had managed to escape and sway next to those sapphire eyes that his gaze always returned to.

‘…A simple chill could turn into pneumonia because your immune system has taken a battering trying to cover so many traumas in your body. You can’t be too careful at this early stage. You’re lucky Captain James is an absolute wiz with these things otherwise you wouldn’t be here today. The war isn’t going anywhere so you’ll get your chance to fight again, probably far sooner than you think.’

‘Crikey,’ he said gobsmacked. ‘Will I ever leave here or ever be safe to join my company again? Am I still on death’s door? I was beginning to feel so well again.’

'You haven't listened to a word I have said, have you,' she scorned, sitting at the end of his bed. 'And there was I going to treat you to a quick wander around the grounds tomorrow for some fresh air. In a wheelchair of course. I have to say, I don't do that for all my patients, but no, I have obviously got my wires crossed and you have absolutely no intention of taking my advice seriously, so you can jolly well stick to the same bed bath and tapioca regime of all the other patients tomorrow instead' and she thumped the end of the bed teasingly and jumped up.

John cried out jerking forward and grabbing at his leg.

'Oh God, Captain Baker, I'm so sorry how unprofessional of me!' she gasped with her hand over her mouth and rushed back to his bedside in dismay pulling back the covers to see what damage she had done.

As she leaned over to see, John had a sudden burst of courage and pulled her towards him, holding her firmly in his arms and quietly said, 'has no one told you what happens to me if I am forced fed tapioca, Sister Hall?'

'No,' she whispered, nervously held in his clutches.

'Well, I suggest that you make sure that the wander around the grounds takes place as was previously arranged lest I am forced to reveal it!'

'I see,' she said knowingly. 'Best you let me go to confirm the arrangements then.'

Their eyes were fixed upon each other and their breathing was heavy. John suddenly realised how close her lips were to his and although the temptation was great, he withdrew his grasp apologetically, completely taken aback by his own forceful actions upon her. 'I'm sorry I don't know what came over me.'

'Oh didn't you?' she said pulling herself up, faltering with her blonde locks. He lowered his eyes with embarrassment and then to his amazement she said quietly, 'that's a shame, I was rather looking forward to what I thought was coming next.'

John, completely speechless, looked around the ward with his eyebrows raised for confirmation that somebody else might have seen and heard what just happened and understood it, because he wasn't sure that he did. Was he going on a date tomorrow in a wheelchair?

And did she mean she was sorry that he didn't kiss her? Or was he imagining things? Nobody answered his queried glances. The nurses in the ward were still very busy going about their business, another casualty arrived from surgery, visitors were coming and going, patients were sleeping or reading and some attempting mobility up and down the ward in some form or another. Apart from the two of them, nobody had seemed to notice anything let alone care. First, he pinched himself to make sure he was awake, then he checked his own pulse which seemed to be racing over the whole experience, he pulled his abandoned covers back up to his chest, took a deep breath, shrugged his shoulders and laid his head on his pillow. He smiled dreamily, unable to believe his luck.

The next morning came and went and there was no sign of Sister Hall and when John inquired as to her whereabouts via one of the other nurses she replied quite abrasively, 'she won't be in today it's her day off, she hasn't had a day off since the Hood was sunk.'

'Oh, I see,' said John quite disappointed thinking he'd obviously got the wrong end of the stick, but later that afternoon to his delight she arrived as promised with a wheelchair and a smile.

'Oh, you're not ready!' she teased gently and helped him out of bed and wrapped him up warmly in his temporary transport. 'I was expecting you in your best uniform.'

'This is the best uniform I have had for months,' John pointed to his blue striped pyjamas, his khaki drill had been a sweat-soaked set of rags for nearly two years and he hadn't seen his dress uniform since arriving in Egypt. 'Not sure I need this wheelchair, I can walk easily enough.'

She pushed him gently back into his seat as he tried to rise, shaking her head. Outside the sun was shimmering through the haze and she pushed him around the sparsely gardened grounds to find a shady area under a magnificent date palm. There she pulled on the brakes and set out another blanket and sat down beside him.

'It's a beautiful day,' he commented politely. 'It's good to be out in the fresh air, thank you.'

She looked around at the dunes and mudbrick homes, picketed by the odd oasis of palms. 'You're very welcome,' she smiled uncertain if he was being sarcastic or genuine, then drawing a flask from her bag and pouring them both some orange juice she handing it to him. 'I'm sorry it's nothing stronger but alcohol is not good for your condition at this time with your medication,' she said wryly.

He took a sip of the juice, smiled, looked up into the sky and took a deep breath closing his eyes and soaking up the warmth of the sun.

'Where is the sea? I thought we were near the sea?'

'Bit too far inland, it's just over there behind that ridge, but if you think I am pushing you all the way over there, think again. Perhaps when you are up and about a bit more we will go and see it. How are we feeling today, Captain Baker?'

'John, my name is John,' he sighed relaxingly. 'Please call me John.'

'So, how are we feeling today John?' she asked.

'Oh much better…'

'Katherine,' she replied. 'But I prefer to be called Katie.'

'Katie it is then, can I call you by your first name, is it allowed?' he requested.

'Out of public earshot, I don't see why not.'

'I thought you had forgotten me this morning, one of the nurses said it was your day off, so I presumed I had misunderstood about the whole thing and you were cross with me,' he said in a relieved tone.

'I always keep my promises, even to naughty patients,' she said jovially. 'And apart from the usual letters home it makes a nice change to have some company.'

'Where is home?' John asked.

'Devon is my home, but I was born in Leeds. You are a Sussex boy I believe?' John corrected her with 'Sussex man!' She had overheard the many conversations that had been taking place at his bed. No doubt the ones with Tom had given the most away. 'We have something in common you and I, if what I overheard the Sergeant Major who comes to visit you was correct. Your father was killed at Cambrai? Mine too, he drove one of those metal monsters. I don't remember him I was but one or two. My mother brought me up completely single-handed for the most part. While I was at school she started working in a factory as a seamstress for Montague Burton. She eventually got involved with designing and worked her way to the top of the company, an exceptional achievement for a woman, particularly a single mother.'

'Sounds like quite a woman,' said John. 'My mother brought me up alone, you see she never married my father, I don't know why, perhaps hoping to do it when the war was over. He never saw me and I never knew him, only through my mother and Tom's recollections do I know anything about him.'

'That is why you and the Sergeant Major are so close?'

'Yes, it's unbelievable, but he was my father's Sergeant and friend and now he's my company Sergeant Major!' John laughed along with her surprise.

'You can't really make something like that up I suppose.'

'I know,' he chuckled and explained briefly how Tom had become so entwined into the family. 'Anyhow with my mother unmarried and with a child, naturally the family disowned her. She brought me up single-handed for the most part, but remarried an American, Ted, not long after and they had a daughter.'

'Sophie?' she asked.

'Sophie,' he confirmed. 'Who I love and adore. We were a small family that relied on each other to survive. It was never easy, Ted died, my mother's father died and never left her a schilling and even today most of the family still don't recognise us. Thank god our uncle looked out for us. Let's talk about something more cheerful, what do want to talk about?'

'Why did you join the army then? Not that it is a more cheerful subject I suppose,' she chuckled.

'I joined the army when I was sixteen, Tom helped me enlist to train as an officer and my uncle pulled some strings so that I would be in his regiment. Didn't really expect to be in the same company though! I think I did it to make my father proud.'

'It's uncanny,' said Katie. 'Who would have thought it, but our lives do seem to have a common theme.'

'Do you have someone in your life, I mean a relationship, someone at home or here even?'

'No real relationships,' said Katie in a very matter of fact manner. 'Too busy really and it's rather ill-advised and frowned upon in these circumstances, it's a single woman's lot. And you?'

'Likewise, too busy and I haven't found the right one yet,' he reciprocated 'Thought I had once but it wasn't to be. So how come you are here then, wouldn't you have preferred to have stayed safe at home?' he queried.

'You're a man that thinks a woman's place is in the home aren't you? I'm disappointed in you John, under the circumstances I would have thought you would have been the first to understand.'

'No, no, I didn't mean that at all!' he defended and then seeing her grin realised she was toying with him. 'I suppose the Home front is no safer at times. I worry about my sister working in a hospital, the things she must see. I just wondered what made you choose this particular avenue?'

'Well, the Matron of the hospital where I was working had encouraged me to enlist. I was very interested in tropical diseases and hadn't long been back from a sabbatical overseas so it seemed just up my street. I didn't know the war was going to break out so I volunteered. I took my Matrons exams and while I was waiting for the results I was offered an interview at the War Office. I never got the chance to find a posting of Matron before I was posted out here. So until they sort out all the commission status I am still a sister, though qualified to be a Matron. At the moment I could be anything between a Lieutenant and a Brigadier,' she chuckled again. 'It's not important as long as I am nursing and helping.'

John was fixated; he hung on her every word, then suddenly realised she might even outrank him. He shivered a little in awe. She saw him and was concerned that he wasn't warm enough despite the intensity of the heat and rewrapped him. He grabbed her arm saying, 'I'm fine, really, I'm not cold, and anyway I couldn't be, not when you're around looking after me.'

'If you're sure,' she fretted. 'I can't be responsible for you catching pneumonia in the desert.'

'Can you imagine that out here in this heat! Honestly, today is the best I have felt.'

'So what about your sister?' asked Katie. 'Is she ok? Do you hear regularly from her?'

'What a mess,' he muttered. 'I was posted as killed, god knows how she is faring back home and what her reaction is going to be when she gets the news.'

'But you're alive?' queried Katie.

'I certainly am thanks to Captain James and your tender care, but she will have been notified that we are dead already. It's going to be an even bigger shock to find out we have come back to life,' he said shaking his head. 'Then there is Anthony.'

'Anthony?'

'Perhaps we should change the subject again.'

'Poor girl,' gasped Katie. 'There have certainly been a fair amount of storms in your young lives so far to have weathered, but in the face of so much adversity I think she'll fare much better than you think.'

'Tom said more or less the same thing,' John sighed. 'I hope your both right.'

'I'm sure we both are,' insisted Katie and she kissed him gently on the forehead and cuddled him sympathetically.

'Is it really a single woman's lot, nursing?' asked John.
He tried to look out the corner of his eye to see if her face would give away a smile, but couldn't quite see as she said, 'it's an important role, it wouldn't do to get attachments or show favouritism. Involvements impair your judgement. Being a sister I must set a good example. Besides, relationships interfere with our work and after all who knows what tomorrow will bring for any of us? I don't want heartache in my life,' she said.

'Heartache?' questioned John. 'Why heartache, I don't understand?'

'Well you know, here today and gone tomorrow, reputations and such,' she said quite forlornly. 'Anyway best get you back, it may have been my day off today, but I have the night shift to contend with.'

Back in the ward Katie assisted him from the wheelchair to his bed, John's bare feet touched the cool hard floor and it shot an aggressive pain and stinging sensation towards his thigh and he threw the rest of himself backwards on the bed. From behind her, through a window John could see the sun setting. Her golden hair was bathed in an amber glow almost like a halo.

'An Angel,' he whispered to himself.

Sophie reached home in the early hours of the morning. The sun had risen but was subdued in its warmth by dark grey clouds as another channel storm brewed. There was a chill in the air and the shrubs and bushes were being blown around by a wild breeze, not a rare event for the month of June. The scent of the sea filled the hallway as she turned the key and pushed the door with the last ounce of effort she had left after a long shift. The claws of the hawthorn bush that grew up the side of the house scratched at the windows and a tapering finger caught her cloak as she stepped inside.

She had left the door ajar and through it out of the sharp breeze, soothing rays of brief sunshine warmed her back as she bent down to pick up the delivered mail. Her normal enthusiasm to search for passed Army stamped letters, from any of the lads as well as those expected from John or Anthony just didn't arise. It had been a long night and she wasn't expecting any more news and for the first time ever she threw it on to the hall table without even glancing at any of the envelopes.

She took herself up the stairs and without undressing, she collapsed on the bed emotionally and physically exhausted. She listened as the Hawthorn continued to scratch the glass and the wind began to bluster, howling at times through the large poplar trees that lined the lane. The door creaked and groaned as it swung back and forth and as it gained momentum she heard the latch click into place. Once she knew the door was shut, she let her eyes flicker for one last time and for what felt like the first time in three days she slept.

It must have been just after midday that the frantic and continuous knocking at the front door roused her from her short sleep. The dark clouds had gathered together now and a distant rumble could faintly be heard over the Downs and out at sea. She reluctantly got herself up and sauntered down the stairs calling, 'I'm coming, I'm coming.' Yawning profusely she opened the door to find Richard and Joy both hopping impatiently about outside as if it was a cold winters day and they were trying to keep warm.

‘You have got to get a phone Sophie, this is ridiculous,’ he blasted as they charged through the door.

‘It’s on my list,’ she said indignantly. ‘Matron’s always saying the same thing and I’ll tell you the same as I tell her when we can afford it.’

‘Spoke to Archie today and he is going to bring one back with him, then there won’t be these ridiculous charades every time we need to contact each other,’ he spurted completely out of breath.

Joy thumped him hard and screamed at him fervently, ‘Get on with it.’

‘There’s been a mistake, Sophie,’ he said excitedly clapping his hands. ‘Do you understand? A mistake at the Ministry, there’s been a mistake, not the first time I might add. He should have been posted as missing!’

Sophie was not sure how that was any better than killed in action, they often alluded to the same thing.

‘Ok, so that is good news, because…’

‘Because we now know John is alive! I had a telegram from Tom, it arrived this morning.’

Sophie felt dizzy and dropped to the floor. Holding the small table with her right hand for balance as her left felt the sweat upon her brow. She suddenly felt cold and clammy and had the urge to be sick. She could hear herself telling Buckland that she had told him so, but right now the feeling of relief was mixed with disbelief and the need to vomit.

‘Well I must say, Richard,’ said Joy positively fuming at his complete and apparent incompetence of handling the situation. ‘That went really well, get the Pickles, it’s in a small brown bottle in my bag, quickly, then go and find some brandy, or something alcoholic, I’ll take it from here!’

Richard fumbled around in Joy’s handbag with a constant battle of trial and error, eventually finding the little brown bottle of Pickles smelling salts. He handed them over and went off to find some brandy. Not knowing where to start looking there either.

Sophie’s dizziness was slowly swept away by the strong smell of ammonia carbonate which flooded her senses, making her cough and splutter.

‘I feel sick,’ Sophie mumbled, ‘Did I faint?’

‘You were close, just sit for a moment.’

‘John is still alive?’ she looked imploring at Joy who smiled and nodded.

‘Brandy,’ declared Richard, arriving on the scene raising the bottle in one hand and a glass in the other, pleased with himself that he had managed to do something right at last.

‘Not for me thank you, I try to avoid the stuff,’ said Sophie furtively.

‘Oh of course, I forgot. Do you mind if I have it?’

‘Of course not Uncle Richard, help yourself,’ she sighed.

Joy looked questioningly at Richard and he mouthed ‘because of her father’ to her from where he stood hoping Sophie wouldn’t see and be offended by what he was trying to say.

‘Terrific news,’ he crouched down beside her. ‘You must be pleased? We were thrilled to bits. Tom told us in the telegram that he has been wounded, but will be back with the unit soon. I don’t know the full extent of his wounds or condition yet, but can’t be serious if he is returning to his unit.’

‘Did Tom not say where or how he was wounded then?’ by now she was back on her feet and although a little unsteady her nursing instincts were kicking in.

‘No, it was quite short,’ he spoke to her similar to a child who had just fallen over, trying to make it all easier for her. ‘You know they are not supposed to say too much, just enough to get the point across.

It’s difficult to know what’s going on over there at the moment. Wish we did, but old Churchill, well he tends to keep these things under wraps until really necessary. You know how it is, everything is on a need to know basis so as not to destroy the good old British spirit and all that. We don’t want to let those Jerry’s in on a bloody thing.’

He took a sip of the brandy and did what Sophie could only assume was a little dance of some sort.

‘It’s alright Joy,’ Sophie said, forgivingly putting her hand on Uncle Richard’s arm understanding perfectly what Richard and Joy were trying to do. ‘I don’t mean this to sound offensive and you’ve both been so very good to me these past few days, but I do realise and understand the predicament we are all in. I feel numb.’

'You'll be fine when it's sunk in,' nurtured Joy. 'Now is there anything we can get for you or do for you while we're here and before we go?'

She helped Sophie take a wander around the hallway to get her trembling legs to work again and was still holding her by the shoulder when Buckland passed through the door, his navy cap under one arm and a telephone in the other.

'I knew he wasn't dead,' she said beginning to smile and turning to Buckland repeated to him. 'I just knew, I told you, I told you that I just knew!'

He grinned and gave her a large embrace saying, 'I couldn't wait to get back and see how you had taken the news, your uncle told me earlier.'

'I just knew,' she repeated, coming back to life with a tear of joy pricking her eyelids.

'You haven't opened your mail today!' exclaimed Joy picking up the small pile of letters from the hall table left there earlier.

Tucking the letters under her arm she guided Sophie through to the parlour and they sat down side by side on the sofa. Joy tapped the letters together and stacked them neatly on the table.

'Tea?' Buckland made his usual suggestion and glancing at everyone he took the apparent hint and went off to make some.

'Now then, what about this mail? Perhaps there is more news from Africa? Good news of course,' hinted Joy. 'And perhaps we could arrange a date to get together soon and start making plans for this wedding?'

'Perhaps,' said Sophie, not really interested in that for now, but then feeling quite repentant for Richard and Joy's genuine gestures, she carefully fanned the three letters apart. There were no official-looking envelopes, it all appeared to be just general mail so she picked up the bulkiest blue envelope with an Arundel postmark first, knowing that it would be from Anthony's parents.

Then raising a smile, she said with a little more enthusiasm, 'This one is from Anthony's parents. I expect he has informed them that he's asked me to marry him, I hope they will be pleased, I only met them once just before he went away, but they seldom keep in touch. What do you think?' she asked Joy searchingly for a positive response.

'Who couldn't love you my dear? And just think, John will be able to give you away,' Joy surmounted.

'I was thinking maybe Tom,' she giggled.

The momentum had now inspired Sophie. Her imagination was running wild and her fingers fumbled trying desperately to open the letter. She was frustrated at the audience watching with anticipation that the letter wouldn't open quick enough. With a huge sigh of relief that it really was from Anthony's parents, she excitedly opened the folded leaves of paper

She began to read out loud, 'Dearest Sophie. It is with the greatest sadness that we forward this news on to you…'

She continued to read on in her head, watched by all who could sense what it contained. It must have been the greatest burden for Anthony's parents to receive and then have to forward on. She thought of her mother and how she must have felt when hearing of Jack's death, she saw with her own eyes the devastation that her own father's death brought her when she was in her teens. The pain she experienced then and the confusion was the same as now. When she received the news of John's apparent death, there was indeed something inside that told her it wasn't possible, that she hadn't felt it. With Anthony, no such connection existed.

'…we were happy to read in the letter we received from Anthony a few days ago the expression of his betrothal wishes to you. We regret with both our hearts that it cannot be and hold our hands out to you for anything you might need…'

Sophie felt that her body was disconnected from her head. Her chest heaved in heavy lunges as she fought back the tears in order for her eyes to scan ahead. Once she had registered the contents she lost all connection to the piece of paper she was holding, like Anthony's hand, it slipped away and drifted slowly to the floor where Joy picked it up. A thousand emotions surged from the depths of all consciousness, her head writhed in pain, fear, anger and confusion.

'What have I done?' she cried suddenly, but her cry also reached the dark depths of her soul. 'What have I done? There is no God, do you hear me God? You don't exist, to me!' she said punching her chest in affirmation and screamed at the ceiling. 'Not anymore.'

She sobbed several times having to remember to breathe because her spirit had been broken and she slowly slid down onto the floor, Joy joining her with her arms around her. Then her trembling hands wrapped themselves around her knees into a foetal position and she dissolved into her innermost sanctuary of shadows.

Joy was blaming herself for encouraging her to open the letters, frantically trying to console Sophie, crying herself and apologising for her own tears, but Sophie was completely catatonic. 'Get a doctor, Richard! This is beyond belief.'

'The phone doesn't work yet,' he said attentively and very calmly continued, 'I'll go and get Mrs Jenkins.'

'I'll go,' offered Buckland. 'She needs her family around her.'

Joy briefly gave him directions to Dr Parsons and Mrs Jenkins' home and with that he left. Joy called Sophie's name over and over again, gently shaking her trying to get some response but to no avail. Almost afraid to leave her alone, Joy decided at least to try and keep her warm and ran upstairs to grab a blanket from one of the wardrobes, returning and engulfing Sophie's suspended adulthood with it, hoping to revive her while she waited for help.

Dr Parsons arrived about ten minutes later with Buckland and Mrs Jenkins, apologising for his tardiness, but he had only just finished the morning surgery at the local general practice. Buckland had explained everything on the way but found himself repeating it all again. Dr Parsons knelt down beside Sophie and unravelled her from the ball she had hibernated into.

'Tragic,' he said ruefully. 'Now young lady, a hospital for this little nurse I think, best call an ambulance Mr Beaumont.'

Before Richard could inform him of the telephone situation, Sophie roused, whimpering, 'I don't want that, I'm not ill, I'll be alright in a minute.'

'No to the hospital then,' the doctor remarked, Sophie sensed the suggestion was merely a ploy to rouse her and he withdrew. 'Shock and the usual I am afraid. Time is a great healer, but she has been through it more than most. Someone will need to stay with her of course.'

All eyes turned to Buckland who simply nodded.

'The Lieutenant is a permanent lodger,' Richard informed him.

‘Well, that would be splendid as long as you are able to be relieved from duties for a day or so, then it is just a matter of time and rebuilding. However, I should imagine that taking time away from duties for someone like yourself will be a bit of a problem.’

Again Richard intervened. ‘Actually no it won’t.’

The doctor sensing the chain of command looked at the two naval officers. ‘Splendid then. Complete bed rest for a couple of days with someone here all the time with you,’ he ordered looking at Buckland with a smile. ‘I will pop back in two days, here is my telephone number for when yours is up and running.’

Joy and Richard offered to take her to the Great Hall, but Sophie protested that she wanted to be at home. Mrs Jenkins offered to call in every other hour, but Dr Parsons insisted that the Lieutenant would suffice and to stick to her normal duties.

‘I will stay the night,’ Joy insisted. ‘Mrs Jenkins and I can make arrangements for alternative nights for a couple of days to help relieve the Lieutenant.’

‘I will be fine, really. Once the telephone is working things will be much easier,’ he insisted.

‘I don’t have a telephone, what if you need me?’ Mrs Jenkins added. ‘Never wanted one of the bloody things.’

‘Well, you are only around the corner anyway!’

Happy with all the obvious attention his patient would be getting one way or the other, Dr Parsons rounded on his patient and helped her back onto the comfort of the chair saying, ‘I’m giving you a sedative to help.’

Sophie winced in response to his haphazard bedside manner and lack of ability to find her vein.

There was no one she could talk to, no one who could explain to her what had happened or what had gone wrong. John had been the one she would have turned to in a crisis as she had done a hundred times before, but she didn’t know where he was or how he was, but at least he was alive, for the time being. So many thoughts were zooming around her mind and before she knew it she was floating, floating on memory’s bliss into sleep. Joy kissed her cheek affectionately and then flicked out the light.

Dr Parsons clipped his bag shut at the door and slipped out into the gusts of the approaching storm.

Buckland and Mrs Jenkins reassured Joy and Richard that they would take the first watch and directed them to the door. Going to the parlour to turn out the main light, Buckland saw the remaining letters still scattered on the floor. He picked them up and looked at Mrs Jenkins.

'Don't open them, dear,' Mrs Jenkins whispered. 'I know what you are thinking, but there really couldn't be any sadder news to protect her from today.'

He placed them back on to the table for Sophie when she was ready to read them for herself.

Buckland watched her in the dark for a moment. Her breathing was so much lighter now as the sedative took hold and the blanket heaved only a little where her chest was. Closing the door, he joined Mrs Jenkins in the kitchen where she had beaten him to the kettle,

'I wish there was something I can do,' he sighed. 'I feel so utterly useless.'

'You're not useless and you are doing something, you are here for her. Crikey you got two days off as well!'

'I've never seen her like that.'

'Of course not,' comforted Mrs Jenkins. 'But I have seen a lot worse when her father died and then her mother. That girl has had too much loss in her life…'

He was beginning to understand the relationship with her brother now. Up to this point it seemed that John held an unusually tight grip upon his sister, an emotional one at that. Buckland had imagined him as a sort of a bully, one who needed his sister more than she needed him, but didn't want her to realise it. Now he saw a little more clearly, John had always been her one constant, a shining star in a sky of darkness that would always be there.

'…What she needed,' continued Mrs Jenkins. 'Was something to look forward to, a happy ending. I hoped that a young man might be the start of a new chapter in her life, but sometimes I wonder if she is going to end up like her mother.'

'Her mother sounded like an unlucky woman.'

'She was a bit. Amazed me her mother, so unfortunate, yet always so happy,' her eyes looked off into a distant recollection. 'I had high hopes for Sophie, I thought I would see her fledge the nest, but maybe not.'

'There is still time for her, still other futures she has yet to discover.'

'Maybe,' she said returning from her memories to the present. 'But that Anthony was everything to her.'

He also felt a tingle of guilt wriggle through his body. He had made no secret of being attracted to her even if he treated it as nothing serious, a flirtatious game that he had always understood to have no conclusion, but with Anthony gone a little sparkle of dark hope manifested. He shuddered at his own perverse mind and how quickly it had manifested a twisted seed. This was not the man he was.

'You alright love?'

'Yes I'm fine,' he said, beating the thought into submission with his more honourable thoughts, the ones he really valued, the ones where he held Sophie when she needed holding, fed her when she was hungry, knocked on her door to check she was alright when she had a bad dream. Not the ones where he was her champion. 'I am tired, I think I am going to head to bed, I want to be awake before she comes to.'

'You do that, don't worry about little miss tonight, I will still be here if she wakes before then.'

There had been no more significant news from the world outside the hospital, John sifted through the newspapers, catching up on events as best he could. The Bismarck had been sunk back in May and Crete had fallen, but none of this was the latest news and most of all he longed for news from home. Sophie had not written to him since before the attack on the ridge and her silence made him increasingly nervous. Tom continued to reassure John that Uncle Richard would have dealt with all the misunderstandings, but John couldn't help but fret that he had left Sophie particularly exposed and vulnerable. He had expected a letter or some form of acknowledgement from her, but to date, there had been nothing.

The only consolation was being away from the ordeals of war and he was getting accustomed to regular sleep often found with a peaceful smile across his face. The nurse and patient scenario was moving on quite dramatically much to the amusement of John's regular visitors, particularly Lieutenant Bailey, who sensed that his second sight mother had known all along and got it right once again. Since their afternoon rendezvous the relationship had clearly developed and gone from strength to strength. It was a relationship made up of suggestions and had not developed physically. They were completely bowled over with each other, but neither had crossed that line yet to admit anything. To John, this made the relationship both frustrating and yet stimulating.

It was late in the evening as Katie pulled the curtains around his bedside, shrouding them in their own temporary world. She tapped him gently on the shoulder and then kissed him on the forehead to awaken him. As he stirred unwillingly from his slumber and opened his reluctant eyes, she was holding her finger across her painted ruby red lips. He smiled a happy but questioning smile at seeing her. She knew John now better than she could have ever known him. She had never said she loved him and he had never reciprocated the same, John wondered if they even needed to. It had not started out that way, at first he hadn't wanted to love anyone, but now he just couldn't help it, it felt right and he just knew that she felt the same.

Whatever it was they were doing, it was both exciting and intoxicating. There was no certainty that they had managed to keep the world around them ignorant. The other nursing staff and doctors had shown no knowledge and despite Bailey's regular teasing, they had managed to keep him somewhat in the dark. If anybody knew or had guessed, it would have been Simon and Tom.

Tomorrow, however, was the day that this desert whirlwind was going to have to end. The hospital registrar and the head doctor had given John the all clear. He would leave in the morning, but he would still have to take things carefully for a week or two. They didn't know what their futures would hold now or where they were going next. For Katie, it meant remaining in a hospital that would feel very much empty, for John, the rumours had indicated Alexandria or Cairo. Wherever he went it wouldn't exactly be just around the corner; he would be gone in the morning and she might not see him again for a long time if ever. There was no more time, every minute now was precious.

'What are you doing here at this hour?' he whispered. 'It's still the middle of the night. I was just dreaming about you.'

'Move over,' she instructed and tidying the bed sheets she sat down on them and curled up beside him resting her head on his chest. John didn't think, the motions and actions that took place now were made with no thought, but a simple impulse of instinct. He pulled her hair through his fingers, grabbed her locks tight and gently pulled her mouth to his and kissed her tenderly. She melted in his arms and her closeness sent shivers down his spine. Her eyes told him that she wanted him and he wanted her.

'Get in,' he asked gently between his teeth as he folded his lips around hers further.

'No,' she said pulling away gently. 'Not here. Not now.'

'I'm sorry,' said John, kicking himself at his thoughtlessness and worrying that he had misread the signs. 'That was selfish of me to even think, let alone say that. I've gone too far.'

'Where are your things, your uniform and the great coat that Sergeant Major Hill brought in for you today?' she cooed softly.

'Under the bed,' he replied quietly.

'Put your great coat on to keep warm and let's go out, you've virtually been discharged it can do no harm,' she simmered.

'Where to?' he eagerly scrambled as he rustled and scurried under the bed amongst the brown paper wrappers of his new awaiting uniform.

'Ssshhhh,' she reminded him and peering through the curtains she beckoned him forward. As they tiptoed across the ward she acknowledged the night nurse, the first hint to John that she had already made arrangements to steal him away and the night nurse even gave him a wink as he passed by. Then Katie grabbed his hand and led him as quickly and quietly as she could from the sideward into the corridor.

Despite his slight limp and aided by a walking stick, they escaped out into the warm desert evening, Katie guiding him fervently to her quarters and her shared room where she revealed she had arranged for a little privacy for the evening.

'She was the nurse on duty, so won't be back until the morning.'

'You know that she winked at me!'

'Did she? She has quite a sense of humour that one, but she is the only one I have told.'

Her room was a very basic and simple shell; she switched on the light to reveal a small crate with a small hurricane lamp predominately placed on top of it in between two camp beds. Two suitcases were neatly packed under the beds and a wooden chair was propped against the end of one of the beds. The walls were a bright white and a ceiling fan twirled at a constant repetitive pace. The barred paned windows, crisscrossed with tape, were covered in sandy dust that obstructed any chance of viewing the cloudless and pink sunset that was slowly merging into the night. Katie took his heavy greatcoat and hung it on the back of the door, then she directed him to the chair and taking his stick as he sat in his hospital pyjamas she propped it against the wall. Disappearing through a door to his right she returned a minute later with a bottle of whisky and two glasses.

John was quite taken aback at her lack of creature comforts.

As if she had read his mind she said in a very forthright manner, 'at the height of war all female nurses are on an alert to leave at a moment's notice. We all keep our bags packed to make evacuation swift, you should have seen us get out of Tobruk, I left half my wardrobe there! But here is home for now.'

The bottle and glasses were placed down carefully on the crate. She moved over to him unpinning her hat at the same time and tossed it casually over on to the bed by the window, she pulled off the mattress and covers from the nearest bed and arranged them neatly on the floor.

'The beds squeak,' she said and they both struggled to contain a chuckle.

Katie then stepped back seemingly pleased with her accomplishments and unzipped her uniform. She pulled it over her head and dropped it on the floor without any undue concern for its remaining cleanliness, untying her laces; she stepped out of her shoes and peeled off her stockings. She unlocked her bra and tiptoed out of her underwear, discarding both items as randomly as she had her uniform, standing completely naked before him. Uncomplicated, immodest and shameless.

John stood up pitching and faltering on the uneven surface of the blanket. He opened his arms and folded them around her as she moved towards him. They stood for a moment embracing awkwardly as John found it a little difficult to balance without any aid still, but she held him as a multitude of emotions bubbled through his veins. She leant her head back and he leaned forward and kissed her neck tenderly. Such grief, such happiness, such excitement, he was totally overwhelmed. She was the most beautiful thing in his life, but he suddenly felt nervous as if he was being watched by everyone.

'Katie,' he whispered. 'You're absolutely sure we won't be disturbed?'

'I told you, she won't be back until morning. Stop being paranoid, you're safe, you're with me, do you want to go back?'

'Katie, are you…' but her eyes were closed and she was murmuring, mesmerized by his gentleness. 'Oh never mind,' he consoled and taking a very deep breath slowly slid to the floor on his knees caressing her body as he went down.

It all just seemed some sort of miracle: Such inexpressible joy as he beheld her beautiful body standing before him. He was so close now but as he reached the floor kneeling he grimaced with pain as it rampaged and sent shock waves through his thigh. Katie came to him again and stood close to his face and pressed her stomach to his lips. He looked up as if for further confirmation, but her eyes were still closed and she was feeling through his hair with her hands. Her body tense with expectations.

Haphazardly he undid the buttons on his shirt and with a clumsy awkwardness and the sentiments that he should have thought about this and done it a few steps further back, he wobbled ungracefully as he tried to take off his underwear. Katie laughed gently as with one leg inside and one leg outside of his pyjama bottoms and in complete disarray, he knelt beside her a frustrated invalid at his clumsiness and so she came to the rescue once again.

He felt more wounded by this moment than all his battle scars put together, but with his confidence renewed by her continued arousal, he languorously made love to her. She groaned in ecstasy at his every movement. Rolling in and out, over and under each other's bodies until the pulsating climaxing rhythms of their intertwining souls were reached. He sat up breathlessly and she elevated herself beside him her arms wrapped around her knees protectively.

'Are you okay?' he asked.

'I'm fine,' she replied weakly.

'Did I hurt you, did I go too far?' he replied, worried by her weak response.

'No,' she said back, but already the tears were flowing and little sobs caused her body to tremble.

He pulled himself next to her and held her for a while. She trembled within his arms and her fingers dug gently into his skin.

'Hey did I hurt you? I didn't mean to hurt you I would never hurt you,' he blurted angrily at himself for his inconsideration.

'No, it's not that, it was wonderful,' she murmured between short sharp breaths and tears. 'What is going to happen to us? I have never been this happy, I don't know when I'll see you again, you're going away tomorrow and what if I never see you again? I don't do this sort of thing what the hell am I doing!' she sounded disappointed with herself.

'I'm sorry, this should never have happened, but I can't help it either, it feels so right doesn't it? It's funny, I was just laying here thinking what a blessing these past weeks have been and how you make me feel. I would never have dreamed or believed it in a million years,' she smiled at him and he kissed her again.

'Tomorrow I will be gone and soon I will be sleeping on the sand, in the sand, under sand, eating sand, walking on sand, cleaning my mess tin with sand and digging holes in the sand, but I'll still have you won't I? I'll hold you and this moment in my heart until the next time, the sand won't matter. Christ, I'm insane with happiness!'

'I don't know where you live, where we will meet next, what if we lose touch, what if you get somewhere you can't contact me, what if the war finishes next week and I am sent home and we can't find each other again, what if…' she went on with more hypothetical scenarios.

Her insecurity comforted him, for her worries mirrored his own.

'Katie, we are happy, aren't we? I'm never going to lose this, or you. Have faith, we can do nothing about the situation we are in or being separated. That's the trouble with war there are no rules. I know it makes it hard for you, but it makes it just as hard for me too. I don't want to go away not when I've only just found you, but this is my life for the moment and yours. I might come back to you all broken and messed up again.'

'I will fix you,' she said and the sounding harsh with herself, sighed, 'listen to me, I keep thinking I am such a mess but aren't we all? I can't wait for this bloody war to be over.'

'Tom once said to me and I think he said it to Sophie the night we left England, "say what you feel, when you feel it, never leave things unsaid, be true to yourself." I don't know why it's always stuck, but it has,' John said.

'That's nice,' she said, turning onto her front to look at him better. 'No regrets, I like that. Your Sergeant Major clearly had a love in his life.'

'Yeah the army,' John chuckled.

'I know we are saying this is not the end, but I can't help but feel that such promises are seldom kept,' she said routing through a bag for a cigarette and offered one to John. 'People say things in the heat of the moment with such good intentions.'

'My intention is to find you when this is all over and never let you go again.'

John was consumed in the bliss of this one moment, he didn't pay any attention to tomorrow and couldn't care less as to what tomorrow would bring, only that Katie had to be in it somehow. He wished to make the most of everything in the here and now. Deeply immersed in the moment, all seemed beautiful as the gentle gust of a sand storm outside and the romantic flicker of the hurricane lamp added to the ambience. This was how he would remember it all, this is what he would take with him and hold on to.

He bit her neck playfully and then tickling her they rolled and laughed together, tangled in the thin white sheets on the floor for the last time.

They both knew the time would end and even the lamp flickered more dramatically as it began to burn the last of the paraffin. Picking everything up they made themselves look more presentable and snuck back to the ward without running into anyone. John and Katie kissed goodnight, embracing together for the last time, both disappointed at being parted, both finding it difficult to let go of each other. Eventually Katie slipped from his arms and he was left there in silence as if it had all been a dream.

Sophie woke late into the night, the sedative now well and truly kicked out of her system. She was still tired, but her eyes were open. She was still in the armchair where she had been left and the storm that had been approaching during the day was on its way out, although the wind was still shaking the trees and the hawthorn bush was still clawing at the windows. It unnerved her to wake up in the dark and she felt for the lamp nearby, illuminating the room in a warm glow.

Was it real? She wondered for a moment, thinking back to the news of Anthony. Off course it was real, the letter from his parents lay on the table nearby to remind her. She reached for it and read the top line. There it was in black and white, there was no doubt, no hope, only the reality. She wanted to crunch it into a ball in her hand and throw it across the room, but she also imagined that one day she would need to look at it again, to torment her memory of what could have been. Like the many things in life she had collected, there would be a place for it and for now that place was an old shoe box that held all her correspondence from Africa. In there she would place it next to the letter of proposal and both of these would be kept separate from the rest, a memento to look back upon in years to come, a story to save and share on a rainy day when her own daughter perhaps had experienced the loss of love for herself.

Buckland had become her very own sentinel and she watched him watch her over the next couple of days. It interested her that instead of going above and beyond as she believed most men do when a damsel was in distress, he continued the same routine, perhaps working out that what she needed was normality. It took a couple of days for her to eat properly, a couple more before she would look at him again as she had once done and when she did a feeling of shame and guilt overtook her. When Anthony had been alive she had struggled to see him in her mind, but now he was gone, like a ghost he was visible everywhere as clear as day, especially when she looked at Buckland. The most painful part was that when she saw him she imagined him to be scowling at her, or simply shaking his head. The more she tried to convince the ghost that she felt nothing for her lodger, the more dejected the ghost looked.

Sophie was not surprised at the number of visits from Joy and Uncle Richard, she was touched at their love as always and she was happy to be rid of Dr Parsons when he popped in as promised. Overall she wanted peace and quiet whilst at home and the hustle and bustle of the wards. The spectators were making her feel she was a zoo animal.

She eventually looked through the remaining letters, supervised by Buckland. Although she would never admit it to him, it was a comfort having him over her shoulder, it gave her the extra strength she needed to open them. The letters, now joined by a few more were work-related anyhow, so there was no need for concern, not that it made opening them any less difficult. One was from her matron at the hospital advising her to take her time, but that she was needed and sorely missed. It was at the hospital that Sophie felt she should be, being needed meant being busy and that meant there was less time to think about her loss. She did, however, agree to some sick leave, more so for Uncle Richard and Joy than anything else.

She told Buckland that she was over the initial shock. It wasn't important that he believed her and the look in his eye did not betray her assumption that he hadn't anyway. In one day Sophie had received news of her brother brought back from the dead in one hand, but had lost her true love Anthony on the same day in the other.

Up until now the only information on John received from Tom, had been that he was alive. A further letter from Tom soon found her and any hope that remained in hiding within her was swept away when Tom himself confirmed Anthony's mortality, tactfully and delicately mentioned, as was Tom's way with reporting bad news. There wasn't much more information he could give her and she sensed how lost he was with what else to right. Usually there was an amusing tale or a description of something exciting, but all were missing from this letter that concentrated on her brother's health as if that was the only positive thing he had to focus on.

Her two days with Buckland had given her time to continue her mother's journey and he had wrestled the countless books down into the parlour room so she could read them more easily and in comfort. By now he had returned to his duties and felt more confident she wouldn't do anything silly, something Dr Parsons had hinted at as he left a few nights ago.

From Sophie's point of view, it gave her time alone, time with her mother whose words at times helped ease her pain and her suffering, whilst at others, she felt a strange entwinement of their lives and it was difficult not to see that they were in the same boat. After John was born, it was inevitable that she would read about Jack's death and with the extra time on her hands, she had reached as far as 1917 now and the letter her mother received from the army of his passing was found with a pressed poppy and cornflower amidst the pages. Her heart felt sore now, understanding completely what her mother felt. It was different from the death of her own father, that had been tragic in a different way, but she could sympathise with her mother's loss of Jack so much more. If she erased Jacks name Anthony would fit in the void just as easily.

'Tom,' she said out loud, realising that he had been missing from the correspondence for some time now.

She scoured the next few pages of the 1917 diary, until nearly a month later she found a letter from Tom expressing his sadness of Jack's death. But why wasn't he with him? All she could determine was that Tom only knew about Jack's death because her mother had written to him, but surely it should have been the other way around. Tom had always told John the details of his father's heroic death as if a witness to it.

She went back over previous pages and there was nothing, until she noticed a separate note written at the top of a page in red pencil that her mother had added so as not to forget, it simply had "Tom, A COY, 2ND MID" She understood it was A company, but the second part she didn't understand. Whatever it was, it still did not reveal why Tom was so late in knowing about Jack's death, surely he was there, at least that is what he had always told them.

She imagined what Buckland would say as if he was over her shoulder, 'I'm sure there are a number of reasons. Maybe they were separated or it might just be the fog of war. The fog of war being…'

'I know what the fog of war is,' she again said to herself.

She reached for some paper and a pencil, deciding to write to both John and Tom there and then. She knew it took a while for her mail to reach them wherever they were in Africa, but hopefully by the time they received it John would be on the mend or maybe even back on duty. Wherever he was he might be interested in her findings and Tom could fill in the blanks. So she set to work with pencil and paper.

When Sophie had completed her essays she placed them in two envelopes ready to send off to Africa. She would be back at work tomorrow and so had to utilise the time she already had. The post office was a good mile away in the village and would be open for another couple of hours. She settled on the idea of calling in up at the Great Hall to show Uncle Richard and Joy her latest discoveries and perhaps her uncle could shed some light on the mystery numbers. Popping in was also the least she could do, they had spent so much time worrying about her, checking in on her and being supportive. Sophie hadn't really returned any of their kindnesses socially, just thrown herself into the diaries and tomorrow she would throw herself back into work.

Joy had felt partially guilty about making Sophie open her mail and hadn't stopped apologising since. She had pleaded with her to go down with her to the cottage she had in Devon for a short break, but Sophie had refused, she couldn't abandon her work, even with Mrs Jenkins' encouragement she was emphatic that she just wanted to stay home. She recalled their gestures, smiled and decided that she would raid the garden of flowers and take a pot of delicious strawberry jam made by Mrs Jenkins to them as a surprise.

With her letters, a jar of jam and a newspaper tucked under her arm, Sophie browsed the garden, snipping a pair of scissors in her right hand through the imaginary air. She eventually decided on some ruby red dahlias which were growing by the gate and set the newspaper down ready, sprawled at a random page. She continued to snip here and there but actual stems this time and wrapped an assortment of vivid blooms into the newspaper and transferred the posy, letters, scissors and jam to her awaiting bicycle basket. She set off for the post office.

Today you would have been hard-pressed to prove that there was a war going on. As she took herself off up the lane towards the main village the birds were singing in a chorus, a rabbit dashed out from the verge and two jays watched the world go by as they sat upon the wire fence of the sheep field.

On arrival at the post office, Sophie leaned her bicycle against the wall outside, trying to keep her flowers from falling out of the basket whilst she headed inside to get her stamps. Within minutes she was assured that her letters were on the way to the desert and returned to the bright sunlit day outside.

'Hello, you!' said a charming voice from behind her as she stepped back from the shiny bright red box embedded in the post office wall.

'Oh, Lieutenant Buckland,' she said with surprise as she turned literally straight into his arms apologetically and crossing his pathway as he mirrored her movements exactly. They both stopped and laughed helplessly at the predicament they found themselves in.

'You're out and about,' he sounded surprised.

'I needed to send some letters,' she said passing him by and pulling her bicycle from the wall. 'Before you start, I'm feeling fine and off to see my uncle. What are you doing here, does my uncle know you are neglecting your duties?'

'Funnily enough he knows exactly where I am, as I am on my way to see him now. Just popping in here to send some post of my own on the way,' he wore a satisfactory smile at putting her in her place. 'Can I join you on the way?'

She looked at her mode of transport and then to his motorbike that sat further down the road.

'I will come back for the motorbike,' he said noticing her stare and then pointed to her bicycle. 'Let me push it for you.'

She nodded in agreement.

It was now early afternoon and the air was warm. As he pushed the bicycle through the village the turning of the wheels created a current that sent the fragrance of the flowers in her basket wafting up to their noses. She felt so much better walking alongside him as he told her of tales at sea. His storytelling reminded her of Tom a little and a small void that had been created in his absence was temporarily filled. There was the amusing tale of Terry the Terrier, a dog that he remembered whilst serving on a destroyer before the war that gave the galley a run for its money. Then there were the gloomy tales of convoy duties, which reminded her that she should be relieved and grateful to have John back from the dead.

She felt awkward for being so happy around him, especially now as the loss of Anthony still weighed heavily on her heart. As Lieutenant Buckland so rightly commented, 'It's good to grieve and for as long as we deem it necessary, but don't forget the living and make them feel guilty for surviving and we must not forget to live ourselves.' Anthony had said something similar to her in a letter some time ago and picturing him in her heart, she blew a kiss to him in heaven and then pushed her feet forwards, trying to keep up with Buckland's fast pace.

As they reached the other side of the village, he had been so successful in his efforts to distract her mind from any heartache, that in that momentary lapse of concentration she had done something that she had forbidden herself to do for the past five years and that was to take the short cut down the lane opposite the butchers. Without realising, she had forgotten to encourage him to head straight and instead followed him to the left. She wanted to slow down and even wondered if she should pretend that the other route was faster, but he no doubt knew the best routes by now as well as she did and with the main village behind her she continued to follow him down the lane. They passed the three stone cottages and then, around the sharp bend at the bottom of the hill they came to the Three Feathers pub.

Suddenly she paused and the laughing and light-hearted mood was blown away by the summery breeze. Buckland took a moment to stop and looking back to her asked, 'You alright, Miss Watson? You look like you've seen…'

'A ghost? Yes, I know.'

There were three things in her life she wished she could forget or wished had never happened. One was the war and its disruption to her happiness more recently, another was the loss of her mother and the sight of the Three Feathers bought back the last dormant nightmare from its resting place in the back of her mind.

The Three Feathers stood in all its ancient grandeur, silent and imposing with the sun shimmering through the drops of dew, caught in the delicate spider webs that encroached and sparkled in the corners of the deep coloured oak doors that were firmly locked shut, keeping out unwontedly customers from entering at this early hour.

The only movement in the lane came from the swishing of the ferns and the percolating trickle of the brook in the deep gully that bordered the lane. Over the brook was the rustling sound of the leaves in the pendulous treetops. As a cold chill began to embrace her body, Sophie noticed that the bird songs had suddenly stopped.

To those in need of thirst-quenching refreshment, The Three Feathers was no doubt a welcome sight indeed, serving real traditional cask ales from the nearby brewery in Lewes. To Sophie however, The Three Feathers gave no such sustenance, only sadness, regret, anguish, disappointment and self-condemnation. Her father had been a regular patron to this watering hole as well as John, but the patronage on both her father and John's parts had been on a social basis only and rarely at the same time.

'Miss Watson?'

'My father drank here,' she began. 'I haven't told you about him and it's a chapter of my life that won't crop up in my mother's diary either.'

'I see. I take it that it's a bad memory and not one for sharing.'

It was a chapter that only herself, her mother, John and Tom knew about. What happened on the night of the 4th May 1935 had never been uttered, although it was certainly at times on their mind.

The First Painful Memory
Sussex 4th May 1935

Sophie's father, Ted, had on the whole been a supportive family man. A successful businessman who had grown up in New England, he had found himself in Britain making prospects for new business at the end of the Great War where most would have thought you could only scrape the barrel for any opportunity, but Ted was shrewd and knew life wouldn't take long to get back to normal. He had been a good provider and had wooed and courted her mother with his suave American confidence. He had adored them both and his beautiful daughter could wrap him around her little finger.

Ted would never have been able to fill John's father's shoes of course, even though John had never known his father. The ivory tower that his memory had been encased in was completely indestructible and the idea of John accepting any other fatherly figure, in this or any other life and least of all by Ted, was completely unattainable.

Needless to say at times family life could be difficult. Helen's continuous effort to unravel some of the idealism she had created and appease the situation with her calm and soothing manner, along with the practical help of Tom was admirable when Sophie looked back on it all. Despite this, John still regarded Ted in a subordinate manner and just never really grew to like him, but he loved his sister and his mother and sweetened his coffee for their sakes.

And so the status quo continued until that was after the Wall Street Crash in 1929. Ted, then virtually became a resident at the Three Feathers drowning his sorrows at every opportunity. The businesses he had established across the pond in his new home spiralled and folded one after the other. Sophie's mother's inheritance given to her by Uncle Richard after their father had died was all that there had been to keep them afloat. A great deal of that had had to be used to bail out some of Ted's debts. John despite being so mature for his age was only thirteen and watched helplessly and with frustration when Ted would think nothing of taking the very last of the housekeeping from their mother's purse to nurture his depression with a drink at their expense. Any respect John had had for the man had become non-existent by then and his mother and sister became a constant worry to him. The situation wasn't helped years later when John had to go away for 5 months training in his first year as an officer in the Infantry, a role that Tom had insisted he should take and one that he felt could turn fortune around.

Family sympathy for Ted's plight had now become indifferent. As time had passed his depressions had become more profound and the only comfort and solace he would accept were from a bottle. Nearly every night he would stumble in through the door of the cottage, occasionally vomiting before he would reach the bathroom, often swearing and shouting abusively at Sophie's mother or both of them if he had been thrown out a little earlier than usual.

He would slur and babble on about how much he didn't care about what he had lost; clearly distraught and enraged at the whole situation he now found himself in and having to sell various other assets that were blatantly dear to his heart. Sophie was too young to remember caring about what the assets were, she was wrapped up in reading and writing scary stories or drawing pictures. All she could remember was that this auspicious self-made man had now toppled from a very lucrative ladder down to having to rely upon an allowance from his wife.

The resentment grew on both sides, Helen's, for his lack of sobriety and submission and Ted's for having to ask her for the money. Ted loved Helen, he needed her, he wanted her, but to her his dependence had become a burden, a heavyweight that pulled her down. Now physically and emotionally she was drained and they couldn't have been further apart. He had become more and more alienated from her and Sophie was helplessly caught in between.

By her teens everything was gone, including his pride, dignity and social standing. Her father had become an embarrassing nuisance and despite all of Sophie's efforts of encouragement, he shouted her down or slobbered all over her profusely. Whimpering his misfortune, immersing the atmosphere with the stench of stale drink, he would overwhelm the very air, clean, fresh air she was gasping for. He clambered and clung to her delicate framework for comfort, murmuring for consolation and some form of encouragement, mistaking her for her mother in his inebriation. It was all Sophie could do at times but to push him away, chastising him softly but sincerely as 'you're drunk again' and calling her mother for help getting him to bed.

It was when John was far away that the situation got worse, all the time her brother was home Ted tried harder to stay sober, especially now he wore the green uniform of authority, but then on the 4th of May 1935, it all came to a head. She could remember as if it was yesterday. The fresh spring air filled her lungs with a flowery fragrance and the constant showers of hard and heavy rain drummed against the windows.

John had been away since January. Her mother was so proud that he had chosen to follow in the footsteps of his father. For five months they hadn't seen him and in those five months Sophie's father had become worse. He spent most of his nights down at The Three Feathers and now he was knocking on the door before opening time, coming home at closing time for a nap during the afternoon and on waking would wander back down for the rest of the evening's spoils. If he was drunk enough, he couldn't think about it. A scotch or two had sung him through the afternoon lull on this particular day and he had run out of funds again. 'Lend me a bob, Soph,' he whined.

'Oh dad, don't go down there again, you don't need any more,' she pleaded. 'Why don't you come with us to the Ball this evening? Let's all go together as a family. You used to love dancing.'

'Your mother wouldn't approve,' he sneered disparagingly. 'It's just a bob, Soph, that's all I am asking for.'

He raised his hands in questioning despair. She refused his request replying that she barely had enough for herself and pretended that she would get into trouble from her mother for giving in. He reacted disdainfully and cursing aggressively slammed the door as he marched out of the house. For Sophie, it created a disturbing atmosphere for the rest of her day and it was raining now.

Her mother was a member of the local women's institute and for the past few months she had been busy preparing for the spring ball in the town hall at Eastbourne. The ball was meant to raise money to help repair the local church roof damaged in a storm the previous year, but had now grown in size to become the event of the year, so much so that hundreds of people were expected to turn up. Both Sophie's mother and the whole area seemed to be buzzing with excitement about the event and Sophie was particularly eager when her mother as a special treat had brought her a new dress. It was beautiful, so very elegant and Sophie looked stunning within it. It flowed so naturally over her young and youthful body and she twirled in front of the tall freestanding mirror in her bedroom. Normally she would have shied away from the mirror, for no matter how many times her mother, father or her brother told her; she just couldn't see the beauty within it.

'My, my,' her mother said from the doorway. 'Just look at you.'

The dress which was a lush and vibrant red started from her bare shoulders, nipped in around her tiny waist and fell down to her feet. It was simple and unpretentious, to some perhaps quite plain, but on Sophie it had become an elegant and perfect statement. Her dark hair was wrapped tightly in a bun crowning her head and her lips were coated in a rich glossy red lipstick. She looked graceful and refined for her young age.

'The boys will be falling over backwards when they see you,' her mother said.

'Mum!' she replied with embarrassment.

Her mother laughed. There would be few lads at the ball her age. The scary thing for her mother was accepting that this gloriously beautiful woman in front of her was still her soon to be sixteen-year-old daughter.

'You need to stop growing up,' she said. She stood behind Sophie and gently placed around her neck a silver necklace, 'You're making me feel old.'

Sophie smiled. Her mother was a great inspiration to her, always managing to get through the hardest of times with a warm smile. She wondered whether to tell her about her father, but didn't want to ruin the moment.

Her mother sighed, 'More beautiful than an English rose.' She looked at Sophie from within the mirror. 'I chose the colour because I knew it would suit you.'

'I know,' Sophie smiled. 'I'm your English rose, but roses can be other colours you know.'

'But I think the most beautiful roses are red. They are full of depth and richness, from claret to ruby they stand out against all the other flowers of the world. Just like my daughter,' she leant her chin upon Sophie's shoulder and put her arms around her cherished daughter. 'Now then, I have to pop along to Annie's to prepare a few things for this evening, I'll only be gone for half an hour or so.'

'The weather doesn't look like it's going to let you.' Sophie remarked.

Her mother looked wistfully through the window pane as if searching for a gap to appear so she could escape without getting caught up in the downfall.

'It will ruin my hair. Oh and there is going to be a special surprise for you this evening at the ball,' she added nonchalantly.

'What surprise?' Sophie looked puzzled.

'It's just a surprise, but I think you'll like it.'

With an animated grin, her mother then walked out of the bedroom and down the stairs. Sophie could hear her Mother putting on her coat and the grating of the door as it opened.

She wondered what the surprise could be and then as she pondered she went back to staring at herself within the mirror. She turned her body to the left and then to the right. The dress was indeed lovely, but she was more excited now about what the surprise at the ball could be. At fifteen Sophie was still more interested in her studies than boys, her hormones had kicked in but they hadn't imposed their emotional velocities yet. There had been no one at this stage in her young life that had caused her heart to flutter, take her breath away or blush and her naiveties remained intact. Perhaps somebody important was going to be there? That must be what her mother meant, that at the ball a special guest would be present. She would be sixteen tomorrow, perhaps the surprise was something to do with that? Someone famous, her thoughts were running away in all directions now.

She looked once more at herself in the mirror and finally managed to smile. She did look wonderful and perhaps for the first time in her life she felt comfortable saying it to herself.

Before long the sound of a hooting car horn brought Sophie out of her temporary trance and she realised that Annie and her mother were outside waiting for her.

She grabbed her mother's shawl from the back of her bedroom chair and made her way down the stairs to the hallway. She tugged at the vacant umbrella in the stand, shook it slightly open so that it was ready to put up and as she opened the door made one last quick glance around the hallway, before flicking off the switch and pulling the door shut behind her. The Ball awaited.

Sophie didn't remember the journey, which was only a short journey, her heart was pounding with excitement and before she knew it they had arrived at The Town Hall. She alighted from the car with her mother, pushing up the umbrella to keep them dry. They waited while Annie parked the car and watched as people streamed in from all directions.

'Oh mum, look at all the people,' Sophie exclaimed enthusiastically.

'I think we will be making a good contribution to the Church roof,' Helen said shrugging her shoulders gleefully. 'A very good contribution.'

Annie caught up with them at the doorway, 'Wow, Helen, you really did sell a lot of tickets' and arm in arm they giggled together all the way into the Ballroom.

Before she knew it Sophie was surrounded by Tuxedos, Ball gowns, sequins and silks. She picked her way through the multitude that was directing themselves anti-clockwise, trapped in sequence with the glittering pirouetting circles of colour that splashed the walls, courtesy of a huge gyrating mirrored ball that rotated in tempo with the music that was drifting through the air from the band.

Sophie smiled a contented smile, this was heavenly.

'What do you think?' her mother asked loudly over the last chord of the current song, as the swirling came to a halt and the applause of the appreciative audience echoed across to where they were standing. Sophie didn't get the chance to reply, in the next instance her mother's eyes had caught a glimpse of someone trying to attract her attention, with an air of surprise and delight her mother was next seen gliding across the dance floor in their direction.

Sophie shook her head in disbelief at the enchanted room her mother had been a part of decorating. Smiling she said to herself, 'oh mother it's magical. You have done a good job.'

As she watched her mother disappearing amongst the throng, she saw her turn, clasping her hand to her lips as if she had forgotten something she turned and directed her finger at Sophie, drawing an anti-clockwise circle in the air and mouthing the words, 'turn around.'

Sophie frowned and looked with some perplexity back at her mother in return. Her mother repeated the charade like sequence again. Then with sudden realisation and clarity of the instructions, she spun around on her heels to find Tom and her brother propped up against the bar grinning at her.

'Surprise little sis,' he bellowed in her ear as she threw her arms around him hugging him tightly. He chuckled and winked at Tom, 'steady on, this might be the only pint I get bought this evening.'

The head of his ale quivered precariously around the rim of his pint jug and then settled back down.

'I thought you were both away?'

'We've got 48 hours to leave, so it's only a short stopover,' then seeing his sister's questioning look and raising his voice an octave higher, he squawked, 'well I couldn't miss my little sisters 16th birthday tomorrow could I?'

He pulled a small package from behind his back and presented it to her with his free hand.

'Not till tomorrow though!' Tom said, his formidable stature stepped forward and gently brushed her cheek with a kiss, which caught a solitary, salty tear of delight as it fell. 'Happy birthday my dear, you look delightful.'

He handed her a champagne glass. Overwhelmed with the whole array she accepted the glass hesitantly but gracefully.

'We will tell mum that it's only lemonade,' John said winking.

'Oh that's quite alright, thank goodness I'm not driving!' she said sipping it courteously and glancing away. There was spontaneous laughter from all of them at once to her cheeky repartee.

Walking over to a spare table, John twirled Sophie around in front of him.

'Quite the young lady, don't you think Sergeant Major? When I left she was a child, now when I return I see a woman,' John bowed.

Sophie blushed almost as ruby as the dress she was wearing.

'What do you think of mum's efforts?' Sophie said, changing the subject as her self-consciousness began to take over. She pointed to the décor and the band, 'She has worked hard.'

'Good party,' John remarked by nodding his head in the direction of the filled dance floor. 'I always thought the women's institute just got up to knitting and things like that.'

His comment got a sound from Tom as if he had scalded his hand, a warning that his comments could find their way to insulted ears.

'It's nothing like that and you know it,' Sophie continued. 'Mum's worked tirelessly for weeks to get this right. Annie's been helping too. Have you seen her yet?' she asked with a little apprehension.

For a brief period of time John and Annie had courted.

'No, not yet,' John mumbled. 'Think it's best to leave it, water under the bridge and all that, you do understand don't you? I'm sure we'll bump into each other before the night is over, but it's all over.'

'Does Annie know this?' she chuckled.

John preferred to avoid the subject and offered Sophie his uniformed arm and asked, 'shall we dance?'

Tom, gracefully half bowing and saluting, made his excuses and headed off in another direction.

Sophie knew that sometimes one could be disillusioned and disappointed when expectations are not met and don't always turn out the way one might imagine them. This was not so as she took her brother's hand and like a nimble deer, she tapped the floor with her toes and heels. To be truthful the Spring Ball exceeded her expectations and more. The surprise of her brother's presence was the icing on the cake. So what had seemed a miserable day when it started, had turned out very well indeed and she danced the rest of the night away like Cinderella.

At midnight came the anti-climax as the band played its last piece. Sophie felt deflated as she watched the multitude of happy faces, many who had drunk themselves into a stupor or were red in the face from so much dancing depart. Annie appeared at Sophie's side just like a fairy godmother, 'time to go Sophie… Hi John, how are you?' she said blushing fervently and gushing into the next sentence to avoid any further conversation. Sophie had seen her looking over at their table all night. 'Sophie, Tom is staying to help your mother with the rest of the clearing up, I think we are pretty much there now so I can take you home. I'll drop you off as well shall I John?'

'Well I'm not sure,' he stuttered.

'There will be no charge! Besides it was Tom's suggestion so he can take the staff car and drive Helen home like a real gentleman,' she added sarcastically.

Without waiting for a response she spun like a mini whirlwind, gathering up Sophie in her path and sweeping her through the doorway before setting her down on the top step of the Town Hall entrance. John landed next to her a moment later breathless from the experience.

'I won't be a tick,' Annie chirped and flicked her long dark hair across John's face as she crossed his path.

'I think there's going to be words,' jibed Sophie, cheekily wagging her finger at him and grinning. 'Rather you than me!'

'Yeah, right, thanks for that Sophie,' he sighed.

'You're welcome,' she replied again and clip-clopped her tired heels to the lower Town Hall steps as Annie's car pulled up.

It was a silent journey home; Sophie dozed in and out of consciousness with the rhythm of the wiper blades as they squeaked and grated from one side of the windscreen to the other. As the purring of the engine stopped outside the cottage gate, Sophie fumbled in her bag for the key to the door. Alighting from the car and raising her umbrella, she popped her head back in the car and noted the coolness of the atmosphere before making her excuse as she attempted to close the door.

'Thanks for tonight Annie,' she whispered. 'John?' she asked enquiringly, wondering if he was going to get out or not.

'Give us a minute Soph, get yourself inside or you'll catch a chill. Put the kettle on?'

'I'll turn your bed down ready,' she said, smiling knowingly and spun the key around in her fingers. Unable to resist, she quirked to Annie, 'be gentle with him, he's my brother.'

'Happy birthday for tomorrow Sophie,' said Annie.

John waved meekly as she slammed the door and made her way up the path.

As she turned the key in the lock, she heard the car pull away. Sophie wondered whether to put the kettle on now or after turning down the beds for their guests. There wouldn't be a lot of time if John had only 48 hours leave, but it was so good to see him. She kicked off her shoes and ran upstairs to turn down the beds.

She heard the front door rattle and realised that she had locked it again on entering, poor John had no key and wouldn't be able to get in. She hurried along the landing and jumped down the stairs two at a time, but as she reached the door it already swung open with force and smashed into the side of her face.

Sophie screeched with pain, cupping her right cheek with both her hands and looked in disbelief as her father thundered into the house uncontrollably crashing onto her and bringing them down like tumbling bricks. He snorted and spat in his drunkenness, completely unaware that his daughter was crushed beneath him, kneeing her groin in his failed attempts in trying to pick himself up. Finally, he fell sideways on to his back and they both lay there side by side. Carbon dioxide gushed from Sophie's airways as the pressure of his knee and body ceased at last. The rain was driving through onto the hallway carpet and the door continually banged against the wall, chipping at the wallpaper on each return.

'Oh Dad,' she groaned and curling in a ball away from the stench of whisky, picked her fractured torso as best she could up off the floor.

Ted was fine; Sophie had broken his fall and for a brief moment soberness seemed to get the better of him. He groaned an apology and she wept.

'Mum won't be long,' she whimpered and still clutching her face, she dragged herself to the kitchen.

As she passed the mirror in the hall she noticed her nose and lip were bleeding, so she aimed for the kitchen sink to get a cloth to wipe the blood away. As she edged away from the mirror her father staggered towards her again, his legs giving away by the hall table and everything within arm's length diminished beneath his torso once again. Sophie in her anguish stood disbelievingly at his wretchedness, a shadow of the man she once revered and knew. He finally reached the kitchen door and haphazardly leant against the doorframe, trying to focus.

Sophie cupped her hands under the running tap and brought them up to the smarting wounds on her face to soothe her cuts. Wincing and flinching as the coolness of the moisture smarted and stung, her eyelashes flicked open and shut to keep out the water running from her forehead. She then leant across the draining board, clumsily feeling for a clean towel before dabbing herself dry.

'You missed a good night tonight, don't spoil it,' she cast him a look of condemnation. 'I'm fine by the way.'

'I'm sorry,' he slurred.

She filled the kettle from the Fawcett and put it down on the range where it sizzled and spurted as if in protest.

Ted tugged at her arm to get her attention and she rounded on him saying between short, sharp breaths between sobs and tears, 'I'm making tea for the others, would you like one?'

'Others, what others?' he questioned, stammering and swaying at the same time in the doorway.

'John, Uncle Tom, mother, I don't know about Annie but I expect not,' she said softly.

'Oh! For Christ's sake, not the bloody cavalry again back from sodding manoeuvres already,' he thundered raising his arms in disbelief and for a brief moment, he seemed wide awake from his drunken trance. 'Hasn't someone shot them yet? Where are they then? Come out, come out wherever you are?'

He called out, mockingly cocking his index finger towards his nose and then around the kitchen space as if calling to an invisible cat and catching himself precariously before he completely lost his balance. He then attempted to salute to his daughter who watched with little interest.

'I think John's saying goodnight to Annie outside,' Sophie croaked as she tried to prop him up as his legs gave way again. 'And Uncle Tom and mum are tidying up at the Town Hall.'

Ted looked at her indignantly, then his eyes flashed and he jumped to attention mockingly. Gripping her tightly she was locked in his vision like a startled rabbit trapped in a car's headlights unable to move.

'I bet they are,' he said scornfully and with that commenced singing Maurice Chevalier's "Isn't it romantic," as his breath petered out, he pushed Sophie away splattering all over her. 'Drink Sophie. Get me a drink.'

'The kettles nearly boiled,' Sophie sighed, taking a deep breath of relief at her new found freedom from his grip again.

‘Kettle, kettle? I don’t want a bloody kettle,’ he screeched. ‘Where’s the whisky?’

He staggered to the cupboards in the kitchen, opening and slamming the doors shut remorsefully as each one revealed to him no glittering prize.

‘Sergeant bloody major,’ he muttered and grunted.

‘You don’t want tea then?’

‘What is it with this family?’ and he lunged at Sophie, slobbered and slipped, punching his chest. ‘It doesn’t matter does it, I don’t matter do I?’

‘Of course you matter.’

‘What’s going on?’ he asked himself and then replied to himself. ‘I’ll tell you what’s bloody going on!’ Then aiming in Sophie’s direction he bleated with a sinister smile, ‘It’s never been me, I can’t do right from wrong in this God-forsaken family.’ He mimicking her mother piping, ‘oooooh Ted you’re drunk, ooooh not now Ted, Ted, Ted, Ted,’ his tone raising up and down in an octave.

‘Please dad, go and sit down, or go to bed.’

Then very snidely he turned on Sophie laughing at her ‘and look at you all dressed up and nowhere to go.’

She sobbed as she stirred the tea. ‘Actually, I’ve been to the ball at the Town Hall, which you were invited to, but perhaps your absence was for the best, we had a wonderful time!’

Both were dazed and surprised at her courageous retort.

‘Actually,’ he mimicked cruelly. ‘Actually, I think there’s more to you than meets the eye Madam,’ he continued vindictively, his eyes were heavy and full of viciousness. Saliva dribbled down his chin, making him look even more sinister.

‘Please go,’ she whispered.

He rose again like a raging torrent and sniped piercingly, ‘we had a wonderful time, we ALL had a wonderful time. I’m so clever, bloody sergeant major and my holier than thou so bloody perfect brother, Helen of bloody Troy and my daughter.’

‘Please.’

He looked at her, poking his chest, ‘my daughter, my lovely daughter.’ He then screamed maddeningly. ‘Well, I sometimes bloody wonder! Don’t you? I mean I wonder, are you actually?’

She didn't know where it came from, but the rage that surged through her body was unleashed before she had acknowledged it. The cup she had found from the cupboard exploded upon the wall beside him as she launched it with an energy she didn't know she had. Another followed until she remembered how much her mother loved the cups, decorated with little blue birds and pink flowers. Instead, she reached for one of the heavy brass pans and found his head.

'No I'm not! I'm not your daughter and never will I be. There is that what you want to hear?' her venomous words came uncomfortably easy to her. 'I wish you weren't my dad, in fact, I wouldn't care who my dad was, so long as it wasn't you! I am so ashamed of you. Do you hear me?'

He fell slumped against the wall rubbing his head where the pan had struck home, whispering something else unapologetically having finally run out of adrenalin, but she couldn't make out what it was that he had said.

Her chest heaved and exhaustion set in. Sophie couldn't bear to face him any longer in his own excitement and she carefully attempted to brush past him as best she could, her heart beating faster and faster and her body still shaking between the sobs. Her back was hurting and her lip still bleeding. She just wanted to get by, but her father was not finished and opened his mouth to lunge verbally like a springboard again.

Hearing all the commotion outside and crashing abruptly through into the kitchen came John. He saw the state of his sister and coming to his own conclusion landed himself between his sister and her father. Shouting and with such swiftness that nobody saw it coming, he belted a punch on Ted's chin. Before he even attempted to repeat his swing again, Ted slid to the floor in a messy heap.

Sophie threw herself at him, wrapping her bare feet around his legs as best she could in her long flowing dress and cried. He assertively unwrapped her and demanded, 'What's been going on here for Christ's sake?' rubbing the knuckles of his right hand.

'I don't know, I don't know,' said Sophie exasperatingly.

'Look at the state of you Sophie, what did he do to you, did he hit you? Sophie, did he touch you? Sophie, what did he do?'

John was grimacing and standing over Ted, waiting for him to get back up. She could have told him that it was all a misunderstanding, but at this point in time she could barely speak through the sobs and was just overwhelmed with gratitude for his presence.

There was no sign of Ted moving and John held his sister, gently brushing her face with the back of his hand with empathy.

Sophie put her hand to her mouth and with a pitiful frown looked at her father. Limp like a rag doll, his body was slumped against the kitchen cupboards.

'It was an accident, he was drunk, the door hit me in the face. You know what he is like, he's always drunk, he didn't touch me like that,' she whimpered. 'I hurt him with the pan I think.'

'Come on let's get him up,' said John encouragingly. 'I didn't even hit him hard.'

As he jostled Ted's frail carcass in an effort to get a hold of him, he suddenly sprang back into life, backing himself into the nearest corner with trepidation.

'Ted are you alright?' John asked, keeping Sophie behind him. 'I'm sorry Ted, I just got the wrong end of the stick there, I thought that... look I'm sorry.'

Ted staggered to his feet clambering up the cupboards and rebuking John, 'you'll be bloody sorry, soldier boy, this whole bloody family will be sorry. Aye, aye, captain.' He then turned to Sophie. 'And as for you, don't worry, you won't see me ever again, you have made sure of that!'

'Dad I'm sorry, I didn't mean…'

Ted glanced at John one last time and mimicked a salute, he then crisscrossed his way past them like a drowned rat. He aimed for the hallway towards the front door.

'Dad, where are you going?' Sophie cried out after him.

'Anywhere but here, it stinks here,' he brandished his arm behind him dismissively.

'Let him go,' comforted John.

'But where's he going to go at this time of night, it's raining and mum will be worried sick. We've got to get him back John, please,' she pleaded. 'In spite of everything he is my Dad.'

'The rain will sober him up, he'll be back in a minute,' John said and he looked at his sister's imploring face, her eyes red and sore from so many tears. 'He won't even reach the gate, Sophie, I promise you, he is completely legless!'

Her eyes told him everything he needed to know and then grabbing a coat from the coat stand in the hallway, he gestured her to stay where she was.

Her feeling of relief was interrupted as John turned to go out of the door and there was a long screeching sound of brakes and a thud. Sophie gasped, exchanging a look of shock and misgivings to her brother they both gasped 'Ted' and 'dad' simultaneously before tearing out of the house. Sophie, charging and splashing carelessly down the puddled pathway after her brother, didn't feel the jagged stones as they cut and punctured her bare feet.

It was a few yards up the road that they found her mother and Tom either side of him. Tom was profusely protesting his inability to avoid the situation and Helen was slumped on her knees trying to cradle him in her arms, calling his name gently in his ear and telling him to hold on. Within seconds of reaching him, Sophie was standing in a pool of blood. It was seeping into the road and filtering into the rainwater that his crumpled body lay upon, dispersing randomly into trickling veins mirrored by the moonlight and mixing with her own as she now noticed the stinging sensation from her feet.

'Find a house with a telephone to call for an ambulance Sophie,' her mother instructed. 'And somebody please go and get Doctor Parsons!'

Tom insisted they could fit him into his car, but it was clear it was too late by then. John embracing Sophie felt her exasperation as she wailed uncontrollably, 'it's all my fault, it's all my fault!'

'Ambulance! Please!' her mother cried again more insistently.

'I'll go,' said John, but as he let go of Sophie and turned he saw that Mrs Jenkins was already running towards them. Somehow she had witnessed the event from her end of the lane. As she reached them she said breathlessly, 'it's alright dears the ambulance is on its way. I used next door's phone and also phoned Doctor Parsons, he is on his way.'

‘I’m so sorry Helen, he was just suddenly there, from nowhere,’ said Tom, desperately trying to understand what had happened in his shock.

‘It was an accident Tom, an accident,’ said Helen tenderly gripping his arm to reassure him.

Sophie was now beside herself, clinging to her brother and calling to her father. His glazed eyes searched in response to her voice, but then as if being called from another direction he looked skywards, his eyes rolled back and slipped away into deaths grasp.

Tom checked Ted’s pulse and listened for any breathing, but there was nothing. He looked at Sophie and Helen and shook his head.

Sophie, devastated, sat in the middle of the road in her elegant ball gown, soaked to the skin and looking down upon her father. Tom took off his tunic and placed it around her bare shoulders, pulling her up and away from the scene gently. John took off his tunic and covered his mother to keep off the rain, then he placed the overcoat he had grabbed from the coat hook earlier over Ted’s body.

Mrs Jenkins ushered Sophie at John’s request into the house and Sophie reluctantly obeyed.

‘Are you sure he’s dead?’ Helen asked imploringly.

‘I’m sure,’ Tom replied, pulling her to his chest in a comforting embrace and then searching to the heavens he asked, ‘What happened here?’

It wasn’t long before Doctor Parsons came running down the dark lane, his slippers soaked and barely clinging to his desperate feet, his umbrella blown inside out. As he reached the scene he could already sense it was too late and so began slowing down to a fast walk as he approached.

The world was still, the rain had stopped and a gentle mist was rolling along the street. The damp smell of the early morning began to rise in the air. The sound of gentle droplets of rain stopped and was replaced by the sound of trickling water as the leftover rain flowed into the gully of the verge. In the distance, a blue tint of light seemed to sporadically turn the horizon on and off and then the silence was broken and everybody was brought to their senses by the clanging bell of the ambulance.

‘Sophie, are you alright? Said the voice of Lieutenant Buckland reassuringly. ‘You’ve been standing here for ages, I called out several times.’

‘What?’ she queried coming to from her memory finding herself back in the shady lane outside the pub.

‘You said something about your father.’

She looked back at The Three Feathers. ‘Yes, he used to drink here.’

‘I already got that part, I think you were going to tell me a little about him, but you ended up frozen to the spot.’

They continued walking. Sophie gave the pub one last glance, thinking to herself that it was about time to let the ghosts of her past float away. She couldn’t continue to avoid places like the short cut to her uncles, just because they reminded her of the past.

She told Buckland everything about her father’s death, going over the details of the memory she had just experienced for the second time and this time it felt good. It was the first time she had disclosed such information to anyone and it felt like an immense weight was lifted from her shoulders as if she was no longer alone as the keeper of the secret. She expressed her guilt quite openly and the complexity of life afterwards, feelings she had only ever shared with Tom.

‘John would tell me that it wasn’t my fault, but what I said to him…’

‘You weren’t to know and your brother is right, it wasn’t your fault. Fate dealt you a harsh deal that night.’

‘God I haven’t thought about that for a long time. I used to avoid thinking about it and it took me years to have a birthday that wasn’t tainted by it.’

‘I can understand,’ Buckland said. ‘I guess the loss of your mother not long after was also just as difficult.’

‘More so I think,’ she sighed. ‘It left me completely alone. You're supposed to lose your parents much later in life. When it happens you have your new family around you that keep you going and comfort you. Both John and I lost everything so soon and so young. We were completely alone and he felt it was his duty to look after me, I was all he had left and he was all I had as well.’

Buckland nodded, understanding more and more.

'I initially thought your brother might have been a bit of a bully, possessive almost.'

Sophie chuckled, 'he is, but I always understood. He was just being my big brother. Now when I look back on it all I think he was trying to be more. Perhaps he felt the responsibility to fulfil the role of our mother and fill the gap of my father. I guess when you're trying to be three things at once you get lost with your purpose.'

She thought for a moment, taking in the warm breeze and smiling at him as he listened attentively to her words. She suddenly realised how lost John was and despite having the army, he had put everything else on hold to be all the things he thought Sophie needed him to be. She had suddenly realised that both of them had been very selfish. She had needed his protective instincts and in turn, she had given him purpose. It was more complex than she initially realised and of course when Anthony had arrived the dynamics of their relationship had been tested.

'Think I could live here?' he interrupted her thoughts with an odd question.

'Excuse me?'

'Do you think I could live here, locally? I'm thinking of moving, after the war I mean. I could get a job, settle down.'

'I'm not sure you could settle down could you?' she jested.

He pretended to have been struck through the heart, 'Ouch.'

'It wasn't meant to offend,' she chuckled. 'But maybe you could, you would have to get to know the locals in a place like this.'

'Well I already know one,' he smiled trying to gauge her reaction from the corner of his eye. 'And she is all that's worth knowing.'

Sophie tried hard to keep a straight face, but there was a smile that was fighting hard to break through and at one point it was on the verge of victory. Buckland had a wonderful ability to lighten the mood, he was funny and loveable and he had a natural ability to make her smile. They talked about everything as they trudged further on up the hill. She glanced at him out of the corner of her eye once or twice thinking how similar he was in posture, build and facial features to Tom, resembling him both physically and personably, but obviously younger.

And just as she did with Tom, she felt safe and at ease with the young Lieutenant. There was nothing to prove to him and she had allowed him to enter her world a great deal faster than she had anticipated.

'Do you know what this means?' She asked and wrote out on a piece of the newspaper, "A COY, 2ND MID".

He studied it for a moment and then said, 'A company of the Second Middlesex Regiment. What did you want to know that for?'

'It's something to do with Tom,' she replied.

'More discoveries from the diaries? I thought Tom was in a different regiment during the first war…'

'Something doesn't add up, something doesn't make sense and I am determined to get to the bottom of it.'

They walked on again until Buckland broke the silence. 'It is beautiful countryside around here, and the coast isn't far, you can smell the fresh sea air every now and then. I think I might stay,' he declared, still thinking about his life beyond the war.

At the first light of morning, John stood by his bedside as Tom helped him to put his tunic on. It was no-doubt second hand but resembled a freshly tailored, clean, smart officer's tunic, its bright shining pips reflecting like golden idols in a lost forgotten land.

'That's better,' Tom said, stepping back to take a look at John as he did his buttons up. 'Your mother was always so proud of your smartness, that's why she wasn't surprised that you joined the Army.'

John was a little surprised at Tom's comment; it was out of character. The more he thought about it the more John realised that he hadn't heard Tom mention his mother for an awfully long time. He looked at him with surprised eyes and the old soldier looked back at him, proud of his captain and clearly elated that he was still alive.

'Thank you, Sergeant Major,' he was clearly a little overwhelmed. 'What news from the company?'

'The company are formed up ready to move out in the next few minutes and the Major's orders are that you report to him as soon as you arrive at Mersah.'

'Mersah?' John was a little confused; he had remembered Simon mention that the company was to pull back to Alexandria, which would have been a welcome break for the men. 'You mean Mersah Matruh?'

'Yes, why?'

'That's halfway to Alex. I thought we were pulling all the way back to Alex during the week?'

'Well, perhaps we are,' Tom replied. 'Perhaps we are stopping at Mersa Matruh for just a day or so, anyway, when you arrive you are to report to him straight away.'

'Sod the Major,' John interrupted. 'I want to see my men first; I will see the Major after I have seen them.'

Simon entered through the ward door and walked over ready to drive John to his next destination where the Battalion was to be based. He caught the eye of Katie who was helping one of her nurses to dress a patients arm.

Katie had dreaded this day, she was pleased that John was well enough to retake command of his company, but she wasn't ready for him to go and her professionalism wouldn't allow her to his bedside. They had said what they had to say the night before. Today everything had to go back to normal, the charade made things easier.

One person who had seen her fighting her inner thoughts was Simon. He had still continued to lend a hand at the hospital and so the pair got to know each other very well. Simon a man of the world was quick to notice that her daily smile grew even bigger when around John. Now he stood staring at her, fully aware that she was dreading the moment that John would walk with him out of the double doors.

'Captain James,' Tom acknowledged with a smart salute.

'Hello Sergeant Major,' he replied. 'My, my, John you look very dashing, all the nurses are looking.'

'Very funny,' John replied sensing his sarcastic tone.

'Well if you don't mind sir I will be off,' Tom said, placing his stiff cap upon his head. 'I've got to get on one of the Lorries with the rest of the mob. I will see you when you get to Matruh and after you have seen the Major.'

John gave him daggers as he emphasised the word "after".

'I know you want to see your men,' Tom explained. 'The meeting with the Major won't take long.' John began packing the few belongings he had into an old battered pack. His silence meant he was sulking and being back to his old petulant self, put a smile on the Sergeant Majors face. 'I will see you all later then,' he said smartly saluting Simon again and walking outside.

Tom stepped out into the brilliant light of the midday sun. He had delayed the company's departure from Sidi Barrani for a couple of hours now and he knew he couldn't delay anymore. Travelling the desert at night was a risky business, despite being a protective cloak from the eagle-eyed Luftwaffe. The men were stacked along with their belongings and weapons into the back of several lorries, all of which lined the main street.

Tom looked into the back of one and was pleased to see several boxes of 303 ammunition at their feet, all of which he had insisted be liberated and bought with them, there was never enough ammunition in the desert, it was at times as scarce as drinking water. He gave them a subtle wink approvingly and the men smiled.

Sergeant Scott was still leaning against the hospital wall taking in the last of a cigarette. 'You took your time,' he said to Tom as the lorries began to move off.

'Just checking on the Captain.'

'He alright? Of course he is alright' Scott said darkly, He's got you to remind him of his brave father, I sometimes wonder if you tuck him in at night.'

Tom rounded on him and before pulling rank at his remark could see that Scott was just plainly tired, sapped of enthusiasm from the desert heat.

'Are you coming with me in the staff car, or taking one of these?' Tom pointed to the last couple of lorries about to pull away.

Scott followed Tom to the car.

'Why do you do it? I have stayed silent for nearly twenty long years now. Why do you do it, Tom?'

'Do what, tell a young man about his father's achievements?'

'No, I understand that,' Scott replied. 'You fill in the pieces, it's not what you do that has troubled me, but how you do it. You elevate him Tom to a pedestal he never deserved.'

'I'll be the judge of that.'

Scott chuckled, lighting another cigarette.

'He was no more a hero than you or me and that boy in there is no longer a boy. He lives off your stories, but we both know the truth and all I want to know is why you do it.'

'Because a son deserves…'

'I get that, I really do. I get why you do it for him, but why do *you* do it, what do you get out of changing the past?'

His words hit home and as they both got into the staff car with Lieutenant Bailey, a long silence enveloped the atmosphere. Tom looked into the rear-view mirror and Scott stared back at him, his face perplexed and still unable to understand Tom's motives.

'I got a letter from his sister yesterday,' Tom began. 'It seems that her mother kept track of things back then and she is going through all her diaries.' He spoke as cryptically as he could so that Bailey would not completely understand. 'She found out that I wasn't about when Jack died.'

'Then she will have a lot of questions,' Scott replied unsurprised.

'I suppose you can't bury everything forever.'

Bailey turned in his seat, 'What the hell are you two talking about, don't tell me you two have had a lover's tiff!'

Scott replied with language that was typically Scott and Tom closed down the conversation.

Instead, he reflected in his mind the events of one winter in 1916. Scott was there, younger and lower in rank, for then he was simply a corporal, although the smoking habit was still the same. Tom wore his three stripes proudly and Jack sat at his desk behind them both, filling in recruitment papers and having them sent off to a place Tom wished he could burn down.

The Somme was over and somehow the three of them had got through it physically unscathed. The regiment as a whole, however, was a very different matter. The only positive event to come out of the slaughter was Jack's bravery at Trones Wood that had earned him the Military Cross and Tom the Military Medal, but as Tom recalled he was not the same man after.

They had been recalled home as their regiment practically no longer existed and there was a need to help drive recruitment. Outside their small office on the ground floor of the town hall, the busy streets of Brighton were beginning to fill with young men who had recently come of age and were ready to join up. As the glass doors were parted, their job began.

Tom and Scott would do the usual routine. 'Good morning, state your name, and how are you this morning Mr Jones? Splendid, can you state your occupation please. I bet that keeps you busy and the army could certainly do with a strong set of shoulders like yours, so why do you want to join the army?'

It had all been one great big fabricated lie and Tom hated being a part of it. Scott would casually continue, far less interested in who he recruited and far more interested in the extra money for each recruit. What broke Tom was Jack's attitude to it all.

'Hello young man,' Tom had said to one recruit. 'What is your name?'

'Henry Keeler sir, but all my mates call me Harry.'

Tom corrected the young man reminding him to address him as a sergeant. He then got busy with the rest of the questions, eventually coming to the two that he hated the most. 'So Harry, why haven't you joined up already?'

It was the guilt so many of them showed for being human that made him uncomfortable.

'I wanted to sir, I mean Sergeant, but I was too young. I've just turned eighteen so thought I would join up now.'

Tom no longer had to ask the second hated question, but if Harry was eighteen, then Tom's eyes were already in need of some serious attention. He studied him more and rubbed his chin.

'Do you have any identification?'

'Didn't think we needed any, my mate was here yesterday and said he didn't get asked for any.'

Tom looked puzzled, there was no way on God's earth that he would have let anyone through without identification, that was the rule. He looked at Scott, who had just asked the same question and been handed all the necessary paperwork by a gentleman who clearly was in his early twenties. He then turned to Jack whose head was still down and looking through papers.

Tom asked the boy to hold on for a moment and went over to Jack.

'Sorry to disturb you, Sir, but I have a problem.'

'You're too nice to them,' Jack replied, he didn't even look up from his paperwork.

'I'm sorry Sir, I don't follow?'

'You're not their father Sergeant, so why pretend to be? We are not here to make them comfortable, we are here to get recruits.'

'Very well Sir, but I have a gentleman who cannot prove his age.'

There was a long pause before Jack sighed and sat back in his chair.

'Hardly a problem Sergeant.'

'Well I know sir, he will have to come back tomorrow, but he informed me that his friend came here yesterday and didn't have any identification either, but his friend was passed. I'm worried sir that someone has recruited an underage boy.'

'I will come and deal with it now.'

Tom was grateful, but becoming alarmingly sceptical.

'Mr Keeler?' Jack began. 'I am Lieutenant Baker, apparently, my sergeant informs me you can't verify your age. Let's have a look at you.' The young man tried to stand as tall as he could. 'Well you certainly look eighteen, but my Sergeant is right, you do need some identification. I tell you what, pop out there and get someone you know to write down that they confirm you to be the age you are,' Tom attempted to protest and Jack held him back with an outstretched hand. 'Do you catch my drift young man?'

'I think so, sir.'

'And when you pop back we will all know that you are eighteen won't we?'

'Yes, Sir.'

'Do you want to serve your country and kill Germans?'

'Yes, sir!'

'Well run along and get me what I've asked for and we will accept you.'

The boy, who Tom had worked out now to be no more than fifteen and that was at a push, ran from the office full of excitement. Tom however, was horrified and even Scott had given him a surprised expression. He realised that Jack had been doing this all week, getting the numbers he needed and not thinking about the souls he was sending to the meat grinder they called France.

He approached Jack once again who had returned to his desk.

'He was underage and I don't think he was the first,' Tom could stay silent no longer. 'That was someone's son.'

'We are all someone's son Sergeant. Look, Tom, I know what you think, but we are short on men…'

'And morals too.'

'If we are to win this war, we need men and we need them from anywhere.' Jacks tone was short, but he refrained from raising his voice. 'For god sake man we are fighting for our survival and it's everyone's duty to put their money where their mouth is when talking about the final victory, see them all out there?'

Tom looked out through the window and into the street at the casual everyday normality he had come to forget.

'I see them.'

‘All of them want results, but none of them is over there making those results happen, armchair generals the lot of them!’

‘I understand Sir that there are many people who should be out there and who aren’t, but that doesn’t excuse sending innocent underage boys.’

‘A little adventure will do him good. I don’t care what you think, I have been tasked with recruiting so many men in such a short space of time. As long as I hit these figures given to me Tom we all get paid and get to stay here a little longer. Let them do the fucking fighting for a change. It’s all a matter of statistics.’

‘A war of numbers? You can’t treat our youth as simple statistics!’

‘A machine gun can fire five hundred rounds a minute and with you here I am barely able to recruit one soldier every ten minutes, of course it’s about statistics, this is a war of numbers and the Germans are winning it!’

‘And what about when we run out of teenagers as well as common sense? What happens when those boys come home broken, what good will they be then?’

‘That’s not my problem, but someone else’s.’

‘You are about to be a father yourself, do you want me to recruit your son next? What do you reckon, recruit him now or give it a year until he is one and he can crawl across no man’s land?’

‘Enough, back to your post!’

‘Post? You will find it’s called a desk and cosy it is indeed. Have you even spoke to her?’ Tom had found his voice now and was becoming bolder.

‘Our years of friendship and your past loyalty is all that is keeping you from being dismissed right now.’

‘I will take that response as a firm no then. I didn’t think you had spoken to her and you should.’

‘Sergeant if you do not return to your post I will have you dismissed,’ Jack stressed unsympathetically.

‘Jack,’ Tom pleaded quietly so nobody could hear. ‘Jack I’m worried about you and I’m worried about Helen. You need to see her and I think you need help. Take your pips off your sleeves for a moment and I will remove these stripes and talk as we used to. Jack, it’s me your friend Tom talking. Jack?’

Jack rose from his seat and with an upsurge of anger that rivalled a volcanic eruption screamed, 'no, no, no, no!' He somehow loomed over Tom menacingly. The office went quiet and Scott jumped causing him to scribble uncontrolled across an attestation sheet. 'No more Jack! There is no more Jack. Do you want to know where Jack is? He is over there,' he pointed out the window towards the sea. 'He is dead Tom, dead along with all the rest and you have now overstepped the mark.'

Tom attempted to protest, 'Sir please, I am just worried about…'

'Well it's not your place to worry about her, or me' and then paused before sighing, 'you're dismissed from the company. You will no longer be a member of this regiment.'

Tom was beside himself, shaking his head in disbelief. Scott had begun to rise from his chair, uncertain as to what he could do.

'I'm having you transferred Sergeant to the 2nd Middlesex regiment, you will be with A company.'

It dawned on Tom that these motions had already been thought through, the choice of unit and the details were very precise. Tom could now see that Jack had been waiting for an excuse to act upon this threat and he had now provided it. Their friendship, one that had been deteriorating slowly over the year had now come to an end.

Tom remembered the sense of remorse in Jack's tone when he told him to leave. He was a man split in two and the old Jack just could not fight the new one. The look on Scott's face was one of confusion, unable to understand why he had not simply continued to follow orders without question, it was the same searching glance he was giving Tom now in the rear-view mirror of the staff car as they trundled out of Sidi Barrani.

'No not a lover's tiff,' Tom finally replied to Bailey having returned from a past he had wished to forget. 'Just a misunderstanding.'

'Hardly.' Scott muttered from the back seat and Tom could not decide if he was referring to the present or if he had travelled in time with him ever so briefly at that moment.

'I hate it when he's right,' John muttered, still angry at Tom's insistence to see the Major before seeing his company, 'but I've waited this long to see them, I suppose I can wait an extra day or so.'

'And what about Katie?' Simon asked bluntly.

'I will thank her in a moment,' John said stopping what he was doing and looking over to her. 'I've really enjoyed her company; she's a wonderful woman so warm and caring.'

'How do you feel about her?' Simon asked.

John let out a long sigh. He wanted to tell Simon that he was in love, but at this time he thought he might not take it seriously. 'She's great, really great!'

It was the best he could do under pressure and Simon gave him an unconvincing look.

'So it's just great then?'

'Well, we have kissed a little.'

Simon let out a long 'ooh,' as a primary school boy would do when someone had been really naughty. 'You kissed, how exciting.'

'I know I shouldn't with everything that is happening with the war, but I can't help it, it just happened. Bloody bad timing for both of us I guess' and he rammed the last of his things forcefully into his pack.

Simon left John to gather his things and walked over to Katie. She avoided eye contact at first.

'Not my place of course, but have you exchanged details?' he strummed casually. From his pocket, he took out a piece of paper and borrowing a pencil from her clipboard he wrote down the battalion details as well as their destination. 'Here,' he said. 'Love, hope or whatever you want to call it arrives in all sorts of ways and can even arrive by mail.'

She smiled, taking the paper and putting it into her pocket she gently kissed him on the cheek, a reward for all his hard work and straightforward thinking.

'There are some people in this world who I truly believe are sent to remind us how good people can be, a bit like an angel. You are one of them,' she said.

It was perhaps the most beautiful thing anyone had ever said to him and for a moment he had to keep his composure. 'John insists that you are the angel around here if I have heard right.'

Katie saw that John was ready to leave and so walked over to say goodbye.

'It only seems like yesterday that you were dragged in here covered with blood and dust,' she said smiling.

'Thank you for everything, you truly have been a blessing.'

'That's all right Captain, it's been a pleasure and I'm very sad to see you going,' she said, trying hard to continue the charade of professionalism.

She fiddled nervously with her hair, rolling long blonde wisps between her fingers. There was an awkward silence as John's cap found its place perched on his head. Both wanted to say more to each other and embrace once again, but it wasn't the time or place now.

'Well,' Simon jumped in chivalrously. 'This doesn't have to be a goodbye, does it? After all Captain Baker, we are not on the other side of the world, are we? We are just eighty miles down the road are we not?' With a smart salute to Katie, he walked outside into the dry desert air.

John stared at her whilst deep down inside his mind was searching for what to say, then he kissed her gently on the forehead and said, 'soon, my darling, Simon's right this isn't goodbye.'

'No, I know,' she agreed still fiddling with her hair only this time from the back of her neck. 'Do you think you will be able to write?'

'I will be on light duties for a while no doubt and I'll write every day that I can to you here.'

'Yes,' she snapped with excitement almost before he had finished. 'Yes, I would love you too.'

'There won't always be time, but I will certainly try when I can. I'm sure I will be able to get back to take you out one evening or we could stay in again?' he grinned.

'Well I will have to check my diary of course,' she returned heartily.

What hadn't occurred to John of course, was that he had little choice in where to take her; they were both staring at each other in the middle of a hospital that was situated in the middle of the North African Desert and both would now be separated by eighty miles of sand. But stuck in a glowing moment that neither wanted to be released from, both had forgotten the desert and its emptiness, in fact, both suddenly felt very free from the isolation they had been so used to in this dreamy silence. At the rear of the ward an urgent call rang out for her and their time was cut short.

'I think you're needed back there,' John said still lost in her eyes.

She looked behind her briefly, 'so I will hear from you soon then?' she asked.

'Of course, you will,' he replied.

She gave him one last glance, this time for longer as she headed to the back of the ward and across her face the warmest most relieved smile one could imagine. John turned and walked away from the comforting environment he had been so used to and then walked down the steps outside to where Simon was waiting in a Humber staff car.

'Well?' he asked, as John threw his bag onto the back seat and slumped down in the front.

'Well, what?' he asked, pretending he did not know what Simon was going on about.

'Don't play games with me, John,' he said starting the engine and pulling out into the road avoiding the clatter of people and camels who filled the streets. 'You know what I'm on about.'

John looked back over his shoulder at the hospital as it disappeared behind a cloud of dust and the bustle of market stalls. As the sun reached the horizon, he thought back to his parting with Katie and how it lacked so much that it would have made a poor cinema classic. There had been no romantic embrace, no final romantic line and the more John thought about it, the more that was ok. Their story was not one written by someone for other people's entertainment, it was real, spontaneous and awkward because sometimes that was what love was.

'It just seems wrong, there's a bloody war going on Simon and all I'm thinking about is a beautiful blonde. And what about Anthony?'

'What's Anthony got to do with this?' Simon asked, there was a frown creeping across his face.

'My Sister has lost the love of her life merely a couple of weeks ago, she thinks I'm dead due to a cock up at headquarters and in the meantime, I'm acting like a romantic fool by falling in love.'

'You mean you have fallen in love with the baby dragon!' Simon gasped pretending that it was all news to him.

John ignored him and continued, 'I don't know how I'm going to explain it to Sophie, how can I tell her I've found love when she's just lost hers. I'll have to leave it a while I think, which is a bit unfair on Katie as I'm damn proud of her.'

'Katie now is it? Moved on quite a bit already then this relationship that earlier was just "great" as you put it earlier.'

The car ground to a halt by the side of the road. John looked at Simon, wondering what had made him stop.

'What's the matter?' but Simon sat quietly for a moment.

'Listen,' he began, turning in his chair with a reassuring smile across his face. 'I don't want to sound like a moaning auntie, but listen to what I have to say. War is an ugly thing John; I don't need to tell you that. Sometimes out of that destruction you can find something beautiful and when you do find such a thing, it's a real waste to let it pass you by, not many people find a miracle like that back home, let alone out here in the middle of the desert and in the middle of a war. Yet there it is right in front of you, staring you in the face.

I know you are upset about Anthony and you're worried about Sophie, there is nothing you could have done about Anthony's death or the loss of your men. Hitler started this war not you and as for Sophie, she will soon find out that you are alright. But let me tell you this. Katie is a ray of sunshine that you need right now, enjoy each other while you can, forget about everything else because it will all come right in the end. The greatest surprise of all is what can bloom in the desert!'

John patted him upon the shoulder, 'you're right.'

The car rattled back into life and slowly pulled away again. John thought deeply about what Simon had said and it was true, through all the fires of war an angel had indeed arrived at his bedside. There was nothing he could have done to save Anthony and there was nothing he could do until the letter explaining the mistake about his death from Tom reached his sister, had it not done so already. He had to make the best of what little there was and made a promise to himself to write to Katie as soon as he could.

In his mind, John looked back on the last few years and decided that he had been beating himself up a great deal over many things. He had done everything he could do to take care of Sophie and tried to keep his promise to her and look out for Anthony, but how do you stop an artillery shell? There were just some things that couldn't be avoided.

The staff car rolled on through narrow streets and then broke out into the open desert and its long never-ending highway that led off into the hazy horizon. Apart from the occasional lorry adrift or staff car, it was empty and the only sound was the rattling Humber as it pushed through the dust and over the lumps and bumps of the track.

The air was especially dry today and caused Johns throat to contract in a bid for water, but with such a precious substance in great demand in God's great furnace, he decided to try and close his eyes and sleep instead to take his mind off his thirst.

He must have dozed off miraculously against all odds in the juddering, jumping, bone-jarring vehicle, but what actually woke him was his body's realisation that the car had stopped. His eyes opened to a wonderful ceiling of stars and the desert around him was bathed in a wonderful night time blue glow, helped by the power of the moon. He seemed to be alone. Looking to the left there was nothing but sand, its ripples reminding him of water, especially now that it was bathed in the blue night light and it brought back the thirst that he had felt during the day. Around him was a blanket that hadn't been their earlier and when he looked to the driver's seat saw that it was now empty. Suddenly the sound of metal on metal caused him to turn in his seat where he saw Simon pulling one of the Jerry cans out from the back of the car.

'You're awake,' he said, his voice was faint and appeared to lose itself in the remoteness. 'Nearly out of fuel so thought I would top up.'

'For a minute there I thought you had disappeared,' John exclaimed his voice still strained with tiredness and thirst. 'Bit pointless to ask where we are I suppose.'

Simon grinned, 'in the middle of the desert, but actually, we are not far from Mersa Matruh.'

'How far?' John asked.

'Don't know exactly, maybe thirty miles, maybe less,' he began quenching the car's thirst with petrol and the trickling fluid which sounded as though it belonged somewhere else caused John to reach for his water bottle. 'Got to drive slowly now, it's easy to drift off from the coast road if you're not concentrating and I certainly don't have enough fuel to get lost.'

He threw the empty can onto the back seat and then jumped back into the driver's seat. He didn't start the engine and instead gazed up at the heavens. There was a long silence, for not a word was needed at this time. John could make out some of the constellations he was familiar with back home, but there were so many more stars out here that it was harder to see the familiar ones.

'So many more out here,' he eventually muttered.

'Clearer skies.'

They fell back into silence again until Simon said, 'I gave her the Battalion details so that she could write to you, of course now I know how serious things are I suppose you had already dealt with that.'

'I did indeed.'

John continued to lean back in his seat and stare at the stars.

'You didn't just kiss either did you?'

John simply smiled, 'it was very kind of you to think of the mail situation. I just hope there's time to write as I promised.'

'I think you will get plenty of time,' Simon said.

'What makes you think that?'

'We have a new general and the way I see it a new command equals a new offensive. They will pull the battalion and many others back who have been in the thick of it for the last year to rest and reorganise for another push. You know how it works. The state our unit is in tells me that that push won't be for some time. We will be behind the lines for a while I think, at least I bloody hope so. So I think you will have plenty of time to write.'

'You might be right,' John agreed. 'The first sign will be new replacements and stragglers from disbanded units and then they will give us a few weeks or maybe a couple of months to train them. Unless we get disbanded, that's always a possibility.'

'That won't happen.'

They both continued to stare up at the sky.

'How's that leg?' Simon asked.

'Fine.'

'Why do you keep flinching then? I noticed when you were in the hospital.'

'I wasn't flinching,' John replied.

'Don't play silly buggers with me,' Simon laughed. 'I'm a doctor and I know that you're still in pain so why not tell me what it is?'

'Alright,' John replied, giving in to his friend's wise all-seeing knowledge. 'It aches still and I get sudden bursts of pain up my thigh.'

'How often?'

'No more than once every day, sometimes I don't even notice,' he was lying, the pain was impossible to not notice. 'It's nothing serious.'

'If it gets any worse you'd better tell me,' Simon replied. 'Sounds like muscle spasms to me, it should be okay.'

Silence returned once again. There was no wind in the desert air that usually blew across the emptiness to remind you there was sound. When it did blow it was eerie and if emptiness had a sound, the desert wind was its voice, but not tonight, even their breathing was remarkably silent.

'Shall we go?' Simon asked, but John was so engrossed in the sight that filled the sky that he decided it was better to stay a while.

'You know,' he began. 'I look at the stars nearly every night, but it's only now that I have really looked at them in any detail.'

'Get lost in them don't you?' Simon replied. 'I take it you're in no rush then?'

John shook his head, 'I'm in no hurry what so ever, in fact, I'm quite happy where I am at the moment.'

'Me too' and Simon took from his pack a half-empty bottle of gin. The sight of it made John laugh out loud.

'I have always said that I would never ask,' John began, 'but please tell me; where the hell do you find this stuff when we struggle to find drinkable water.'

Simon responded with a chuckle and began to pour some of the alcohol into his tin mug. John who was by no means a big drinker pulled his mug out and accepted some of the sweet nectar. The mugs clashed together and the gin dribbled down their dry throats.

'I can't tell you,' Simon replied, his teeth reflecting the strong night-time glow through his cheeky grin. 'You might think badly of me and besides, if anything happens to me I want to leave some kind of mysterious legend behind, a legacy if you like.'

Another few mugs were enough to empty the bottle. Simon threw it onto the sand by the side of the track. The empty bottle landed on its side and rolled for a few feet but didn't break, Simon stared at it. 'A few hundred years or perhaps a few thousand years and someone will dig that up no doubt.'

Again John laughed, but this time at the idea of an archaeological expedition over a gin bottle. 'I doubt it. Who would come all the way out here and start digging around?'

'I don't know someone might be interested,' Simon replied. 'How do you think they found all those tombs over by the Nile? Someone might get excited by it.'

'Over a gin bottle?'

'Alright perhaps not over a gin bottle, but maybe someone might be a little interested in what happened out here.'

'Again I doubt it,' John replied pessimism in his tone.

'You're beginning to sound a bit like Lieutenant Keyes,' Simon said jumping out of the Humber and beginning to wander around on the sand. He walked on for a few feet into the dunes.

John jumped from his seat and followed him, trying for some unknown reason to walk in his footsteps. A few more feet from the road and Simon dropped gently to the floor stretching out his legs in front of him. It was as if he were lying on a comfortable imaginary mattress, an everyday item that he had forgotten the feel of. John dropped down next to him, the Sahara sand swallowing his fingers.

He wondered how many more endless nights spent under the glorious heavens, in scorpion and snake-infested dugouts there would be. He enjoyed the long drawn out nights under bright stars that twinkled endlessly, occasionally shooting across the firmament like a random rocket that had gone astray from a firework display. Whilst he missed home, each day the desert began to claim him more and more, so much so that it already began to feel like a part of him. His mind began to convince itself that this was what the rest of his life was going to be like and he was beginning to accept it. He wondered less and less if he would ever see England again and it was thoughts of Sophie that would bring him back to his senses.

If anything happened to him, if he was killed this time, it was here in these lonely arid plains that he would remain. Out here he would be lost forever, under the sand. Everything that had happened here in this desert over the past two years except for Katie, was beyond anger and tears and he felt uncertainty in his heart. He missed his new love already and suddenly felt lonely, empty and sad.

'A lonely place to rest,' he muttered, unaware that his thoughts had been vocal.

'Yes, but what a monument you would have over you every night.'

Simon waved his hand across the sky as if presenting the stars as a gift.

'So I take it you have been listening to the preaching's of Lieutenant Keyes then?' John asked with a sarcastic grin.

'I try not to really, some of the things he has running around in his head are not great for morale, seems to me he has little faith in our great crusade out here.'

'Our great crusade?' John repeated.

Simon loved his history and used it to compare and contrast much of what was going on around him.

'Yeah, our great crusade to rid the world of evil.'

'Oh, I see. I think what Keyes is worried about is that no one will remember or appreciate what we went throughout here,' John said defending the absent Lieutenant. 'I think he is worried that we all be forgotten.'

'Nonsense,' Simon said. 'They'll be filling history books with us for years to come. Perhaps even produce films!'

'Maybe,' but John was not convinced. He imagined the History books being filled with the names of great battles and generals, but like Keyes, he was not so sure their individual names would live on. Would the children of the future know who he was, would they know Anthony?

Simon had told him when they first arrived in Egypt about the Persian king Cambyses II, John quite liked him in a funny way, he was cruel and barbaric or so the Greeks would have people believe and in a way that made him more memorable. He had sent an army into the desert, not far from where they were, towards the Siwa Oasis and the tale went that it was swallowed up by the sands of the Sahara. John knew the tale and perhaps many in the future would, but the individual names, their families, they were just pawns on a chessboard, long to be forgotten and remembered only collectively as an army.

'They won't remember our names,' he muttered. 'They won't know about us.'

'That's not important though is it?' Simon replied, already beginning to realise that Keyes had a line of reasoning and that his own argument was rapidly running out of steam. 'I suppose you have a point. They will want to read about how it started, how it finished and how many Jerry's we butchered. They won't want to know about the individual people, will they like Doctor Simon James, Captain John Baker…'

'And Lieutenant Anthony Thomas?' John chipped in.

There was a pause of memorial silence. John's fingers played with the grains of sand by his side, holding handfuls of it before letting the thousands of grains run between his fingers until there was nothing left.

'This war has to be fought,' Simon said breaking the silence. 'I wouldn't say that about any of the other parties I've attended. You couldn't mix it up with the last one which was a bloody waste.'

John didn't doubt that, although in his mind he saw all wars as a waste. Like Keyes, what he began to worry about the most was that the lessons of this war would not be learnt in the future, much as the lessons of the last one hadn't.

'I know we must fight,' John agreed. 'I am just worried that the lads and many like them are just as expendable to history as they are to the Army. I worry we will be remembered by the future as simply soldiers, born as soldiers to die like soldiers. No one will know that we were bakers, farmers, writers, musicians, doctors and ordinary men. Just ordinary men.'

Simon rose to his feet, the soft sand sprawling in every direction under his boots. He helped John up and they both headed back to the staff car. Simon's hand found itself perched atop John's shoulder.

'That's our destiny all the time that we wear the uniform. It's the job of our children and grandchildren to ensure our names live on,'

Simon said softly. 'But I'd rather fight with Sister Hall and her band of ferocious nurses any day,' he winked.

'Hands off, that baby dragon is mine,' John chuffed back and as the engine rattled into life and breaking the silence, they sped off, now a little later than they should have been.

Reunion

As dawn broke Simon had pushed the staff car to its limits. As it turned out, Mersah Matruh had been less than thirty miles away and so the journey had not been as long as they had expected. Outside the town, an old disused airfield stood overlooking the rocky coast on a raised plateau. A pair of huge aircraft hangars came into view. Their bared metal carcasses framed and towered the skyline like rib cages stripped clean of their wooden flesh. The bombed out remains of the aircraft were still inside, black and charred.

Around the once active Italian airfield stood a barbed wire fence. The laying of wire had become a popular and active past time of wherever the armies had set foot. John had decided it was like ivy, as it seemed to sprout up and surround absolutely everything and everywhere, this included around the few remaining scattered huts and tents.

A gentle breeze from the sea caught the tents in its path and caused them to sway like little sails of an armada of ships. The battalion had only been a few miles ahead when they had left Barrani, but because of the enjoyable pause both John and Simon had enjoyed beneath the stars, the Battalion had already arrived and struck up camp.

Beyond the airfield was a sight that John had not seen very often, the sea. For a man who had lived all his life only a few miles from the sea, it was always an emotional sight and he breathed in deeply hoping his senses would smell and taste it with the help of the fresh wind that swept up over the car's windshield and whistled round his face. The sea was a glorious canvas of different hues of blue, light and dark, gentle and deep. A mix of colour that no proficient artist could ever be able to master and recreate and in his impromptu thoughts the rich earthy red rocks of the desert replaced the white cliffs of the Seven Sisters.

'Are you alright?' Simon asked.

John filled his lungs addictively with the fresh salty sea air several times and then groaned, 'doesn't that just smell and taste so good!'

'It certainly does,' Simon chorused.

'The only thing missing is the fish and chips,' John jollied.

'Over there,' Simon began, pointing towards the western edge of the airfield. 'Not fish and chips, but those tents belong to a company of the South Africans. I got acquainted with them back at Barrani,' he said with a cheeky smile. What he really meant was that he had located where the drink was stored. 'Useful chaps to know if you take my meaning.'

'Where is our battalion and my company?'

'We are up ahead and your company must be over there on the far eastern edge,' Simon pointed, but John could see he wasn't really sure. 'We will find them.'

The car's wheels revolved slowly to the main gate surrounded by MPs and anti-aircraft batteries. Once inside they soon found D Company.

'Where do you think I am going to find the Major?' John asked, jumping out and grabbing his pack. The scorching sand seared through his boots and burned his toes. Simon pointed to a large tent next to one of the aircraft hangars and as John looked in the direction that he was pointing, he could see a small board with 'Battalion HQ' written hastily in black paint. 'And you?' Where will I find you?'

'Don't worry about that, I'll find you,' Simon replied revving up the engine and pulling away with a comical and dismissive wave goodbye.

When John entered the tent the Major was sitting at a small table at the back, whilst Sergeant Martin sat on one of the collapsible canvas beds reading a small manual. Corporal Southcott, the Majors normal aid seemed to be missing and in the rush to Matruh, it appeared that only a few of his things had been brought along and left in a small pile in the corner.

The Major jumped up with delight when he saw the young captain, 'John!' he called out as if an old long lost friend had been rediscovered. John saluted, but the Major ushered him into a seat to relax. 'I'm sorry I couldn't come and see you in the hospital. I have been away for the last few weeks in Cairo, but I can see quite clearly that you're better already.'

'I completely understand, Sir, you're a busy man, you have a battalion to run, but thank you for your concern and the gesture, I feel as fit as a fiddle now, thank you.'

'Yes,' he said slowly fiddling with his paperwork, 'but it's the men that make the Battalion; we are a well-oiled machine which is why we have managed to survive for so long.'

'Couldn't agree more, Sir.'

'I'm sure everyone has been filling you in on what's been happening?' asked the Major stoking his pipe with his baton perched under his armpit.

'They have sir. I would like to add that Lieutenant Bailey let slip that we were due to be sent back to Alexandria is that true?'

'Well supposedly, but that's still to be decided. It's looking more and more likely each day that we will end up staying here. Bloody rat infested place!'

'That's a shame. I can remember just how much the men liked Alexandria when we first docked there,' John said remembering the city from two years earlier and how much the nightlife had been to the young men's taste. The Major gave him a look that suggested he remembered it a little differently. 'I'm looking forward to regrouping with my men and catching up.'

'Quite, quite,' shuffled the Major uncomfortably across the table, like a bluffing card player who has just realised that the game is up. 'They haven't told you have they? The true cost of Battleaxe?'

His voice became a little hoarse with nervousness. Major Love knew how important John's men were to him and he was aware of his commitment and closeness to many of them, friends as well as compatriots. Family almost.

'Sergeant Major Hill didn't tell me the exact casualty figures Sir, they were yet to be confirmed,' John said. 'I understand that many were missing, as I and Captain James were, so there is a hope that some will be in an Italian or German POW camp somewhere, or possibly mixed up with another unit.'

'John,' the Major's voice turned into one that reminded him of his old teacher about to inform him that not all was right with his test. 'There were only four men listed as missing from your company and one was you.' John suddenly felt as though his body was shrinking, getting smaller and smaller. His heart thumped nervously and every beat jolted his body. 'Unfortunately, your company took the heaviest casualties. Nobody anticipated what was going to happen. It seems intelligence on that ridge was a bloody shambles and no one had picked up the movement of an element of the Italian Trieste division. I think it was the 7th Bersaglieri with motorized support.'

'It was,' John croaked, struggling to find his own voice. 'One of them called an ambulance for me. How many have died?'

The Major reached into his top pocket and calmly took out a box of matches and lit his pipe. 'It wasn't your fault John, the enemy artillery was far too concentrated in that area and the tanks, well they just weren't up to the task.'

'How many?' John demanded.

The Major put away his matches. Having coaxed his pipe back into life he called to Sergeant Martin for the paperwork and swivelled it around on the table to face John.

'Out of sixty-five, nineteen were killed in action, fourteen were wounded, five severely. I don't know if the other nine will be back in time for when we go back out there and of course three are still missing.'

John was aghast, it had reduced the company from an already under strength size to merely thirty-one men in total. He was now certain that his men would be disbanded and used to strengthen other units.

'What? That can't be right. That's impossible that leaves me with only thirty-one men. There must be a mistake sir?'

Major Love looked at him and shook his head saying, 'If only it was so.' The list of names was long, too long even for his liking and had been on his desk ever since he had returned from Cairo. Major Love was now pacing around the tent ineptly swinging his baton with one hand and the cherry scented smoke of his pipe spiralled from between his teeth, as if he were on a Sunday afternoon stroll in the park.

John was seething, anger rising from the pit of his stomach and he blasted full pelt at the Major, 'but that means my three platoons will be down to roughly ten men each when they should be thirty strong! Three platoons have become three sections!'

'There will be no disbandment, I know how much D Company means to you and I assure you that you will not be disbanded. I am trying to sort out replacements, but it doesn't look like we will have any for a week or so. It may be longer than that. We were lucky to get Lieutenant Moore back and thank God we did otherwise you would be an officer short,' he blurted out defensively. 'It's a tragedy, John and we never know what to say to each other when these shocking revelations crop up. I am sincerely sorry. I know how incredibly close you were to many of the men.'

The Major's words were sincere and warming, but John wasn't listening any more. His anger had turned to numb disbelief; he couldn't bring himself to look at the list.

'Who are the three missing men?' he asked.

'Thompson, Wright and Corporal Orchard, that cheeky chappy young lad. I was quite fond of Orchard myself as it happens, fellow boozer and all that! I know you were very close and what that young man became was all because of you, what I am trying to say is, there is a chance that he is alive and well.'

John wanted to hide from him that Orchard was dead. The strangest feeling overwhelmed him, as if by not saying so and keeping his name on the missing list kept him alive a little longer, but it didn't really change anything.

'Orchard is dead,' John informed him rubbing away the sweat from his forehead.

'Are you certain of that?' the Major asked.

'Yes, he died trying to save me. Captain James buried him.'

The Major marked a black cross against Orchards name on the list. Muttering to himself that it was a damn shame and something about a stolen box of tobacco.

John had forgotten to inform Tom or Lieutenant Bailey about Orchard, perhaps he hadn't forgotten, perhaps mentally he had cut that memory from his mind hoping it would go away and turn out to be just a bad dream. He was slightly surprised that Captain James hadn't recorded it with them, but then Simon had been the mainstay of the hospital theatre the past couple of weeks and hadn't had a minute to himself.

'I would like you to note that Corporal Orchard's heroic actions and sacrifice should be recorded in dispatches, Sir,' John said. 'Perhaps we could recommend him for a medal, something for his family to hold onto. I was thinking of the Military Medal.'

'Of course, I will look into what we can do for him, give the details to Sergeant Martin and he will take the appropriate action,' the Major said and then he looked at the corner of the tent where Southcott's small bag and folded up spare uniform stood. 'Considerable losses, John, Battleaxe gained nothing and the casualties have been high, too high. That's why we have been pulled off the front line, to rest, regroup and train up the replacements when they arrive.

I am going to use your company as a reserve company until it is back to full strength again. We also have a new General in command now, General Auchinleck, so you can expect a few changes. Take my advice John, light duties for the next few weeks and train up the new ones coming in.'

'Disbandment sir, please can you just confirm…'

The Major held his hand up. 'I promise you it won't happen. I'm, sending you the majority of replacements, just train them up.'

John nodded in agreement. Noting the Major's contemplation over Southcott's belongings, his uniform protruding a pair of medal ribbons above the chest pocket.

'Corporal Southcott, Sir?' he asked referring to the uniform in the corner.

'Hit with shrapnel. A damn fine aid and a good friend. I'm going to send the rest of his belongings home to his family. Another funny little character wasn't he?' John smiled in agreement. 'Been with me for three years,' the major continued. 'You know, he was terrified of every battle we ever got involved in, hated this whole war but he never left my side. That's courage for you. No place in history, but it earned him a place in my memories. Doesn't seem worth it does it?'

'That's an honourable place to be Sir,' John put in, an attempt if there ever was one to convince himself of his own doubts about memorials.

Major Love gestured Sergeant Martin to leave so that he could be alone with John.

'I don't like seeing lists like that, no more than you do and that's not the only one I have had to read through. I have tried very hard to keep lists like that one to a bare minimum. I have always tried to keep the casualties down, keep the men out of trouble.'

'Of course Sir, I know and the men know too. We are well aware of your recognised experience in warfare, Sir.'

The Major whispered in a confiding manner, 'I had heard that there were whispers and opinions as to my abilities to lead. Have you heard them? Too old and all that rubbish and that I would panic and freeze at the first sign of trouble.'

'No, Sir I haven't and don't agree. I wouldn't have thought that rumour to be true and wouldn't give it the time of day. I can assure you that any opinions of the sort would not come from my company,' exclaimed John in a pacifying way.

'Oh yes, John, there have been speculations going on all over the place and I am referring back to the day we left England. Well now they know that is not the case,' he retorted his jowls puffing out like an old bullfrog.

'They know sir; you have shared the same hardships as they have and been available whenever you are needed. The men highly respect you, to say the least,' he cajoled.

The Major smiled and then looked at the list that was still in John's hand. 'John I don't want people to think of me as incompetent. If I knew that the enemy positions were that strongly defended and had been reinforced, I would have fought hard to have stopped that attack going in. You know that don't you? The last thing I wanted to see were those boys being cut down like that.'

His experience from the first war began to show through. The Major had seen things in Mesopotamia that he never wished to see again and evidently operation Battleaxe had brought back the hardships he had witnessed at Kut in 1916. John understood it was easy to blame yourself, to feel responsible for your actions and the decisions you make, despite the fact it was handed down from others. John felt answerable for the names on the list, even though he was coming round to the idea that there was little he could have done to save his men. He also knew that had it not been for Corporal Orchard, he would have been on the list himself. They all were just following orders. The massacre was not chargeable to the Major. The attack on the ridge was just another of the many mistakes and failings in war, but he was taking it personally today.

'We all want to make someone accountable and put our fists in their face for what happened,' John began. 'But as much as I hate to admit it, the ridge was just another badly planned military blunder, badly assessed intelligence. Another waste, another sacrifice. Like Gallipoli or Kut.'

The Major looked rankled when John mentioned Kut. He was angry with the staff at the top today, just as he had been over twenty years ago.

'Too rushed Battleaxe,' the Major said softly. 'The Prime Minister is in a hurry for a victory and victory takes time. He is in such a rush to beat the Germans that he has put a new general in command of the Eighth Army. Damn politicians!' He slammed a fist on the table. 'They just don't understand how difficult this all is, completely out of touch with it all.'

John watched as the Major withdrew a photo from his chest pocket and passed it to him. The photo was of a young handsome Lieutenant. On his arm was a white band with what would, had the photograph been in colour a red cross. The young officer was standing in front of an old brick building wearing a beaming, youthful smile.

'You?' John asked.

'My brother, we did look alike,' the Major replied. 'Battleaxe is not the first time I have seen things go wrong. We were both young medical officers in 1916, we were at Kut in Iraq during the first war. At first, everything was alright, the Turks surrounded our positions, but we had enough provisions to last a prolonged siege, providing relief would come. The men fought with everything they had, like knights of old and a crusade of immense proportion. No one came and after months we began to realise that there was no escape, no way out.'

John could feel the Majors acrimony rising as he reminisced.

'It was that fantastic idiot General Townsend, his pride and need to be some kind of great hero that destroyed us. Our supplies dried up like the desert that surrounded us and we had to surrender to the Turks. Starving we were and totally out of ammunition. If I had known what was coming I would have saved a bullet and shot myself. The torture we endured was beyond the call of duty. We were put into camps and died in the thousands from disease and neglect. I buried my brother only a few weeks before we were released.'

'I'm sorry sir.'

'I don't ever want men to suffer the way I saw those men suffer and I have never since cared for politics or military leaders who think it is their God-given right to be the next big hero for our country. Sitting on their arses and making decisions from the comfort of their armchairs, treating those below them as mere statistics. The heroes are the ones that we forget, the ones that get left behind.' He slumped into his chair and waved John dismissively. 'I'm getting too old for this, anyway, enough of me and my sorrows, I just wanted you to know you are not alone. I'm sure you are keen to get back, I won't keep you any longer.'

'Thank you, Sir,' John said, handing him back the creased Sepia photograph. He saluted and stepped back out into the heat of the day.

Tom was waiting for him outside with Sergeant Scott who hadn't seen John since the attack. Scott's wrinkled leathery face, normally so forbidding had transformed into one of happiness and relief.

'Good to see you again, Sir,' he shook his hand, an unusual gesture from him. 'I hear the nurses have been giving you their full attention!'

John grinned; Scott's face may have changed all though be it temporarily, but his dry humour was still intact.

'Thank you, Sergeant, it's good to see you too.'

'Shall I form the men up sir?' Tom asked.

'Yes, why don't we form them up over there by the beach.'

'But the beach is mined, sir!' Tom replied.

'By the beach, not on it Sergeant Major,' John smirked. 'It will be good for them to get some sea air.'

Their spirits were surprisingly high as John stood amongst most of them. There was no need to shout to make himself heard as he had done on numerous occasions before, there were too few men left. They were pleased to see him though, one soldier calling out, 'welcome back' and the remainder calling out, 'here, here' in response. John stood in their midst clutching the piece of paper with the list of names on it in his right hand. It shook a little due to nerves as although he knew the amount lost in his company, he didn't know exactly who was on the list, but the absent faces around him allowed him to compile a sad list of his own.

As the patter ceased and everyone became quiet, John began to speak to them. He talked about their training and sacrifice, there actions that would make their country proud. He didn't lie, nor did he give cold hard facts. If anything it was honest and humble and Tom's nodding head showed he approved.

'I have no doubt in my mind that you have given your very best and are some of the very best that the British Army has to offer,' he told them. 'Wherever our next fight takes us, I know we will succeed and take back more positions from the enemy and hold it. That was one hell of a fight on the ridge and I was proud of every one of you. I don't think anybody will ever understand what went on here, but us few. They will never understand the hardships we have shared and the suffering we have gone through, but we will all have our own stories to tell and as for those who will forever remain here, we won't forget to tell their stories for them.'

The list of names weighed a ton in his hands as Lieutenant Moore volunteered to read out the Lord's prayer. Those that were sitting, scrambled to their feet and joined in, their heads bowed and as the end approached, John looked for the first time at the dirty white sheet of paper and then read out the names.

'Private Curtis, Private Dean, Private Dowling, Private Elliott, Private Harrison, Private Jones M, Private Jones T…'

His voice trembled a little, both the Jones' had been brothers, the only sons of Margery Jones, a wonderfully vibrant lady who worked in Johns favourite Bakery in Eastbourne. He suddenly saw her as he pushed the bakery door open, the little bell that always felt as though it would break announcing his arrival. 'Good morning Captain,' she would say. 'How are my boys doing, not causing you any trouble are they?' Of course, he was always off duty when he would bump into her; he would be busy buying a nice fresh loaf so that Sophie could make her special cheese sandwiches. He could never confess that the Jones boys were a troublesome and mischievous pair, always playing tricks and getting into some kind of trouble with Sergeant Scott. Truth was that John would put up with any of their mischiefs now if it could bring them back.

'Private King, Private Marsden, Private Medhurst, Private Robinson, Private Smith A, Private Woodgate…'

His voice was beginning to fade now as the sudden realisation that his entire command platoon had been wiped out, with Woodgate and Dean gone there was only Scott and Hill left to accompany John.

'Lance Corporal Lewis, Lance Corporal Murray, Lance Corporal Yates, Corporal Patterson, Corporal Woods…'

He knew he had to add Orchard to the list, as his name wasn't there and as he announced his name, there were communal sighs and gasps of disappointment. It was final now and there was no doubt anymore, he had also passed the way of heroes.

Now there was just one name left to be called and that was Anthony's. Like a horse at a jump that is beyond its capability, John shied away from reading it. His face showed no emotions, he never let his men see them and no matter how much they clawed and tormented him within, he always managed to hold his composure, inhaling as much oxygen as his lungs would allow.

'And Lieutenant Thomas A.'

They all stood to attention in honour of the fallen. Noise carried a long way in the desert, day or night and so did silence. There was an eerie peacefulness whilst the men thought about their friends, their comrades, their brothers, while down below the cliffs the marine blue of the Mediterranean gently lapped and washed up on the rocks.

Sophie's hands flicked through pages of her old photo album. The precious memories of the past found on each page were protected by a thin layer of tissue paper, which made them seem older than they really were. Some of the older snapshots fell out and gently landed upon the floor as if begging to be looked upon and remembered again. There were pictures of family and loved ones. Images of her mother, her brother and of course there were depictions of her father from happier times.

In the early days, he had been an attentive man full of energy, teasing and tormenting her with tickles at play. He loved the English seaside and so did she and there were glorious memories stirring in her head of seaside days and sandcastles. Her fingers trembled delicately around the edge of his portrait. He hadn't always been a drunken sot and her mother's diary of 1919 had shown a heroic side to him.

Destitute, disowned by her family, unmarried and with a child, her life should have been a tragic tale then, but she had met Ted who had also been disowned by his family for going to fight with the American army in France. Most men, if not all men would have looked the other way, but he saved her and married her in a year where the whole world wanted a fresh start. The photographs proved that beyond question most of her younger years had been vibrant and full. Fate had dealt them all some harsh cards as a family, her father just happened to be the weakest hand of all. Her heart felt the pangs of guilt and a twinge of pity looking down on the sepia snapshots of time. A cold sharpness swept over her being, she shivered and quickly skipped the page.

Thereupon the next page stood John on the day he had been presented with his first army uniform next to Tom. An impressive pair they were, with Sophie's mother squeezing in between the two soldiers, her arms around them both, her eyes full of delight, pride and happiness, her nose crinkled almost touching her pursed lips in a kissing action.

Sophie missed John and would often sift through the many letters he had sent her, which had now come with more regularity as he had explained his recovery to her. She would read them and in her head hear his voice as if he were by her side, explaining the desert, what Africa was like and remembering old memories. She was delighted at the news of a woman he had met and although he was his cryptic self, Tom filled in the gaps that John was too shy to fill.

Sometimes she would rehearse what they would talk about when he returned. It seemed a crazy thing to do at first and for a while, she felt silly until she realised that the house felt less empty when she imagined her brother in the room with her. But for now, both John and Tom were gone.

She gazed back at her mother in the photo, she was gone too. Everyone was gone. The melancholy atmosphere could be overwhelming. Was it her? Did she have some kind of essence in her body that poisoned anyone who touched or got close to her? Was there a family curse? With too many ghosts, she snapped the album shut resolutely telling herself not to be so stupid.

'Curse?' Buckland called out from his chair, Sophie had come to calling it his throne now.

She must have muttered it out loud and not noticed. 'It doesn't matter.'

'If you think your family is cursed think again! There are families out there that are in worse shape, try to remember that, it helps believe me.'

'Sometimes it feels that way.'

'Of course it does when you look back and can't change anything, but I think you are a long way off having a curse inscribed above your tomb door.'

'What do you think it would say, the inscription?'

He laughed, 'I don't know, but it would have to be in hieroglyphs.'

She watched as he settled back to his newspaper and rubbed his chin with thought. It was odd, she had noticed all of his little quirks and found them now very endearing. When he was thinking he rubbed his chin or his forehead and she knew now when he was going to do it, even before he did. When saying something important he would look down at her a little, she called it the professor gaze, as he always looked as if he was looking over imaginary spectacles. She knew she was fond of him, but how far that fondness extended she had yet to know.

'It needs time my dear,' Mrs Jenkins told her as she was washing up.

'Time? I don't think I follow you,' Sophie replied, but she knew the old woman wasn't stupid and even Buckland had officially christened her with the title 'The Oracle.'

'With the Lieutenant and don't say you have no idea what I am talking about! I know you, my dear, better sometimes than you know yourself.'

Sophie struggled to contain a chuckle. 'I don't think you have anything to worry about there.'

The Oracle grinned whilst plunging her hands into the sink. 'If you say so love.'

'No really,' Sophie's laugh became more nervous. 'There really is nothing to worry about there. My heart is with Anthony and always will be.'

The Oracles knowing smile remained, she was plainly not convinced and the longer it remained there the less convinced Sophie became. Mrs Jenkins placed a plate upon the side and then proceeded to wipe away the remaining sods from the surfaces and her hands with a tea towel. 'That is the first childish thing you have said for nearly three years,' she said.

Sophie had already spent the morning sifting through the many letters Anthony had sent her. His letters were now wrapped altogether and tied up with a red ribbon with a photograph strategically placed on the top. She had tied the ribbon loose enough to draw one occasionally to remind and remember what might have been.

A part of her wished she had never met him, that love had not brushed upon her heart and left it a now empty void. Yet another side to her felt more fulfilled as though she had gained something out of the sorrows and pain. Better to have loved and lost than never loved at all she tried to remind herself. She was conscious that she shouldn't have any feelings toward the future, it was a selfish emotion and prompted an immense and overbearing feeling of betrayal that these feelings were at the expense of poor Anthony's life. Like a forest fire, there was something growing out of the ruin left behind by the flames.

She hated thinking it, but her relationship with Anthony had seemed so childish in comparison with the friendship she now had with Buckland. She reprimanded herself for even trying to compare, for they were not the same.

Buckland had once asked her what Anthony was like and she noticed on several other occasions when it had come up in conversation, that her description was almost identical, as if reading a prepared script. She began to realise that they had barely known each other and that was alright, she thought, as they had originally had the rest of their lives to find out more, but now with him gone, there was a horrible realisation that there were so many missing chapters to a book that had ended.

Buckland had almost trumped Anthony with his mere being, he had proven that love did not need to be a fairy-tale romance and was not just for the young. It could be rekindled with such simplicity using a professor's gaze, a newspaper routine and a silly joke. She had got to know Buckland better than she had gotten to know Anthony. She didn't want to admit it, but was eventually forced to acknowledge that her relationship with Anthony had been a reality fuelled only by letters. She had never been with him physically and no plans for a future had been committed to. It was with a guilty conscience that she had lost a man in her life, but not lost a life with him. She would never forget him and would always honour him as her first true love, bestowing other imaginary titles upon him, many of which made the most presentable war graves seem half-hearted.

She had a second chance now and it was with that in mind sometimes that she would lay in bed, knowing Buckland was only feet away through the door. She would feel her body, her soft hips and firm breasts with her hands, imagining they belonged to his, beating away the image of Anthony to continue exploring what Buckland might explore, touching and biting her lip to keep quiet. At first she would cry into her pillow afterwards, still pierced with remorse, but eventually, it was only the pleasure she felt at the end.

What Sophie hadn't noticed at first was that after each day and each night she was getting stronger. She had begun wearing a familiar brave face and smile. The same brave face and smile her mother would wear to get her through the toughest of times. The war, its autonomy and the experiences it had bought had made her stronger. Perhaps it was that she had finally grown up.

'You know war is a terrible thing,' Mrs Jenkins said. 'But out of it we change and we grow stronger. You have really grown up Sophie, you are a wonderful and brave woman, I couldn't do what you do in that hospital every day and I am telling you now that when your brother and Tom get home, well, I doubt they will recognise you!'

Tom's Letter

Sometimes it almost seemed an eternity till dawn peered over the horizon of the dunes of the desert. The nights were bitterly cold, wintry in fact and those lucky enough to have beds would shiver, those without would shiver too with the added irritant of feeling every grain of sand in the desert grinding against their bodies, between their vestments and invading every crack and crevice you could think of. It was a constant presence and a constant nuisance. Despite the ground sheets supplied to alleviate the problem and keep the shifting sand at bay, every particle still sprinkled and sparkled from every cranny of their tightly woven blankets, falling dustily with any movement back to its mass, to be picked up again and settle inconveniently somewhere else.

Today's dawn started as a false dawn and John was stirring from a restless sleep still dressed in his shirt and trousers, putting names to faces in his mind and re-enacting the already spent day. The sky had begun to lighten and he checked his watch with a squint, but it was too dark to see and he decided to go out for a stroll.

He wandered, thinking to himself, his hands tucked in his trouser pockets. He kicked at the sand beneath his feet imagining a football into a goal, but then as if it had just suddenly changed its mind completely the sky began to darken and he looked at his watch again. It was four in the morning and he shrugged his shoulders and started to wander back. He had never experienced anything like that before and he'd been here for two years. His mouth felt dry again and he went back into his tent to search for water.

He came back out with a bottle in his hand and had put his jacket on as there was still a chill in the air. He went to the furthest edge of the campsite, placing the bottleneck down in the sand he stepped back a couple of yards and sat down. He pushed his hands down into the desert sand and felt about. Within the perimeter of his outstretched arms, he picked out all the debris and small stones, aimed and threw them one by one at the bottle, chipping, chinking and clinking it with every hit.

Then again as if the sky had had a change of heart, it began to lighten a lot quicker and finally revealed a thin red bright strip that began to get wider and wider, forming shadows about the camp where an object crossed its path.

John looked to his left and right at the makeshift tents and the scenery around him, watching the shadows rise and fall. He thought of Katie and how this awesome sight needed her audience. 'Katie,' he sighed to himself and resentful at her absence he threw another stone intensely hitting the bottle fiercely and knocking it over, but it gave him no sense of relief. He wanted to be with her, there or anywhere, even here where he sat sprawled out across the sand. He could smell the aroma of her perfume and taste the sweetness of her skin as he closed his eyes, the picture was still fresh in his mind from the last night they spent together and his heart ached.

His hands reached back into the sand and this time he felt an unusual rock, quite large, the same size as the palm of his hand. Instead of a smooth surface it had sharp creases and folds. He pulled it up from its sandy grave to see it glitter in the dim light. It was a beautiful pink crystal and resembled an almost perfect rose bloom, reminding him of the kind his mother grew. John had seen one once before in a bazaar in Cairo. 'Selenite,' Tom had called it, but it had another name and the locals referred to it as a Desert Rose. John rolled it around in his hand before placing it into his pocket with the intention of taking it home for Sophie, she loved little things like that.

He closed his eyed as a gentle warm breeze gusted across the desert. He saw Katie again in his mind. When he opened his eyes, releasing himself from his torturous thoughts, the real dawn had begun to lighten the sky and as the tip of the blood red sun began to shimmer on the horizon, the long shadows began to creep ever faster across the sand dunes like an army of scurrying scorpions. It would be warm and light soon and he glimpsed at his watch for the third time within the last hour, a little fearful of what daylight might bring.

The desert had become the suns anvil by midday. Sweat soaked bodies staggered through its fiery haze. Each man had his rifle and a full load of equipment as they stumbled on through the searing heat. The replacements had arrived two weeks previous and were still unaccustomed to desert life, John had spent a lot of time toughening them up and Scott had been left in charge of acclimatizing them, but now they joined the veterans in their first true test of endurance. A few seemed to cope well; their shirts turning a dark khaki colour the same as the veterans as the perspiration seeped through, whilst the others staggered like drunks across the rocky floor.

John paused for a moment to watch them pass, encouraging them to keep pushing forward and Tom stood alongside.

'Have you given the newcomers the tea and coffee talk yet?' John inquired.

The tea and coffee talk was part of Tom's welcoming pack, it was a true account of a Sergeants experience in the field that cost men their lives and if he thought it could save any of his current men or that of any other company's men, he would tell it to all the newcomers and today would be no exception.

'Thought I would give it on the way back Sir when they're even more tired and knackered, when they are resting and I have their full attention. Can't afford to have anyone fainting yet other than through hard graft can we sir?' he chuckled.

A few more miles and the company were back in Matruh. Exhausted and permeated bodies fell about the roadside, necks reaching back, as near empty water bottles trickled their last drops into wide open mouths. There was gasping and panting to the extreme and the rhythmic inhalation and exhalation of the soldier's breathing filled the air.

Extra water was brought out from the airfield to quench their thirst, but given out sparingly. It was still a precious resource.

The new recruits, although clearly not to the same fitness as the veterans, had done well. They had managed to keep up with the others and a couple had even been able to outperform a few of the old hands. John was pleased.

'They did well,' Tom said.

'Indeed,' John replied. He was a little out of breath himself. 'I presume its tea and coffee time for the new recruits and then have the men get back into camp and have some rest for the afternoon, I think they deserve it.'

Tom gathered the new recruits within hearing distance and began his tale. 'This is the story of Frank and Joe and the flask of tea or coffee, why didn't they know whether it was tea or coffee? Well thereby hangs the tale!

It is a true fact that a hot drink can quench your thirst better than a cold one and this particular day Frank's thirst was unbearable. Joe had shared his water ration very generously and as they were trudging through the desert back to their camp, very much like we have done today only more sedately. Frank espied and picked up a thermos flask that he thought perhaps had fallen out of one of the Officers trucks that kept zooming up and down on their route.

When they all stopped and very much like us all sitting here, his thirst not having abated, he tried to undo the flask top hoping to find some tea or coffee or in the very least a nice cold drink, but to no avail. The top wouldn't budge. His mate Joe offered to give it a go and open it and as he took hold of the flask from Frank a young and fresh Lieutenant just out of training grabbed it from Joe saying "Pathetic, give it here for goodness sake I'll do it."

The officer got up and walked away trying to get the flask top off, leaving Joe where he sat speechless. But he couldn't unscrew it either and by now this little flask had become quite a speculative item. Others were showing an interest and volunteering their strengths. From a distance, the Sergeant coming towards them was wondering what was going on as quite a small crowd had gathered around the performing Lieutenant, who had now put the flask up to his ear and was shaking it to hear if there was anything in it. The other volunteers were by now jostling around the young Lieutenant and jeering and jibing at his inadequacy and there were even odds on by this time that the flask was, in fact, the General's secret tea time tipple and he would be for it!'

The veterans smiled as Tom continued, having heard the tale so many times already, whilst the new recruits with curiosity upon their faces listened.

'As the sergeant got closer he realised what was going on and shouted desperately at the young Lieutenant to throw the bloody flask as far away as he could and the men to get as far away or down immediately. But it was too late and the Thermos flask detonated. With a thunderous blast, a cloud of dust and sand dispersed North, South, East and West and when it settled the young Lieutenants head, shoulder and the arm that held the flask had gone. The poor Sergeant that had shouted to save them was dead, and there were three other blokes, one fatally and two seriously injured in the crater that the bomb had made.

Frank wasn't thirsty anymore and Joe, Joe was grateful that the Lord smiled upon his good intentions on that day and that he didn't get the chance to try and open the flask. He thanked the good Lord above and if he would continue with his watchful eye upon him, he promised he would go to Church every Sunday when he got home. The moral of the story of Frank and Joe? Bottles and Flasks found in deserts spell, No!'

It still tickled John every time he heard it. Tom had such a way with his stories. They had fascinated John and Sophie and his mother all their lives, even the serious ones had a slight sense of humour within the moral.

'Do you know this Frank and Joe and are they still alive?' someone asked.

'Indeed I do and indeed they are,' Tom replied. 'That's how I got to tell the story.'

'So what's with the bottles then?' someone else jibbed.

There was a groan from the crowd, but Tom continued, 'Well it isn't unknown for our nice Italian and German enemy to sometimes leave the same sort of present in a wine bottle in the sand. Same scenario just different flavour,' the Sergeant Major enthused sarcastically.

'God,' someone else said rhetorically, 'and there was me thinking they were only good at making ice cream!'

There was absolute uproar and there ended the lesson well and truly learnt.

Soon the men were lazing about in the camp, taking a much-deserved rest.

John had decided that they should be allowed some leave and so as evening fell many disappeared into the town, not that there was a great deal to do in Mersah. Most in fact, decided to stay in camp, crowded around their tents and shelters, playing cards and sharing memories of back home. John and Tom stood watching and listening to some of the replacements.

'Not quite the same is it?' John said almost in a daze, but Tom knew what he meant.

'No it's not. They all seem good lads and there is work to do, but they're willing. You can't help but miss the ones we lost, but we'll all be brothers in arms again before long.'

There was more laughing and the cheerful clatter of tin mugs. Low burning hurricane lamps spilt light upon the sandy floor. From within the cheerfulness, the haunting sound of Corporal Orchard's jokes could be heard lost in time.

From out of the crowds of troops Sergeant Scott appeared, his face was red and his nostrils flaring like an angry bull. 'Bloody bastards,' he raged as he approached. 'Someone has nicked my bloody cigarettes and my bloody matches!'

He was not happy at all. To separate Sergeant Scott from his tobacco was a serious offence and punishable by almost certain misery at his hands, if he ever found you out.

'I've got spare cigarettes,' he continued. 'But no bloody matches and the ciggies were my Navy cut ones as well, can you bloody believe that?'

'Do you want my matches?' Tom asked.

'Oh, you're a diamond,' he said resolutely.

'They're settling in well then, the replacements? I'm glad you've got total control and they haven't found your Achilles heel yet,' Tom quipped, forcing back an erupting smile.

'Yeah well, it's only a matter of time.'

He sounded like a pantomime villain and John had to turn away for fear of breaking into hysterical laughter. He admired how Tom could stand there so straight-laced, but one thing was true, there were new characters forming already within the family unit. The air and the atmosphere was lighter already.

'The Sergeants revenge will be swift and sweet,' he rued gleefully rubbing his hands together. 'Tomorrow's another day.'

'You know who it is then, do you?' asked Tom soberly.

'Not exactly,' Scott retracted.

'You are sure you haven't mislaid them anywhere? Or are you sure that they have definitely been, what's the word? Chawed?' he teased quizzically.

John was beginning to think that there was more to this conversation than met the eye and he was intrigued.

'Matches?' said the agitated Sergeant pulling the palms of his hands towards himself, but to Tom, it simply indicated his nicotine levels were at crisis point.

Tom reached into his shirt pocket which bulged out from his chest. It was crammed with small sheets of paper, matches and his small dust goggles tin. As he withdrew the little matchbox a small half folded envelope fell from his pocket and floated down onto the desert floor. John reached for it whilst Scott wandered off with his new matches, cursing as he went on the hunt for the culprit who had stolen his Navy Cuts. It was then as the envelope was in his hands that he noticed the handwriting on the front. It was his mothers.

'Thank you, Sir,' Tom said, taking the envelope from John's hands before he had time to digest what he had seen. He put it back in his chest pocket along with all the other items.

John was slow to react and it took a moment for him to realise that he had seen that envelope before, its pink colour and crinkled age gave it away and suddenly it dawned on him.

'Wasn't that the envelope you took from my mother's chest of drawers to be posted on the day she died?'

'That's correct,' Tom replied. 'Now I'm sure you've got things to get on with, I know I have, so I will leave you in peace.'

'Wait, Tom, if I remember correctly that letter was to be posted to Uncle Richard, it was about Sophie's future or something,' he said wryly, the scene playing out clearly in his mind. 'What does it say?'

'You know what it says,' Tom replied calmly.

There had been doubt in John's mind ever since his mother gave the same response to his query when he asked her many years ago about its contents. That same doubt floated to the forefront of his mind again having never completely receded.

'You didn't post it?' he stated, he juggled in his mind trying to fit all the pieces of the unresolved jigsaw into place, something didn't make sense.

'I did not post it,' Tom agreed.

'Why not? You promised my mother, I heard you.'

'I didn't need to post it,' he remarked quite casually in return. 'I went to see your Uncle Richard and I delivered the message personally.'

'But it was my mother's letter to him, for him, for Sophie; surely he would want to keep it if they were her last wishes, why didn't he keep the letter, even for Sophie as a keepsake and a reminder of my mother's request for him to look after her?'

John knew that Sophie would treasure the letter and have it as a keepsake, it was the sort of thing she would do, a constant reminder of her mother's last wishes of how she wanted things to be.

Tom was in the midst of walking away but paused.

'Your Uncle Richard copied the letter, it's always been there up at the great hall, but I asked if I could keep the original letter because your mother was very precious to me too. I have little more than memories of her which are beginning to fade.

This was his kindness to me, that I might have something to carry with me that still keeps the link alive between us, that reminds me that I am still part of the family, that I am still necessary and that I still have a place and purpose. I hope you understand and can see where I was coming from. A selfish act of course, but for me a necessary one.'

'I see,' John said withdrawing honourably but reservedly. 'Tom, did you love my mother?' he suddenly came back candidly.

Tom fell silent for what seemed an eternity and then sighed, 'with all my heart.' His reply to John's took him by surprise and then he said with a sorrowful sincerity, 'but she only ever truly loved your father and there was nothing I could do about that.'

He tapped his chest pocket twice and inhaled deeply. John was frozen to the spot. Suddenly so much of the past now made sense, he was astonished he had failed to see it before.

'I never gave it a thought,' said John ashamedly.

'About what?' asked the Sergeant Major.

'That you might want a memento or token of my parents when you had spent more of your life with them than I ever did,' he concluded. 'Was there anything she might have wanted you to have, to leave behind for you?'

'There was a small benefaction that I can think of, but it's not appropriate at this time and I'm not ready to claim it yet,' Tom said cagily and leaving that as his answer he walked away, unable to give John a chance to ask anything more.

'You should have said,' called out John regretfully. 'Tom please wait a moment. I feel awkward now and that I have offended you and injured our relationship somehow.'

Tom turned back to him again, 'I am not offended and we have crossed too many bridges and walked too many of life's paths for something as silly as this to come between us. It will wait for another day.'

John let him go, for the day had started twice all ready for him and it was getting late.

It had been a long day for Tom too and he wanted to rest his weary eyes. Lying upon his collapsible camp bed he tried to close them and drift away into sleep, but he couldn't. He kept thinking of the envelope and how it had fallen out of his pocket in front of John. It had never fallen out of his pocket before. Normally it was so well wedged in with his goggles tin and pay book that it was impossible to budge. But it had fallen out and fallen onto the floor in front of John as if wanting to be discovered.

He quickly put the thought out of his head; an enveloped letter couldn't possibly have a mind of its own. Yet the coincidence continued to burrow into his mind causing his eyes to twitch with frustration so that they couldn't find the sleep he desperately needed. It had also happened at the same time Sophie had begun to write to him about her mother's diary. He had yet put pen to paper in order to explain his absence at Jack's death.

'Perhaps it's time,' he said to himself feeling the envelope in his pocket, but he couldn't bring himself to even think about showing it to John. The letter had the power to heal vulnerable and still open wounds, but also had the power to destroy and Tom hadn't yet mustered the courage to administer such medicine. It could be a new beginning or it could be the final straw. Helen's last wish may have to remain as unfinished business. He didn't want the family to suffer any more than it had done already.

As the evening light began to fade on yet another day, the reflecting blue of the sea began to change into a gentle lilac. Patches of small clouds threw shadows over the tranquil waters causing it to turn a deeper red and purple. The sunset was always splendid out here in the desert; it was as if it couldn't possibly be the same sun as the one back home. The stars too, although only just beginning to shine, also seemed to be of a different sky.

Suddenly the stars went out as searchlights cut into the sky and an air raid began. The silence was shattered by the continuing wine of the siren, the warm glowing hurricane lamps were quickly extinguished and any romantic meanderings were scattered like a fox in a chicken coop, no longer lingering in the surreal atmosphere. Air raids were becoming more frequent in retrospect almost every night.

The raids were nowhere near as intense as what Sophie had described in her letters that were happening in London back home, but they still put a nervous edge on the men. Tonight they were trying to hit Sidi Barrani off in the distance. During the height of the day Stukas had tried to hit a pair of destroyers just of the coast, but daylight raids on Mersa Matruh had cost the garrison and outside the airfield a stout battery of anti-aircraft guns always gave as good as they got.

Now the Italian bombers were beginning to carpet bomb the settlements during the nights. The skyline lit up as if someone was striking a boxful of matches one by one from East to West and the Italian bombers kept on ducking and diving and dropping their loads with the anti-aircraft guns booming their discontent in return. More and more distant bonfires appeared on the horizon and it was looking more and more like a celebratory evening for Guy Fawkes.

A few took shelter in the dugouts provided and some dared the caves that were found under the sand. Tom, as with many had become numb from years of bombing and besides the raiders were attacking Barrani and so, for now, there was little danger to them here, but he knew that John worried about Katie who was still there in the midst of it all. Tom begged god for her to remain safe, as he could personally do nothing but watch Barrani taking a beating out in front of him in the distance.

With all the goings on and John and Katie still fresh in his thoughts, he returned to his tent and with his lamp as low as he possibly could get it without being unable to see, he searched amongst his things for a pen and paper. He had decided to write to Sophie and explain everything. He had nearly lost John once and his number could be up next. Whilst he might regret the decision tomorrow or worry about the consequences, something made him realise that it was now or never. He knew if he asked Sophie to keep his disclosures private she would. That then still gave him time to think about how to talk to John and Sophie would undoubtedly give her opinion on how to do it, should he need her help.

As he wrote he thought he felt a hand on his shoulder, but there was nothing. A shiver ran down his back and a small gust of wind blew open the flap to his tent. If Helen had a ghost, it was here and she was spurring him on.

Unknown to Tom, John had also set to writing, only this time to Katie, attempting to arrange an evening out when he was next on leave, there was only a little paper left, so the letter would have to be short.

He had already received a letter from Katie suggesting a time and a place and he had every intention of being there. Despite the obvious difficulties of the air raids, the close proximity of the battle zone and of course the endangering distance of such liaisons. Without making any promises and limiting any waiting time to half an hour as a precautionary and safe measure, he wrote a touching and warming response, indulging the paper with tact and sincerity, his unrequited love and future prospects. It would leave her with no illusions other than the truth. She was never far from his thoughts.

She had put a small photograph of herself into the last envelope, which helped John remember just how beautiful she was. He had the photograph in his hand now, his eyes riveted to the image longingly. A part of him wanted to place it on the small table he used as a desk for the entire world to see, but she wasn't his to show off. Officially no commitment had been uttered or promised by the other, even though he was sure their feelings mirrored each other's.

When he had finished he didn't give a second thought to reading it through, he had no photograph of his own to give, so he drew a caricature of himself on the reverse of the envelope, hoping the comical gesture would suffice. He was quite a dab hand at cartoons and caricatures and while still at school he had been encouraged constantly by Miss Webber his teacher to follow his artistic flair, but to no avail. It was the army for him and always had been.

He peered through the tent flap into the chilly evening air and grabbed a hapless soldier that was passing by to take his letter.

'Pop this in with the rest of the company mail will you.'

With that done he breathed a great sigh of relief. It felt good to have tied up letters and loose ends.

The Second Painful Memory

Sophie had now almost finished her mother's diaries, reaching 1935. Each scrapbook had revealed so much she had never known. She had purchased a new scrapbook and the loose clues were now being reassembled into a book of her own. There was a new development with Tom's last letter, for he had now broken the silence and each letter he sent cautiously filled in the gaps until there was almost no doubt anymore.

'There is a spring in your step.' Mrs Jenkins had noted.

Sophie merely smiled, Tom's last letter had asked her to stay silent and to allow him to explain more when he returned, or at least give him time to explain in a more detailed letter, which time had yet to permit him to write. She would honour their agreement and besides, there were still some missing pieces, for not all had been perfectly placed in the jigsaw she had created of her mother's life. The pieces that were missing however, were obvious and Sophie struggled to contain her excitement as she thought she knew where the story was going and more excitedly, the story was now about her brother.

So it was that she settled down to read the last diary and it was then that she noticed the large volume of blank pages halfway through. Of course her mother's story ended in this year and the only one left qualified to write the last chapter was Sophie herself. Her mother's last entry was insignificant, an evening with Uncle Richard and a visit to her father's grave where she forgave him for all the wrong he had inflicted upon her. She had taken red roses to put on his grave, the first visit she had ever paid to him. After that, the story went blank, but Sophie knew the last chapter and her new found bravery allowed her to reflect upon those last few days that her mother was alive.

1936 was a leap year and amongst many things it had been an eventful year to date. The news had been broad and long. The Hoover Dam a colossal physical achievement had been completed. It was both the world's largest hydroelectric power generating station and the world's largest concrete structure costing a total of 112 deaths to date.

More alarming, Nazi Germany had reoccupied the Rhineland, a clear breach of the post-war agreements made at Versailles, but Britain and France were distracted by Italian aggression in Abyssinia and so far the reaction in Britain had been mixed, generally regarding the remilitarization of Germany as harmless.

Edward VIII had succeeded his father as King of the British Empire. He was still a bachelor, but for the previous few years he had often been accompanied at private social events by a lady called Wallis Simpson, the American wife of a British shipping executive. Instead of going to Balmoral in the summer months as would be the traditional norm, the King and Mrs Simpson had decided to holiday together in the Eastern Mediterranean on a steam yacht. The cruise had been widely covered in the press and it was rumoured in high society that Edward intended to marry Mrs Simpson as soon as she was free to do so. The file for divorce had commenced so she could marry the King and it seemed to be on the tips of everyone's tongues.

Perhaps it was because the world seemed ablaze with excitement that at first Sophie had thought little of her mother's illness, after all mum had been ill before, prone to colds, bronchitis and generally run down. She had never been quite right since Ted's death and they had all put it down to stress. This time it was different, after a week of a recurring cough and pains in her chest after a cold, she knew it was something more.

'I'm going to get the doctor,' she told her mother.

Her mother shook her head and told her it was just a cold that had been going around and nothing that some honey, glycerine and a hot water bottle wouldn't cure.

After two restless nights of watching her mother break into hot and cold sweats and a cough giving cramping pains that made her recoil in pain, Sophie became very afraid and decided to ignore her instructions. She ran down the road the following morning to the next row of cottages where Doctor Parsons lived, after gasping almost inexplicably about her mother's condition, he gathered up his black leather bag and returned with Sophie straight away.

'Hello, Helen, it's Doctor Parsons,' the doctor whispered gently arousing her senses. 'Very naughty is this Helen. Not part of our bargain you know, let's have a look at you then.'

‘I’m alright, no hospital,’ Helen rasped and whined desperately gasping for air and resisting his advance towards her by grabbing one of his hands.

‘Well we’ll argue that one out later, but you’ll live if I have my way,’ he soothed in a jovial manner but with a concerned smile.

His gentle and mild bedside manner put Sophie at ease as he examined her mother thoroughly from temperature, pulse and blood pressure, listening to her chest and heartbeat through his stethoscope of which she seemed oblivious as she drifted in and out of consciousness.

‘How is she Doctor Parsons, is it bronchitis again?’ Sophie asked anxiously. ‘What’s wrong with her, I wanted to come yesterday but she kept saying she was alright and not to bother you.’

‘Yes, well that’s your mother all over, not wanting to bother anyone, a silent sufferer,’ he sighed. ‘I think you ought to call your brother, Sophie. Oh no, you don’t have a phone here do you? I’ll pop back home then. In the meantime young lady, we’ll make your mother as comfortable as we can.’

With a groan he stretched down to his bag pulling out a glass vial, a syringe, cotton wool and a bottle of some kind of astringent that Sophie screwed her nose up to at its pungency.

‘How sick is she?’ asked Sophie now alarmed

‘Very, very, sick,’ said Dr Parsons sympathetically.

‘Shouldn’t we call for an ambulance then or something? What are you giving her?’ Sophie questioned.

‘Something to ease the pain and this is where your mother wants to be,’ the doctor peered down his glasses knowingly and assertively. ‘At home. Now I want you to get a bowl of warm water and a flannel or sponge to cool your mother down, let’s try and get the temperature down a bit, shall we? She is very dehydrated Sophie so we need to get some fluids into her. How about some tea or some orange juice or just some nice fresh water, not too big a glass or cup and help her to sip it not gulp it, do you understand?’

‘I understand, but what do you mean this is where she wants to be. Surely she should go to the hospital if she’s very sick?’

Helen groaned despairingly at Sophie’s reactions, Sophie thought she was calling to her and flopped by her bedside.

‘I’m here mum, I’m here, Dr Parsons is going to get John and I’m going to get you something to drink. What would you like, tea, orange or some nice fresh water?’

Helen’s eyelids dropped and raised, slightly frowning through trying to focus. She whispered, ‘Oh Sophie, I’m sorry. Water would be lovely, thank you, you’re such a good girl,’ she praised.

Sophie kissed her mother’s forehead saying, ‘back in a tick,’ but as she left the room she loitered outside for a moment, overhearing Doctor Parsons.

‘I’m very disappointed in you, Helen,’ Doctor Parsons scolded. ‘This is not what we discussed. You promised me that you would come and see me more often. Surgeries aren’t just for sick people you know. When was the last time I saw you for a check-up?

Such sensitive chests need a little respect. I warned you just a hint of a cold or a virus unchecked could lead to pneumonia one day and look at what we have here, a bad case of it I can tell you. I should have seen you many days ago dear girl, always the martyr. Should be a hospital job though, Helen,’ he muttered shaking his head.

‘It just crept up on me very suddenly,’ she divulged faintly with a weeping sniff in between her words.

‘These things have a habit of catching up with us unchecked. Well if we are not going to go to hospital…’ he blurted raising his hands in surrender, ‘I am very limited here, this is a nasty one Helen so you’ll have to do as you’re told, I am supposed to be the doctor here after all. Let’s keep your strength up, plenty of rest; you need to get some goodness inside you. I’m going to ring John’s barracks now and send for Barbara the district nurse to collect some other bits and pieces to make life a little easier, a drip for a start to get some fluids into you. Do you want me to contact Richard?’

Helen grabbed his arm again as he arose from her bed.

‘No nurses, no drips, I’ll be fine,’ she implored him. ‘No nurses.’

‘It would be irresponsible of me not to provide the care you need in your condition Helen and against my medical ethics. So if the mountain won't come to Muhammad, Muhammad must go to the mountain, my dear. It will be all right’ and he tapped her hand comfortingly and left the room.

Helen sighed cupping her hands over her face ruefully. Her face was drawn and her skin as pale as ivory and every breath was becoming more of a struggle. The thoughts milling around in her head were reflected in her eyes that resembled deep pools full of sadness. Her agitated hands turning and turning. This was not the way it was meant to be, so much fuss over a little cold.

'I should have come to you sooner,' Sophie whimpered as Doctor Parsons followed her down the stairs.

'You shouldn't assume responsibility at your age, Sophie. It's not your fault. Hopefully we've caught the pneumonia early enough and as soon as we get all the medication on the go we should see a pretty good improvement in the next few days. Your mother will be fine,' he said reassuringly.

'Thank you, Doctor Parsons,' she smiled.

'Perhaps we could get Mrs Jenkins to rustle up some of her splendid Scotch broth to attack those taste buds and kill the loss of that appetite of hers while I'm gone, eh?' he pampered kindly.

'Splendid idea, I'll pop up the road and get her straight away,' she beamed.

Doctor Parsons tapped his jacket pockets and looked all around him, a habit he had when he couldn't recall what it was he was going to do next. Then as if someone had flicked a switch, he raised his index finger in the air, triumphantly saying, 'barracks number, my dear, is it to hand?'

'Oh, of course,' said Sophie apologetically dashing to the sideboard and pulling out the middle drawer searching for her mother's address book. Although they had no telephone, her mother kept anybody's details methodically in a little red notebook in case of emergencies. Sophie scribbled down John's barracks number and handed it to him.

'So you are off to Mrs Jenkins and I have all I need to call your brother. Now then,' he digressed turning around in a circle. 'Are you sure you'll be alright; do you want me to contact your uncle at all?'

'No, if you're going to contact John he'll be here sometime tomorrow, but you're coming back tonight aren't you?' she queried disconcertedly.

'Oh, yes, just a few things to tidy up and I'll be back to make sure your mother is settled for the night. Barbara will be here first thing in the morning and she will watch her noon and night throughout tomorrow until I can get here after my rounds. But we are all organised now, am I right, young lady? You're the night nurse tonight. Any problems before I return and you must come and get me.'

'Right you are Doctor Parsons, I'll do my best!'

Tucking the piece of paper in his breast pocket, he opened the front door and took his leave.

After placing her order for Scotch broth with Mrs Jenkins, who was extremely concerned about the plight of her mother and insisted on coming round every other hour to see if there was anything she could do until the doctor returned. Sophie busied herself around the house.

She would pop up to see her mother on a regular basis, who was now constantly fading in and out of sleep and Sophie decided rather than sleep in her own bed that night, she would make the corner of her mother's room a temporary bed for herself in order to keep an extra eye in the event of any change.

Mrs Jenkins popped her head in and out as promised and despite the delicious aroma of the Scotch broth; it had been more than Sophie could do to coax her mother with more than a dozen spoonfuls. At about ten thirty later that evening Doctor Parsons called in with a drip and some more pain relief to help give his patient a thorough night sleep.

'How did the soup go?' he asked as he finished connecting the drip feed.

'Mother had a little, but not enough to feed a sparrow,' said Sophie worriedly.

'Things will look a bit brighter tomorrow once she's a bit more hydrated. Suppressing the cough and a good night's sleep might help a bit. I suggest you get your head down as well young lady.'

'I'm going to stay in here, just in case she needs anything,' Sophie stated.

'I can stay as well if you want?' he said compassionately.

'Do you need to stay?' asked Sophie cautiously.

'No, not at all,' he said dismissively. 'Just thinking of you, if you're worried about it at all?'

'I think it will be OK and John should be here soon. You think she'll probably sleep through the night don't you?'

'I will be very surprised if she doesn't,' he consoled.

'I'll be fine, there's always Mrs Jenkins who has already said she will stay.'

'Bless Mrs Jenkins,' said Doctor Parsons, his eyes looking to the heavens. 'I'll bid you goodnight then Miss Watson and see you tomorrow, I'll see myself out.'

Sophie put on her nightgown and settled herself down in the corner for the night. Her mother's breathing had certainly relaxed and she seemed more comfortable. In the still of the night with every intention of sleeping with one eye open, she could faintly hear the drip of the saline solution and the rhythmic ticking of the clock beside her pillow. It wasn't long before the repetitive echo lulled her into a sound sleep of her own.

The rapping at the door woke her with a start and she grabbed haphazardly for the alarm clock from the floor, which she had knocked over in the night to see what the time was. It was just before seven thirty. She scrambled to her feet, glanced over at her mother who was stirring and ran across the landing to the stairs and down to the door.

It was Barbara the district nurse.

'Hello Sophie, I'm on my way through to see an expectant mum,' she waggled her fingers excitedly. 'Sounds like today's the day, so just in case I get delayed before the midwife arrives I thought I'd pop in early and see how Helen's getting on. How are you Sophie, coping OK?'

'I'm fine, mum's just beginning to wake I think,' she yawned.

'I won't disturb her, I will just take a peek and report back to Doctor Parsons.'

Sophie escorted her up the stairs and they entered into her mother's room. Sophie stopped in dismay as if her feet were glued to the spot. Her mother was awake and sitting up coughing up blood and mucus around her. Barbara took charge immediately and seeing Sophie's shock she kept her busy ordering her about all over the place to fetch and pass water, bowls and towels.

'Sophie, we need an ambulance,' called the district nurse. 'Sophie, go and get Doctor Parsons, run to his house, he doesn't start his rounds for another half hour, go, Sophie, go now!'

Sophie had descended deep into the recesses of her mind, those words, this whole scenario had played out before only that it wasn't her mother saying the same words this time it was someone else. Again, just like last time she didn't want to go, she wanted to stay, stay here with her mother. She wasn't going anywhere.

'I don't understand,' Sophie stuttered weakly.

'There you go, Helen,' the nurse encouraged her mother, settling her back down clean and comfortable and puffing up her pillows to give her a little more height. 'Are you still here?' enquired Barbara as she heard Sophie's feet shifting on the floor undecided as to their function. 'Sophie, sweetheart we need an ambulance and Doctor Parsons!' She squeezed her arms firmly but gently as she looked deeply into her tearful eyes and said, 'can you do that for me, Sophie, for your Mum?'

Sophie absolutely beside herself with fear turned on her heels and ran as fast as her feet would carry her. She ran all the way down the lane to Doctor Parsons' house. Her heart pounding up into her throat, she banged and banged on the door sobbing when she reached it and sliding down to the threshold with each thump becoming weaker and weaker as she became more and more distraught.

Mrs Parsons came to the door and screeched to the back of the house for her husband, 'come quickly its Helen's girl.' She pulled her up off the ground and hugged her tightly whilst trying to guide her inside the house.

'No, no, I've got to get back, I've got to get back otherwise she'll die, just like he did, let me go, I've got to get back to my Mum, please let me go,' she pleaded trying to regain her composure.

She had to get back to be by her mother's side. As Doctor Parsons came to the door he knew she was remembering vividly the spring of last year and she was; the beating rain, the screeching of the tyres, the dull thud and the stench of whiskey. Doctor Parsons ran through the rain in his pyjamas as soon as he had heard what had happened, his case of medicine in one hand and an umbrella in the other. The rain had been so cold that night it was like droplets of ice upon the back of Sophie's neck. He swept Sophie up in his arms, his black bag hanging from his elbow and started to hurry up the lane.

Sophie's ears tuned in to the sound of thunderous horsepower coming up the lane from behind them, wheels splashing through the puddles. It was a green Bentley motor car, Tom's car.

As Tom pulled the car up alongside them John could see that something was seriously wrong. He could read his sisters face immediately. He jumped out of the car and grabbed his sister from the struggling Doctor's arms who ran on ahead.
Sophie's mind was numb and without realising it she was still in bare feet.

'What is it with you and no slippers,' John said as he looked down at them, they were cut and bleeding. Tom carried on the remaining few yards and pulled up alongside the front gate. Leaving all their belongings in the vehicle he opened the gate for John who was now carrying Sophie and followed them into the house.

Sophie was crying again, her face full of fear and her tiny frame shaking from the deep desperate breaths it needed. John held her as tight as he could. He didn't need to ask. The feeling in the air, the Doctors haste and the expression on his sister's face was enough to tell him that things were far from good.

'What's happened?' he asked, his hand around her cold shoulders and gesturing Tom to get something for her feet.

Sophie's hands clenched around his waist scrunching up his smart uniform. 'It's happening all over again, I think Mum's dying,' she sobbed, barely able to say anything at all. 'She was a bit better last night after Doctor Parsons had been, but this morning there was blood everywhere, so much blood! John, she really is very sick, and its pneumonia.'

Her body lurched as if suffering from violent hiccups. Surprisingly John was calm; his heart felt heavy and his ears seemed to hear almost every sound as if they had been magnified several times, but he kept his composure, he had too. He could feel his sister's heart throbbing against his chest and he could feel her desperate attempts to breathe with some kind of ordered rhythm. She was his priority for she had only just got over her father, it had been just over a year since the incident and now this. He wondered how much more trauma this family and his little sister could take.

He snuggled her warmly, 'hey, it'll be OK little sis, she's as tuff as old boots our Mum.'

'John,' whispered Tom. 'I'm going up if it's OK with the doc.'

He passed him a warm flannel and John began to gently wipe the blood from his sister's feet. She winced as the soft cloth found the deeper cuts and grazes.

'I will come with you, bear with me a moment.'

Mrs Jenkins had arrived after hearing all the commotion and took Sophie's feet into her hands. John then followed Tom upstairs. They crept along the landing and pushed open the bedroom door. Much to his surprise, after all the commotion down the road and the sense of urgency of it all, there was a peaceful stillness in the room as they entered with a nod of approval from Doctor Parsons. The district nurse acknowledged them as she grabbed her hat and cape to leave.

'How's the trouble maker doing, doc?' Tom asked sincerely. He sat beside Helen and stroked her cold delicate fingers gently, John compared his mother's small delicate hands against Tom's large calloused hands.

'Crisis over, I think, but someone's got to talk some sense into her,' the doctor grumbled and started to roll his sleeves back down. 'Someone needs to convince her that she needs to be in the hospital. This is an acute form of pneumonia; the hospital is an all-round better place to be Tom. She won't listen to me. That's why I rang you and John.'

'Mum,' John began. 'Let's take you to the hospital.'

'Fuss, fuss, fuss,' muttered Helen.

'You're scaring Sophie and me, don't you think the doctor is right?'

'Your son is right,' Doctor Parson gently interrupted. 'Poor Sophie had enough to contend with last year. Think about what she must be thinking. She's still a baby, it's been a tough year for all of you. She thinks she is going to lose her mum and it was only last year… well, enough said.'

He looked apologetically at Tom.

'No offence taken,' said Tom, rolling Helen's hand around in his warmly.

'Anyway, breakfast calls before surgery; I'll be back around midday and see if we can't get this unwillingly patient into a clean and comfortable hospital bed by this afternoon. I'll make the arrangements as soon as I get back to the house.'

Helen wailed weakly, but her protestations were falling on deaf ears now, with Tom and John in the room Doctor Parsons had his champion's seal of approval.

Sophie and Mrs Jenkins were sitting on the small wooden bench that sat against the wall under the living room window cradling each other as Doctor Parsons and John came down the stairs. Tom remained behind to watch Helen.

'Crisis over for the time being,' the doctor said. 'When I get back I'll make arrangements for her admittance for this afternoon with the cottage hospital, I should have done it yesterday, so she must go John for her own sake. Home is not the best place for her now. She needs a firmer hand than mine. Get Tom on the case, she will eventually listen to him,' he chuckled.

'Thanks Doc,' said John as he saw him to the door.

'You know where I am if anything changes or you have any doubts, where is Barbara, has she gone?' he asked of the district nurse.

'I think there's a baby due somewhere,' explained Sophie. 'She had to meet the midwife or something.'

'That'll be Mrs Bell, no doubt, number six on the way. I think her husband's aiming for a football team! See you later,' he said and away he went.

'Has anyone called Richard?' asked John.

'No, Mum said not to,' replied Sophie.

'Let's go and see what all the fuss is about,' comforted John and they headed upstairs.

As they entered their mother's bedroom Tom was kneeling on one knee as if at prayer, rubbing Helen's aching back whilst his mother was whispering in his ear. When she realised that they had entered the room she discontinued what she was saying and kissed him on the cheek, whispering, 'Promise me, Tom?'

'Of course I will Helen, you know I will,' he said earnestly. She gave him one last testing look. 'I promise,' he repeated, staring at her virtuously.

'Thank you.'

She flopped relieved back upon her pillow and he went to the chest of drawers beneath the window. John and Sophie watched as from the top right-hand drawer he withdrew a small pink envelope and showed it to her. She confirmed his action with a nod and he placed it in the top right-hand pocket of his tunic. Feeling a little awkward about the situation he was in, he gestured Sophie and John towards their mother.

'I'll go and put the kettle on shall I?' he asked with nervous merriment. 'How about we find some biscuits as well Sophie?' he encouraged tickling her behind the ears and nodding his head towards the door trying to get her to come with him and leave Helen and John alone for a moment.

'Biscuits? But you know where the biscuit tin is Tom' and then realising his intention, she quickly remarked, 'oh, yes, I see, Mrs Jenkins has found a new home for them, I'd better come and help you.'

A brief look at his face told John that Tom was finding this all very difficult. There was more emotion in his face than he was letting on. The sternness no longer remained; instead, it was replaced by one of frustration and worry.

'Are you going to tell me about the letter?' asked John quite defiantly to his mother, his empathy and concern for her welfare misplaced for the moment.

'Let me look at you,' she murmured stretching towards him. You are so like your father, but are those another set of pips on your shoulders? Congratulations my darling. I always knew you would go far.'

'Thank you Mother, you know full well I have been promoted to Lieutenant recently, you were there at the parade and you are trying to change the subject.' He folded his arms quite irritably and then seeing her sadness he felt guilty and fell to his knees beside her, apologising. 'I'm sorry, I didn't mean to sound so harsh.'

She ran her hand through his hair. 'You are so loved.'

'So the letter that Tom has just taken out of the chest of drawers, is it important?' he repeated quite agitated.

'Don't you trust me, John?' she whispered quite frankly. 'It is something that I have asked Tom to do for me.'

'Why can't I do it for you?' he retorted like a spoilt child.

'Because I've asked him to do it for me,' she remarked quite astonished at John's challenge.

'To do what exactly?' he continued in this cat and mouse act.

'To post it.'

'To whom?'

'Really John, does it matter?' she sighed disappointedly, but she knew once he had a bee in his bonnet he wasn't going to stop buzzing around the honey pot.

'To me, yes,' he said perturbed.

'You already know what the contents are.' She sighed. 'Ah well, I suppose it won't make any difference now. If I don't pull through this the letter I have given to Tom is to be given to my brother Richard with instructions for Sophie's future. She is still very young John and you are growing in the army. If anything happens to me what will you do? Give up the army to look after Sophie, that wouldn't be fair when you have so much potential.

I have asked Richard to be her benefactor and I am sure he will look after her when you sometimes just cannot be around. The army is a vocation I know all about. It becomes a man's wife, life and sacrifice and I don't want and Sophie wouldn't want you to be hers. We have discussed this before.'

'Have we? I don't remember, but I could still have posted it for you,' he said indignantly.

'Oh John, stop! Tom has been our guardian angel through thick and thin, how will he feel if I take back the instructions now,' she argued benevolently and now tiring quite dramatically continued. 'He will ensure that it reaches the right destination at the right time. You will have other things to contend with,' she reassured him and closed her eyes to stop the conversation going any further; she started to cough uncontrollably again and then afterwards fell back exhausted.

Realising his childishness and audacity as she lay there gaunt and frail, John felt an even bigger twinge of remorse and poured out his apologies at full throttle.

She opened her eyes and stroked his head that was lying by her side. For a moment while he was looking up at her, he couldn't quite decide from her languishing smile whether he had been completely outwitted and deceived, or whether she was just comforting his fears with her own.

'Mum, one more thing, you know we all love you, don't you? And we want what's best for you?' he cooed sincerely.

'No, I won't go,' she spluttered feebly. 'Ambulances always arrive too late.'

'Oh God, Mother, sometimes you really are impossible!'

'She's pulling your leg now John, aren't you Helen?' came the jovial boom of Tom's voice through the bedroom door, a tray of cups of tea balancing precariously between his thumb and little finger like a waiter. He winked at her and said, 'she goes to the hospital and I post the letter. Isn't that right madam?'

Helen smiled and agreed.

'Oh, well thank God for small mercies,' John sighed with relief. 'Thank you for the tea Tom, two sugars for me.'

The ambulance arrived just after dinner. Barbara the district nurse had returned before noon from Mrs Bell's false alarm and was seeing to Helen upstairs. Mrs Jenkins had fixed them all lunch and Sophie was packing some things for her mother's journey and stay in a small brown leather suitcase. John and Tom were reminiscing downstairs around the photo album when the porters were transporting Helen down the stairs on a stretcher and out to the ambulance.

'You are all coming with me aren't you?' Helen beseeched them.

'We'll be right behind you Helen,' assured Tom.

'Thank you, Tom, for everything, you've always had a very special place in my family's heart, you've been wonderful,' she said to Tom pulling out her arm from under the tight sheet with difficulty and grasping his hand, squeezing it with what little strength she had left. 'It needs time and when you feel it's right.'

Tom didn't know what to say, he looked in so many directions as if lost and although John convinced himself his mother was delirious from the drugs, Tom seemed to understand every word as if it were a code.

'I'm so proud of you,' his mother looked over to him now, a weak but beautiful smile upon her face. 'You do know that don't you?'

John walked over to her as she was put down by the front door, she grasped his hand as a tear seeped from his eye and ran down his cheek. Her eyes were tired, but still full of love and adoration.

'Where's Sophie?' she called softly

'I'm here Mum; I've got your bag.' She raised it high to show her.

'Look after each other,' she said.

John turned to look at his little sister. She was still trying hard to hide her pain and sorrow. Her mother beckoned for her to come over and then it all seemed to happen so slowly and yet so beautifully.

'My children, my beautiful children,' she said softly. 'How I love you both.'

'Let's get you in this ambulance,' interrupted Barbara efficiently. Sophie her mouth wide open just stood there. 'Do you want to ride in with your mother to keep her company, Sophie?'

'It's too late,' whimpered Sophie.

'No, it will be fine,' said Barbara encouragingly. 'There is plenty of room.'

'No, it's too late,' repeated Sophie. 'She's already gone.'

Their mother's hand that still clutched John's went cold and limp.

'She knew,' Sophie whispered. 'She knew she was never going to leave this house.'

The silence was dull and heavy. Tom's eyes were firmly fixed on a spot on the floor unable to believe what he knew had just happened, then he gripped Sophie quickly and held her tight in his giant arms to soothe her distress, but she was impassive and detached.

Barbara, checking Helen's pulse and breathing, firstly shook her head in amazement and then shook it again at John to confirm that Sophie was right. Helen had given up the fight. Mrs Jenkins drew her apron that she had been drying her hands on up to her face snatching her breath in dismay and crossed herself. Barbara then closed Helen's eyelids respectfully and drew the blanket over her peaceful face.

Tom caught the district nurses hand quickly, 'don't do that,' he said abruptly. 'She doesn't like the dark' and then realising that he had stepped out of line, apologised.

The porters continued through the door and John stared at Tom, absorbing his reaction and trying to make sense of it. Tom could see John's fixed gaze and he walked into the living room opening the curtains fully that had been only slightly ajar so that sunlight could shine through.

'You mother never liked the dark,' he said staring at the panes of glass. 'When your father died I promised your mother I would look out for her and you. I owed it to Jack who couldn't be here for you. I'm failing to protect you all, I'm sorry John, I'm so sorry.'

'She knew, didn't she? That she was… ill.'

'I don't know; I just don't know. Your mother has a way of knowing things that we were oblivious to.'

John had never seen Tom cry. Trying to fight back his own emotions was difficult, especially in the light of seeing the sincerity of Tom's on full display for the first time in his life. Sophie drew her knees up to her chest and encircled them with her arms and rocked, wrapped up in the embrace of Mrs Jenkins.

'Oh God, Uncle Richard!' exclaimed John. 'Tom, the letter,' he gasped.

Tom pulled from his chest pocket the letter he had taken from the drawer earlier.

Wiping his tears away Tom said, 'you need to take Sophie in the car and get yourself down to the hospital with your mother; that's your rightful place. I'll get myself up to the Great Hall.'

'We could go together,' John winced.

'Indeed we could, but that's not what your mother asked of me,' he squatted down next to Sophie and said. 'Are you going with your brother?'

'Yes,' she nodded.

'Up we get then,' he said tenderly, tears rolling down his cheeks. 'There's a lot to be done tomorrow and we are only half way through today.'

August turned to September and September to October. It was hard to tell what time of the year it was, as out in the desert there was no change in season. When November finally came, there was no hint what so ever that winter was on its way. John missed the seasons, they were a comforting reminder of the repetitive consistency of life. The Sahara lacked an autumnal blush, its reds and ochres were not the same as the trees back home.

In spite of several unsuccessful attempts to rendezvous, Katie and John's affair of the heart had been confined to pen and paper. Time restrictions, planning, training, the limited boundaries on John's part and increased shifts and workloads due to high air raid casualties on Katie's, had kept them apart, but you would never have known, such was their smitten, seductive and passionate language, expressed as they made love to each other in every letter that they wrote and exchanged.

John was pleased that Sophie was writing regularly again, she had found a new lease of life and thrown herself into her work; it kept her busy and she seemed to have gotten over all the shocks and misery of the months past. He sensed a new inner strength and quality of Sophie's writing. She was quite assertive in her letters, more understanding about matters and at times more inquisitive. He noticed she had a lot of questions and some of them quite intrusive. Although she had been pleased to hear that he had found comfort in a romance, he never divulged much on the subject. Despite her new prying nature, her descriptions of the changing seasons and village life back home kept his imagination alive and overall with the apparent contentment of both the ladies in his life, he could go about his day with a new sense of calm.

The Company was still training outside Mersa Matruh, but many of their nights were spent further out in the desert and trenches that surrounded the town, watching for saboteurs and any possible surprise raids. It also got the newer members of the family into the routine of living in the desert.

The Company headquarters dugout was not nearly as cosy as the last one John had slept in before attacking the ridge. For a start it had no roof. It was a shallow dugout made deeper by adding extra sandbags around it. Over the top of the many scattered old ammunition boxes, the small rickety table and many of John and Tom's belongings was a camouflage net. Both Tom and Scott slept in the dugout alongside their captain and both detested the idea of having no roof. It made them sitting targets for the flies again. As well as being plagued by aggravating insects the sand would begin to pile on top of the blankets and it made them feel like pork chops on a grill and so the vicious circle continued, move or be roasted, move or be swarmed upon.

'Bloody sand,' groaned Tom, breathing through his pullover which he was using as an air filter.

'Bloody flies,' whinged Sergeant Scott. 'But at least we don't have that bloody rat in here with us again.'

It had been a long time since the discovery of the little Gerboa in the last dugout. John found it strange how easily he remembered the name they had given him and every now and then when there was a small noise, he would look to see if Harry or one of his distant relatives was there.

It was the 10th of November when the Major came to see him; John was having a shave, using the remainder of his tea as water for his razor. Nothing was wasted out here.

'Morning John,' he said cheerfully.

'Morning Sir. Sorry be with you in a minute,' he said starting to pack his razor away although he was only half done.

'Oh don't worry about that just carry on, I have some news.' The Major made himself comfortable on an old ammunition crate and started laying out a map across the table. 'There's going to be another attack to relieve Tobruk.'

John with half his face clear of bristles turned giving the Major a look of alarm. He wished he was joking, twice the Eighth army had tried to punch through to the Rats of Tobruk and twice they had been mauled by the desert fox. As much as John wanted to break through to the garrison, the British record so far had been far from perfect.

'I know, I know,' the Major replied reading his thoughts, 'but this time I'm confident it will work. It's to go ahead on November the 19th although we won't be deployed until twenty-four hours later. Our objective is to capture a small settlement called Sidi Omar and then drive onwards towards the port.'

John wiped his face and walked over to the table.

'And?'

The Major pointed to the target. 'Hopefully,' he continued. 'Elements of the 7th armoured division should have taken it already the day before and when we arrive all we will have to do is hold it whilst the rest of the division drives on towards Tobruk. When you arrive you should find a handful of tanks from the 44th armoured brigade. What I am saying is this time we won't be alone.'

'So we are babysitting this position?'

'Not quite how the Brigadier put it, but yes.'

'Great it all sounds so simple,' John said sarcastically.

'It is really, most of the frontline will erupt with action. I was at the briefing with General Auckinleck yesterday and there has been a real shake-up from the top. He is a very clever man our new general and I will tell you this, he has the men at heart. No more risks and gambles. There is a full briefing this evening so you better come along with Sergeant Major Hill and get the full picture.'

'What's the plan called sir?' John asked.

'Crusader.'

The name seemed appropriate; the whole effort to relieve Tobruk had almost become a crusade. The Major left him as it approached midday. John had planned to take the company to the rifle range again, his aim to keep his men as the best shots in the battalion. 'A' Company had been firing their rifles all morning in an attempt to improve their accuracy, especially since a shooting competition had been arranged for the following week. As they began to trudge back towards them, John knew it was time to send off the first of his platoons.

The range was not what one would have expected. There was no big embankment to absorb the stray rounds or a comfortable shack which would shield you from the overpowering sun; just a large dune of sand. The targets were a combination of the usual boards with bullseye rings, empty food cans and small piles of rocks painted white and stacked like little pyramids. If you could cause the pyramid to tumble, then you were doing well.

John and Tom watched each platoon as they did half an hour on the range. The men lay upon the ground across a small ridge of sand and fired across at their targets midway up the opposing dune. The shooting was pretty good and small clouds of dust kicked up around each pyramid, but it took the average rifleman three or four rounds to bring the stones down. Not a good start for the finest shots in the battalion.

John walked back and forwards behind his men. The heels of his boots sunk into the red sand as he watched carefully their fall of shot. Some fired too high and others too low, but all eventually hit their targets well as they adjusted.

'Bit of a slow start,' Tom muttered. 'Especially the new lads. As for the rest, I think we have the finest rifleman in the regiment. What do you think?'

Over Tom's shoulder John noticed a scurrying figure behind him in the distance coming towards him across the dunes.

'Sod the regiment Sergeant Major,' John replied. 'I think we've got the finest riflemen in the whole Division.'

'Well we will know next week when we have our firing range sparring against 'A' Company,' Tom said. 'I saw them this morning, some of them are good, but not as steady as ours.'

'I think we will hold our own, but we don't have time on our side, especially with these new boys.'

'There is always the in-company boxing tomorrow,' Tom added.

John turned his back to the shooting and whispered out of earshot of the men. 'Boxing might be all we end up doing. We are going for Tobruk again and there is a briefing tonight.'

Tom's face lit up at the thought of battle again. He had been biting his nails along with the new recruits to lock horns with the enemy again.

Meanwhile, the distant figure had now evolved into a young lance corporal. He gave a smart salute and then dropped down to the ground out of breath. Tom helped him to his feet.

'Lance Corporal Mills Sir, Royal Army Service Corps. Are you Captain John Baker of D company?'

John saluted back, 'yes Corporal what can I do for you?'

'Well actually it's this sir' and he held out a small envelope. 'Couldn't find you all morning and I have to get back to Alexandria this afternoon. Was going to leave it with B Company...' Tom gave out a disapproving grunt, B Company had been accused of theft on more than three occasions in the last week. 'I had the same response from your quartermaster who pointed out where you were. I promised the lady that I would hand it to you personally. I don't normally walk halfway across the desert to deliver mail personally, but this seemed rather urgent.'

Tom passed him his canteen.

'A lady you say?' John asked.

'I was in Sidi Barrani this morning delivering medical supplies and mail. I promised her I would stop here on my way back to Alexandria.'

He passed the letter to John, Saluted and then walked away back across the sand towards the town which could be made out in the distance.

'Brave lad, such a shame,' Tom said ruefully.

'Why's that, do you know him?' John probed with interest.

'Never seen him before, but there is a ruddy great big minefield over there between him and the town if he goes that way,' Tom replied with a sinister grin.

With a tremendous shout, John stopped the firing and ordered his men to empty their rifles, place them on safe and take a rest. One private under John's orders, skittered across the sand in order to catch up with Lance Corporal Mills and warn him of the minefield and show him the safe path through.

With the men rested John turned to his correspondence that was obviously from Katie, but before he began peeling back the flap he realised that he didn't recognise the writing on the front. It had to be Katie he thought, but the writing suggested otherwise.

'Well we all know who that is from,' Tom said, pushing out his chest to imitate the bust and waistline of a woman's figure, pouting his lips and drawing in the air a love heart with his hands.

'Jealousy will get you nowhere Sergeant Major,' John sighed.

Tom pulled from his pocket a letter he had received from Sophie the day before and waving it in the air teased, 'I've got one too from my girl' and pranced off like a horse leaving John shaking his head in wonderment of him.

The letter as he presumed was not from Katie, it was from the Matron of the Sidi Barrani Hospital.

He read the letter and then read it again following each word carefully, checking what he had been reading as at first he couldn't believe it. His heart beat faster and harder before it sank into the pit of his stomach. A cold and sickening feeling swept across his body. He felt dizzy and perspired as if struck with a cold. He wanted to fall to his knees as the weight of the letter and the news it contained was as heavy a burden as the list of lost men and comrades he had held not so long ago.

'No,' he whispered to himself and repeated the word defiantly to himself over and over again. 'No.'

Tom could sense his mortification and see his wretchedness from where he was sitting and bounded to his aid.

'Tell me, John, John, tell me is it here or home?'

'Here,' John gulped feeling the lump in his throat strangling him now.

'Katie?' Tom quizzed and John nodded.

He couldn't say the word and couldn't move. The letter fell from his shaking hands and Tom picked them up, reading it and exclaiming, 'Jesus Christ.'

She was missing, that's all the letter eluded to and it was basic and to the point. Matron Denning explained that she had been working in the POW wing of the hospital when it was hit during an air raid. Katie had been trying to get some of the walking wounded to the shelter, it was here that a German prisoner, wounded, turned on her and stabbed her in the back in an attempt to escape, but that wasn't what killed her.

Katie had been evacuated home and the matron had packed her on-board one of the destroyers ferrying wounded out to a homebound hospital ship. It was hit by a dive bomber and sank in minutes.

'Dismissed, back to barracks!' Tom bellowed to everyone within earshot. 'Sergeant Scott get these men out of my sight!'

'Sorted Sergeant Major,' returned Scott automatically seeing for himself the private predicament on display.

'Talk to me John,' encouraged Tom as they walked together away from the firing range, 'open up son, just let it out.'

'Is it me Tom?' John stuttered. 'Everyone I try to protect…'

'It's not you.'

'It must be. I have this effect on everyone I get close to. I kill them. I'm a jinx, a hex, a bad luck charm. Mum, Anthony, I bet I even killed my father! What is it with me? She was the one, I know she was. I loved her, I truly loved her,' he howled his head in his hands.

Tom put his arms around him, comforting his stifled words, patting and rubbing him firmly across his shoulders. 'She loved you too and was where she had to be. She would have done everything she could to have stayed alive. Strong type is Katie. Believe me, she is a survivor if I ever saw one. There might have been a chance that she made it, John? She might have survived the sinking, there is still hope.'

'Hope? She was stabbed and then went down with a bloody ship Tom!' His heartache was replaced by venomous anger. 'Chances are pretty bloody slim, you know as well as I that missing is a word used in letters because they are too afraid to write dead!'

'Well we thought the same of you not that long ago and here we are. This desert is just as full of miracles as it is despair.'

'Sodding lists,' he dribbled, his teeth biting his lips to keep his emotions from virtually bursting openly. He rubbed his hands through his hair several times the tips of his fingers pushing down hard and almost scouring his scalp. 'Not possible, not possible at all, she said in the letter that all survivors accounted for and she wasn't on the list. Sodding, sodding lists!'

'Not accounted for yet,' Tom tried one more time.

'Fucking war!' he spat and took himself away from Tom, scrunching the letter in his hands and throwing it as hard as he could and as far away from himself as possible. 'Roll on Tobruk,' he shouted at the air indignantly. Scowling maliciously and hurting from his core he said cruelly, 'Now it's really personal!'

Tom watched him walk back to the company. He paused and picked up the letter, trying to flatten it back to its original shape as best he could. Reading its contents again he placed it in his breast pocket, next to the letter John's mother had given him the day she died.

'Still hope,' he said as if to her ghost.

Buckland arrived back at the cottage when it was quite late. The moon was full and the path bathed in its white glow. He hung up his coat on a hanger and placed his cap upon the hat stand.

'Mrs Jenkins? It is ever so late, what on earth are you still doing here?'

'Oh hello love!' she then broke into a whisper. 'Don't tell little miss, but I left a few of my chores the other day, so I am making up for it tonight.'

'And Sophie?'

'You know where she is. Reading through more of her mother's diaries. Weeks now she has been glued to them and she has years left to get through them all. Barely moves from them.'

'She is going to work isn't she?' he whispered with a wink. 'Why don't I give you a hand, help you out for a bit so you can get home.'

'No, no,' she protested. 'This is what I am paid for, at the end of the day I have to make the most of the job whilst it exists.' Buckland gave her a morbid expression. 'Well let's face it love, this kind of work isn't going to last forever, especially with every invention that comes along. Technology is constantly changing, it did after the last war and I shouldn't imagine this one will be any different. I dread to think what we will witness by the end of all this.'

She waved a wooden spoon around as she gestured to the world around her. Buckland smiled, there was something so wonderfully comforting in the elderly's resistance and scepticism of the future. He would no doubt be the same when it was his turn, cherishing the modern world he knew as he trembled in the wake of the new one he would no doubt stand before.

'So,' she began again. 'Apart from being long, how was your day?'

'Oh Mrs Jenkins, you know I can't possibly talk to you about all that, careless talk and all that.'

'Lieutenant,' her tone was that of a strict school teacher. 'I am aware of that. You could have just humoured me. Try saying something like it was a nice day, or it was a fairly good day. Give it a go sailor.'

'In that case, I had a fairly good day then.'

'There you go!' she teased and giving her a smirk he left her to her chores.

Sophie sat on the floor surrounded by what appeared to be letters, photographs and all manner of correspondence. The bulky diaries were in a pile next to her. Her face was studious, scanning every word her eyes locked onto, taking in each and every meaning. She even had a notepad now and Buckland could see that it was full of scribbles, words and lines.

'Confusing family tree?' He said breaking the silence.

'You're telling me,' she replied not even lifting her head from her work.

'Better than reading them up there?' he pointed to the roof.

Sophie nodded, 'I was always a little worried I would kick over the hurricane lamp and set the house on fire.'

'Never seemed that clumsy in the hospital.'

He coughed to grab her attention and pointed her in the direction of the carriage clock on the windowsill. When she saw that it was past ten she sighed and closed the diary she was looking through and began tidying up. She called for Mrs Jenkins and apologised.

'I didn't realise the time,' she said. 'Mrs Jenkins I am so sorry, I had no idea I had been in here that long, you need to go home. Why don't you take Wednesday off? You have done more than enough tonight.'

Mrs Jenkins gave Buckland a wink and then departed to get her coat.

'So how is the family history going?'

'Odd, so very odd,' she began. 'She really loved him.' When Buckland looked confused she continued. 'Jack, not my father, although of course she loved him too, it's written all over the pages of the later diaries, but it was a different kind of love. It sounds strange, but I never ever thought of Jack as a real person, he was John's father and so my world was never consumed by him. It was always my mother and father. I never really took much notice of Jack, if anything I was always so very envious of John, his father always sounded so much better than mine. Every time Tom would tell one of his stories, Jack was always so brave, a real hero and almost superhuman. My brother would lap those stories up. Jack was always a mythical legend in the family.

Yet something is wrong. Whilst I am not disputing Jack's bravery, the description of him here is quite different. I can't help but feel that this Jack is very different to the one that Tom always told us about.'

'Well Tom would have known him better over there in France, there is bound to be some inconsistencies.' He added.

'Even though Tom was posted to another regiment?'

He didn't have an answer for that. 'Ok you have me there,' he said plucking the newspaper from the side table and leaning in the doorway. 'Maybe as you read on it will make more sense.'

She rose from the floor, finishing the last little bit of tidying as he stood watching her and pretending to be engrossed in the cover story of the newspaper.

'Have you ever had that feeling that you have been living in some kind of fairy tale?' she asked as she attempted to pass him through the doorway. 'As if the reality you thought you knew was just all one big dream?'

It wasn't planned and nor was it expected, but before he knew it he had said 'yes,' leant forward and placed his lips firmly upon hers. She didn't pull away, not at first. She kept them there and he could see as he looked upon her eyes that they were closed. He wanted to drop the newspaper and place his hands around her waist but worried this moment would end abruptly if he did, he refrained. She tilted her head a little and slowly her lips opened, inviting him to continue and so he did. He felt her exhale on his cheek and her hair tickled his forehead.

No sooner had the moment come and he wished for it to end. He tried to wriggle into her mind and in there he imagined her thinking of Anthony or thinking him no different to other men. The minute he imagined himself to be in there, the more he feared what she might think of him. It was Sophie however who pushed him gently away first.

'I am very lonely in my soul, but I am not ready for this and neither are you,' she said. 'You will feel like you are filling Anthony's shoes and I will feel uncontrollable guilt that will undoubtedly ruin everything.' It was as if she had read his mind precisely.

'I am sorry, I don't know what came over me.'

'Don't be sorry,' she put her hand to her cheek. 'If it is meant to be then it is meant to be and I don't think any less of you. It's just that it is not the right time yet. Reading those diaries has taught me I never fully knew my mother and I want to know who I am before I make any more commitments.'

'Or mistakes.' He sighed.

'I don't think you would be a mistake, I know who you are and I know you would make me very happy or die trying. In return, I would expect you to have me for who I am and I have only just begun my story.'

Journey To The Front

'Get dressed and ready to move out,' came the shout. The air was cold and chilly. The early morning wind moaned and wound itself throughout the camp like a wailing old woman, kicking up tent sheets and camouflage nets like laundry left on the line whilst each man packed up his belongings ready to embark upon the Lorries.

It had been raining throughout the night and there was an air of surrealism about the place. Nobody had slept at all through the night, as the tension of knowing that this was no exercise had gripped even the bravest of souls. Nobody knew or could even haphazard a guess as to what they would be marching into. With a last frantic effort to write letters, update diaries the order for 'everyone on board,' followed.

Simon watched as John went over their destination one last time on the small crumpled map which he laid upon the bonnet of his Humber staff car. Tom sat behind the wheel waiting for the order to move out and after a few last minute questions and corrections, the column, with the Humber in the lead pulled away following the Lorries of 'A' company into the abyss of sand.

The Lorries crawled along in bottom gear in a jolting and bone-shaking motion. The men bounced up as far as gravity would allow, only to be thrust back down just as forcefully landing on the hard slatted wooden seats again and again. Tom wrestled the Humber over the jagged rocks and potholes that lined the roads. The dust from the trucks in front was making it difficult to breathe as it spiralled and corkscrewed around the open staff car. John pulled his jumper up through his tunic and held it around his mouth and face, he could feel the grit in his mouth and the sand in his eyes and both he and Tom were wearing eye shields. Visibility was poor enough as it was.

Bomb craters from the many nights of heavy bombing scarred the surrounding landscape with big black scorch marks. Matruh itself was still gripped by the night and as the convoy progressed through its silent streets not a soul was to be seen. As the column headed into the desert leaving the town behind in shadow, the distant sky began to light up with a pale golden glow. The stars were still plain to see in the sky above and the dunes that stood like magnificent monuments were still in shadow towering above them.

Johns left boot rested on the wheel arch rim of the staff car and his studded boots began to flake parts of the paintwork off with the vibrations of the vehicle. He stared ahead, watching and waiting for the appearance of the sun.

'Beginning to lose 'A' company sir,' Tom said and looking ahead John could see clearly that 'A' company was indeed pulling away.

'That's alright Sergeant Major; we know where we're going. Besides, it's probably for the best that the battalion doesn't bunch up, particularly now it's getting light, but try and keep up if you can,' he replied.

John's face showed no emotion, no concern, nothing, he felt empty from within. He continued to stare ahead only moving to look in the direction of where he expected the sun to soon reveal itself. Finally it did, bursting out between two distant dunes, overpowering and catching everything in its path with its intense warmth. The shadows suddenly scuttled backwards leaving nothing but rich earthly colours behind that drifted and changed as the shadows receded. The rising and shimmering heat haze distorted the occasional little green shrubs and the towering dunes of sand in the distance.

Tom was disconcerted by Johns silence; he had barely said anything throughout the journey so far. He knew what it was that was playing on his mind; the loss of Katie had been an unexpected blow and John was still reeling from the news inside. Tom understood completely, he too had lost someone he loved, but even with that in mind the dumbness was still difficult to carry. Nothing could be done now and there wasn't really much more anyone could say. Everything had been said so he respected the silence.

The Humber bounced on through the dust and it seemed an eternity. They rolled on through the emptiness which was broken only by the occasional scars of war. Burnt out vehicles and dismembered artillery frameworks were now sculptured scenery on a barren landscape, they were shining and glinting piercingly in the sunlight where they had been facing the desert winds and the paintwork had been stripped or worn away to reveal the original shiny metal carcass.

They passed small villages with names of which nobody would remember and gravesites where a once unfruitful soil had now become forever England.

By now 'A' company had all but disappeared except for a distant dust cloud. Tom had decided to switch his eye shields for his more uncomfortable, but effective goggles as the ground became even harder, baked by the sun and the dust began to rise up in stronger agitated motions.

As the day went on they passed near to Sidi Barrani over to their right. The town couldn't be seen but was marked by plumes of polluting grey and black smoke rising in the distance. Tom wouldn't have noticed that was where they were but for a small barely visible distressed signpost that pointed the direction out to him.

John glanced briefly in its direction.

'I don't know, John, whether you will appreciate what I am about to say,' Tom began. 'Words cannot express the grief one feels when one loses love, but it is one of the last things your mother said to me and I think it is time to pass it on because it's as true now as it was then. You see love begins with a smile, grows with a kiss and…'

'And ends with a teardrop,' John finished the sentence for him.

'Ah, she had already told you,' he sighed disappointed that his words would be of no comfort.

'No, she never told me that, it was something that Katie wrote in one of her letters.'

'Katie wrote that?' Tom sounded surprised. 'I was just trying to break the silence.'

'I know, but we don't have to talk Tom, sometimes there just isn't anything to say is there?'

He patted his old mentor graciously on his shoulder as the Humber bucked and pitched ever onward choking the column relentlessly behind. As the column of lorries marched tirelessly on, every soldier's eyes were now watering with the windswept dust and it would have been difficult to tell at that precise moment whether John's eyes, also already inundated because of the dust, were redder with soreness at the sands tireless constancy or because of perhaps an additional tear.

‘I loved and lost once,’ Tom continued. ‘I know I told you all of those stories about the girls I met in France, but I never told you that there was actually one woman in my life I really did love.’

John was taken away from his heartache for a moment. ‘I could certainly do with one of your stories right now.’

Tom was on the verge of opening up, the words were on the tip of his tongue, the confession bounding out of the door, only to be pulled back. If John required a story and that would help, then he would oblige.

‘Did I ever tell you about the little French tease I met outside Calais? It was after the war.’ And so Tom embarked upon another story, this one as fictional as all the others he had told both John and Sophie over the years. All of them to disguise the truth that now only Sophie had access to in a letter that would find its way to her.

The truth could wait. John now smiled contently at the comfort of what he thought to be an old familiar tale.

'You knew!' Sophie seldom lost her temper to anyone, especially Uncle Richard. She was relieved that Joy was out today as no doubt she would have calmed the situation and right now Sophie wanted rage, pure rage.

'You need to calm down,' Richard protested, he had been caught by surprise as she burst through the doors like an angry wind. 'Knew what?'

'They had an affair, my mother and Tom and you knew all along!'

The diary under her arm didn't lie and although Richard had no idea how she had gotten this information, he poured a scotch from the drinks globe and slumped defeated in his chair. Sophie had been putting the pieces together for some time now, but the last pages of her mother's diary revealed not only her uncle's involvement, but so much more it shook her to the core.

'It was brief, so incredibly brief Sophie.'

'Why didn't you tell me?'

Richard ran his hand through his hair. 'It's hardly my news to give you, it's my sister's history and that of Tom's, not mine.'

'Well my mother is dead and the only person who can help me understand what all this is about is you,' she demanded.

Richard looked more sternly at her 'and what about Tom, have you stopped to consider his feelings on the matter?' Sophie's sigh suggested otherwise. 'I thought not. Do you think Tom would want me blurting out his secrets when he is not here to defend himself? Of course not.'

'I'm not angry with Tom, I just want to understand what I'm reading in here.' She pointed to the diary and Richard's eyebrows raised dramatically. 'I found her diaries and she wrote everything down. I know everything, I just need you to help me understand.'

Richard paused, sipping his scotch and thinking to himself. He looked down to the floor and then up to the ceiling as if the answers were written somewhere else.

'Jack changed, he changed a lot, to my mind he became quite a bully. On the few occasions I saw them together that autumn he was quite polite, but behind closed doors he was cruel. Any goodness in his soul was taken away on the Somme and buried there. Naturally your mother turned to Tom for support. All I know is they wrote to one another, quite a bit I think. She helped Tom through his troubles and he helped her through hers. I don't know what the content of the letters was and I suppose that isn't important. They became friends, something unusual between a man and a woman in those times.

Like many friendships it became more, but as far I am concerned that was when it came to an end. The minute they acknowledged they had feelings it came to an end and it was Tom who called it off. The following year they went back to the front and Jack was killed at Cambrai. Tom didn't come home until 1919, long after the war ended.'

'But it didn't stop,' Sophie added softly. 'The affair, it didn't stop.'

'I assure you it did Sophie,' Richard concluded. 'Before Tom had even gone back it stopped, before Cambrai it stopped and that bloody awful mess at Passchendaele.'

'I meant Tom never stopped loving mum,' Sophie added.

There were tears welling in her eyes as the reality of the story began to hit home and Richard fetched her some tissues.

'Of course he still loved your mother, it was always obvious, at least to me, perhaps because I knew. I am surprised you never saw it yourself, but then you were always so innocent and Tom and your mother were always very good at hiding it. I saw it. And it's clear now that even your father could see it, although he could never prove it. Did it never occur to you, some of the nasty things he said? The poor man thought you were Tom's, he confronted me about it once.'

Sophie felt a lump in her throat, a part of her hoped it was true, for Tom would be the father she dreamed of, but then she remembered the poor plight of her own father and how such a revelation would humiliate his memory.

'Is Tom my father?'

Richard shook his head confidently. 'No, but does it make sense why he said those things? Of course it does, but you wouldn't have seen it at the time because Tom had done such a good job of rewriting the past, to protect himself and more importantly your mother.

You see as time went on a spider's web was woven and the more stories that were told the more impossible it became to be untangled from the lies. But it was done so that your mother would not be dishonoured, because they were afraid you would be ashamed of them.'

'I would never…'

'Easy it is to say now with hindsight,' Richard interrupted, pouring himself another scotch. 'As children, you were more fragile and there was so much upheaval in your lives, the fiction became more necessary and more impossible to double back on. Can you imagine the damage it would have done to your mother's marriage to Ted? Your feelings may not mirror the feelings John might have on this news. I am not condoning their actions, but the story went on and you all went along with it, for better or for worse.'

'The truth has to be told now,' Sophie said, emotionally exhausted.

'You must understand Sophie. Tom was a man driven by guilt, for betraying his commanding officer a man he served and his friend. Tom needs to serve someone and he has more than made up for his errors by serving your family.'

'That's the reason they fell out and Jack sent Tom away to another regiment, isn't it?'

'I can't confirm that. All I know is that Tom never forgave himself for the betrayal. His attempts to reconcile Jack and your mother weren't going to happen, so the next best thing when your brother was born was to honour Jack in death for the sake of the child.'

'His penitence.'

'I guess you could call it that.'

'Why didn't my mother wait for Tom? After the war, they could have been together and made it work.'

'You know the answer to that already. My father disowned my sister and until he passed away I couldn't intervene or help. Your father came from a good stable background and offered to marry her, it was an opportunity I know no other woman in your mother's position to have ever had.'

Sophie understood completely and admired the way her mother had managed to turn her destitute life around under the circumstances. Her mother was a survivor and it filled her heart with a radiant warmth to imagine her father, whose past had been blighted with drink and jealousy, to have been the hero for a brief moment of time. She had for a while been happy with Ted and for a while they had been a loving and happy family. It had helped bring his story to a finish with a renewed added sense of recognition.

Tom might have come for her mother under different circumstances, but Jack's retribution had done its job well and Tom's unit was one of the few to have stayed in France after the war. Ted was in a better position to provide, having a wealthy family and making so many investments during the boom in the 1920s. Tom could never have provided what Ted had been able to provide and then she remembered something Mrs Jenkins had once said, that Ted could never live up to Jack.

She had been mistaken, it was Tom that Ted could never have lived up to. He could never have lived up to Tom's ability to have saved Helen emotionally, to say and do the right thing when it counted. Tom wasn't just her mother's hero but became John's, he replaced Jack unwittingly becoming his inspiration and motivation, something Ted had never been able to do. Tom had become the father Ted could never have been during his last days to Sophie, as the depression in the states pulled him to The Three Feathers on a daily basis.

Tom had always been their constant star. All this time he had been her mother's champion and Sophie and John's role model. Sophie was frustrated too, that the whole time he had been the families dependable and wise knight he had said nothing. It was a romance that never truly was and nor could it ever be. It was this that made it all the more so beautiful and yet all the more tragic. A love that only novelists write about.

'You know sometimes I wish things had been different,' Richard said. 'Tom would have been good for you mother and good for you all. His faults and they were few, made him one of the most honourable men I have ever known.'

'Do you realise what all this means for John?'

'I warn you, Sophie, this will do very little good for your brother at the moment. Do you understand that? It will simply discredit Tom and could do damage beyond our comprehension.'

Sophie walked over to him and thrust her mother's diary onto his lap. It was already open to the page she wanted him to read and she pointed to one of the last entries her mother had written.

'I disagree,' she said calmly. 'Read this, it describes a letter she wrote weeks before she died. My mother knew you see, I don't know how, perhaps that sixth sense she often went on about, but she knew she was sick and knew it was serious. She wrote a letter and it tells you here exactly what its contents were. You see, whilst I realise now that Tom's stories were a journey he took us on that had good intentions, he wasn't the only one who lied.'

Richard scanned the contents of the page cautiously, adding together each piece of the puzzle to the pieces he already had. Finally the picture was complete, it was now whole and both Sophie and Richard could see it in its completeness and it was astonishing.

'Do you see?' she asked. 'There is nothing I can do about this in a letter. This is not the kind of news I should be the one breaking to him.'

'Out there,' Richard said, raising from his seat and gazing out of the window. 'There is a man in the dark and another man whose suffering I could never imagine.'

The night drew near, the sound of rumbling and thundering guns and the distant flicker of light pointed out the battlefield. The company had arrived at their start point. They had spent all day and much of the night driving through the dust and dirt. Each man was covered from head to toe. They had stopped only to top up with fuel and water for the radiators, so each soldier's back was breaking and their eyes fighting to stay open from the exhausting and painful conditions of the journey.

'A' company was over to the left, crowded around their Lorries. The other companies somewhere over on the right just pulling up from their long journey. There was no time to unpack as they would be heading off first thing in the morning. John sat in his seat in the Humber staff car, staring at a pair of scorpions that were duelling on the sandy floor. Both were the same species and even the same size. It was strange to think of them mimicking the war, where the only real difference John could see between his men and the enemies, was the language and uniform.

'Hello John,' called Major Love, his baton raised high in acknowledgement.

'Sir,' John responded.

'How was the journey? Mine was bloody uncomfortable and bloody hot, feels like my back is going to break any minute.'

'Same here sir, the men are exhausted, it was a long drive,' John replied. 'There are a few that are dehydrated and parched, some sore shoulders and blisters, but mostly everyone is fine. I'm surprised we weren't hit by enemy aircraft. Talk about vulnerable. It felt like a constant waiting game. With no cover, all we needed was one enemy plane and it could have taken us all out in one hit!'

'The RAF have dealt with that I expect,' the Major looked down at the scorpions and cringed a little. 'Ever eaten scorpion?'

John looked at him with surprise and almost laughed in disbelief, 'No sir I haven't why?'

'Me neither. When I was a prisoner in the last war, the Turks barely fed us anything. The things the men would attempt to eat in order to survive was astonishing, including scorpion. I will never be taken prisoner again. We are going to hold here till first light and then advance towards Sidi Omar.

John, there is one more thing. I'm putting your crowd in first, I want your company to lead.' It was news John could have done without. 'Sidi Omar is only a few miles away; the 44th armoured brigade engaged the Germans to the south of this location today, turned out they belonged to elements of the 21st Panzer division which of course alters things and although our tanks should be on the outskirts of the settlement in the next few hours, knowing the Panzers are in the vicinity is a bit of a game changer.

You know the procedure and you can remember the briefing. Your company will replace and go in first instead of 'A' company; I need experience and the best. Your boys are the best. Can I count on you and your men?'

John sighed at both the compliment and potential death sentence, but there was little he could do, someone had to go in first and it might as well be his company.

'Of course sir,' John replied.

'Oh and my commiserations, John. Simon informed me a few minutes ago about your lady friend, you sure you are up to it?'

John didn't answer but continued to stare at the duelling scorpions. The Major too gave them one last glance himself and cringed at the sight before leaving.

With the night nearly over and the three lieutenants informed of the change in plan they got themselves ready to move as the sky began to pale. The night had seemed short and John had been unable to sleep again at all. In all none of the men had really slept, the night was cold and their nervousness made them feel even colder. Part of them wanted the dawn and the warmth of the sun but a part of them knew the dawn would bring another eventful day of hardship, maybe their last.

'He wants the best,' John told Bailey as he rolled up the map they had been looking at under torchlight.

'Well he has the best alright,' Bailey chirped. 'But what about the rest of you, are you going to be joining me?'

'I see nothing has dampened your spirits.' John replied.

He threw the map into the back of the car and nodded at Tom to start the engine.

'Nothing to it,' Bailey said. 'As you have already said, it's a holding action just to prevent a counter attack. Light resistance if any at all.'

'Like the last show? You and I know better than that. Stay ready, stay alert.'

John temporarily put his loss of Katie behind him and concentrated on his job. There was a battle to be fought in a few hours and the men were full of patriotic spirit, they cajoled each other with fighting talk that would make anyone feel sorry for whoever would be defending Sidi Omar. John was warmed by their courage as always, but sceptical. If tanks had been spotted and engaged that same day, where were they now?

Within a few minutes the orders had been barked yet again and the Bedford lorries were rolling forward again through the sand with the staff car at the front. Tom pushed the car forward slowly so as to keep dust as minimal as possible; dust would often give away the position of a vehicle particularly now they were closer to their goal. There was a whole sense of déjà vu again about the day.

'John,' Tom called above the rattling engine. 'Sidi Omar is just up ahead, we will need to stop and disembark soon.'

John peered through the hazy heat of the morning and up ahead he could see the small settlement, it was still far and he could only just distinguish the few mud-brick buildings and a small mosque. It wasn't much and appeared to be more important to the map than the actual desert.

'I know this might seem completely inappropriate and the wrong time, but there is something I have to talk to you about John, just in case,' Tom called at the top of his voice.

There was something in his voice that made John feel very nervous as they passed over a hidden rock which threw him to the other side of the vehicle.

'Just in case?' he frowned and bounced back towards him. 'Tom I don't think there is anything to worry about, we all know you are bulletproof. The men think you were an army experiment that went wrong, or right depending on your point of view.'

Tom gave out a chuckle and slowed the staff car down.

He then spoke with a voice weighed down. 'I don't really know how to begin, I haven't really known for a long time. After the last battle and nearly losing you I should have said something then. Actually there is no perhaps about it, I know I should have said something then, but for whatever reason I didn't. You see it's about the letter, I want to explain about your mother's letter.'

'The letter she gave you when she died?'

'Damn it, it's not really even about the letter either, it's about you, me and your mother.'

'I know you loved her,' John replied, he had been putting some of the pieces together himself. 'And for what I think it's worth. I believe she loved you too.' His comment threw Tom completely and his look of shock gave John a satisfactory smile. 'Wow, you're not speechless are you Sergeant Major? That will be a first.'

'I wasn't entirely honest about its content,' Tom continued.

'I think I already know Tom,' John said. 'I've been so consumed by grief and worry that when I stop and think about it, well it's obvious. In fact I think I have always known and just never acknowledged it. Perhaps because I never saw it with my own eyes until now when all those years it had been right in front of me. You loved her and she never knew.'

'Close, but that's not the whole story. There is more to it than that.'

'We are too close and open here,' John said returning them to the war. 'We have come in at the wrong point on the map. Change direction and head over there, we can disembark behind those rocks as we have no cover here. Just have to hope the bloody place is empty after all. Sorry, Tom, you were saying that there is more to it than that?'

Before Tom could answer the ground erupted around them with enemy artillery. The car was tossing and turning to the left and the right, sometimes being lifted into the air as if it were only a toy. As John turned in his seat to look at the infantry in the Lorries behind, he could see them being straddled by huge columns of fiery sand where the shells were crashing.

Jesus Christ!' Tom screamed trying to dodge the craters that were appearing all over the desert floor.

The air was choked with dust and blocked out the sun. Fragments of rock flew through the air tearing through the canvas covers on the Bedford's and ripping through flesh. There were cries of fear and screams of pain.

'Shit! Stop the car!' John yelled.

Tom almost turned the Humber on its side in order to avoid another crater, but there was another he didn't see in time. The car crashed down into the hole and crunched into the crater wall. John managed to hold on for his life, but Tom was thrown across the bonnet. His body flopped like a rag doll across the front of the vehicle, but like a man possessed, he was up in seconds checking on John.

'You okay?' there was blood flowing from a cut on his face.

'I'm fine,' John replied grabbing his kit from the back of the car, but before he could check on the Sergeant Major, Tom was up and charging towards to lorries trying to organise the men.

Ahead through the dust John could just make out muzzle flashes from the settlement. They were sporadic which although signified that there were only a few enemy soldiers around, it also meant that the Company would have to fight for their first objective. It was not part of the original plan, but the Major's concerns had now been justified.

'Out, out, out!' Tom shouted as he ran from lorry to lorry.

The men spilt out from the vehicles, their equipment rattling and weighing them down. A few were badly wounded and dragged from the vehicles including Lieutenant Keyes who's arm looked as if it had been mauled by a lion. 'I'm all right,' he called out and gathered his platoon ready for action.

Still men were bundling their way off the trucks. John watched helplessly as one corporal was assisting his men off the third truck when a bullet struck him through the chest. He drew a sharp breath out of surprise and for a moment carried on assisting his men as if nothing had happened, until he dropped to the floor in a lifeless heap, his lungs like a torn balloon losing its air.

There was no time to dig in and the riflemen fired back at the muzzle flashes from the mud brick buildings taking cover in the now frequent shell craters. The deep sounding crack from the 303s and the chattering Bren guns was a good sign that although the company had been caught by surprise, there was still a fair fight to finish.

There was little time to act as the enemy artillery rounds got closer and closer to the now stationary trucks. Sidi Omar was only a few hundred yards away and they had been caught out in the open. John was quick to see a way around the problem and ordered Keyes to attack around to the north of the settlement whilst the remaining platoons put down covering fire and slowly advanced.

The drivers of the lorries with their human cargo delivered, began to beat a hasty retreat out of the fray, but one got caught and the driver slumped down over the huge steering wheel.

The biggest concern now was that they were alone, the supporting tanks were nowhere in sight. Within minutes Keyes and his platoon had begun to head towards the northern side of the settlement, German soldiers holding the position were put into a crossfire. On seeing this advance John pushed the rest of the men forward.

'Fix Bayonets!' the order was repeated again and again and John could hear the tell-tale clicks of the blades finding their housings on the end of the rifles.

'All right boys,' Tom yelled. When he saw the remaining two platoons hesitate as the sound of the whistle finally caught up with his ears he roared, 'Let's go!' and through the fog of the sand and the dust, the men charged.

Any apprehension or doubts felt earlier by these men seemed to have disappeared. Their bayonets glinted in the sun and their blood-curdling cries filled the air overpowering the thudding, exploding enemy artillery. It was to do or die, there was no more time to think about it. Their hearts pumped their blood with extra force around their bodies and the hairs stood rigid on the backs of their necks. The enemy began to fall back as the men approached and it became clear to John that Sidi Omar was only lightly defended. Something didn't feel right.

The enemy, now identified with certainty by their green and sand tunics as Germans, fell further back towards the western edge of the settlement on an area of sloping ground. D Company began taking positions around the settlement even digging fox holes in some cases and capturing prisoners, but still, something felt wrong. The Germans had the high ground and although they had been quick to beat a hasty retreat, they now held firmly to their new position.

'Position is almost ours,' Tom reported, he was covered in dust and blood and had firmly gripped in his right hand his revolver.

'We've got to get that high ground Sergeant Major,' John instructed.

'I will try and push Second Platoon further forwards and see if we can force them out into the open.'

He ran towards the northern edge where Keyes was positioned, bullets zipping up and down and ricocheting through the narrow streets.

To the south Lieutenant Moore had put his platoon into some of the buildings in order to protect the southern side of the position. In the centre around John who took cover in a small alleyway, Bailey and his platoon had taken cover themselves in the buildings. By now reinforcements had now arrived and were pulling up in the centre of the settlement. After disembarking miraculously without any casualties or so it appeared, they took over the northern area of the position. John was relieved by their arrival and no longer was his company alone.

Shell after shell hit the ground which shuddered and shook displacing all and sundry, each explosion made the sand rise like a foggy blanket that they couldn't see through, let alone the enemy, but it appeared that John's men had the upper hand for now.

Grateful for the reinforcements from 'A' company and with 'B' company now also arriving, John took stock of the situation.

'Where's our tank support?' he said out loud.

They were due to link up with their steel support and advance north. Instead the secured settlement was in fact still filled with Afrika Korps infantry and the tanks were nowhere to be seen. John's orders were to take, hold and then advance with the tanks. At this rate they would be delayed.

Sergeant Scott ran to and fro, checking on each platoon whilst Lance Corporal Pearce, John's new wireless operator, listened carefully to his headphones for any new developments.

'Getting there,' Tom reported skidding across the main road that crossed through the settlement as the enemy tried to cut him down. 'So far 'A' company have taken a position to the north. I have moved Lieutenant Keyes back here to give us a hand.'

'Good,' John replied. 'We have got to find a way of dislodging them from that high ground.'

'I would suggest we keep them pinned down until our tank friends arrive.'

John agreed, it shouldn't be a problem as it appeared now that they had simply caught some stragglers, it was the only possible explanation for such a small defending force. He crouched down leaning against the corner of a stone building, beside the main road that ran through the settlement. Apart from the shelling which had become a little lighter and the occasional rattle of machine guns his men seemed to be gaining the upper hand.

'I don't like it,' John commented nervously.

'Let me guess,' Tom began. 'The position was taken too easily and resistance was light, I was thinking the same thing, not that we have taken the whole position yet. Look on the bright side, those Jerry's aren't going anywhere. Although if you have inherited any of my intuition over the years you will be wondering what's holding up the armoured support.'

'Sir!' John's new radio operator called out urgently. 'There's talk on the radio of tanks approaching from the south-west.'

'Our armoured support no doubt, time to relax,' Tom exclaimed.

Running towards them through the dust and sporadic enemy fire was Simon. For the first time since John had known him he had his tin helmet on his head, it wobbled from side to side and behind him came two of his medics.

'I'm glad you're here,' John replied. 'Have you got a minute to see to Lieutenant Keyes, he is over there,' John pointed to a stone building a few meters away.

Simon nodded and ran through the hail of stones and shrapnel towards it where inside he found Keyes against the wall, cradling his bloody arm, but still in command. To the south-west the sound of tracked vehicles could now be heard and a cloud of dust pointed out their exact approach. Their prayers had been answered, the armoured brigade had arrived.

‘Thank god,’ Tom said. ‘Now we can get on with what we came here to do and get on our way to Tobruk. I will get the men prepared.’

‘Still need to deal with these stragglers before we can move off,’ John reminded him. ‘When that’s done we can have a quick break and count the cost.’

The men began cheering and waving their tin helmets in the air like bowler hats to welcome their armoured support.

‘Tell the men to rest easy,’ John said turning to Scott, but as quickly as he had given the order he revoked it.

The tanks appeared over the gently sloping sand, but to everyone’s horror they weren’t British.

‘Bloody hell Panzers!’ Tom cried in astonishment.

‘Tell the men to hold fire!’ John screamed. ‘Let them come in closer.’

‘Where the hell are our boys?’ A young replacement almost cried like a desperate child.

It all began to make sense now. The way in which the enemy had withdrawn and then held the high ground even though they had been outnumbered. The whole time they had been delaying John’s men in order to sandwich them between themselves and the now fast approaching panzers.

Tom began to rush about and give orders to Moore. Meanwhile, John, with his new radio operator at his heels like a yapping dog, ran towards the other platoons which he felt would be closest to the oncoming battle. The Panzers rumbled towards them like giant metal dinosaurs with Afrika Korps infantry swarming all around. They were slow, but their long-barrelled guns were sniffing the air for their trapped prey.

There was only one way out and that was back into the desert behind them. But they weren’t going back, they had come here to take Sidi Omar and help relieve Tobruk and although the besieged port was another sixty miles ahead, the relief had to start somewhere and John was damned if he was going to let a few steel monsters stop him. Katie also filled his mind and he pulled the bolt on his rifle to release an empty cartridge and load a fresh round, ready for his first shot of revenge.

He arrived behind Bailey who was sheltering to the side of another building and as he arrived he tumbled to the floor due to a combination of exhaustion and the weight of his equipment, but the Panzers had spotted him. Shells tore into the side of the building, spilling their occupants with horrific screams. Machine gun rounds peppered the walls causing mud brick and stone to flake like falling snow all around them. John grit his teeth.

'Calm down, you will be fine,' John reassured himself. 'Lieutenant Bailey?'

'Here John.'

'Where's your Anti-Tank team?'

Bailey pointed to a shell crater over to the right in the open. Inside it was the crew of an anti-tank rifle and even from where John was crouching he could see them nervously peering from their positions awaiting their orders. Without thinking for his own safety he leapt across the sand, bullets seeking him out and dived into the crater with the two apprehensive soldiers.

'Sir, this won't make a dent in that!' the first said very jittery.

'Do you want to live?' he asked and they looked puzzled as they nodded. 'Good, if you want to live today that tank has to go! Listen to everything I am about to say. I want you to hold your fire until I tell you.'

'For how long?' the second gunner asked, fidgeting while aiming to fire.

'Until I tell you!' he repeated shaking his head.

'Sorry sir,' he replied. 'You sure this will work? They are bloody big tanks, bigger than the last ones we shot at.'

John peered over the lip of the blackened crater and before him was the lead panzer. It rumbled through the sand its cannon trained on the building behind them. A flash was followed by a roar as the shell passed overhead, ploughing into the building showering the three men in lumps of rock and dust. Bullets continuously kicked up the ground around them.

'Jesus Christ Sir, now?' the gunners, feeling anxious and intimidated were beginning to waver.

'No damn it, wait till he is closer, you've got to make it count. You might only get one chance,' John continued to watch, he worked out that the tank was about one hundred and fifty yards away and for the rifle to be effective he needed it in closer. 'Steady,' he called still peering over the lip of the crater, 'steady.' In his mind he roughly counted down the yards, one hundred and thirty, one hundred and twenty, and one hundred and ten.

'Sir?' The gunners were wetting themselves with anticipation and worried sick to take the shot.

John continued to watch and slowly he lifted his rifle and trained it on one of the advancing infantry. The German soldier was walking to the right of the tank, if he saw the muzzle flash from the anti-tank rifle they would be finished. John took careful aim, seeing Katie in his mind and imagining this to be the same German who plunged the knife into her back.

He squeezed the trigger. The Enfield jerked into his shoulder and in the distance the soldier fell lifelessly to the floor. He aimed to the left where another German soldier was looking for where the shot had come from, but before he had a chance to guess, John let off another round which punched through his chest and sent him down upon the dust.

'Now!' John screamed and with a magnificent crack the anti-tank rifle fired.

The shot hit below the turret and bounced clean off.

'Again, Again!' John roared.

Another shot bellowed, but with the same result. The Panzer was now aware that it was a target and began firing back in their direction. A shell tore its way through another building behind them and another exploded into the sand just ahead of them.

'Relocate!' John said pulling himself up and running back amongst the buildings.

The boy's crew followed him, dragging their thirty five pound weapon between them. A few yards later and John ordered them to fire again, this time at the tracks of the tanks, but still the rounds bounced off as if they were made of rubber. A few more yards and again they fired, but still no effect.

The whole time buildings broke apart and shells were falling and exploding all around them, wounded men were beginning to be picked off in the streets as they started to appear in the doorways as masonry and shrapnel caused the casualties to clear out of their hiding places. Many now opened fire, aiming for the supporting infantry as they were the only targets they could hit, but the tanks were now closing in and taking their time to tear the buildings apart until there was nowhere left to hide.

'Here,' John yelled pointing to a shell hole in between two buildings. The position was perfect as from this spot the tank was merely sixty yards away, maybe less and not only that, but it had started to move northwards exposing the weaker side of its armour.

'Hit!' he screeched and with a flash the tank burst into flames. The crew began to bail, some on fire waving their arms frantically. It was an awful sight to see and a horrific way to die, but there was little pity in his heart and John lifted his rifle and with what appeared to the rest of his men as kindness, he picked off the screaming and burning men.

He then turned back to the anti-tank team. The two privates were watching the burning hulk with shock and surprise.

'Well done lads, got the hang of it now?' he congratulated. 'Let's get another!'

'Sir, we didn't shoot it.'

John looked again at them and then to his surprise noticed that the magazine for the gun had not even been loaded yet. He gazed back to the burning tank in time to see a second panzer explode. Looking cautiously to the south-east he could see why. The shot had come from a British tank; their armoured support had arrived at last. A loud cheer erupted as John lowered his head in relief.

As the Germans were swept up and forced to retreat, John returned to the main heart of the settlement. He found Tom at the same time that a British tank rumbled into the street. It caused him to smile as from either side of it, every so often from the rubble and ruin of battle, his men smiled with relief. Tom was up a small alleyway to his left and Simon was cowering in a doorway, both watched the metal beast and their smiles revealed the white of their teeth through their dust-covered faces.

'Germans appear to be falling back sir,' the radio operator called out from behind him. 'Small pockets of resistance. 'B' Company will take lead and dislodge the enemy from the high ground.'

'Job well done,' Tom called out.

'Indeed it is…'

John had barely finished his sentence when all of the air in his lungs seemed to be sucked out from within him. His body lurched forward from the impact and upwards with the shock. It was as if a red hot poker had been thrust into his shoulder, but only this time had travelled the entire width of his body and thrust out from his chest. It wasn't a red hot poker, but a bullet and another soon ripped through his thigh, the same thigh that still occasionally had a shooting pain from his last wound. This red hot round caused his legs to buckle and like a confused drunk he collapsed on the floor.

It had been an easy mistake to make, the Germans were on the run, but from the high ground the trapped Afrika Korps infantry from earlier was making a break for it and had now appeared at the end of the main road, the very road that John had not thought to take cover on whilst watching the fast approaching cavalry.

Tom in despair broke cover and dived upon John to protect him from any further fallout.

'John? Come on John, wakey, wakey, breathe man; don't be silly now come on!'

John's eyes were bulging from his skull as he tried to breathe. The bullet had passed through the lower left collar bone and therefore Tom worried that it might have passed through his lung or damaged his heart.

The pain that welled up inside the old Sergeant Major was immense. His eyes uncontrollably were bursting with tears and his words were slurred with panic. Simon had also broken cover and even with stray bullets still flying down the road, dived next to Tom dragging him to the ground.

'Stay down,' he ordered Tom and then turned his attention to John. 'Not again John, this will be two drinks you owe me now.'

He ripped open his shirt and before him he could see the exit wound. It was huge and had punched out a massive chunk of flesh from his collar bone area, but it was difficult to see if the bullet had in any way damaged the lungs. John was still struggling to breathe.

'It's hit the lung, its hit the lung!' Tom panicked.

'I don't know,' Simon said desperately. 'It's difficult to tell, it might have just ruptured the lung. It might have missed.'

‘But he’s struggling to breathe,’ Tom cried. His hands were upon his head in despair and looking around he could see fear gripped faces all around. Another bullet cracked past and then another even closer. ‘This isn’t right; he’s struggling to breathe!’

‘It could be shock!’ Simon said with an angry tone, he needed hope not despair. ‘What’s got into you Tom, not in front of the men.’

‘Sergeant Major get the hell off the road!’ a private called out, but Tom wasn’t going anywhere.

‘Come on, John, please!’ Tom begged whilst Simon plugged the wound. ‘I’ve got to tell you about the letter, about your mother and me.’

John continued to fight for air, he looked at Tom’s face and the world around him seemed to blur. The sounds too began to fade. He could sense Simon’s rough handling through the juddering movements, but could not feel it.

Simon continued to frantically stop the bleeding, another bullet whizzed past kicking up dust as it went.

‘Your mother never told you and she never told me until the day she died, you must hold on so I can tell you, please!’

John’s face was getting pale and his breathing shallow. Simon couldn’t tell yet if it was a good thing or not and turned his attention to the leg. There the bullet had quite clearly shattered the bone and Simon knew that should John survive, that this time there was a big risk he would lose his leg.

‘Private!’ he called pointing to a lone rifleman huddled up against the wall. ‘Private I need your help.’

The boy ran across and knelt down next to him. In front of him, the ever distraught Tom was trying to keep John awake, Simon had never seen him so consumed by fear before.

‘Private do you know how to make a tourniquet?’ he asked the young lad who nodded affirmatively. ‘Well get it done,’ he instructed, pulling all the necessary bandage and linen from his bag and he returned to John’s chest whilst Tom babbled on.

‘Is he going to be okay, please tell me he is?’ Tom asked.

‘I don’t know Sergeant Major; perhaps you should get back to your men, it’s all under control here, they need instructions from you right now you’re leading the company.’

‘I can’t lose him, Simon, I can’t.’

‘I’m doing everything I can,’ Simon replied frustrated and as he did John’s eyes closed.

Tom saw them close and feared the worst, in his heart he knew it was all over. Simon continued to keep trying, but Tom’s heart had already lost hope. He clutched at John’s hand.

‘My son, my precious son, I'm your father. I'm your father, John....’ he fumbled hastily to pull out the contents that were firmly wedged in his top pocket, to reach the letter from John's mother.

Simon's face fell, he paused as Tom tried desperately to communicate with John as he slipped away into unconsciousness. His words fell only upon the ears of Simon and the men around them.

‘Please forgive me,’ he pleaded desperately, as he flapped the letter frustratingly in front of John's closed eyes. ‘It was before I went back to France, she never told me that you were my son, not until she was dying. I have been trying to find the right time, oh God, it's all too little, too late. This is not how it was meant to be!’

‘I think I can save him,’ Simon said calmly gripping Tom’s arm to reassure him. ‘I think he is going to be alright, but I need you to lead the men.’

It had no longer become a fight to save a friend and fellow soldier; it had also become a fight to save a son. Simon pushed all his medical training into gear trying everything to keep the soldier alive but fate was watching.

Another bullet tore its way up the road and this time struck Tom. He barely flinched as the round punched through the centre of his back. In doing so it exited through his chest, splattering his life over Simon and the young private still trying to make the tourniquet. Then in seemingly slow motion, almost as if time had come to a standstill, Tom’s eyes full of pain, sadness and knowing, caught Simon's devastated glance. In response to his confused frown; all Simon could do was return a dismayed smile and comforting nod of reassurance that he was doing everything he could.

As Tom fell forwards Simon caught him and whilst Tom struggled to gasp his last gasp of desert air Simon whispered, ‘I will tell him, Ive got this old chap, everything will be fine.’

As Tom's life left him his body slumped over the body of his son, the letter covered with blood-stained fingerprints still firmly grasped in his hand. Simon pulled it from his grip and delicately placed it into his breast pocket.

A Desert Rose

1942 - Sussex, England

It was drizzly and grey outside and there was a blustery mood about the day. Sophie's mother would have called it a spring cleaning day, but Sophie had resigned herself to catching up with her correspondence. She had written once a week to John but nothing had come back for months now. The news of what had happened on the advance to Tobruk had reached her by Lieutenant Bailey, now in command of John's company and she had still not come to terms with the loss of Tom. It was like losing a father again and in many ways it had been more difficult.

She had been so exhausted from so much loss over the years that she had almost developed an immunity to the pain, or so it would seem upon the surface. Deep inside she hurt and it was an ache that never went away. For now she really must put pen to paper, promising to write to Bailey and Simon who she knew were still out in the desert and headed for a pile of envelopes balancing on the dining table.

Buckland continued to take it upon himself to become Sophie's minder and keeper in John's absence. Sophie allowed the charade to continue, like John he was a man who needed to feel needed and his concerns were a comfort. Their moment of awkwardness over the kiss had passed now and he remained a true friend and companion, retaining his cheeky and charming nature. The relationship was purely platonic and any future, which she had promised she would consider was still a possibility. It gave him hope and despite its fragility, hope was necessary at these times in any form. There was still no lack of trying on his part, but there was a mutual understanding that no matter how much they flirted with each other, neither were truly ready. Commitment, romance or opportunity, however, Sophie looked at it, would be left for time to deal with.

There was some good news in the cottage. Buckland had been promoted to commander, a position he had not necessarily been seeking but had nevertheless proved himself capable of. Uncle Richard was of course well acquainted in Ministry circles and there were rumours that Buckland had been granted the position through his good graces. However, Uncle Richard insisted that he had achieved his promotion purely on his own merit without any input from himself.

Today Buckland was picking her up at five o'clock to take her up to the Great Hall. Further good news had been received that Joy's daughter Katherine was back in England and coming up from Exeter. Katherine's war had been just as traumatic as her brother's and Sophie was thrilled to finally meet her. Joy was throwing a tea party during the evening in celebration for the occasion, although Sophie sensed there was more to it than that.

Sophie finished her letters and placed them in envelopes ready to post. She looked upon the new bookshelf she had made and ran her fingers across the spines of the several diaries her mother had made. They were now the pride of place in the centre amidst the photograph albums, bathed in a brief ray of morning sunlight through the window.

There was no Mrs Jenkins today, although she too had been invited to the Great Hall and Buckland was also absent as he was still on duty. She had to make her own tea this morning, a strange concept now as she had got so used to Buckland's constant offers, perhaps he could sell tea after the war, she wondered amusing herself.

She gazed out the kitchen window, the cold misty air surrounded the back garden and the orchard beyond, smothering it like a blanket. The light was dim and the cold was causing Sophie to shiver and she wrapped herself tightly into her bathrobe. The house was also cold and slightly damp. She had got up unusually early today even though she was off duty this weekend and the crisp sharp air that seemed to seep in from under the front door, despite the presence of the draught excluder, was nipping at her heels.

Still quivering from the cold Sophie walked back through into the living room on her toes and glanced upon the letters on the living room table that she had received from Africa. She had been sorting them and in some cases deliberately evoking the pain. Some were from Anthony, a few from Captain James, but the largest pile was from her brother and Tom, all neatly stacked in order of receipt.

The last letter she had received from John was from last November, telling her that Katie had died. She had written several times since then, but each time she had received no reply. For a while she had continued to convince herself that there was nothing to be alarmed about, however, the usual reassurance she would take in knowing that Tom would be by his side was no longer a comfort that helped her sleep at night. For now, she simply blamed the absence of news down to the U-boats that prowled offshore, it left the possibility that her letters or his were at the bottom of the sea.

It was just after Christmas that news came via Uncle Richard again. He received confirmation that John had been critically wounded in the taking of Tobruk. Bailey's letter arrived soon after confirming Tom's death. There was no doubt anymore.

She also received a long letter from Captain James, who felt it necessary to inform her that John was alive, concerned there might be another misunderstanding as before. His letter was a permanent and repetitive apology. At the time he had done all he could for her brother and after many minutes had been forced to make the decision to leave them both as he couldn't have done any more for them in the firing line. He had to leave John in the hands of the stretcher bearers who took him back to the nearest field hospital. His duties had forced him to move on to other casualties in the field when the advance picked up the pace again. When the battle had ended he had lost John's whereabouts and to date, he did not know exactly where he was or how his condition was.

Sophie knew he was still alive, but four months of silence had now passed and she had to admit that there was a twinge of doubt in her mind.

Christmas had been and gone and although it wasn't the first Christmas she had experienced without her brother and Tom, their neatly wrapped unopened presents stored each year for their return frequently reminded Sophie of the spent time. Although she knew Tom wouldn't be coming home she couldn't bring herself to remove his present that Christmas and it remained under the window even now.

'Stop worrying,' she reassured herself and she began to pace the living room deep in thought about where John could be trying to keep warm.

Alongside the letters was a small pile of newspapers, anything which mentioned North Africa had been pulled out and saved in order for her to build up a bigger picture of what was going on out there. She had made a scrapbook of the cuttings and it sat next to the diaries. The latest news had been the success of operation Crusader and how Rommel's Afrika Korps and the Italians were on the run. Somehow Sophie was not convinced. The media liked to make the news as positive as possible, as by now everything imaginable had been thrown at Britain and at Sophie. She was a well-educated veteran in the ways of propaganda by now and remembered how much everyone had praised the evacuation at Dunkirk. From Folkestone hospital, she had not seen the same story everyone else saw on the black and white cinema screens. Her view had been of white faces, shredded green serge battledresses and vibrant crimson.

The country had been at its lowest ebb during 1941 and now in 1942 there was more disastrous news from the North African campaign, with the hungry Desert Fox on the counter-offensive and the Allies in retreat, the whole campaign appeared to go backwards and forwards and neither side appeared to break the seesawing motion of the conflict.

The fear of invasion had begun to subside and with the cottage so close to the sea this brought Sophie great relief as she imagined herself to be in the way of the Germans if they did arrive. Instead the only invasion of late to break the peace and quiet had been the influx of Canadian soldiers to the area who were clearly gearing up for something. Otherwise all remained the same, the local signposts which had been taken down years before were still absent and causing confusion for motorists and the Home Guard were still constantly on the prowl.

She had got used to the long shifts that followed an air raid siren. Raid alerts usually started these days at around 9 pm and lasted until 6 am. Sophie was now in her second year of nursing and she couldn't believe how quickly those years had gone past. Her salary for the first year had been very helpful as she was pretty much self-sufficient from that point on. Now she was doing very well for herself and Buckland's rent covered Mrs Jenkin's wages. Any spare money enabled her to enjoy the occasional night out, she particularly liked dancing, a past time that Bella had taught her.

She sat down on the floor next to the living room table tucking her bathrobe under her feet. Reaching out, her hand took the first envelope from the top of the pile of letters from Anthony. Her beautiful deep brown eyes scanned the rough manly handwriting. In the letter he told her over and over again how much he missed her and longed to return. Anthony talked of the future and she closed her eyes to recall the memory. She wasn't sad anymore and it wasn't a morbid action, she was proud of him and his sacrifice and the letters brought happy memories not sad ones.

Suddenly there was the sound of a vehicle pulling up outside. She rose from the floor and walked to the front window peering through the hawthorn bush brushing the ledge. There was still an eerie mist lingering, but the sun was breaking through in bright shards and through them, her eyes focused on a large dark green army ambulance.

Sophie didn't know what to make of it. She wasn't on duty this weekend. The ambulance had stopped and from the back she could see although not very clearly two men opening the back doors. The mist hindered any chance of seeing who these men were and after a few seconds it became clear that one was a field nurse.

She jumped to the front door. Opening it the cold mist outside flooded the hallway, grasping at everything with its icy fingers. Her bare feet reluctantly stepped out onto the path and then jolted back in for the comfort of the slippers she always forgot to wear. Whilst her right hand still clutched at the door frame her left hand and contorted body hastily tried to juggle her feet into position, her eyes trying desperately to focus through the mist.

There was the sound of a man's voice, but it was distorted, so there was no way of telling who it was. There were the distinctive whack and groaning squeak of wooden crutches, there was no mistaking it, Sophie knew the sound well enough.

The gate opened with a creek and the fog dissipated a little so there was a chance to see clearly who was approaching. It was a man and either side of him was a medical officer and a field nurse. They helped him through the gate and up the path.

She didn't recognise the medical officer and the nurse was not from the hospital where she worked, but there was something about the man in the middle whose head stayed low. He stood poised for a moment resting upon the crutches as judging by his pose he was unused to using them. His hands were pitted and sore from the inexperience of carrying the weight of his body. His face was thin and weary and as

Sophie searched beyond his hair to his eyes that was when she realised who it was. There was a look of relief and tearful happiness as he smiled weakly.

In desperation she pulled her slippers on and ran as fast as her legs would carry her towards her long lost brother.

As she approached he attempted an ambitious step towards her, this time without the aid of the help that had accompanied him, but he lost his balance and fell with a crack onto the path. It was a pitiful sight; Sophie couldn't help but think and looked upon the crippled soldier.

John laughed and said sheepishly, 'got to get used to these.'

He tried to pick himself up and pushed away from the helpful gestures of the orderlies, but his sister held him firmly and helped him to his feet. Her emotions now cascaded intensely from her soul, the cold air biting at her watery eyes. Sophie held him as if to never let him go again. He felt thinner than she could remember and certainly more fragile. She was beside herself with relief and sobbed in his arms as he too unloaded three long years of locked away emotion. It felt good to feel his arms around her and to hear his thudding heartbeat, it meant he was real. It had been a long time since she had seen his face and the war had changed him, he looked worn, tired, drawn, older and wiser. Her hands couldn't stay still as they squeezed his shoulders and then his waist as if checking that he was all there, just in case there had been a mistake. She had been hoping for this moment ever since the war had begun and now it was here.

Her soft silky hair fell against his cheek and he closed his eyes smelling it. When he re-opened them there was peaceful relief and she sensed that the war was not far behind those eyes of his.

There was so much to tell, so many painful and tragic memories, but there were many other days to reflect upon them, right now they let their tears free and cried as if they had never cried before. Sophie pulled away and clutched his relieved face in her hands. She stared into his eyes. Her hands, slowly and gently caressed his face, checking that her eyes were still not deceiving her.

The culmination of his journey and all that had gone before contained in every tear, he spluttered, 'I've lost them, I've lost them all and I can't go back and change it. I failed, Sophie and I can't put it right.'

'All is right with the world now,' she murmured gently in his ear stroking his face passively. Then vigorously she ruffled her hands through his hair. 'Anyway. It's my turn to look after you now.'

The orderlies, before leaving, helped her to get him inside and she settled him in a comfortable chair in the pantry, rushing around and fussing over his every wince or groan. When she was finally convinced that all was well, she sat in front of him wanting to fire a hundred and one questions at him about Who? What? Where and why? But she knew that it would all have to wait for another day and at his own pace. He was home and that was all that was important for now. Keeping him warm, comfortable and feeling safe was the best medicine in the world. She touched where his leg would have been with a tear in her eye and he grabbed at her hand.

'I'll get used to it, I've got a spare. I'm thankful to be alive, apparently there are major breakthroughs on artificial limbs and I should have no problem getting sorted pretty soon,' he said assuredly.

'I know,' she said.

'I'm sorry I didn't write, I had things to get through,' he apologised lifting up his scarred hand and arm. As well as the bullet wounds to his chest, shrapnel had punctured his arm, leaving him blemished on one side, but it would heal with time. 'It was just a little difficult and I was feeling too sorry for myself until recently.'

She stood up and kissed him on the forehead. 'No matter, I was always here rooting for you.'

'I barely recognised you at first,' he grabbed her arm and she stopped mid-track and just out of the blue he announced, 'Tom was my father Sophie, not Jack.'

He fumbled about in his shirt for a letter. Sophie had never seen it before, but her mother's words had already told her its contents.

'Where did you get that from?'

'I was sent back to Alexandria,' he began softly. 'It took a while, but Simon managed to find out where I was and sent it to me. You know some of those awkward times after mum died when he half said things? I guessed that there was something, but it must have been tormenting for him trying to find the right words and a way of telling me.

When I look back I think I actually knew in my heart when I saw them together, but I always thought it was you that was his daughter, not me his son. Poor Tom, I would have accepted it so easily and now he will never know. We loved him didn't we Sophie?'

She wanted to point to the diaries and tell him she already knew, but as he passed her the letter he had received from Simon, the letter their mother had given Tom, it wasn't the right time. She read them with tears in her eyes and a sorrowful glance told him that she felt the same.

'We'll always be honest with each other and never hide any mishaps like this won't we?' She implored. 'I am happy with my lot John, but think how different it could have been if they hadn't both been so frightened of the truth.'

He looked puzzled at her and then sighed with a smile, 'you already knew.'

'I wanted to write to you, I just didn't know how…'

'It's ok,' he stroked her arm reassuringly. 'That's the saddest part isn't it? That it was all so unnecessary.'

He suddenly leant forward and pointed to his small pack that had been left by the orderlies near the door. Sophie approached it and he gestured her to a small pocket on the side. As she reached inside she felt something unusual, a solid lump with sharp jagged edges. As she pulled it from its hiding place she realised it was a beautiful crystal.

'What is it?'

'Even in the desert rose's bloom. I found it one morning at dawn.'

'Looks just like a rose, what a beautiful thing,' she wondered.

'I thought you would like it. Sometimes the desert surprises you with its gifts.'

The telephone rang and it made them both jump, especially John as the phone was a new edition to the house. Sophie answered to hear the voice of Buckland on the other end, confirming their arrangements for later that afternoon. As she informed him that her brother was home he gave a cry of joy on her behalf.

'I don't know what to do at the moment, shall I call Uncle Richard?'

Buckland went quiet for a moment on the other end before suggesting, 'It might be a good idea unless you want me to do it? Are we still going to be attending the tea party?

'I would still like to attend, but John's arrival… I don't know, let me speak to Richard first. I have a funny feeling there might be a change in plan.'

'Ok, I have to go, will catch up later.'

There was a click as the phone went dead.

'Have I messed up something you were going to be doing today?' John asked.

'No, no, not at all, that was a friend of mine, Lieutenant, no it's Commander Buckland.'

'Our new lodger? I remember you writing about him now.' John said. 'I can't believe you cleared out mum's old room.'

'I needed to free up some space, Mrs Jenkins helped.'

'How is the old battle-axe?'

'Same as always, she will be over soon as we were going up to Richard and Joy's for tea this evening. Joy's daughter had quite an ordeal like you and she is coming up from Exeter with her newborn daughter. Uncle Richard will be so pleased to see you.'

John smiled. 'He won't be expecting me.'

'Well from what I can tell on the telephone there might be a change of plan.'

'So Richard and Joy are grandparents?' He asked.

'Wonderful news isn't it?' she fumbled and faffed.

'I didn't know that Joy's daughter was married,' John said. 'I suppose I wouldn't, none of us has ever met her! I thought she was a real career woman? Fancy that, is Joy pleased?'

Sophie was lost for words, she only knew Katherine through letters and even then she had only written to her occasionally since embarking upon her nursing career. In some ways she knew only as much as John did.

'I would assume so.'

'I feel rather guilty, I have never really bothered to ask about her and there we are always feeling like that black sheep. I'm sure she's a very nice person though if Joy's anything to go by. Have you met her?'

'No, apart from a few letters. I was going to meet her once, but it was the day you all left the docks at Newhaven so I missed her. Joy keeps her cards close to her chest and doesn't really give much away. I think Joy has an estranged relationship with her. I suppose she must have got married, got pregnant and come home to have the baby. I don't really know, I don't think Joy does either, it all seemed a bit of a shock when she rang and asked to come up and see them.'

She giggled.

'What's so funny?' John asked puzzled.

'Well you know I really like Joy and all that, she has been an absolute star to me throughout the past few years, but I can't help but think that her daughter is a bit of a loose cannon. I think it's rather put her nose out of joint. Lady of the Manor, an estranged daughter, secrets and all that sort of thing, it's just not what I expected of Joy,' said Sophie mischievously but not maliciously, for it only endeared her to Joy even more and besides it added more excitement to her family.

'You should still go,' John said yawning comfortably in the chair as Sophie lit the fire. 'Don't mind me I'll be fine for a couple of hours and anyway it will be good for me to get accustomed to the old surroundings and I've got a lot of thinking to do.'

He stretched happily relieved to be home at last.

'I need to ring Uncle Richard and tell him the good news. I'm surprised he didn't know you were coming home actually?' she tutted. 'I must also tell Archie if there is a change in arrangements.'

'Who is Archie?' John roused suddenly.

'I mean Commander Buckland,' she replied correcting herself for the second time.

'Life's complicated sometimes,' John said. 'There isn't always any rhyme or reason for how it is. Tom was always saying, "That's how it is!" God, I miss him.'

Sophie sense that Tom's loss was going to be the biggest gap of all. It had always been the three of them and now they were reduced to two. The family had diminished and needed a new sense of life to bring it back, a new chapter to make the previous hold meaning. It crackled warmly. As she turned to tuck the blanket around him in his chair, he was already asleep.

His face was peaceful, the war was far away for him now and as she gazed upon him she made up her mind to stay at home. She picked up the phone to call Richard and Joy, Styles answered as usual and informed her that Commander Buckland had called with the news about John just minutes ago and that they were on the way to the cottage. She should have been pleased, but there was a feeling of dismay, she was not ready to share him yet or have any disturbances for her brother, at least not on his first day home.

It did not take long for the knock at the door to come and selfishly Sophie delayed opening the door, gazing at John one last time in their moment of solitude. Joy was beside herself with excitement and was obviously over the initial shock and disappointment of her daughter's circumstances. She cradled her granddaughter proudly in her arms as she stepped over the threshold. The baby was as sound asleep as John was. She was closely followed by Joy's daughter who astounded Sophie with her beauty. Katherine appeared slightly subdued, embarrassed about turning up on the doorstep unannounced and pardoning her mother's actions and excitement. Behind them came Buckland and Richard, followed by Mrs Jenkins who couldn't wait to see John.

Richard was completely exuberant and flapping excitedly he asked, 'is he well enough for a shock and up for visitors?'

'Probably not,' Sophie defended indignantly. 'He's still very unwell, he's lost a leg Uncle! He is tired and weak and he's got to register with Doctor Parsons tomorrow.'

Mrs Jenkins had already snuck past and into the living room, she soon returned whispering. 'He's asleep, keep it down.'

'He fell asleep not long after he was dropped off,' Sophie explained, ushering them into the kitchen. 'Generally he seems pretty with it, he doesn't seem to be struggling with his emotions or anything but he's asleep at the moment, exhausted.'

'Tea?' asked Buckland.

He had his usual cheeky grin on his face, knowing that it was his usual punch line, but Sophie also noticed the smiles upon the rest of the family. Naturally they were all pleased John was safely home, but they seemed excited for another reason. Only Katherine seemed nervous.

'What's going on?' she asked warily.

'I need to speak to him privately,' Richard urged. 'By the way, may I introduce you to Katherine, Joy's daughter.'

'We just met on the door. Uncle, what is going on?'

Richard turned to Katherine and ushered her forward, the poor woman seemed as confused as Sophie was. 'Katherine this is Sophie, Sophie Watson. Captain Baker's sister' and he raised his eyebrows in a knowing fashion.

Katherine stepped back in astonishment and by now Sophie was aghast with the apparent madness that she seemed to be surrounded by.

'Please Uncle, what is going on?'

'Sophie this is Katherine Halland, but in the medical profession also known as Katie Hall.'

Sophie felt sick, confused and stunned at the same time. The penny had dropped and it was clear now that all of them had only just realised the connection. Katie's face had gone white as she too realised what was transpiring around her.

'We didn't realise until she arrived a few hours ago,' Joy said. 'We didn't know where to begin and so here seemed the best place to start.' She turned to her daughter, helping her fit together the gaps that were now plainly visible. 'Katherine was a sister in Sidi Barrani hospital, she looked after John back in July last year.

'John wrote to me about you,' Sophie croaked. 'He thought you were dead.'

'I was injured and supposed to be evacuated by boat. I developed a fever so don't remember much, but there was not enough room on the boat that was taking the wounded to the hospital ship so they took a few of us back off and left us on the dock to be transferred to another boat. Of course I was listed on board the original ship that sank. Ironic I should be posted as lost at sea, especially after meeting your brother when he was posted missing.'

'I never knew many of the details as there were so many things going on here as well,' declared Sophie. 'Joy never let on that you were lost at sea, how did you get home and the baby?' she asked Katie.

'Well, that would be why my mother is a little angry with me. When I registered as a nurse so many years ago, I registered as Katie Hall, not by my birth name, so my mother was never notified at her Sussex address.'

'Not that I would have known much anyway,' Joy interrupted, gently bouncing the baby in her arms. 'You barely write anyway.'

Katie rolled her eyes, 'they eventually got me on a hospital ship and I stayed on board for nearly three more months recuperating and of course I realised I was pregnant by then. I couldn't believe how stupid I had been,' her mother nestled up next to her as if it was not an issue. 'I was evacuated eventually back to England and reached home before any more misunderstandings took place.

I couldn't get any word of John, I tried to write to his Sergeant Major as I knew they were close but had no luck. I also tried Captain James, but again no luck. I didn't realise we were all connected, it never occurred to me and obviously never occurred to any of us either.'

'Fate,' Buckland chipped in.

'Fate,' Sophie smiled back.

It all made sense, John had been informed she was dead and so no more letters came or went to Sidi Barrani. Katie had become a non-entity for want of a better expression and meanwhile John's unit had moved on, everything had changed, the losses were high, the fighting was fierce, there was no possibility of contact being maintained.

'Neither of us expected to be cut off from each other so violently,' Katie said. She was now agitated, looking constantly towards the door that she knew John was behind. 'I had no idea until now what this all meant. I didn't know how to get in touch with him and couldn't write until I got back here. I got back in January and rested at home in Exeter. The baby came early and I wanted to keep her so I came up to Mum's to explain everything and that's when I saw the photo of you and John on the piano. I couldn't believe it and still can't. It'll be alright won't it? He will want to see me won't he?'

Sophie was trying to hold back her emotions, 'he's in the parlour.' She pointed to the door that Katie had been glancing at since arriving, 'but he's lost his leg and more importantly he has lost Tom, he had only just found out he was his father, so I think this is all going to be a bit much you know.'

She nodded understandingly, 'it's ok, Richard and mum informed me.'

'He is so very tired and I don't know about his emotional state.'

'Nothing I can't fix,' she said and gently opened the door to the parlour.

Katie stood looking down at John, here they were against all odds once again and she couldn't help but wonder if fate was indeed involved. She knelt down in front of him tidying the blanket that had become dislodged, just as she had done the last time he had been wounded.

'John, I need you to wake up,' she called gently and stroked his face. 'Wake up John.'

John stirred at the sensation of her touch and then his semi-consciousness told him that this sensitivity was real, not imaginary and his eyes began to flicker.

He looked at her, blinking repeatedly until his eyes were open and he wasn't dreaming. He was startled at the sight of her and uncontrollably he wept.

'My Angel.'

'Yes,' she smiled.

She took his hand and brushed it against her cheek and reassured him that she was really there and then she kissed him gently on his lips. His heart was pounding and he was confused, he wanted to respond but he was afraid it was all in his mind.

'I thought that I'd lost you,' he said hurt. 'I thought you were gone.'

'I thought that I'd lost you too,' she consoled.

'But the letter I received, it said… I never stopped thinking of you,' he declared. 'I never stopped loving you.'

'And I never will,' she vowed.

'As I am now?' he beseeched. 'My leg Katie I won't be any good for anything.'

She hushed him as the rest of the family entered the room. John was swamped by the loving embrace of Mrs Jenkins, his first comment being that he had missed her cooking and would later have to tell her how food in the desert compared. He was surprised at how Uncle

Richard had tears in his eyes and his heart warmed when he shook Buckland's hand and saw the devotion in his eyes that he had for Sophie, her future was still not written.

The biggest surprise of all was Rose. She made a strange gurgling sound as Joy lowered her into his arms. Her eyes were closed and she wriggled gently in the warm blanket she was swaddled in.

'I remember you telling me that your mother called Sophie her English rose,' Katie said. 'So I called her Rose, except she is a Desert Rose.'

'Like the crystals,' John smiled.

John felt the baby's soft cheek with his finger and a tiny hand reached out and grabbed it. It was a firm grip and he looked at Katie who gasped, 'You're the first person she has done that too.'

'I know what it means,' John said looking at Sophie.

It took a matter of moments for John to see into his new future. There would be picnics upon the South Downs overlooking the blue of the sea as a family day out. He saw Katie's hair blowing in the sea breeze and little Rose attempting her first steps. He saw the wedding they would have in the same church his mother had got married in and their first dance whilst Sophie whispered in his ear at how proud Tom would have been.

As for Rose, when she was old enough to understand everything and the poppy's swayed gently in the spring fields alongside the cornflower on a warm afternoon, he planned to sit with her, he thought, remembering those who had gone before with fondness and pride. He would tell her of the friends and comrades that had been lost through the tragedy of war. He would tell her about her grandmother, her defiance against illness and her grandfather, Tom, the bravest soldier he ever knew, the greatest role model and friend. The most loving father.

But Tom was not lost and even now he was very much alive in John's heart and mind. When Sophie would suggest he was looking down upon them both, John would agree with a gentle nod. In his mind he could see Tom driving the old Humber staff car across the golden plains of the desert and as the sun began to rise over the distant dunes, he would turn to greet its warmth with a smile whilst being bathed in its glorious heavenly glow.

He would instil in Rose the importance of who and why she came to be, but most of all, where it all began and finished. He would tell her how she came to be their precious Desert Rose.

Printed in Great Britain
by Amazon

44433717R00223